Footprints in the Mists of Time

BY S.N MAHACHI-HARPER

ISBN: 978-1-908690-14-2

DEDICATION

This piece of work is dedicated to the following people whose footsteps merged with mine in a remarkable way:

Thokozile Dhlamini-Vudzijena, for a wonderful friendship which in itself, is a virtual journey. Only larger and firmer footsteps can erase earlier footprints. Yours have remained large, firm and defiant.

Sophia Chiwara, neither the mystery of death nor a permanent absence can erase the footprints cast in stone on the remembered paths of previous journeys. The memories of yesterday break through even the thickest of mists. Soar on, fly high.... Je ne sais quoi, as you would say.

Janet Wiscot-Mugwagwa, through the thickest mist and upon the longest journey of all, the footprints have refused to be winnowed away and left to fritter in the wind. Thank you, Amake Rati.

ACKNOWLEDGEMENTS

Kupukile Mlambo, for the support, the encouragement and the invaluable friendship that is constant and consistent, I can't thank you enough, mon cher ami.

Victor Mahachi and **Cynthia Mahachi-Dengu**, for encouragement and assistance here and there, zikomo.

I acknowledge the following songs; *APhiri Anabwera* by Zex Manatsa, *The Servant Song* and *His Labours Here Complete* from the Methodist Church hymn book.

Foreword

When I received a request to write a foreword to *Footprints in the Mists of Time*, a *tour de force* novel recently written by Spiwe Mahachi-Harper, I hesitated, wishing to disqualify myself from such a mammoth undertaking. Beyond being just a consumer of literature, what could I, an economist and banker, have to say on any literary work, especially this particular one, I wondered. I had been privy to earlier drafts and had seen the manuscript transform into a novel that one Zimbabwean writer and critic, Memory Chirere, has dubbed Zimbabwe's longest novel to date in any language. To write a foreword to the novel was, however, an entirely different matter, yet I was also conscious of the great honour bestowed upon me.

The novel, which is essentially about labour migrations in Southern Africa can be read through multiple lenses. There is an extended debate, often couched in broader economic, political and social terms, on the causes and effects of migration on the receiving and sending countries. Spiwe Mahachi-Harper contributes to this debate in novel form and tells the story of the lives and experiences of migrant workers at a mine in Southern Rhodesia. It is a story told through the voices of four generations of a migrant family from Nyasaland. For Spiwe, herself a Zimbabwean living in Great Britain, the story of migration is more than economics and politics. It is above all a human story. Migrants are people with dreams, desires, hopes and plans. Their struggle is a common human struggle, but one that is lived and experienced in foreign lands, with all the attendant challenges of alienation, loss of culture and crisis of identity. Migrants lead exilic lives suspended between

home and away, always mentally projecting the geography of another space separate from the one they physically inhabit.

Spiwe's characters endure lives carved out of marginalisation, alienation and disdain. In their new adopted homes, they are looked down upon by their white employers and they are shunned by the locals who refer to them with such derogatory identities as *Mabhurandaya* or *Manyasarande*. When Dhairesi, the feisty grand-daughter of the patriarch migrant, Bhaureni falls in love with a local Shona boy, Tatenda, she has hopes of marrying him. She is soon disabused of any such ideas by her own community, and even more brutally by Tatenda's aunt, Amai Moyo, who makes it clear to her that Tatenda's family would never accept a daughter-in-law *"who has neither totem nor acceptable roots."*

Running through *Footprints in the Mists of Time* is the theme of culture and identity. The migrants at Patchway Valley Mine live at the cross-road of cultures. They hail from different countries, tribes and clans. They also have to contend with the dominant local Shona culture. While the older generation of migrants resist assimilation and do all they can to retain cultural purity, the younger generation yearns to conform into dominant as well as trending cultural idioms. The result is cross-cultural and intergenerational conflicts. Spiwe captures the complexity these cultural conflicts and identity crises in the life of Dhairesi, the spirited grand-daughter of the patriarch migrant labourer. All Dhairesi yearns for is to emulate local Shona girls, have a Shona name_ and Fadzai is the Shona name she adopts for herself_, fall in love with a local Shona boy, and not have

to practice the dated rituals of her people, such as initiation into womanhood or being forced to shave off her hair in honour of the dead. She wants to follow a culture that she and her young friends call *"isimanje-manje"* or modernisation. The result is all too familiar. In the end Dhairesi cuts a tragic figure, accepted by none and rejected by all. Her Shona friends refuse to call her by her adopted name, her community treats her as a freak, lumping her together with the disabled and the mentally unstable, and her wish for marriage to Tatenda ends in rejection and disappointment. She yearns for acceptance, independence and identity but finds none.

The novel is not only about hardships, conflicts and shattered dreams, it also about hope, determination and the future. Spiwe closes the novel with the voice of Mavhuto, the great grandson of the patriarch migrant labourer, who left his Nuhono village in Nyasalanda and travelled many months to the mines of Southern Rhodesia. Mavhuto demonstrates the same that same spirit, a determination to break with the past, and for him it is a determination that transcends everything. It is a spirit born out of a realisation that this adopted land that they inhabit, the new Zimbabwe, is also their own. Mavhuto does not need to go back to Malawi to trace the histories of his people because this piece of earth beneath him is his own patch as well and from it, he will trace the footprints of his people through the mists of time. From this patch of earth that he has claimed as his own, he will make other destinies for himself and his progeny, his own footprints in the mists of time.

Spiwe is a talented story teller. Zimbabweans will be familiar with her other works, such as *Echoes in the Shadows* or *Trials and Tribulation*, all told in lucid

language and in gripping tones. In *Footprints in the Mists of Time,* she gives an honest voice to migrants, allowing them to narrate their hopes, their pain, their despair and their dreams. It is our story, a human story in this era of globalisation and human movements.

Kupukile Mlambo, Ph.D. (Econ)
Deputy Governor, Reserve Bank of Zimbabwe
Harare, Zimbabwe (4 September)

Reviewed by Memory Chirere.
The Herald (May 2013)

Title: Footprints In the Mists of Time
Author: Spiwe N Mahachi- Harper

If Wellington Kusema's novel *Dzimbabwedande* is the longest Shona novel at 108 264 words, then Spiwe Mahachi-Harper's new novel, *Footprints in the Mists of Time,* at a whopping 181 008 words, is the longest novel by a Zimbabwean! It is both a show of immense narrative tenacity and talent. This is a 419 broad paged historical novel written as an alternative to dry history with facts and figures. This story is written with a deliberate desire to tell and present arguments on the lives and times of generations of migrant African labourers who settled in Southern Rhodesia before it became Rhodesia, before it became Zimbabwe. They drifted from the then Nyasaland, Northern Rhodesia and Mocambique to work on the mines and farms of Southern Rhodesia. This book follows about four generations, beginning with Bhaureni Nyirenda's journey from Nuhono village in the Nkotakhota District of the then Nyasaland early in the century to settle at Southern Rhodesia's Patchway Valley Mine in Gatooma District. This links Zimbabwean history with the histories of her neighbours and makes nonsense of the present day boarders. This is a story about the oppression of people and their consistent dehumanisation, leaving the conscious reader with a suggestion that Africans have travelled a very long road of suffering. This is a story about the anxieties of people brutally isolated and trapped in localities far away from their original

homes. This is a story about moving on and even drifting without finding an anchor and with no ability to return to the source. This is a story that defines the nature of colonial exploitation in Southern Africa. This book reminds me most of Alex Huley's *Roots,* the saga of an African family in American slavery, in demonstrating that all people displaced by capital become chattels and not humans. And the process of being turned to an animal begins when your tormentor makes you doubt the humanity within yourself. Pushed out of his village by the desire to work and be able to return and pay taxes, Bhaureni Nyirenda realises while in Southern Rhodesia that: "I was nothing and a nobody but just a lifeless limb detached from the rest of the body. Back in Nuhono village (in Nyasaland) I also left behind my soul, without which I felt empty and hopeless, like a piece of dead wood cast adrift in a river and left at the mercy of the forces of nature, to sink or float." He leaves behind a wife and children and is never able to return to them even when he thinks he might return soon and very soon. The mine system sucks him, never giving him enough to survive and retrace his steps. The return journey would be as tragic as the first journey because one does not want to return with nothing to show. From Bhaureni to his son Masauso, through to grandson Chakumanda and great grandson, Mavhuto, the migrant labourer is reminded by the indigenous Shona people and the white man of not belonging to Southern Rhodesia. This happens, despite shedding tears and sweat in the mines and suffering, to death from the dreaded respiratory diseases from spending a lifetime in the

dusty underground. This novel also reminds me of Edward Kamau Brathwaite's poetry in *The Arrivants* and *Mother,* in demonstrating that all displaced people survive on memory stored in both the mind and in the genes. The migrant community re-enacts home through their languages and enduring cultures. Knowledge is handed down from father to son. But towards the end of the four generations, a grandfather says to grandson: "You, Mavhuto, can retrace the footprints of your great grandfather back to the warm heart of Africa... Malawi. Only animals fail to trace the trail of their births through the ages." This shows how they wish to pay pilgrimage to the land of their birth even when they know that they are now based here. This is going to be an important novel for Zimbabwean literature. Zimbabwean fiction rarely puts the migrant and his offsprings at the centre of the narrative. But here is a novel written from their point of view. *Footprints in the Mists of Time* is Spiwe Mahachi Harper's third novel after *Trials and Tribulations* and *Echoes In The Shadows*. The author is a trained teacher and holds a diploma in French Culture and Civilisation. Currently, she stays in the United Kingdom, dividing her time between Zimbabwe and that country.

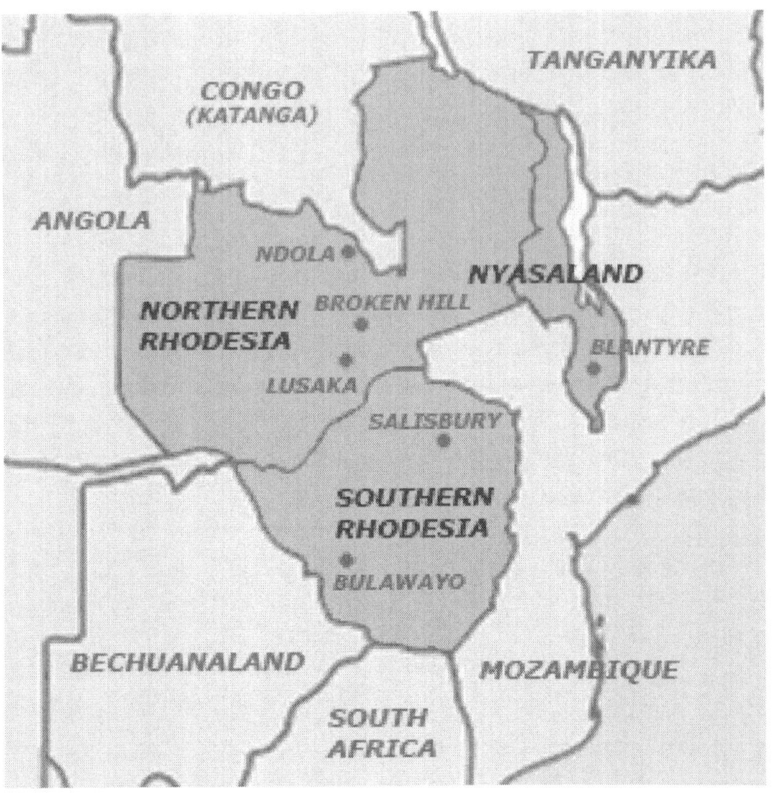

THE FEDERATION OF RHODESIA AND NYASALAND

(SOUTHERN AFRICA DURING THE COLONIAL ERA)

CNN CABLE NEWS NETWORK
Monday, Jun. 19, 1972
Disaster at Wankie

A cable car was hurled like a giant cannonball from the No. 2 mine shaft of the Wankie Colliery in north western Rhodesia, burning a row of papaya trees before it came to rest 50 yards away. That was the first sign of the disaster. An explosion, possibly emanating from a dynamite magazine, had devastated the major shaft of the mine that produced all of Rhodesia's coal. On or near the surface, four men were killed instantly. Hundreds of feet below, 426 miners —390 of them black, 36 white—were trapped amid rock and deadly methane and carbon monoxide fumes.

For 15 hours, rescue operations were tragically hampered by gases seeping from the mine head. Police urged a crowd of mourning African women to move out of range. Eventually the officers of the colliery, which is owned by the Anglo American Corp. of South Africa, decided to clear the shaft by pumping air in to push the fumes deeper into the mine; the decision permitted the rescue effort to begin but inevitably reduced the chance of finding anyone alive.

There was never any sign of life in the three-mile tunnel. Rescue teams listened in vain for "pipe talk," the tapping of men who have somehow found sanctuary in pockets of fresh air. On the third day, the Mine's Manager, Sir Keith Acutt, announced that all hope was lost, adding, a bit speciously, that indications were that the missing men had

"died instantaneously and were not aware of what had happened." The final death toll is expected to exceed 430, making Wankie the fifth worst coalmining disaster in history. At the mine-head, the wailing of the African women continued.

The worst: Honkeiko Colliery, Manchuria, 1942, 1,549 dead; Courrieres, France, 1906, 1,060; Hojo Colliery, Japan, 1914, 687; Omuta, Japan, 1963, 458 dead.

Excerpt from the book *"The Reluctant President"*, The Memoirs of the Hon. Clifford Dupont, GCLM., ID. Pages 222-224. Published by Books of Rhodesia Publishing Co. (Pvt) Ltd 1978. ISBN 0 86920 183 2. © C.W. Dupont.

"In June, 1972, one of the greatest natural disasters to hit the country took place, when an underground explosion occurred in Wankie No.2 Colliery. Four hundred and twenty-six miners lost their lives - thirty six Europeans and three hundred and ninety Africans. Apart from the one hundred and seventy-six Rhodesians who died, there were ninety-one Zambians, fifty-two from Mozambique, thirty-seven from Malawi, thirty Tanzanians, fourteen Britons, twelve South Africans, nine from South West Africa, four from the Caprivi Strip, and one from Botswana. The disaster provoked reaction throughout the world, and messages of sympathy poured in from all quarters, and included those from Queen Elizabeth, Sir Alec Douglas-Home, the British Foreign Secretary, the Pope, and the Prime Minister of South Africa, Mr. B. J. Vorster. I visited the colliery the following day, and I think this was one of the most depressing and indeed most distressing days I have ever spent in my life. The wives of the African miners were wailing. Most of the European relatives were in a severe state of shock, and one felt completely helpless at not 'being able to do anything to relieve their distress.

The whole country was stunned by this disaster, and with the well-known generosity of Rhodesians, various

organisations as well as individuals immediately set up funds for the relief of those who had been affected by the disaster. The Wankie Disaster Fund came into being. The response from all sections of the Rhodesian community was instantaneous and overwhelming. Contributions varying from small silver coins donated by Africans to large sums given by commercial firms and organisations were received. The main object was, of course, to provide for the welfare of all of the surviving dependants. In view of the fact that so many of the African victims came from outside our borders, a great deal of trouble was experienced in tracing relatives, and eventually a special representative was employed to travel around the country to endeavour to locate those who had either returned to their Reserves, or were being looked after by their own families. He succeeded in tracing no less than one hundred and eighty, but even so he was considerably restricted in his efforts as a result of the disturbed conditions in many parts of Rhodesia due to terrorist activity."

For history to come alive, one needs, above all, to know the social implications, the individual human story_ the reasons that impelled people to leave their homeland, the successes and tragedies they experienced in adapting to the hard and challenging life…

(Kate Caffrey, Great Migrations 3)

Etched at the very back of my soul
Is the shadow of a mighty dream

Of weary clansmen in a foreign land,

A home within the vast wilderness.
The hope of an enriched life burning
Flares like a fire beyond the horizon.

S.N Mahachi-Harper

TABLE OF CONTENTS

Mavhuto's Story
(1975- present day)
Patchway Valley Mine, Kadoma

"*Ma*Mpofu...[1]"

The voice quivers, catches in the throat, struggles then tapers off into a barely audible sound as it mingles with the darkness around me.

"Shhh... *a*Nyirenda." The soothing tone of a strong voice drowns the feeble wheezing. "I am here. Try not to talk, otherwise that will tire your lungs and make the coughing worse."

"Water, *ma*Mpofu."

The two voices merge in the dark. One reaches me as if from the other side of a small hill; feeble and raspy like a tired and breathless wind struggling to break free. The other, boisterous in normal circumstances, struggles to be reined in but succeeds in becoming only a barely subdued whisper in the night. Grandfather and his second wife, *ma*Mpofu, are in the room where they sleep. A brick wall separates that room and the one in which I lay down during the night. The latter is used as a sitting room by day. On this night I lie in the dark, my reed mat placed next to the wall. Though my ears struggle to catch the words coming from the other side, my mind however, clearly envisions the old man lying on his bed. His hollow and lifeless eyes look with despair at a world that has shrunk to just four walls, and one that has taken everything from him and given nothing in return.

Grandfather's skeletal frame, with knotted grey hairs on his head, reclines half-sitting and half-lying on the straw-stuffed mattress. This image of the old man is the

1 *ma*; honorific term for females, precedes the totem

one that I had lived with in the last few months. But that is my mind pulling me back to the events of the past. The sounds of Grandfather wheezing and calling out belong to the days just gone. Today, at this moment in time, it is the voices of wailing women that cut into the night. A sharp pain tugs at my heart as I realise that Grandfather has not called, and he never shall. His voice shall never again struggle against his chest. The tortured chest shall never again labour to rise and fall with a barely noticeable rhythm that marks time with each beat of the heart, separating the past from the present.

* * *

This moment…
  suspended in time…
    neither the past nor the future…
      not yesterday, not tomorrow,
        but just this moment in time,
          stuck between yesterday
            and tomorrow, refuses to linger.

It draws me back to the past before it shoves me, unprepared, into the future.

Gloomy spaces, both filled with horror, one of a tragic experience and the other of anxious uncertainty, fill my mind and shut out the present. The past floats across my mind and brings forth the memory of a hot afternoon when humid air breathes and shimmers like a silvery blanket billowing in the wind, after which, showers of rainfall bring a welcome coolness. A short while later, the setting sun casts a coppery glow that lingers momentarily after its rays have glided over the point where the sky

touches the dark brown earth. My shadow has retracted beneath my feet like a snail into its shell. When the showers stop, I lift my bare feet with ease and they leave faint footprints.

Temporary.

Transient.

Here today, gone tomorrow.

That was a few days ago. Today, at this moment, *ma*Mpofu's grief gathers in her mouth and is hurled across the room where it hits the wall opposite with a resounding heaviness before it floats back and settles among the mourners gathered around the body of the old man.

* * *

When Grandfather started coughing, *ma*Mpofu and I had assumed it was just the usual coughs and colds everybody else occasionally suffered from due to changes in the weather. But the old man's cough had persisted. He rattled mostly at night and well into the early hours of the morning. When he was still coughing a month or so later, he had to be persuaded to go to the local clinic where the nurse gave him medicines and tablets of different types, one after the other. When this did not seem to help, Grandfather was referred to the visiting doctor. The white doctor and his black nurse aide came periodically to deal with the more serious health issues deemed to be beyond the capabilities of the Red Cross-trained nurse who attended to the black Mine employees. The doctor said the persistent coughing had something to do with the weak insides of the old man.

In the beginning, Grandfather's illness caused no alarm. He coughed, he hawked and he spat out phlegm.

Because we could not see the damage to his insides, we took it for granted that it was merely a matter of time before he regained his good health. He had been examined by none other than a white doctor, after all. It was generally assumed that white people knew everything and were said to possess knowledge superior to ours. What they could not put right, no one else could, so we waited patiently for Grandfather's niggling cough to go away. We had great hope that it would, especially on those days his face lit up and the coughing subsided. Despite that, his wife *ma*Mpofu, and I found it exasperating at times to be completely powerless to do anything about his coughing. The old man hated it when people referred to his illness as if it were a permanent state of his condition.

"It is the dust that makes you cough, *a*Nyirenda. It makes your condition worse. Why do you keep going down the shafts when your chest is this weak? Just tell your bosses you need time off work," begged *ma*Mpofu.

"Only a coward will lie down and let illness take over his life," he retorted.

This was during one of the many cold winter evenings we spent in the outside 'kitchen' warming ourselves by the fireside. *Ma*Mpofu and I often took turns to stoke the fire and keep it going until the burning embers glowed red. Every winter night after the evening meal, I would select a few of the biggest embers and put them in a shallow metal tin. I would fan them until there was no more smoke coming out and I would then take this *mbaura* into the house. Making sure there was nothing nearby that could easily catch fire, I would carefully place the tin on the floor of the middle room. We left the two interior doors open so that the warmth could spread to the other rooms. By the time we went indoors to sleep, the house would be rid of the chilly air without being exactly warm.

"And do what, if I do not go down the shafts?" demanded Grandfather, making a feeble attempt to stick out his weak chin in defiance.

"If I do not go to work what do I do here, *ma*Mpofu, chase after the hems of your skirts? And what do we live on? We need money for *chingwa, mereki, ndimpupu.*[2] Mavhuto's education costs a lot of money. There is also the issue of school fees, the building school fund, the uniform and the never-ending little things such as writing books, exercise books and pens. All that costs money, *ma*Mpofu, and lots of it. Where would the money come from if I stop working? Who does not know that *abwana*[3] pay us only for the work done per shift? Every shift counts, in case you do not know that already. Each shift is money earned and each missed shift is money lost. No work, no pay. It is as simple as that. I have to go down those mine shafts if I am to get my wages. So for each shift I am scheduled to work, I put on my overalls, my gumboots, my helmet and with a torch in hand, I turn up for work. And I work hard. Always. I am not a lazy man, nor am I a coward."

"Why don't you take just a few days off then, only a few days, *a*Nyirenda? Will the whole of Patchway Valley Mine grind to a halt just because of your absence? Why, even the hardworking Mashona people say *kufa kwemujoni kamba haivharwi.*[4] All this boasting about never missing a day of work due to illness is misplaced loyalty to *abwana* who do not care whether you live or die. What loyalty or gratitude have your employers ever shown you, *a*Nyirenda? You insist on driving yourself to breaking

---

2bread, milk and maize meal

3the bosses

4The death of a white policeman does not result in the closure of the police camp

point, yet you know that once you are no longer of any use to them, they will lay you off with nothing more than six months' wages. They will not hesitate to wave you away from this place and, before the wind has erased your footprints from the path that leads out of this compound, they would have moved someone else into your house. You need to take care of your health," *ma*Mpofu admonished her husband.

"Woman, has it not occurred to you that the reason I drive myself so hard is to prove to *abwana* just how useful I still am, despite my age? Do you really think I do not dread *chigumura*? How else am I to evade the fate you have just described if not by working my knuckles off? I have no wish to give my employers a reason to cast me away. No, at least not so easily. And letting them know that I am too ill to work is one sure way of doing so. We still need a roof over our heads and food in our stomachs."

"And you think that overworking yourself when you are ill is the answer, even if it kills you?"

"What choice do I have? You tell me, *ma*Mpofu."

"Just try and take it easy for now, for our sake, if not for your own, please *a*Nyirenda. Very soon, Mavhuto will look old enough to start work. He can soon take your place underground. It is the only way we can avoid being thrown out of the house should you face *chigumura.*"

"Never!" screamed Grandfather. "No descendant of mine shall give his life to the mines. Has this Mine not sucked enough of my blood as it is? No, *ma*Mpofu. That will not happen. Not to Mavhuto. The Mine has reduced me to this wretched shell that I have become, so it might as well finish me off. But it does not have to claim yet more of my descendants."

"In that case why don't you ask to work on the surface where there isn't that much dust? Surely there must be some other jobs you can do?"

"I do not think so," answered Grandfather shaking his head. "What type of job would they give to an old man like me? I cannot learn a different line of work. Too old. All I ever learned was how to wield the pick-axe and swing the shovel."

"*Old!* You talk as if you are a white-haired old man tottering towards his grave, which of course you are not, otherwise *abwana* would have retired you a long time ago. Surely, there must be something they can give you to do *kumiro?*"

"*Kumiro*! Do not forget that the mill is where they crush all those stones to get to the precious gold which *abwana* worship as if it is their God. They want a different breed of men there altogether. For one thing, the fires are said to be hot enough to melt metal. Can you try and imagine such heat?"

"Can that be true?" I asked, speaking for the first time now that the conversation had moved on to a safe topic.

Both Grandfather and *ma*Mpofu turned towards me, the former with an amused expression on his face, and the latter with undisguised annoyance.

"In my village in Zvimba, well-mannered children do not address their elders unless invited to. And more importantly, they do not interrupt the conversations of adults, *nxi,*" admonished *ma*Mpofu.

"*Ma*Mpofu, the boy is not a child anymore, at least he is not so young that he cannot join in our discussions," said Grandfather. Turning towards me, he asked, "Mavhuto, how old are you now? Thirteen, fourteen?"

"Just turned fourteen, *Asekuru,*" I answered, not too boldly in case I invited *ma*Mpofu's disapproval for the second time within a moment.

"You see? This one here is a boy, soon to be a man," Grandfather chuckled with obvious pride. *Ma*Mpofu mumbled something about *vabvakure* having no manners and failing in their duty to discipline children from an

early age. The old man dismissed her mutterings with a feeble wave of his hand before continuing with the tale of the mill as if the brief interruption had not taken place.

"Those who work at the mill say they sweat and wipe their brows all the time and that the heat makes them feel dizzy. Their throats are parched most of the time in that place they describe as a living hell. That would make me go mad. That, and the tight security. Imagine being under close watch by those eagle-eyed watchmen. I would hate to be checked, searched and frisked each time I left the premises as if I were some common thief. "

"But *a*Nyirenda, you know there is a reason for all that now. With the recent incidents of mine labourers stealing bits of smelt gold, what do you expect?"

"Why would anyone want to steal those useless bits of stones anyway? We grew up with them under our feet and picked up some on the way to school. We kicked them about and crushed them to free the glittering bits embedded there. They were all over the place then, so what is different about them now?" snorted Grandfather. "The stones were of no value to me then and they still are not, even today. What I do not understand is why these young men of today want to take what belongs to *abwana,* and always has done since our fathers started working in the mines. Who buys those stones from our misguided young men, and what do they need the money for? To buy those useless wirelesses they perch on their shoulders, and with which they blast our ears with the sounds that crackle out of them? Look what the result is now; strip searches, *nxi*! I will work down under where I am not treated with suspicion."

"I still do not think it is advisable to continue breathing in the dust underground. It does not do your lungs any good. Surely the *miro* is preferra_"

"Hai, wosanitsutsa, maMpofu[5]*!"* Grandfather screamed at his wife, which immediately set off a bout of coughing. For a moment, we were alarmed. In the days prior to that discussion, the old man had found it increasingly harder to control his temper, which he seemed to lose at the slightest provocation. I was baffled by the gradual change in his mood in general, but *ma*Mpofu, at whom the outbursts were always directed, managed to calm him down and he would revert to the gentle, mild mannered Grandfather that I knew.

"Your Grandfather must be in pain," *ma*Mpofu would calmly whisper. "Men rarely cry when they feel helpless, Mavhuto. They get angry instead and lash out."

Before the illness, Grandfather had always spoken softly. Only rarely did he raise his voice in exasperation, but with the gradual deterioration of his health, he became a different man. Like *ma*Mpofu, I too wished he would stop working, but he had the obstinacy of a donkey. He could have asked to be moved to the mills where gold was smelted, but he hated the tight security which at times required that the miners turn all pockets inside out, remove their gumboots, shake them and turn them upside down. Whenever there were suspicions of gold nuggets being smuggled out, the searches could be very thorough, requiring that miners strip completely and stand with their hands stretched away from their bodies.

"Can you imagine me, *ma*Mpofu, old as I am, stripping to my bare skin and standing at attention in front of those young security guards?" snorted Grandfather. "'Hands up, *a*Nyirenda. Turn around. Open your mouth.' *Ha ha,* as if one would hide stones under the tongue! 'Remove your gumboots, turn them upside down. And now...., drop your trousers!' Eyi, I would rather go hungry, *ma*Mpofu, than suffer such indignity before those

5Don't argue with me *ma*Mpofu

youths who underwent their *jando*[6] only a few years ago. I would rather be laid off, thrown out of my home and left on the outskirts of this compound for the vultures to pick whatever is left of me than submit to such humiliating searches. If that is the kind of gratitude *abwana* think I deserve after all these years of shedding my blood, sweat and tears for their stupid stones, then so be it. No, *ma*Mpofu, I shall continue to go down those shafts even if it kills me."

So for a few more months, Grandfather kept on going to work. He also started talking about the land that his father had left behind many, many years ago. I listened patiently as he talked. When someone one cares about is ill, and there is nothing one can do about their condition, sometimes patience is the only meaningful thing one can give them. So day after day I listened as the old man's voice droned on. The same desires and wishes, hopes and dreams, regrets too, were expressed first in a quavering voice, then in a raspy whisper as the months went by. I could not understand the old man's obsession with a past he had not shared. Grandfather knew about the old country only through the memories of his father and those of the other elderly migrants who spoke with nostalgia of a homeland they were destined never to see again.

The more frail Grandfather became, the more he talked of the urge in him to fulfil his father's wishes and look for his clansmen back in the Nkhotakota district of Malawi, in Nuhono village to be precise. It is difficult to say when exactly Grandfather's illness began because he was always strong and brave.

"Whatever problems may be tearing your heart apart, be sure to bury them in your chest, Mavhuto. Smile with the sun, sing with the birds and the world will certainly look better. Even your problems will begin to pale. A man

---

6circumcision ceremony for boys

must be strong in his actions even though his body might be dictating the opposite. And remember too, that we men are different from women. We do not whine at every little ache and pain. We do not lie down and listen to every searing cramp in the stomach, every throb of the head or to the twinge of each pulled muscle. We are strong, Mavhuto. You must always remember that," Grandfather used to say. He had never been bedridden for as long as I could remember. Once in a while he suffered a headache and caught a cold, but it was nothing to keep him from work.

One humid night, several months after Grandfather had started coughing, I was woken by a rattling sound. I thought it was an animal howling somewhere outside. I had never heard such a sound before. Then it became clearer and a lot nearer. The wheezing and whooping sounds were coming from the other side of the thin limestone-brick wall that separated Grandfather's bedroom and the sitting room where I slept. The old man was at the height of a fit of coughing that went on and on, punctuated now and again by *ma*Mpofu's soothing voice. After what seemed like an eternity, the coughing subsided. Grandfather's feeble voice croaked, "*Madzi*, *ma*Mpofu. Throat…. dry." I threw off my blankets and got up to go and fetch the water that Grandfather was asking for. At that instant, *ma*Mpofu flicked on the light in the living room. If she was surprised to see me awake she did not show it.

"Mavhuto, get some water for your grandfather. He is thirsty," she said.

I shall never forget the sight that met my eyes when I walked into Grandfather's bedroom. The old man was sitting up in bed with his head slumped forward. The chin rested on his chest, below which protruded emaciated ribs. Shrivelled brown skin covered the ribs like a tight-fitting shroud. A pillow was positioned behind his back to prop

up his gaunt frame. I realised at that moment just how frail Grandfather was. On the floor by the sagging bed lay a crumpled handkerchief that was soaked with spittle and frothy phlegm. I stood rooted to the floor, my lips unable to mouth the fears seated in the pit of my stomach. The specks of blood were unmistakable. I threw *ma*Mpofu a terror-stricken look but her steady gaze refused to acknowledge the fear in my eyes and silently cautioned against commenting on the horror before us.

"Rub my feet please, *ma*Mpofu. I cannot feel them," croaked Grandfather. Just as his wife bent down, he rasped, "My chest, *ma*Mpofu, there is fire in there."

"Try and take it easy now. Here, take a sip. The water will make you feel better." Propping Grandfather's head up with one hand, *ma*Mpofu brought the cup to his parched lips. The sight of her helping the old man with such tenderness made me regard her with new eyes. Despite the occasional malice towards me, she was capable of showing tenderness towards those she cared about.

"My insides, *ma*Mpofu *wanga*… they are on fire. When I cough... it feels... they want to… come out through my mouth. My lungs... congested." There was more wheezing after that.

"Shush *a*Nyirenda, the more you talk the worse it gets__"

"My throat..."

When Grandfather finally drifted off to sleep, his shallow breathing making his chest move only slightly, *ma*Mpofu picked up the soiled handkerchief and motioned me to follow her into the living room. When I looked at the clock on the wall, it showed a few minutes after two o'clock.

"I hope he will have at least a few hours of sleep. He sleeps better in a sitting position when the coughing gets that bad. This is the worst it has been at night. He normally coughs that bad only during the day upon his

return from work," explained *ma*Mpofu. We were whispering because the walls were thin.

"When I am at school," I observed. That explained why I had not noticed before just how much worse Grandfather's condition had become.

"Yes."

"*Ma*Mpofu, was that er, is that blood, I mean did he cough up all that?" I pointed at the handkerchief in her hand.

"Yes, and this is the third time it has happened. Three times in one week, imagine. When it happened the first time, Nurse said we were not to worry unless it happened several times over a short period of time."

"And now it has," my trembling voice betrayed the fear in my heart. "We have to tell Nurse in the morning."

"If he lets us, which I doubt," said *ma*Mpofu.

"But if that is the only way he can get treatment why would he object?"

"The way he sees it, it will result in him being removed from his home and kept in isolation at the Annexe Hospital in Gatooma. That hospital is your grandfather's worst nightmare. He dreads it worse than he does retrenchment."

"But he will get treatment," I cried.

"Of course he will, but only God knows if the treatment will help him now. It might be a bit late for that. I do not know how we can convince him that it is the best thing to do." *Ma*Mpofu and I were quiet for a while, each of us lost in our individual fears. *Ma*Mpofu sighed and said, "Go back to sleep, Mavhuto. Tomorrow you and I can talk to him together."

I crawled back under my blankets but sleep would not come. For a long time afterwards I lay awake, my mind filled with thoughts of the horror that was unfolding before us. I was still awake when the first cock crowed. I lacked the strength to fold my blankets and face the day. I

decided to miss school so that *ma*Mpofu and I could deal with the urgent issue at hand as soon as the clinic opened. When I went in to see Grandfather, he had no recollection of my presence in his bedroom the night before. He looked a lot better and my relief was immense. He did not argue when I told him that I did not have to go to school that day. After he had washed his face and eaten his porridge, *ma*Mpofu broached the subject that was uppermost in our minds.

"*A*Nyirenda, if you remember, um… the first time we saw specks of blood on your phlegm__,"

"I do not remember," he growled and threw his wife an eye that dared her to contradict him.

"Ah, surely you must remember? You know when you coughed non-stop till__"

"What about it?" Grandfather made a weak attempt at adopting a no nonsense tone.

"If you remember well, Nurse said we would only need to worry if you coughed up blood again within__,"

"So who says I have?"

"Three days ago and last night, you__,"

"*Hai, ma*Mpofu! Do not start annoying me now. *Sha*! Not on a morning when I feel a lot better than I have done in a long time. Don't! Am I not suffering enough as it is? Should you be making up sensational tales of the cough-and-spit-blood disease just because I have developed a mere cough?" *Ma*Mpofu held her head in her hands and sighed. For the first time in my life I felt sorry for her. She had lived with the old man long enough to know how stubborn he could be.

"*A*Nyirenda, I beg you, Mavhuto and I only want what is good for you. We want you to get well but that cannot happen unless the doctors look into your chest. And for that you need to go to the African General Hospital in Gatooma__"

"*Ya*, after which, the doctors there will bundle me off to the Annexe in Bherina African Township as if I were an old, broken-down tool that can no longer be repaired and therefore ought to be discarded. Who does not know that if you cough up a bit of blood the doctors there put you in isolation as if you have the disease of rotting fingers and toes? *Ma*Mpofu, if you are tired of looking after the useless creature that I have become, I beg you, just pack up and leave! I will bear you no grudge. I shall forever be grateful for the care you gave me in the last few months, but do not attempt to drive me out of my own home. I want to take my last breath here, in this house, not locked up in some jail *abwana* try to pass off as a hospital. From what I know, a hospital is a place where people go to get better, yet no one we know has ever come back from the Annexe walking on his own two feet. Everybody in this community knows that the doctors over there give you an injection with poison to finish you off," panted the old man. When neither *ma*Mpofu nor I commented, he demanded, "Why is it that only ageing African labourers are sent there? When *a*Bhauti's wife went to visit her husband there, she says she saw no *vazungu*. Not even one! That place is where they send those labourers that the mines are too slow to finish off. I am not going anywhere, *ma*Mpofu. *Iyayi*[7]."

Instead of arguing further, *ma*Mpofu offered Grandfather some tea, which he gladly accepted, and said, "You see now why I refuse to be away from home? Who would take care of me the way you do, *mukazi wanga?*" And there the matter rested.

When Grandfather started coughing and spitting frothy blood, we knew that his body had finally succumbed to the disease of the mines. It was a disease that ate away the insides of the body while its victim

7 No

continued to work, oblivious to the damage slowly taking place within until, in most cases, it was too late. Grandfather knew how bad his condition was because he had seen it all before in other miners before him. They called the ailment the 'cough-and-spit-blood' disease.

For a while after that night, Grandfather would get better before getting worse again. He kept going to work whenever he could, which was more often than not. I started spending more time keeping him company, and less on playing football with my friends. In the mornings when Grandfather did not go to work, *ma*Mpofu would bring out his wooden stool from the bedroom and place it near the wall outside. Our house faced east and therefore received direct sunshine on cold winter mornings. The old man and I sat by the wall while *ma*Mpofu cleaned the house. We basked in the sunshine, our long limbs stretched before us. *Ma*Mpofu used to joke that if we continued to sun ourselves like strips of meat carved and hung out to dry, our legs would soon develop dark patches and look like the coat of a leopard. "You are going to get *mbare*, you layabouts. Only lazy people bask in the sun long enough to develop those dark patches." After a few chuckles and a bit of banter, Grandfather's wife would leave us alone and get on with the work around the house. The wall was one of the places on which serious conversations in our home took place. Apart from that wall in the mornings, there was also the place under the mulberry tree whose large evergreen leaves provided shade in the hot summer afternoons. In the evenings we sat in the outside structure that served as a cooking place. Grandfather and I also shared special moments alone while chopping wood, watering vegetables, tending the flowers bordering the yard, or as we weeded our fields on the outskirts of the compound.

We were basking in the sun by the wall one morning when Grandfather said, "Not once did I imagine that I would one day get this disease. I saw myself either facing *chigumura* like many others before me, or being presented with a *njinga*[8] as reward for long service, and the offer of a one way railway ticket to Malawi, the land of my people. The land of my dreams! If only you knew Mavhuto, how often I have dreamt of that!" For a moment the eyes became watery but the threat of a deluge was killed in one quick blink. It was the first time that, to my knowledge, the old man openly admitted that he had contracted the dreaded disease.

"Take note of this now, Mavhuto *muzukuru.*[9] In the mines one does not retire. A few lucky labourers do, but the majority of us just become useless due to illness or premature ageing, then the mines spit us out, after which we are then ordered to move and make way for younger blood. We hold on to the shovel and keep going for as long as we can before passing it on to the next lot. We grip the shovel, reluctant to let go for we have nothing with which to steady ourselves once our hands are empty. It is an act stemming from the fear of an uncertain future rather than from pride in the job or devotion to it. Young men with strong bodies, stamina and fresh blood coursing through their veins step in and take up the shovels and pick axes. They continue with the race while those before them collapse, panting and sweating, at times never to rise again. It is like a relay, this existence of ours. Fortunately for those of you people growing up now in a country where the black man rules, things are changing, *muzukuru.* There is no reason for you to join the race. Going down those shafts day after day, digging and shovelling in those

---

8bicycle

9grandson

stifling tunnels is a laborious job, and the most perilous I can think of, yet it pays very little. It is no better than slave labour," complained Grandfather. "Labouring in the mines and on the farms is what our people had always done. We did the hardest jobs. In any case what choices did migrants like us have? We had no homes in the village to move back to, and no land to till in order to sustain our livelihoods, our own lands being a whole world away. We had no money either with which to buy houses in the black peoples' townships. What was one to do, save give one's life and service to the ungrateful farmers and mine owners? But you, *muzukuru wanga,* can now get an education and get a good job in future, thanks to independence."

Grandfather had continued going to work off and on for several weeks. Then one day, his supervisors told him not to report for work until he was well enough to do a full month's work without breaking his shifts. Eventually, he had to accept that though his mind was willing, his body was no longer able to cope. It was not an easy situation for him to accept and it made him miserable. He still tottered into the surrounding farmlands but only rarely and for brief periods at a time. After a while, Grandfather's body seemed to weaken drastically. He found it difficult to do simple everyday tasks that most people took for granted. Walking made him wheeze. Bending down to pull out weeds triggered a bout of coughing that lasted a while. Carrying even a small watering can left him panting and struggling to breathe and gradually, Grandfather found it difficult to stand for more than a few minutes. Each morning, *ma*Mpofu took a reed mat and some blankets and placed them outside for him to lie under the mulberry tree. From his hollow sunken eyes, the old man watched the small world that Patchway Valley was, pass by. His friends and fellow migrant workers visited as often as they could and they

told him amusing tales of events taking place in a world he was slowly drifting away from and losing touch with. Though he never disclosed the true nature of his illness to outsiders, it soon became obvious to those closest to him that Grandfather had contracted the cough-and-spit-blood disease. With total disregard for their own health, his workmates colluded in a silent pact to keep the Mine Management from knowing the truth. Away from him they spoke in hushed whispers about the fatal disease but in his presence and with his wife, they talked about *a*Nyirenda's back that troubled him, and how lying down most of the time made breathing difficult, resulting in endless coughing. *Ma*Mpofu gave that same explanation to whoever asked.

One day around sunset, the sweaty figure of one of our neighbours shuffled into our yard. The unpleasant odour from his overworked body was one that everybody in the community was familiar with, but which no one could ever get used to. We recognised that smell as part of our existence. The sweaty stench defined the miner, his job, his fears and the hopelessness of his situation. It wafted into our noses as *a*Mwanza dragged his weary feet towards us. His gumboots were covered in quarry dust and an empty flask and a helmet dangled from either hand. It was obvious that he was coming straight from the afternoon shift. He came over to the mulberry tree where Grandfather lay on a reed mat and *Ma*Mpofu sat by his side, fanning flies away from his red, watery eyes.

"Mavhuto *muzukuru,* get a chair for *a*Mwanza," Grandfather's feeble voice said.

"Do not worry yourself, *munyamata*[10]. I will be okay with this," said *a*Mwanza as he dragged a big stone from nearby and sat down on it next to Grandfather. He put his

10 Boy

flask down on the grass and balanced his helmet on his folded knee before turning his attention to *ma*Mpofu.

"How are you, *ma*Mpofu?"

"We are faring well, *a*Mwanza. How about you, how are you?"

"What can befall us? It is our invalid here whom we worry about. How is he today, and the pains that trouble his body?"

"He bears them from one day to the next. What else can one do?" answered *ma*Mpofu.

"*Hai, ma*Mpofu," said Grandfather. "I am still alive, and I can still answer for myself. Am I so ill that I have lost the power of speech? Wait until my lips are permanently stilled, then you can speak for me."

As I got up and went into the house, the sound of their chuckles at the lighthearted banter followed me. I was raised to move away and from within earshot when adults came to visit. *A*Mwanza did not stay long, for when I came out a short while later, he was leaving.

I went back and sat by Grandfather's side. He looked livelier than he had been before *a*Mwanza's visit.

"This concern by my kinsmen, more than anything else, touches me deeply. It fills me with pride," he beamed. "You see Mavhuto *muzukuru,* the many ways in which our lives are enriched?"

"You tell us, *a*Nyirenda," cajoled *ma*Mpofu.

"We may be poor but no one can say we neglect each other. We have love for each other and we care about each other's well-being. What can be more important than that, especially in a foreign land? Our people may not live in big houses, they may not own large farms, nor do they drive those fancy cars that *abwana* value more than their kinsmen, but so long as the same words roll off our tongues, and our feet beat the same path, my people's lives are enriched. We are not greedy."

"Oh yes you are, why else would you be so far away from your homeland, the land of your fathers?"

"Get away, *ma*Mpofu. Should we say then that even you are greedy? If I remember well, you do not come from these parts yourself. My people do not want everything of anything they lay their eyes on. They just want enough to survive. *Bwana* is so greedy he is forever competing with his kinsmen, whom he is suspicious of most of the time, which is why he would rather have a dog as his best friend. Do you hear that, Mavhuto? An animal, hahaha, his very best friend, ha ha ha! Even in our poverty we at least have each other. So who says our lives are not enriched, eh?"

On the days that Grandfather sat up and laughed, we dared hope for his recovery even though we knew the disease led to death if it was not diagnosed early and put under control. My mind was yet to accept that the old man would soon die. He had always been strong. Though I referred to him as the old man, it was not because of his age. Signs of ageing only appeared prematurely when he started wasting away because of the disease. His skin became thin and wrinkled like a shrivelled tomato and his eyes looked as if they would pop out of their sockets each time he blinked. At times the coughing got so bad that his ribs ached and his eyes welled with tears that he was always quick to blink back.

Gone was the will to survive that had seen Grandfather and generations of his fellow migrant workers endure the hardships of the mines. The old man had lived a life that was both wretched and hard as he laboured for meagre wages year after year in the harsh, dangerous gold mine shafts for John Mack and Co. He lived among locals who shunned migrant workers whom they often referred to as *Mabhurandaya.* Grandfather always said that he and the other migrants had survived only through sheer strength of will. It was a world in

which men became old as they reached their middle ages. Grandfather did not to know that he would eventually give up the determination to trudge on as the disease that destroyed him from within took control of his life. A couple of months after the Mine Management had told him to stay away until he was well enough to do a good day's work, the old man became bedridden. There came a time when all he did was wheeze and groan. No words uttered. His feeble and vain attempts to hawk and spit out phlegm reduced *ma*Mpofu and me to tears as we watched helplessly while he grimaced in pain. When it became obvious that Grandfather was dying, the elders in the community were summoned. The men who had stepped into his bedroom with brave faces, their jaws set and showing strength of both body and mind, left shortly afterwards with downcast eyes and slackening chins that almost touched their chests. They mumbled their goodbyes as they went past *ma*Mpofu and me.

* * *

Yesterday, just as the sun was setting, *ma*Mpofu and I knelt at either side of the man who meant a lot to both of us in different ways. Although we had doubts that it would save Grandfather, we had decided to ask the Mine Management for transport to take him to the African General hospital, twenty kilometres away. We were going to make the request the following day. I watched as *ma*Mpofu dabbed her husband's brow with a damp towel. There was tenderness and compassion in that gesture, which I found hard to associate with *ma*Mpofu. I was still watching her when I felt Grandfather's hand grip my arm with such force that I almost squealed with delight that he was regaining his strength and therefore getting better. He

muttered something that I could not make sense of and took a long breath. I smiled as his face relaxed. *Ma*Mpofu's hand froze with the damp towel on Grandfather's temple. I was puzzled by the look of shock on her face. I was still trying to figure out what had stunned her into such stillness when she snapped out of it, threw her head back and howled like a wounded animal. Her scream shattered the silence and my heart also into tiny sharp fragments. Grandfather was gone. Her wailing said it all.

At my age I understand what it means to die but the knowledge had not prepared me for grief, nor did it prepare me for the pain that is ripping through my heart right now.

* * *

Impenetrable darkness…
suffocating stuffiness…
an oppressive odour!

A strange and bewildering feeling envelops me. I struggle to stay afloat in a dark bottomless well, my eyes firmly closed. I am scared, even though I cannot place the source of my fear. The sombre sounds of women wailing slowly penetrate my senses. I recognise the voice of *ma*Mpofu; hoarse, self-pitying and raised to barely above a whisper. It filters into my ears like water trickling slowly down the sides of a well. Striving to master some kind of bravery I am far from feeling, I open my eyes. A bright star stares directly at me from above, unblinking. The voices of the wailing women become distinct, and assume form. They fill the void. I snap out of the nightmare, trance, madness, wild thoughts or whatever it is that had temporarily replaced awareness of my surroundings. My mind registers the stuffiness, the darkness and the odour. The nightmares and the realities of the horrors are impossible

to separate for now. I struggle to face the present and put aside all thoughts of Grandfather's illness, with little success as my mind keeps going backwards and forwards in time.

* * *

After months of playing a twisted and cruel game of life and near-death in our lives, the claws of death finally descended like a huge dark shadow. But before then, the claws had hovered and lingered for some time. They then began to descend before temporarily withdrawing, as if taking delight in tempting their quarry with the miracle of a last minute reprieve. The claws of death were slow, deliberate but determined. Death enveloped the old man's body and his mind. He was a poor labourer who had nothing to bequeath to me, except the story of his people.

Last week, on the day that turned out to be Grandfather's last one outdoors, I should have sensed that he was not long for this world. Dark clouds suddenly gathered in an otherwise clear sky and hovered menacingly above as shadows merged with objects and got swallowed gradually beneath them. *Ma*Mpofu and I were sitting outside, flicking flies away from our legs. We had helped Grandfather back indoors a few hours before, and he had promptly fallen asleep. *Ma*Mpofu and I quickly rolled up our reed mats and rushed indoors. We watched with amazement as dark clouds continued to gather and glide slowly above with an allure that belied everything else around. Beneath them, the fury of the gathering storm whipped the branches of trees first one way_ bending them until they almost touched the ground_ then, like gymnasts stretching stiff limbs, they bent over in the other direction when the gust of wind

changed course. The less pliable of them grunted and groaned in protest. The swirling wind, enraged by its failure to uproot the trees, scooped leaves, bits of paper and other litter off the ground and tossed them high into the air. For a brief moment the whirlwind held the litter in a twisting column, the centre of which spun the papers and leaves round and round.

The image brought to mind a film I had once watched, of a man guiding a dance partner through a pirouette; the embrace suffocating, yet intimate, like a love-hate relationship. Then in a final gesture of victory, the whirlwind unfurled with deliberate slowness and released the litter into the skies where it floated aimlessly before eventually landing on the ground and scattering in all directions. The high pitched voices of excited children at play could be heard in the distance singing, *'Mvura naya, naya tidye mupunga!' Ma*Mpofu and I had only just finished fastening the windows when the skies opened up and a sharp crack resounded high above the asbestos sheets of our roof. The children danced and sang on, oblivious to the quavering voices of their panic-striken mothers urging them to take shelter indoors. *Ma*Mpofu and I were momentarily shocked into immobility, but we soon hastened to remove or hide any items that were red in colour. It was generally believed that the colour attracted lightning. Outside, the sky quivered and roared relentlessly as the thunderstorm descended like millions of sharp whips and pelted the ground with hailstones. The house creaked and growled as it struggled to resist the onslaught. The children's voices were drowned in the deluge, and their quick feet carried their light frames indoors with no further prompting from the mothers with drowned voices.

Before long, pools of rain water had collected on the ground. The raging waters swooshed and swirled. Like serpents uncoiling and stretching from spaces that had

become too small for their massive forms, newly-formed rivulets threaded down the remembered paths of previous journeys. Snaking around houses and hissing furiously, they scooped and swallowed the litter that the whirlwind had scattered all over not so long before. From the safety of our houses we watched the furious serpents hug the debris tight, at times rolling from side to side and upside-down, wiggling and wriggling without once losing their grip. A love-hate relationship; sensual, intimate, yet suffocating! Small stones were swallowed with minimum fuss as the serpents roared and hissed, enraged, past those trees and boulders that resisted their force and stood their ground. They charged at whatever stood in their paths. Then as suddenly as the thunderstorm had started, the onslaught abated, then died down. The demons, now calmed, flowed serenely towards the tarred road, their hips swaying and mesmerising, leaving us wondering if we had merely dreamed of their belching and spitting. The sky had quickly reverted to its familiar and reassuring blue and white colours.

The calmness of the slow-moving waters in the distance belied the chaos in our front yards. To the left, the makeshift kitchen in our neighbour's yard had been uprooted. It rested on one edge, the side tilted towards the ground but without touching it. It hung suspended like the image of a man captured in the lens of a camera while in the act of losing balance and falling forward, but before making contact with the ground. The big mulberry tree on the edge of our yard had finally bowed to a mightier force. Its trunk had split into two, the top and the bottom. The top had come all the way down to touch the ground though it had remained attached to the lower bit by a thin bark and jagged splinters of wood. The leaves touching the ground made a canopy of green foliage. I was still standing in the doorway watching in amazement when

*ma*Mpofu's voice broke through the silence from behind my shoulder.

"Something unusual is going to happen," she said. It was a statement, not wandering thoughts.

"Huh?" I mumbled, confused.

"To begin with, it rains when it shouldn't at this time of the year. The rain falls hard but only briefly, then lightning strikes and destroys this big tree that has withstood many onslaughts before. This is an omen, Mavhuto. The gods must be telling us something though we do not have any idea what it is. Such an extra-ordinary thunderstorm normally precedes an extra-ordinary event."

We stood and surveyed the damage in silence. Before she turned to go back into the house, *ma*Mpofu shrugged her shoulders and said, "I wonder what it is."

I stayed and continued to look outside. I noticed that smaller and not so strong trees than the big tree in our yard had somehow withstood the onslaught. Our huge tree lay battered, bruised and broken. Nothing more was said of it.

Soon afterwards, young voices full of life and expectation filled the air as children rushed outside to play. They could be heard screeching, shouting, jumping and splashing about in the now barely moving pools of rain water. Too old to join them, I watched from the veranda, remembering how it had been when, as a child, I too had played outside after the rain. We used to jump into the muddy brown waters, to the chagrin of the adults, and pretend that we had a swimming pool, just like the whites who lived on the other side of Patchway Valley Mine. It did not matter that their pool water was clear while ours was muddy, we merely wanted to enjoy the moment before the waters dried up. We splashed about, splashed water over each other, and felt all kinds of debris under our feet; bottle tops, wood chips, nuts and bolts, bits

of wire, bottles and whatever else had been swallowed by the little rivulets during the rainstorm. At times we skidded and lost our balance on the slippery mud. It was not unusual for bottoms to land on jagged little stones that grazed bare flesh. Our worst fear was to fall on our faces because falling on sticks and jutting stones meant not only bruises on the face or injuries to the eyes but also swallowing large quantities of the dirty water.

For a day or two after the rains, the ground became hazardous to the children and the adults alike. There was the risk of skidding and, as the ground slowly sucked the rainwater, it got even more slippery and more dangerous. The stagnant waters became breeding grounds for mosquitoes. Snails crawled from these waters and invaded homes where they left slimy, silvery trails all over. Frogs croaked and leapt from place to place, into houses through open windows and doors, into shoes, under the beds, and at times with a snake in pursuit. Days later, the putrid stench of rotting frogs, lizards, snails and whatever creatures had drowned in the muddy little swamps would pervade the humid air. Mosquitoes were the worst problem. One could never avoid their bites, and in some cases, one contracted malaria, and occasionally with fatal consequences.

As it turned out, *ma*Mpofu was right. The heavy thunderstorm was an omen, to me at least. Maybe Grandfather's death was the event heralded by the storm. Or maybe the event is the uncertain future that awaits me. I am alone and lost. I do not have a father. I never had one. During my early childhood, insults were often hurled at me as the bastard son of so and so, yet no one claims to have fathered me. I grew up without a mother either. The woman who was later introduced to me as my mother came too late in my life for me to feel anything towards her other than the respect adults expect from children who are well mannered. I acknowledge her as Dhairesi, the

daughter of my beloved grandfather. I give her the respect due to her as an older member of the family, but I have never been able to bring myself to call her Mother. I understand and accept that she is the woman in whose womb I nestled for nine months_ so I presume because nobody told me I was born prematurely_ therefore I am bound to her by blood and by the umbilical cord through which her body nourished mine. That makes her my mother. However, we are not bonded to each other. On the rare occasions my thoughts turn to her, I regard her as *that* mother-woman. That is what she is, the mother-woman. I should have a kind and loving grandmother in the background to take care of me. She ought to be here today, soothing away my anxieties. Sadly, such a person does not exist. From what I gathered as I grew up, my grandmother died some time before my birth. No one mentions her anymore now. To Grandfather, her one time existence was like a long forgotten event too painful to re-live, and for everybody else, her memory has become a faded image that is completely out of focus with the present and is best left at the back of time.

Grandfather took another wife in the year the mother-woman got pregnant with me, so I was told. I grew up calling this woman *ma*Mpofu because she resented being addressed as *ambuya.* But then *ambuya* is what one calls the wife of one's *asekuru*. *Ma*Mpofu complained that it made her feel old. She preferred that I addressed her by her totem, so I learned to call her *ma*Mpofu. She was a widow with twin daughters whom she brought with her to live with us. The girls were a few years older than me. *Ma*Mpofu did not have children with Grandfather, which made me the youngest child at home. I was adored by the old man but resented by his wife. Although he never actually said so, I assumed then that the old man doted on me not only because I was the youngest but also because I

was the only blood relative he had. Whenever Grandfather was at work, *ma*Mpofu treated me like the abandoned fatherless child she never failed to remind me that I was. I do not suppose she did it out of malice but, in her mind she was just stating the truth as it was. Grandfather made up for it by being kind and loving but that did not still the rumblings of my stomach. He never knew that I was denied food in his absence and if he thought I sometimes looked miserable, he probably assumed it was because I missed having a mother. It was true that I longed for a mother who would sweep me into her arms and wipe away my tears whenever I grazed my knee or hit a toe against a stone.

My heart yearned for a mother who would swing me onto her back and take pleasure in my exaggerated squeals of delight. I longed for a mother who would insist on piling my plate with food even as I protested that I was full. I yearned for a mother who would indulge me in a way only a mother's unconditional love can. My heart desired a mother who would adore me regardless of the stupid things I did sometimes, and beam with pride at my achievements, however minor. Now the very woman whose presence I had hungered for during those early childhood years is inside the house, sitting beside *ma*Mpofu, wailing and beating her chest in grief for the father who loved and cared for her. After years of yearning for a mother, the mother-woman suddenly turned up one day like a miracle once desperately hoped for, but long since given up on. That was three years ago. In all the years she was away, Grandfather never spoke about her. He behaved as if she did not exist. Maybe he thought she was no longer alive and did not wish to speak ill of the dead. Whenever I asked him who my parents were, he always gave the same answer; that he was my father and my mother, both rolled into one. He would tell

me to stop worrying about such issues and I was supposed to be satisfied with that reply. With time I stopped asking, though the answer was far from satisfying me. My imagination ran wild regarding the issue of my parentage. Maybe my father had perished in the mines, or he had perhaps moved away to another mine with my mother, I thought. I imagined too that I had never had a father or a mother, and that I had descended from Heaven in a chariot of fire just like the Biblical Elijah, except that my chariot had travelled in the opposite direction, or that I was a special child rescued from the river like baby Moses, which made my existence a mystery to the whole community. If that were the case, Grandfather could not be blamed for having no answers for me.

There were occasions too when I imagined my birth to be far less intriguing. Maybe I was rescued choking and sputtering from a horrible pool of faeces in a pit latrine after being dumped by some desperate girl who had no desire to keep me, and for whom my birth was bound to be a source of shame. The possibility of that being the case was high. After all I was born during the period when it was common for unmarried young girls to conceal unwanted pregnancies, give birth in secret and proceed to dump their newborn babies. *Ma*Mpofu talked of babies that were dumped on church doorsteps, on rubbish dumps and in bushes.

"I know for sure that in the towns some of these heartless girls flushed their newborn babies down the toilets like faeces. The corpses of the unfortunate babies were swept away and buried forever in the sewage, unless the drains became blocked a few miles away. The babies that were found alive were the fortunate ones. Their mothers were not completely heartless. They did not kill their infants before dumping the bodies," explained *ma*Mpofu. Could it be that I was one such child, hauled

from a garbage heap where I was thrown together with other unwanted rubbish and left for scavenging dogs to fight over? I wondered. Perhaps my mother was some desperate woman whose husband had died in a mining accident, leaving her with no choice but to wrap me up warmly before depositing me on the doorstep of a kind, childless couple. I imagined Grandfather and his first wife as that couple. Since nobody explained anything to me, I could only guess. I wanted to believe that whatever had happened to my parents, they had borne me out of love. Hints were dropped here and there by outsiders but nothing definite was ever said.

So I grew up knowing nothing about my parents, until the year I turned eleven years old and the woman they said was my mother turned up. It was then that Grandfather started talking about her in my presence. Most of the time he spoke fondly of his daughter, but there were times when he could hardly mask his bitterness. I got to undertand at that point that Grandfather loved me more than anyone else, having turned his heart away from the daughter who had increasingly caused him endless shame and anguish. There was no doubt the old man had suffered a lot of pain because of her, but one thing was certain; he deeply cared for his daughter. When she returned from the wilderness, the father and daughter reunion must have equalled that of the biblical prodigal son and his forgiving father. Everybody assumed the excitement engulfed me as well, and a great mother-son bond was expected instantly.

Although I had yearned for a mother as I grew up, often fantasising that I had one, when she eventually appeared I was confused and hurt. I had no idea how I was supposed to cope with being motherless in the morning, then having one dumped on me by the afternoon. Instead of being overwhelmed with joy, it was rage that engulfed me. I had considered my mother to be

dead all along. I had wept for her for many years, yet somewhere out there the woman had been alive and well. I tried my best to call this person *Amayo*[11], but since this was a title by which I had never addressed anyone, by the time I turned eleven my tongue had become too stiff to roll out the word without effort. The word stumbled in my mouth each time I tried to let it glide off a tongue that refused to co-operate. I tried practising saying it in the privacy of Grandfather's bedroom; *Amayo-o, Amaayo, Aamayo!* The word came out strange, whichever way I said it. It came off my lips like trapped stale air struggling to escape from an unwashed mouth. The son whom the mother-woman had abandoned in infancy refused to be resurrected from her dead and buried past. Today, at this point in our lives, at the point of our shared grief, she still remains the-woman-supposed-to-be-my-mother; the mother-woman. *Amayo*. Up to today the word still fills my mouth and threatens to choke me. The tongue, unaccustomed to it, continues to reject it. The teeth remain clenched, trapping it within. The word struggles and dribbles like spittle down the sides of my mouth and the meaninglessness of its sound escapes into the nothingness above, quickly evaporating into thin air.

It was Grandfather who was both mother and father to me, which is why his death leaves me lost. The little I knew of death had been, until now, the sound of beating drums through the night and the voices of women wailing with a sharpness that pierced through the heavy funereal air in the Mine compound. The road that leads from the compound to the graveyard passes right next to our house. That meant I could also watch the slow procession of grieving adults on foot snaking its way to the graveyard to bury the dead. The whole thing had an air of mystery that also made it both frightening and intriguing at the

---

11Mother

same time. As children, we had watched the processions from behind twitching curtains, our minds filled with curiosity and fear. With Grandfather's passing away, death has now assumed a new meaning in my life. I am no longer just peeping at it from a distance, secure in the knowledge that it only happens to other people. I am staring at it from up close and it stares back defiantly. I keep hoping that I am going through a nightmare and that with the rising of the sun, I can rouse myself and shake off the horror of a mind visited by a macabre vision in the dead of the night.

There is no one I can talk to here, someone who understands how I feel. I need to know if the pain will eventually recede. If it does, I would like to know how soon that is likely to happen, but no one comes near me, not even the mother-woman, not that I wish her to. No one talks to me. Instead, I hear expressions of sympathy offered to Grandfather's widow and to the mother-woman.

"*O-o, nichifundo kwambili mubale wanga*[12]," mourners say to Grandfather's widow as they take her hand in theirs to pass their condolences. "We know it grieves you that your husband has departed to the land of his ancestors, but take comfort in the knowledge that he is now at rest. Our kinsman had suffered a lot in these last few months. We all go the same way; different times, different ways but the same route, sooner or later. It is for the best that his soul is now at rest."

"*O-o, nichisoni,*[13] *a*Dhairesi. What will you do now about Mavhuto? Poor, poor you!"

All around me are voices saying, "*nichisoni a*Dhairesi, *nawo mavhuto ma*Mpofu, *nichisoni… nawo mavhuto…*

12I am sorry for your loss my kinswoman

13 With deepest sympathies

nichisoni... nichisoni... mavhuto..." over and over again. *"Nawo mavhuto...."* On this occasion my name has slipped into one of its several meanings.

Outside, I crouch and rest my back against the wall. This is the same wall against which Grandfather and I used to sunbathe in the mornings. I had not realised before that from that same position at night one could also bask in the enchanting halo of the moon gliding slowly across the sky. From here words reach my ears. They tumble from one mouth to another like a carefully threaded string of beads and fill the funereal air around until it becomes like a suppurated wound, eating into the core of my being. Nobody seems to notice as I make my way to the door of the house from where I watch wailing women seated next to the corpse. Grief is all around me in its many varied forms; loud shrieking, sniffing, sombre faces, silent tears, resignation and anger. On what feels like numb feet, I go back outside where grief seems to have no discernible feature. Shuffling lifelessly in the dark from one place to another, I am a dark shadow in the night; aimless, invisible and without purpose. The night is cold. I join one of a few groups of men sitting around log fires that will burn all night. The men are discussing the digging of the grave.

"Go and look for some other place to sit, *munyamata,"* says *a*Gwazimba, the man leading the discussion. "We are busy here with important issues, nothing suitable for young ears such as yours." So I shuffle away again, in whatever direction my feet lead me. I slump against the wall of the house, my throbbing head in my hands. A gentle hand rests on my shoulder, startling me.

"You have to be brave Mavhuto," a voice whispers quietly in front of me. "This is not an experience unique to you. At some point in life, everyone loses someone they cherish. You ought to bear your grief like a man. Now wipe your tears." Through my tears I see the distorted face

of *a*Mwanza. I do as he says and wipe away my tears, trying to master the bravery I am far from feeling. I can still hear the women wailing in the house. Grandfather's widow weeps at the horror that her life has become. Whenever she wails, the other women join in, sharing her sorrow and acknowledging the pain they know she must feel, and the bleak future that awaits her. The women weep at the realisation that it could easily have been them in that situation. They are horrified by this fate that might one day be theirs too. *Amake* Chabwino[14] wails the loudest after *ma*Mpofu. Following the death of her husband at the Annexe a year ago, she now lives with her son and his quarrelsome wife. *Ma*Mpofu laments the fact that she is now homeless, but she can always go back to her village, I think to myself. The mother-woman will go back to the farm where she lives with her boyfriend, husband or whatever it is she calls him. I have no doubt in my mind that I do not fit into the plans of either of the two women from this moment onwards.

I spend the rest of the night outside, lying by the wall and away from everybody. I am still there when the cocks start crowing and the place comes alive with the sounds of women banging cooking utensils together as they set about preparing the first meal of the day. The women indoors can be heard singing softly. The sombre tones of the song overwhelm me and the bravery I had previously mastered hours earlier deserts me. I desperately try to do as *a*Mwanza has advised, but I struggle to still my breaking heart. The effort to hug my grief to my chest hurts even more. Burning tears threaten to cascade down my cheeks. A drop escapes and rolls down. I try to wipe it away before anyone notices but another follows, and another one. Before I can blink there is a deluge of them, enough to drown me in my sorrow. I give up and dash to

14 Mother of Chabwino

hide behind the makeshift bathroom commonly known as a *chinjausi*[15].

Nearby, a group of women is making some fire. I had not expected anyone out there. Suddenly feeling ashamed of my visible weakness, I clutch at my chest and endeavour to tuck my grief inside. I suppress the sobs threatening to turn into howls and almost choke from the effort. No one had ever told me that it would hurt this much. A few heads turn in my direction before hurriedly looking away. Some of the women click their teeth with indifference. Others say, 'Poor Mavhuto. Just leave him alone. He will be all right.' They all soon go back to focus their attention on seemingly more important issues such as the preparation of the day's meals and the collection of firewood and mealie-meal from the various members of the Nkhotakota Burial Society.

"*Uyenera kurimba ngati muntu wamamuna.*[16]" More or less the same words are repeated to me, over and over again until I want to block my ears. After some time I join some of the men sitting on logs around the fire. It is a different group from the one that spent the night there. The men who sat with *a*Gwazimba during the night have been gone for some time, probably to get some sleep before they turn up for the midday shift at the Mine. Those gathered here now have probably just come off the four o'clock shift, barely an hour ago. I know some of them from when they visited Grandfather but there are others I do not remember seeing before. Anyway, one's loss in this community is everyone else's. It is therefore not surprising that even those who knew Grandfather remotely or just by name, have turned up in large numbers. The whole community comes together in mourning like one big

---

15change house

16You ought to be brave, like a man

family devastated by shared grief. As more and more men arrive and sit around the fire, I am slowly pushed to the outer edges. It is from the outside that I mourn the death of the person who was at the centre of my life. *Ma*Mpofu says that her people have an adage that goes, *'Afirwa haatariswi kumeso*[17]*,'* yet these people here glare at me as if to probe my eyes for the depth of my grief. Their unflinching gazes chart every reflection of emotion on my face as if they intend to later describe in graphic detail the extent of my pain. To them my grief is like some kind of performance in a passing tragic show. The less discreet do not even bother to speculate out of earshot about what will happen to me. They discuss me as if I am not there.

"Maybe Dhairesi will finally take him with her to the farm now that her long-suffering father is dead."

"What choice does she have? He is her son after all. It is about time she started being responsible for the unfortunate boy. But that may not be possible because from what I hear, Dhairesi did not tell that useless man she calls a husband about the existence of the boy. Those who know all about it say that Dhairesi intended to make a fresh start, and claimed that she had never had a child, and that the little boy in her family was a brother born in the complicated labour that resulted in their mother's death. Can you imagine that?"

"*Eyi*! I pity the poor boy. Perhaps his father will now come forward and claim him as his son," ventures another.

"Who is his father anyway? I doubt that even Dhairesi herself knows." Enough! I want to scream as I move away to shield my ears from a verbal onslaught my heart is too fragile to bear at the moment. It is obvious the whole community knows that Grandfather's death of is the worst

---

17He who is stricken by grief should not be stared in the face

tragedy of my life. They know too that the mother-woman went away and left me to be raised by her father and her stepmother, and that she had made up with Grandfather three years ago, but they do not know about the absence of the spirit of kinship between us. Nothing binds me to the mother-woman. Her return took place while I was at school, so I do not know how the reunion of father and daughter went. Whether there were tears, pleas for forgiveness, recriminations or relief and joyous celebrations all round, I have no idea. All I know is that by the time I got back from school, Grandfather was in a very happy mood. A woman_ a stranger whose face had a vague familiarity I could not place_ sat on a reed mat in a corner of the sitting room. *Ma*Mpofu went about doing her house chores and did not appear to be concerned about the events unfolding around her. When this stranger was eventually introduced as my mother, my chest did not rise in excitement. Instead, my tongue filled my mouth and lay there, heavy and lifeless. A week later, the woman my tongue had failed to address as Mother went back to whatever place she had come from. *Ma*Mpofu said she lived at a farm some distance away. From that point onwards, Grandfather and his wife started talking openly about her, sometimes in my presence and at times when they thought they were alone, which was how I came to know about the mother-woman's life, past and present.

* * *

I remember the night Grandfather and *ma*Mpofu discussed the mother-woman for the first time in my presence. Grandfather had come off the shift that worked from midday to sunset. *Ma*Mpofu was blowing air into hot cinders to fan the fire and get it going. The three of us were sitting around the fire in the makeshift structure Grandfather had put up to serve as a kitchen. To make

these structures, which almost every household has in some corner of their yard, one removes the bottom and top parts of a drum, then cuts through one side of the hollowed out drum, from top to bottom. The iron sheet is then flattened. Several of these are used to construct the walls. Wires are threaded through holes punched into the sheets to keep them intact the way the womenfolk sew together pieces of cloths to make patchwork quilts. A flat roof is achieved by laying a few of these sheets on top of the four sided structure. Heavy stones are placed on top to keep the roof from being blown away by strong gusts of wind. Those who can afford it have a cement floor, but most people simply place plain bricks on the ground to keep it from becoming muddy when it rains.

On this particular evening of the talk of Grandfather's daughter, the old man had just had a bath and was therefore feeling refreshed and in a good mood. By the look of things, it was going to be a while before we had our evening meal. *Ma*Mpofu, kneeling and bending down, was blowing air into the embers to get the fire burning more brightly. The more effort she made, the more the embers emitted smoke, and the more desperate she became. Sitting opposite, I tried without success to wave the smoke away from my eyes. Through the thin film of tears welling in my itchy eyes, I watched fascinated, as the two round mounds on *ma*Mpofu's chest swung forwards and backwards like giant paw-paws swaying in the wind.

For a brief moment she rested her bottom on the heels of her feet as she panted heavily, gasping for air. She filled her cheeks with air, bent down again and blew out the little air in her lungs. Her cheeks sucked inwards slowly, like a deflating ballon. Each time she bent forwards, her chest came down low, almost sweeping the sack spread on the bricks on which she knelt. Conceding defeat, *ma*Mpofu gathered herself up and tied the headscarf tighter around her unkempt, tightly coiled hair. She then undid her wrap-

around cloth that had become loose and tightened it more securely like one steeling herself to do battle with a resilient adversary. Without uttering a word to either Grandfather or me, she rolled her huge frame out through the door, wiping her eyes with the back of her hand as she disappeared from sight. She was soon back with bits of wood in her short, stubby arms. Careful not to smother the embers, she pushed the wood on top of them through the sides of the rectangular iron fire frame upon which sat two black pots and a gallon of water. I offered to blow the fire. *Ma*Mpofu accepted the help and was grateful. As the flames flared up and licked the bottom and sides of the cooking vessels, she sighed with visible relief.

"Phew! For a moment there I thought my sadza was at risk of becoming under-cooked," she cackled.

"*Mbodza, iweyo ma*Mpofu? Never. I am yet to eat under-cooked sadza from these hands of yours. And how many years is it now, *ma*Mpofu, since you came to me?" asked Grandfather in a light-hearted mood. The old man was sitting to my right on a three-legged wooden stool. Gnarled fingers with grime-embedded nails gripped thin knees that he repeatedly knocked together in a steady rhythm. Grandfather was of medium height and slight build, and regardless of how much he ate, he never gained weight.

"How can you not remember when I came here, *a*Nyirenda? Was that not the same year that your troublesome daughter got pregnant?" replied *ma*Mpofu.

"It was. Yes it was."

"1974, in the middle of that year, or maybe towards the end, I am no longer sure. My memory fails me these days," said *ma*Mpofu. She went down on her knees in front of the fire and lifted the lid off the pot in which maize meal porridge was bubbling vigorously. As soon as the lid was taken off, one of the bubbles shot up and landed on *ma*Mpofu's right thumb. She instinctively

yelped, threw the lid back on and quickly stuck the said thumb into her mouth to cool the burning. Grandfather chuckled as if he found the whole thing hilarious.

"The fire is too hot and the flames too high. That is what makes the porridge bubble with such fury," explained *ma*Mpofu before proceeding to slightly pull apart some of the burning wood and separating the red-hot embers. The flames receded instantly. "This sadza-cooking business requires a lot of skill, Mavhuto, a fact that is not appreciated by most men. Most of you can tell the difference between well-cooked sadza and bad sadza but you know nothing of the trouble we women go to in making it. A poor fire results in under-cooked sadza. Too hot a fire burns it. And one has to dodge these hot bubbles that shoot up as soon as one lifts the lid, *eyi*!"

Neither Grandfather nor I commented, but we both watched as *ma*Mpofu went on to lift the lid with her left hand, cautiously this time. Using her right hand, she scooped a cupful of maize meal from the woven basket beside her and sprinkled it thinly over the bubbling porridge. Satisfied that the fury of the liquid had been quelled, she put the lid upside down on the floor to her left and moved the basket containing the maize meal to that side as well. *Ma*Mpofu gradually proceeded to ladle more maize meal into the pot with her left hand. She used a wooden spoon to gently stir the mixture, using her right hand, as it thickened. Prior to her explaining the cooking process, I had never really thought much about the task of cooking sadza, but watching *ma*Mpofu so intent at it, I could see there was more to it than just random adding of maize meal and stirring. After a few circuits of stirring, she would pulp the thickening paste against the inside edge of the pot using the wooden spoon.

"This is to prevent lumps from developing and hardening, which would spoil the sadza if allowed to happen," she explained. Beads of perspiration formed on

her brow and held. Then they got bigger, failed to hold and gradually made their way down the sides of her face. She tugged at a corner of her wrap-around cloth from under her knee and wiped the sweat off her face with it. She tucked the corner back under the knee and continued stirring the porridge which gradually thickened to a smooth paste with each scoop of maize meal that she added. The glow of the fire cast shadows against the wall of the kitchen. The bloated figure of *ma*Mpofu was slapped against the wall behind her where, like a puppet, it moved sideways, upwards and downwards.

"Under-cooked sadza, or sadza with lumps is the worst thing one can serve. In the village where I come from, brides are sent back to their parents' homes for serving less than perfect sadza. And there they remain until they master the skill of cooking properly to the satisfaction of the groom's family."

"How can a girl be sent back to her people for such a minor issue? You Mashona people make too much of a fuss over nothing. *Nxa*!" snorted Grandfather. "I am glad I stopped my daughter from seeing the Shona boy she was friendly with years ago."

"And what good did that do, *a*Nyirenda? Look at the miserable life the girl leads today. No wonder she stayed away all these years. Not once did she send word asking about her son Mavhuto here. We only heard about her through rumours, most of which were from unreliable sources. The silly girl was last here shortly after we got independence. She probably thought it was freedom from her duty as a mother." I cocked my ears to hear more.

"Ahh, my poor daughter, Dhairesi! The first time she left, her boy was two years old. Then it was two whole years before we saw her again. Then she would come and go after long periods," mused Grandfather shaking his head. "Life has not been kind to her. It is true, Mavhuto *muzukuru,* that from time to time I got news on the

whereabouts of your mother. I am sure she would have come back more often had there not been a war raging out there. Those were dangerous times for people of all races."

"*A*Nyirenda stop making excuses for your daughter. War or no war, Dhairesi just had no interest in her son. You could put a raging river between a mother and her child and the mother would do everything in her power to get to her child. But of course your daughter was always a different kind of mother. Her head was turned by that stupid man of hers."

Grandfather's demeanour changed instantly. A far away look came into his eyes. "I could have told you about your mother back then, Mavhuto, but I did not wish to torment you with thoughts of what was destined to rot out there. My daughter opted to be like a leaf that detaches itself from that which nurtures it and is left flapping in the wind. What she failed to realise is how soon that leaf wilts before it starts decaying."

"*A*Nyirenda, the decay in your daughter was what eventually made her decide to come back. It was obvious to everybody that the Dhairesi who went away a bubbly young woman came back aged and worn out, *hahaha, hehehe!*" remarked *ma*Mpofu with undisguised glee. "But that does not surprise me. Life on the farm must be hard for that girl. She was spoilt and never could bear hard work. Extremely lazy she was, that Dhairesi. Labouring on the farm has certainly aged her. It is hard to believe she is the same girl who used to walk as if there were thorns on the soles of her feet. The palm of your mother's hand was like the skin on the bottom of a newborn baby, not calloused like mine. But just look at those hands now. Gnarled like those of an old witch, I tell you. The cracks on her feet are worse than the legendary deep groves on Jakopo's heels. *Maiwe,* your daughter, *a*Nyirenda has aged well beyond her years."

*Ma*Mpofu knelt by the fire and rested her big bottom on the back of her heels. With what seemed like a lot of effort, she laid out three plates on the floor in front of her. She stirred the sadza a few more times, replaced the lid but left one side slightly open to let out steam. With the practised efficiency of one who did the task everyday, she dipped the wooden spoon in a cup full of water, removed it and used it to scoop out some sadza that she carefully put onto one of the plates. The sadza did not cling to the spoon as before. Again, *ma*Mpofu dipped the spoon in water, shook it then proceeded to pat the sadza on the plate. The result was a smooth round mound of sadza on one side of the plate. She repeated the process with the second plate, putting two scoops in it and three in the third. The portions were for me, for her and for Grandfather, in that order. While she did this I went into the house. By the time I got back with a dish of water, *ma*Mpofu had scooped a tripe and vegetable stew next to the heap of sadza in each plate.

"I blame that horrible man she eloped with, that stupid man with the equally stupid name. Bigboy, or somethingboy or the other," said Grandfather as he washed his hands in the dish I held up for him. When he had finished, he stretched his hands over the fire and wrung them before flexing his scarred knuckles. Drops of water splashed over the hot embers and made them sizzle, to *ma*Mpofu's annoyance. She complained that smoke was bound to rise and fill the little kitchen and make her eyes itch. As soon as Grandfather was done, his wife handed him his plate of food.

"*Ma*Mpofu, I ask you again. What name is that man known by?" Grandfather asked as he balanced his plate on knees that peered through the holes on his worn out trousers. He dug his right hand into the sadza and picked a morsel. I never ceased to be fascinated by the way he kneaded it between his thumb and the other fingers. He

pressed the thumb into the ball he had made and a small depression formed, into which he folded in the stew. His arm rose in an arc from the plate to his mouth.

"Twoboy. His name is Twoboy." *Ma*Mpofu's voice cut through my preoccupation.

"Yes, *ma*Mpofu, Twoboy Limao it is. A silly name for a stupid man,' Grandfather remarked while chewing at the same time. I stole a furtive glance at *ma*Mpofu to see if she would admonish him for it, but she appeared not to notice and yet she never hesitated to pounce on me if I dared to talk with my mouth full.

"I hear he was one of twins, hence the name Twoboy."

"Is that so?" snorted Grandfather. "So what did they name the other child, Oneboy? I do not care what stupid name that farm labourer goes by, but it reaches my ears that he beats up my daughter even when she is pregnant. And that, I do not like. If Dhairesi were not such a stubborn person, I would not hesitate to break her husband's jaw and demand that she comes back home. But knowing her as I do, the stupid girl would probably take the idiot's side and humiliate me in spite of my efforts to drag her out of her life of misery."

"Your daughter always shied away from anything strenuous, and you know that very well. That was why she ran away from here. She was too lazy to do anything for herself or for her son here. You spoiled that girl too much *a*Nyirenda, letting her talk back to you as if you were the child and she the parent. Her *husband,* if you insist on calling him that, beats her up for being lazy, no doubt. When she came back one of her front teeth was missing. She claimed it had decayed and had to be pulled out. Ah, how can one lose front teeth at such a young age?"

"*Mabodza*. Lies, lies. All lies. That is Dhairesi's greatest problem. Her mind cannot separate lies from the truth. It was obvious she had been badly beaten up yet she insisted

nothing of the sort had happened. That husband of hers is a bloody *mambara,*" said Grandfather.

"I suspect she gets beaten up because she is untidy. *Uchapa,* Dhairesi. Untidiness. She never used to see the need to separate her shoes from the cooking utensils. Her combs were all over the place and we were forever picking strands of her hair from the maize meal, sugar, salt and many other places. No man tolerates lack of hygiene, especially where food is concerned. As for her numerous pregnancies, I fail to understand why she persists. After all, she conceives only for the soil. No wonder that useless man she calls a husband beats her up."

"Of course Twoboy *is* her husband! They have been together for more than ten years now," argued Grandfather.

"Call him whatever you wish but that man did not pay *lobola* for your daughter," sneered *ma*Mpofu. "He did not pay even the worthless one cent coin with a hole in the middle, the one that is now out of circulation. In what way then can their union be called a marriage when nothing was received from that useless layabout? The two are merely co-habiting. *Vari kubika mapoto mumapurazi*! It is probably better that way. Who knows, if Twoboy had married Dhairesi, maybe he would have long since returned her and demanded his money back. As it is I am sure he tolerates her because it makes his life easier. He does not need to save *lobola* for some other woman."

That evening was about three years ago. It was through such casual references to her that I came to know a bit about the mother-woman's life. I have this image of her as a beautiful young woman with a big afro hairstyle, an impression I got from a grainy black and white photograph taken outside Checkers Supermarket in town. At the back was a stamp in purple ink; Kidias Studios - Gatooma. Grandfather showed me the faded photograph

soon after his daughter had gone back to the farms. It was all he had to remind him of the daughter he loved in spite of the pain she caused him those many years ago. There is no doubt that the mother-woman was beautiful, once upon a time, but when I look at her now I see only a caricature of the woman she used to be. Nothing remains of the famed beauty of her youth. Her skin is dry like ground that has not received rainfall for years and her knuckles are scarred and knobbly. Her cheeks are sunken and hollow. The mother-woman looks like someone who has been starved for weeks. She walks with a slight stoop, and when she puts her feet down it is as if she is not sure whether she wants to turn left, right or go straight ahead. Although she is said to have given birth to me when she was in her teens, the mother-woman looks as if she could be my grandmother. Her eyes stare into the distance and appear to have no spirit as they sweep right past me, as if I still do not exist. The mother-woman does not acknowledge my presence now, just as she decided not to reveal my existence those many years ago when she eloped with Twoboy Limao. She had done a thorough job of wiping me out of her life to start all over again elsewhere.

"My wayward daughter made the greatest mistake of her life by shunning our way of life. And that, Mavhuto *muzukuru*, is the one thing I hope you will not be tempted to do. No good will ever come of it, believe me. Your mother tried it but how did she fare?"

"She got what she went out looking for, that daughter of yours *a*Nyirenda," said *ma*Mpofu.

"Mavhuto, just remember that your way of life is like your shadow. You and your shadow are inseparable for life. You can never detach yourself from it. You can hurl yourself upwards as high as you can, but you soon land, and your feet reconnect with your shadow. Only the shadow can detach itself from you. It scuttles away quietly

as you expel your last breath but it soon returns to lie with you in your final sleep. But your mother thought she could escape it, and sought to discard every shred of everything that defined her as a girl of the Chewa tribe. Dhairesi was full of nonsensical ideas about love. She would not be dissuaded from staying at the farms with the man she claimed brought meaning into her life, but judging from what she has been through, that love dream of hers must have turned into a nightmare. She must have imagined that as the wife of a foreman, her position and that of her husband would place them above the rest of the farm labourers. My poor daughter did not know how the mind of a *muzungu*[18] works. Foreman or common labourer, *sorongo uli blaki, uli blaki basi, semu revhuru!*[19] The Dhairesi you see now is very different from the girl of her youth, Mavhuto."

* * *

One Sunday, after we had just had our afternoon meal, Grandfather and I sat in the shade of the mulberry tree. *Ma*Mpofu had gone to fetch some firewood with one of the compound women whom she was friends with when the old man told me that he wanted to tell me more about my mother, and about our way of life. What he had to say was best said in the absence of *ma*Mpofu, or else we would never get anywhere with her endless interruptions, he said.

18a white man

19So long as you are black, you are just black, therefore same level.

"Our way of life which had been simple and orderly was turned upside down when *simanje-manje* breezed into our community with the boys in bell bottoms and platform shoes," the old man began. "Your mother, whose natural beauty had won her many suitors from our tribe, started smearing red colouring on her lips, the purpose of which I could not understand. She argued that it made her look more beautiful. That baffled me as I could not understand how a transformation that made one look like an animal that had just fed on the carcass of another could be described as beautiful. The *Ambi* and *Bu-tone* creams that she applied to her face made her skin so light you could almost see the dark veins beneath. Your mother looked hideous, Mavhuto. Try to picture her with a light face and limbs so dark they looked like body parts borrowed from various people and pieced together. With red paint on her cheeks and lips, she looked like a *chigure*[20], a clown indeed! I hated what my daughter had transformed herself into, but she liked the new Dhairesi. 'It is lipstick and Pond's,' she announced with pride the first time I saw her like that.

'*Ponzi*! What is *ponzi*?' I asked.

'It is called Pond's Vanishing Cream, *Ababa*. It is used so that any spots and blemishes on the face can vanish.'

'You stupid, stupid girl! Don't you realise it is only your beautiful black skin that will vanish here, and the pride that goes with it?'

'*Ababa!* Must you criticise all the time everything that I do? Can't you see how beautiful I look with make-up and my long shiny wig? Now I can toss my head back and feel the long hair brush against my shoulders, just like the white madam,' giggled Dhairesi with undisguised pride.

"How I wished I could take the said *lipistiki* and write on her forehead, 'Chewa, Black and Beautiful Without the Hideous Paint'. Everyday, my daughter went off to the

20 Masked dancer

jubhokisi[21] at the shops where she wiggled her bottom unashamedly in public like some shiftless and immoral woman. I was ashamed of what she had become, I must admit, but she was my daughter and I loved her. As the only living relation known to me, I did not wish to drive her away, but she constantly and endlessly tested my tolerance and my patience.

"It was not easy *muzukuru,* raising a girl on the verge of womanhood on my own, especially after her mother had been dead only a short while. Dhairesi was considered to be one of the most beautiful girls at Patchway Valley Mine. She stood straight and tall, and had the build of what a properly fed African woman ought to look like, not just skin and bones, or lumpy folds of flesh that roll out in waves from the chest to the hips. Her skin was dark, smooth and without any blemishes. When my daughter walked, her feet hardly touched the ground. Her gleaming white teeth flashed a smile that entranced grown men and filled her peers with envy. I was proud of her and I hoped that a good husband would come along in good time. A number of suitors had approached me; widowed and divorced men who wanted her, and one or two who wanted her for their sons. Had I not felt protective towards her, I would have done what any responsible father does and ignored her protests and wishes and married her off as soon as her breasts started budding. Instead, in my weakness I just watched as the stubborn girl shunned all her suitors, preferring to follow a dream that was nothing but a mirage. She rejected men that most girls would have happily settled down with, and insisted instead on falling in love with a man of her choice, an idea that was as unbelievable as it was irresponsible. I should have been more strict, but when you lose one of the only two children you have, you cherish the surviving one even

---

21 juke box

more. There was nothing I would not do for your mother. My concern for her increased after your grandmother died. Mavhuto *muzukuru,* your mother *anali nimwano*[22] right from childhood. She was born several years after her brother. Mind you, in those days by the time one child started learning to walk, the mother would be carrying another in her womb, but Dhairesi took her time coming. She was the child your *ambuya* and I had longed for as a playmate and sibling for your uncle Chakumanda."

"You had two children, *Asekuru*?" I asked, surprised.

"Not only two, *muzukuru.* Your *ambuya* and I had more, but only two survived; your mother and her brother. I know that I have not mentioned my late son to you before. That is because his death left a deep scar where my heart sits. I only have to scratch lightly and the pain buried within rises to the surface. I would rather not talk about the past now, Mavhuto. That is a story for another time."

After a short pause, a deep sigh, and a faraway look in his eye, Grandfather continued relating the story of his wayward daughter.

"There was hardly anything her mother and I would not do for that girl, except of course give in to her irrational demands that we abandon our way of life. We indulged her more than we should have done, but we adamantly refused to allow her out to play with other girls and boys at night. If I was a strict father it was out of concern for my little angel. My concern turned to fear after we lost her brother. Dhairesi, however, did not see it that way. She accused me of being too controlling.

'Why won't you let me grow up like other girls of my age?' she repeatedly argued.

'If you were grown up as you insist you are, you would be married and settled with a family of your own

---

22she was stubborn

like other young women in the compound,' I told her, but she was extremely stubborn. She refused to undergo the *chinamwali* ritual, can you believe that!" exclaimed Grandfather. I shuddered. No one, as far as I knew, dared defy the elders on such a serious issue. *Chinamwali* was only whispered about as a highly secretive and mysterious ritual undergone by every female child of the Chewa tribe at puberty. The gravity of the decision taken by the mother-woman to shun it was therefore immense. "She became the first woman in our community to ever rebel against initiation," continued Grandfather.

"Dhairesi thought our way of life was outdated and backward. Everything that was a symbol of our people caused her embarrassment, and we were suddenly beneath her. Can you imagine anyone denying themselves, Mavhuto? Yet your mother did just that. Her friends became those of the local tribes. All of a sudden she did not want to speak the Chewa language anymore. We spoke to her in our own language and she answered us in Chishona. She even wanted us to stop calling her Dhairesi and call her Fadzai or Eriza, or something like that, but your *ambuya* and I refused. We were proud to be who we were. We could not shed our identities and our traditions any more than we could detach ourselves from our shadows. We tried to explain this to our daughter, with great patience at first, until we got so exasperated with her stubbornness that we began screaming at her. The more we did so the more your mother rebelled. My daughter stopped plaiting her hair the traditional way our women folk do. Instead, she adopted a strange hair style that made her look as if she was constantly carrying a charcoal-burnt calabash on her head.

'You want me to remain forever *Mubhurandaya,* with *chuma apa, nyora apo!*[23] Why, why indeed do you insist on

23beads here and skin engravings there.

shackling me to the past that everyone else is desperate to shed?' She lashed out one day, leaving your *ambuya* and me hurt and bewildered. This was after your *ambuya* had suggested taking her to *Ambuya a*Firipo to have tribal marks engraved on her cheeks and forehead to enhance her beauty and mark her out as belonging to the Chewa tribe.

'But what is so wrong with our way of life, Dhairesi *wanga*?[24]' asked her mother. 'What is there to be ashamed of about our traditions? Our culture is a mark of distinction, our pride. It is the one thing that identifies us. Our traditions hold us together and set us apart as a people_'

'No, *Amayo,* no! Those outdated customs are the bane of our existence,' screamed your mother with such force I physically recoiled.

'To think that my own womb, this womb of mine unleashed such horror into our lives!' wailed her mother, clutching at her stomach. 'When I think of all the tears I shed as I buried one stillborn baby after another, and the joy I thought was mine when eventually the heavens heard my weeping, and gave me this girl, I wonder whether we would have been better off with the tears and the sorrow that we had become accustomed to. At least our kinsmen sympathised with us during those times. Now all they do is smirk. This force that is forever fighting against us, one that we are too weak to tame, is probably punishment for not accepting the fate the gods had dished out to us.'

"Your *ambuya* lamented on and on, pleading with her daughter to be more like other girls who were the pride of their mothers, but Dhairesi took no notice and stormed out of the house. So your mother remained Dhairesi in this home though she became someone else outside. We could

---

24my Dhairesi

not keep her from being whoever she wished to be, but we refused to let her impose her ways on the family. Sometimes I wonder whether my decision to let her have her way encouraged her towards a life that I condemn. But then you can tie your children down only to a certain extent. At some stage one needs to let go. Anyway, in the case of your mother there was nothing we could do anymore. We had tried everything. Who knows when a child stops being a child? According to our people, a child remains under the guidance of his or her parents, to be guided now and again through the twists and turns of the journey that life is, to the day he or she dies. It is not so though with you children of today. You have become our parents; with knowledge beyond our scope, the kind of knowledge one can only gain from hours spent with your noses buried in your books. Now we just watch helplessly while you peel off our customs, layer by layer, discarding what you consider to be the husks and throwing them among the chaff as you move on with your lives, like my daughter did.

"When Dhairesi refused to undergo the sacred and time-honoured ritual, we were shocked. Your grandmother asked *Ambuya a*Firipo to explain to her that the locals she admired so much and wished to be so much like also had their lives rooted in the customs of their tribes. We tried to make her understand that they observed their traditions even more strictly than we did ours, which is why they branded us '*vanhu vasina tsika*[25].' This did nothing to change your mother's ways. She had become too much of '*intombi yesimanje-manje.*' The tribal dances that her peers participated in and derived much joy from, your own mother shunned, opting for the *jaivhi* of the new way of life. 'Bump jive' is what they called it. When her mother died, I thought the grief that seemed to

25A people with no manners/traditions.

consume her would make her realise just how wayward she had become. Instead, she emerged from that grief more stubborn than ever. That was after a few weeks of religious zeal that I had no idea what to make of it. But that is not a story for today.

"It took me a long time, Mavhuto *muzukuru,* before I realised that my path and that of my daughter were taking different directions in a lot more ways than just her refusal to observe our traditions. I should have realised it sooner and it should not have come as such a complete shock, yet it still left me shattered when I learned that each time I left home to go for my night shift, your mother also left the house.

"It pained me further to learn that the whole of Patchway Valley Mine had known for a long time what I had no idea was happening with my own child."

"*Aha*?" I urged Grandfather on.

"One of the young men signing off from the shift as I was signing on called out to another that he knew why Giribhati was off in such a hurry and that it was because Dhairesi was waiting for him. That was a big shock, and very embarrassing too. I longed for the ground to open up and swallow me. That night I worked the longest shift of my life. Rage bubbled in my veins. I almost suffocated as I struggled to breathe. I could not say if this was due to the dusty rocks I was breaking or to the pain within my chest. I was angry. Each time I hit the rocks with my pick-axe I imagined that it was Giribhati's head I was bashing in. I despised my own daughter for bringing such shame on me and for the first time in my life, I regretted siring her. I wished her body had enriched the soil at birth just as those of her siblings before her had done."

"Did you beat them up?" I was alarmed that Grandfather, a man who hardly raised his voice in anger could be driven to such fury. On the other hand I hoped he was about to regale me with the details of a heroic fight

between him and the said Giribhati. I pictured brave Grandfather punching and kicking his enemy, leaping into the air and headbutting him before leaving him sprawled on the ground and drowning in his own blood. He would have fought heroically, just like Bruce Lee whose films I enjoyed watching at the local bioscope.

"No, I did not," said Grandfather, shaking his head. So no action-packed drama then, how disappointing, I thought. "But during the whole time I was shovelling away underground, I wished the tunnel would collapse on me and end my life lest I killed someone and had blood on my hands. By the time I emerged the next morning, my rage had subsided. I thought back to what my mother used to say; 'You cannot beat evil out of anyone unless that person is ready and willing to discard the evil themselves and embrace something better in its place.'

"It was a full week before I was calm enough to confront my daughter. I explained to her that she was bringing disgrace upon herself and me in the community. Your mother showed no remorse whatsoever, Mavhuto. Instead, she defiantly told me that things had changed and she was not going to let herself get trapped in the past. After that I could only watch with exasperation while she tried to live her life the modern way. I made a very hasty decision then and took a woman into my home. At least if there was an adult keeping an eye on her while I was at work, then your mother would not be all over the compound like *chitsiru*[26]. At least that was what I had hoped for. I wanted a good, stable family life for her. You could say that I married *ma*Mpofu more for my daughter's sake than mine. Unbeknown to me, it was already too late." Grandfather got up from under the mulberry tree where we were sheltering from the scorching sun. He went indoors and emerged later with a straw hat. I knew

26A silly, wanton girl.

he was going out to the fields just outside the Mine compound. He wished to be alone with his thoughts, away from everything and everyone. During this time, he would take a walk out of the compound and into the surrounding bushes as he reflected upon his life.

"You know *muzukuru,*" said Grandfather as he briefly stopped by the tree, "the reason I gave you the name you answer to was so that you would not lose touch with your people and their ways, nor should you try to detach yourself from your shadow. It is a futile exercise, but in the event that you achieve the impossible and manage to evade your shadow, always bear in mind that you will eventually be united again when you die. Your shadow will surely come and settle once more on your lifeless body and follow you into the grave where you will merge again as one.

"The name that I gave you, Mavhuto, is the shadow that will follow you always. It is a reflection of the person that you are, and a constant reminder of the plight of our people in a foreign land and, within our own souls. As for your mother, I chose to learn from the adage of the Mashona people that goes, '*Ane benzi ndeane rake, kudzana anopururudza.*[27]' I learned to close my eyes to the decay in her and chose instead to focus on the few good traits that still endeared her to me. It was the only way I could save my heart from bleeding to death, for no loss is as heartbreaking as that of a child who still lives anywhere else but in their parent's heart."

Grandfather used the straw hat to cover his balding head and walked away into the scorching midday heat. On numerous occasions, I watched him wander off to be alone with his thoughts, but sometimes he took me with him. He said those sojourns into the neighbouring

---

27he who has a lunatic in the house ululates whenever the lunatic dances

farmlands were necessary if I was to grow up as all men should, with a clear head for thinking and away from the maddening noise of womenfolk beating cooking pots together. On those occasions I came to understand Grandfather a whole lot better. Whenever he went off on his own, he returned looking older, but when I accompanied him, we would both come back laughing and smiling. Life continued like that until several months ago when we first saw the signs of the dreaded disease. Today, as preparations are made to lay the remains of Grandfather to rest, my thoughts drift back to the many conversations we had between us.

* * *

One afternoon during the hot dry months, Grandfather and I sat in the cool shade of the big mulberry tree in one corner of the yard. A gentle breeze swayed the yellowing leaves, providing a cool wave of fresh air. It was still a month or so before the start of the rainy season, but we had already started clearing the small field in which we grew corn, pumpkins, roundnuts and sweet potatoes. Grandfather and I had worked in the field all morning. He and *ma*Mpofu always said that work was best done in the mornings before the heat weakened our bodies and reduced our efficiency. On that particular Saturday, Grandfather and I had worked till just before noon. After our midday meal we brought stools from the house and sat watching *ma*Mpofu washing the pots and plates. The washing place was next to the outdoor kitchen where *ma*Mpofu always had a drum of water, and it was my duty to make sure the water level never went down to less than half. She used two dishes to do the washing up; one filled with warm soapy water and the other with cold plain water that she used to rinse the plates in, before placing them on a flat iron sheet to dry. This metal sheet, which

*ma*Mpofu called a 'dara', was laid on top of a drum. On windy days we placed a heavy stone on top to keep it from being blown off.

For a long time, Grandfather had sat with his eyes closed. I thought he had fallen asleep, so I watched *ma*Mpofu busy at her task. So engrossed was I in watching the shimmering folds of heat cascading onto the metal sheet next to her that I did not hear Grandfather speak at first.

"Have you fallen asleep, *muzukuru*? You are not responding. It is the heat I suppose. It wears you out," his voice jolted me to attention.

"*Iyayi Asekuru,* I am awake."

He had gone on to talk with longing about the village his father left behind in the land of the great Lake Nyasa in what was then Nyasaland.

"Do you know why the locals call us *Manyasarande,* Mavhuto *wanga*?"

"I do, *Asekuru.* It is because they regard us as inferior. They call us that when they are insulting us," I quickly replied. I knew what I was talking about, for I had been called *Munyasarande* often enough.

"Does that offend you?"

"Um, not all the time, but there are times when it does."

"Mavhuto, from this day onwards I want you to know that there is absolutely nothing to be ashamed of in being called *Munyasarande or Mubhurandaya.* You need not be annoyed either. Wear that tag with pride, for it is an acknowledgment of your roots."

"*Asekuru,* I do not understand!"

"You will when I explain. Now, listen carefully *muzukuru*. In the land of our forefathers is a huge body of water that has sustained the livelihoods of our people for generations, so my own father told me. Lake Nyasa is what it was known as ever since our people could

remember, so our land was called Nyasaland, because it was, er, is the land of the great Lake Nyasa. The inhabitants of Nyasaland are referred to as *Manyasalande.* Those particularly from Blantyre called themselves *Mablantyre*. Still annoyed to be referred to as *Munyasarande,* eh?" asked Grandfather.

"So, in other words, it means someone who comes from Nyasaland or Blantyre? Is that how we came to be called *Manyasarande?"*

"Ekizekiri![28]"

"But they say it as if it were the worst insult!"

"Most of the time it is intended to hurt and humiliate, but that just goes to show how little these people know. Bear in mind though that it was not they who labelled us *Manyasarande*. It is our forefathers who proudly introduced themselves here as people from Nyasaland. If the locals call you *Munyasarande* in the mistaken belief that it is offensive, then it is their problem, and it stems out of sheer ignorance. Mind you, our people are not that blameless either when it comes to name calling."

"But we do not call them anything offensive, *Asekuru*."

"Yes we do, *muzukuru*. We do, even I do. It is our people who labelled the locals *Mashambadovi,* which they resent." That was true, and I collapsed in a fit of giggles as I remembered the incident of the two girls in my class who scratched each other's faces because one of them had called the other *Mushambadovi*. "Instead of emulating their cleverness at extracting oil from peanut butter, which they then rub onto the skin to moisturise it and keep it smooth, we mock them and refer to them as those-who-bathe-in-peanut butter. *Hahaha!* Hilarious indeed!

"Enough of all that nonsense, now. Where was I by the way? Oh, I remember. I was telling you about our fatherland, when it was still called Nyasaland. That was a

28 exactly

long time ago, before the winds of change started sweeping across the huge forests and savannalands of Southern Africa. The Zambia and Malawi of today were carved out of those vast lands and were called Northern Rhodesia and Nyasaland. There were two Rhodesias then; Northern Rhodesia and Southern Rhodesia, one on either side of the great Zambezi River," explained Grandfather. "From what our all-knowing teachers taught us, the two countries were ruled as one territory by the Queen of another country, and together with Nyasaland, they called it the Federation of Rhodesia and Nyasaland. That was some time after a man with a Bible in one hand and a gun in the other came across Mosi-oa-Tunya, the great falls on the Zambezi River. He was awe-struck by the falls, which he claimed to have discovered, and called them Victoria Falls after the woman who sat on the throne back in his homeland. For my people though, the great river and the great falls with their thunderous smoke had always been there since the beginning of time.

"Mavhuto *muzukuru,* our people did not need a ghost-like form from faraway lands to come and tell them about the mighty river. The existence of the long river with no source or ending went back ages, to the time of our fathers and that of their fathers before them. It has always been there, sustaining the livelihoods of the numerous tribes on both sides of it, who grew up in its shadows and buried their dead in its caves. Zambezi, the river with the roaring waterfall, Mosi-oa-tunya[29], may have been a great discovery, a mystery and a wonder to the white man from a land ruled by a woman, but to my people, it was part of our heritage; sacred and revered. The mighty falls have served always to remind my people of the power of our gods over our lives through its daily thunderous roaring and the thick smoke that accompanies each echo. The

29The smoke that thunders.

white man wasted no time before poking his long pointed nose into its depths and mysteries. Exploration! That was what he called it. *Hahaha!*" Grandfather's laughter was infectious, so I laughed too, even though I was not quite sure why.

"Despite the white man's explorations, the Zambezi and the Mosi-oa-Tunya refused to yield their secrets to strangers. I hear that up to today, the white man is still baffled by the legend of Nyami Nyami."

"What is Nyami Nyami?" I asked.

"Ah, *muzukuru*, how it pleases me to know that there are some things you can learn from me, an uneducated old man," chuckled Grandfather. "I suppose all they teach you in school is how to speak English with your noses upturned as if you smell faeces in the air."

"So who is this Nyami Nyami?"

"*What*, not who! Nyami Nyami is said to live in the depths of the Zambezi River, so the legend goes. Some say the thunderous noise that can be heard echoing through the Zambezi Valley is the sound of the great serpent sighing. Its breath produces the thick mist that rises from the bottom of the waterfall whenever this river god roars. Nyami Nyami, though revered and regarded as the sacred Snake Spirit of the great Zambezi, has the body of half fish and half snake."

"*Asekuru*," I whispered, "would I be able to see this creature if I were to go to Victoria Falls today?"

"Maybe, maybe not," shrugged Grandfather.

The old man went on to talk about giant snakes, calm lakes, raging rivers, waterfalls and his people, but all that held little interest for me. These tales belonged to an era too far removed from mine to concern me beyond mild curiosity.

"In these modern times, you the educated ones remember events by dates, unlike in the times of my

ancestors. Back then, significant events divided time into three distinct phases; the past, the present and the future. For example, we would say that an event took place before the year of the flood that took the life of so and so, during the drought or after the white man did this or that, and so on. Famines, bounteous harvests and the deaths of tribal chiefs or kings served as milestones that marked time. My poor father *ali kumanda*[30] did not know the year he left his homeland, but he was certain it was several rainy seasons before *Nkhonto yaHitila*[31]. As you can guess, he did not know either the exact year of my birth, but things are different nowadays. You should learn the new way of doing things but without shedding all traces of the past," lectured Grandfather.

I did not live in the shadows of the great river and I had never heard its thunderous voice nor seen the smoke that resounded with a roaring echo, so did not care much for the river to which I had no links in any way, I felt. Grandfather however, had different views. He argued that we were the sons and daughters of Mosi-oa-Tunya, and that the smoke that had sustained the livelihood of our people continued to do so to this day. He also claimed that this same great river was the basis of all our troubles, for it was in following it after being mesmerized by its greatness that the white man stumbled upon my people and claimed them, together with their land, for his queen, after which he started demanding that they pay taxes. I did not take much notice of these rumblings because I was used to them. It was the same old tale over and over again all through the years. The older Grandfather became, the more sentimental and self-pitying the rumblings became, and the more determined I vowed to detach myself from

30 Who lies in his grave

31Hitler's War

his dreams and regrets. The old man had great dreams and grand visions, but I feared they were nothing but mere delusions. He believed in the dream that his father had hoped to realise and he envisioned himself bridging the gap between the past and the future. I had no such illusions. I believed that the past belonged in the past and that the future was better without the ghosts or the burdens of a long gone era. I was happy just existing in the present.

"The present has no meaning if it has no roots firmly embedded in the past. The past is what gives us focus for the future. Mavhuto, if you understand the past first, you will have all the answers to the future for it is the history of our people that makes us who we are today, and it is that same history that will shape our future," Grandfather used to say. The old man had an obsession with an era he had no links with. His greatest desire was to venture to Nuhono village in Nkhotakota District in search of his father's people. It was an idea as futile as it was impractical. Here we were, four generations removed from the family his father had left behind, and with no contact made in all that time. It would be a miracle if the village still stood as his father had left it those many years ago, let alone the homestead. The Malawi that exists now is undoubtedly very different from the Nyasaland of almost half a century ago. A lot had happened since the winds of change started blowing across the whole of Africa. I was content to stay where I was. It did not make sense to go searching for my kinsmen in faraway lands, poking among skeletons for blood kinship when I had no links with the living; the man and woman who brought me into this world. All that changed when Grandfather contracted the disease of the mines; tuberculosis.

Now that Grandfather is dead, I understand the importance of what he was saying all through his life. I need to belong, and I need someone in my life. I need links

and roots, none of which I have. The woman who gave birth to me is just like dead wood drifting in no particular direction. Besides, I hardly know her. I know the neighbours better than I know her. Apart from Grandfather whom we both adored, we have nothing in common. To understand the mother-woman and to know her I have to go back in time, to the past and take it up from there. I have to go back to the year of my conception and reach beyond the days of her childhood. That way I may be able to find out what hardened her heart to the extent of erasing all traces of my existence from her life. Perhaps I need to delve deeper and further into the time when her mind was still innocent and her intentions pure at heart. Then maybe we might be able to share the future.

The woman who looks at me now with no recognition in her lifeless eyes cannot be a mother if she does not have a child. I too cannot be a son if I never had a mother. I was indeed a much loved and adored grandson, but I was never a son. Yet here we both are today, mourning the man who was the most important figure in our lives. The bond that tied us together snapped a long time ago and lies buried in the dust and ashes where Grandfather's body shall soon be laid to rest. The old man's remains shall soon return to the soil, leaving his spirit to wander at will over the hills and mountains and rivers and lakes and forests and…! The winds shall blow his spirit beyond the horizon. Grandfather used to say quite often that a bridge that is not made use of soon collapses. He was the bridge that linked my past to my future. He was the present that could reach out to the past and stretch to the future, drawing them together to make the present meaningful. With the bridge gone, it no longer seems possible to go back in time and try to uncover my roots. The hopes of many migrants remain nothing but wishful dreams. Grandfather leaves this world full of regrets over a past he

could not recover and a history he could not re-write. It is perhaps time I find out how I came to be here today, but that is a long story, one that has passed through the tongues of people of various generations far removed from mine. Just as the rains that fell last week removed all traces of Grandfather's footprints, nothing remains of the trail by his people from their motherland to this place.

BHAURENI'S STORY
(1899-1952)
Nuhono Village /Southern Rhodesia, Patchway Valley Mine

Forty-five long years! That was how long it took me to realise that my life was a journey that went on and on. And what a never-ending pursuit that was! I was always on the move, making only brief stops along the way before carrying on to some place, somewhere... wherever! Sometimes I never really knew where I was headed, and with time, I ceased to care. I just trudged on in a bid to satisfy a persistent itch on the soles of my feet. At times I did so with a clear goal in focus. I pursued that goal which, like a mirage, enticed me further away until I lost myself in an obsession well beyond reach on the distant horizon. My journey, or rather that of my people, started just after the beginning of the century. Maybe it began long before that, no one knows for certain now. I can only remember the tales told about my clansmen who wandered from one fertile patch of land to another, moving only when the grazing land for their livestock was exhausted. It is said that at the turn of the century, my people became less nomadic. They settled down briefly before the itch drove them to move on again, this time along the railway line from many parts of Nyasaland to Southern Rhodesia on foot. For my people, it was not only the shifting from one place to another, but that of their destinies and of their dreams as well.

Over the years, villagers talked with awe and pride about the bravery of their kinsmen who wrestled wild animals in the harsh forests of Southern Africa. Back then the forests were wild and beasts roamed at will, ruling with the savagery of their instincts. Not everyone who left

to seek their fortunes in the mines made it. Some lacked the physical stamina to undertake such a long and exhausting journey, and were left behind at the mercy of the untamed terrain. Some were bitten by poisonous snakes and died while others succumbed to malaria and sleeping sickness. It was sad that men who had fought and killed lions were defeated by the fatal bites of mosquitoes and tsetse-flies. It was a long and arduous journey, but it was one that most young men felt compelled to make. With the coming of the white man also came the need to pay him certain amounts of money every few months for one thing or the other. Tax is what they called it. That need drove men away from their villages and tore families apart. From living a free life, my people found they had to pay for almost everything. It was tax for the livestock we kept, tax for our miserable huts and tax even for the strip roads that we never used. We preferred to pull scotch carts on our own age-old paths in the forests. None of us could understand why we were compelled to pay tax for roads that meandered and made the journeys even longer, and which we did not use and did not want. These roads also made us feel exposed and more vulnerable.

Much as we had wanted to protest, my people chose instead to obey and go and work for the money with which to pay the required taxes. After all the word had come from God's own messengers, and my clansmen had a morbid fear of the God who was said to be invisible, yet very powerful. He was able to see and hear everything we did. The promise of inheriting the earth was rather appealing too, so we took comfort from it. No one thought to ask why we should need to inherit that which already belonged to us anyway. By paying the taxes they said we would be 'giving unto Caesar what belonged to Caesar'. None of us had heard about this man Kesari, but we were made to understand that the taxes belonged to him. Also, if we were to believe in a god we had never seen, it made

sense to believe too in this Kesari. We therefore made an effort to raise the money and pay him his dues. So my clansmen tore themselves away from their children, their wives and their age-old crafts to go and work for the white man.

When a man takes the decision to leave himself behind, he makes the greatest sacrifice of all. Almost half a century ago, I did just that. I left myself behind; my children, my wife, my siblings and my parents. I left everything and everybody, my whole family. I left behind the very people who defined who I was. They were my flesh, my blood and my life. They were the basis of my existence and without them, I was nothing and nobody, but just a lifeless limb detached from the rest of the body. Back in Nuhono village I also left behind my soul, without which I felt empty and hopeless, like a piece of dead wood cast adrift in a river and left at the mercies of the forces of nature, to sink or float. I was blown by the winds of change and dragged further and further away from the source of my existence, and from everything that defined who I was. I became rootless, and had no purpose in life save to follow one mirage after another. With time, I went far beyond the horizon and failed to find my way back. But I was not alone in the wilderness. I was simply one of many who had started out for the mines, none of us with any intention of staying away for more than several months. Generations later, we were still away, our dreams less focussed but our hopes well defined and quite distinct. Forty-five years was how long it took me to realise that one never really touches the mirage. It entices from a distance, only to elude swiftly as one draws nearer, until one is finally sucked and lost in the mists of time.

Like most young men in my village who felt the pressure to earn money for taxes, I decided to go to Southern Rhodesia where work was said to be plentiful in the mines. The wages were said to be good too, and far

better than what the white man paid for working in his house doing women's work back in Lilongwe. When I told my parents of my intentions, they were shocked.

"Bhaureni my son, *kushupika sikubhurara*[32]. No one ever died of a life of hardship as far as I know. How can you want to leave your village, all your clansmen and the land of your fathers, to go blindly into the wilderness where none of your ancestors ever set foot?" asked Father, bewilderment and pain clearly visible on his wrinkled and weather-beaten face.

"*Amuna wonse ali kupita, Ababa*![33]" I replied.

"*Amuna wonse,* how right you are!" shrieked Mother. "And the result? These villages here are full of orphans and widows whose fathers and husbands are swallowed by the horizon from time to time. The young women lose their husbands to distance and time, and now you too wish to lose your soul to foreign lands and leave your children without a father, and their mother without a husband! Poor Kamwendo, what fate can be worse than becoming a widow of the living dead, and at so young an age? Have you considered your family and how your departure will affect us all? The young men who left this village a few seasons ago have not been heard of, since. Does that not worry you?"

"It is too far, Amayo, and they are probably on their way back here by now. It has been two harvest seasons since their departure."

"That is too long for their families to be without them, with no news of them for that matter," argued Father.

"*Ababa,* men have been known to leave their families for far longer periods than that when they go to war," I said.

---

32 hardships do not kill

33 All the other men are going, father.

"In matters of defending their homes, their womenfolk, their children and their livestock, yes indeed. Men sacrifice time with their families to protect them, but these are peace times. There is no reason to leave your family, none at all.

"I am not happy about your going. After all, you are my only son and by virtue of that you become the head of the family when I die. Tell me, Bhaureni, if you go and never come back, who will look after the interests of the family? Luckily, your sisters are all married to good and responsible men who I have no doubt will look after them well. You cannot foretell though, what misfortune might befall them in future. I wish their husbands long lives but I am not the creator. Should any of your sisters become widows at a young age and not wish to marry the brothers of their late husbands, it would fall upon you to give them a home here, their paternal home, and to look after them until they die. There is also my sister Nkhope whose troubles with her husband I need not tell you about. Everybody in this village and in other neighbourhoods knows that her marriage is volatile. Were it not for my intervention and my threats to skin Kamanga alive should he dare knock out anymore of her few remaining teeth, he would have killed her by now, or he would have long since chased her away and married a younger woman. Bhaureni, as my only son you have the responsibility of looking after the welfare of the whole family, close and extended, and taking over responsibilities that I have. A family is as good as dead if it has no head. The homestead itself becomes a playground even for cowards to flex their muscles about."

I wondered how I could convince my parents that my going should be seen not as desertion but as a huge selfless sacrifice that would be of benefit to the whole family. I looked at my hands. They were calloused and the skin was hard from ploughing the land, cutting down

trees, chopping wood, hunting and doing the many various tasks one did to survive from one day to the next in the village. The white man wanted us to pay taxes, but we did not have the money. He offered us jobs in his house, to work for his family so that we could earn money and pay the taxes. He created a problem, then handed us a solution, one that meant young men had to leave their villages to go and work. Those who took up the jobs donned aprons and did the cooking, cleaning, washing and all other chores in the house. It was reversing the order of things and many proud men abhorred the idea. I failed to understand why I should leave my wife in the village to go and work as the wife of some family in town. It was unheard of among my people. I was not afraid of hard work. After all I had always worked hard for my family, but to desert them in order to slave for another was hard to accept. Many other young men in the villages and I agreed that if ever we had to earn the money required, we would rather do so in a manly way. No aprons or silly headscarves for us, but overalls and helmets.

"I shall certainly come back, I promise you," I said, bringing my thoughts back to my parents who were still struggling to absorb the shock of my decision. "No one, as far as we know, comes back from the mines. Of the young men who disappear into Sauti Rhudhizha[34], the only contact we have with them is through hearsay or in our dreams, where our minds refuse to relinquish their link with those who were once a huge part of our lives. Those mines are bound to be death traps, and the work back breaking. From what I hear, the young men who work in the mines are made to dig large holes deep into the bowels of the earth, some of which stretch over a distance that one walks from this village to the next, or even beyond. All those horror stories we hear from those

34Southern Rhodesia

who work in the copper mines of Noti Rhudhizha,[35] do they not deter you? Despite their years of toiling in the mines, what fortune do the returnees bring, apart from a wardrobe and a bed? Is it worth abandoning one's family for, eh, my son? Most of them come back as invalids, to be looked after by the very families they had neglected for years. Noti Rhodhizha is far enough, and here you are talking of going to Sauti Rhodhizha which is said to be even further away. Nobody who has dared to venture there has been known to return, yet that is the place you want to go to. If you must go, why not go to the Copper Belt?"

"Because *Ababa*, from what I hear, there is not much demand for mine labourers anymore. The mines are said to be getting exhausted_"

"Exhausted? What nonsense!! The mines are getting exhausted indeed! And you believe that? The mines do not get exhausted Bhaureni, it is the mine labourers that do. By the time a mine is said to be exhausted, you can be sure it would have exhausted whole generations of your people into the ground. My son, the mines will suck your blood, chew you thoroughly, and swallow you whole before spitting out only a lifeless and exhausted shell. If you are lucky to survive that, it would only be to embark on the slow, arduous journey, not back to your welcoming homeland, but to a cold and unfriendly grave far away from the land of your ancestors," said Father.

"I cannot understand this desire of yours to leave behind all that is dear, meaningful and familiar to you in the quest for lands your forefathers never even heard of. The bones of our people have always been laid to rest in the land of our ancestors where our umbilical cords continue to enrich the soil for generation after generation, bonding our bodies to our homeland till eternity. Now

35Northern Rhodesia

you want to allow the absurd demands of the white man to uproot you from it and scatter you all over the world like raindrops. In those foreign lands, who will look after you when the mines eventually spit you out and shun you? Who will sing a song for you on that final journey when your soul detaches itself from your body? Must you go and die like a slave, homeless, shunned and uncared for? Must you be buried like an animal, with no rites performed for the peaceful transition of your soul from this world to the one our forefathers inhabit? We do not let our souls leave this earth without committing them to our gods, ever. Yet you want yours to just fritter in the wind like that of a wild animal! Who knows anyway if your bones will find a resting place, ever after?" Mother asked.

I wanted to give my parents some sort of reassurance that I meant it when I said that I would be back. I knew my duties as a son, husband and father, I wanted to add, but I kept quiet.

"What about us, your relatives, we of your flesh and blood? Do you expect us to lay our heads down at night and have untroubled sleep despite having no knowledge of where you are or how you are? Our anxiety would know no bounds and our souls would be condemned to eternal anguish and heartache. I know that I speak for your mother as well when I say we shall feel lost and empty. Your leaving would be like losing a limb. I would feel the pain forever throbbing at the core of my heart for that part of me which is no longer there. When, and if you do go, I shall commit your soul to the gods of my fathers for I know that to me you would be lost forever and my eyes would never see you again," sniffed Father.

"*A*Nyirenda, the proverbs of our forefathers advise caution in the words that fall from the mouth of an adult. They are sacred and do not fall flat on the ground, so let us desist from uttering that which we do not wish upon our son should he insist on leaving," Mother remarked, her

head bowed and tilted to the side in deference to her husband. "It is best not to cast a shadow over the dreams of your son however much you may disapprove of them. Bhaureni is your own flesh and blood, and should a single drop of his blood flow, it drains you just as his sweat enriches you too. I also think we should accept and appreciate the drops of blood in the same way we would appreciate the fruits of his sweat. My mouth may not say so, but my heart bleeds as much as yours, *a*Nyirenda. Yet I am prepared to wish him well and let him go, even though our hearts may be heavy and our minds troubled. Should he go, no day or night shall pass that my heart will not grieve while he is away. Tying him here against his will would only make him miserable. Maybe you ought to give your son the chance to make his own mistakes so he can learn from them and become wiser."

"*Amake* Bhaureni, if you his mother, the one who carried him in your womb for several moons, are happy to let him go, then so be it. I hope the spirit of his forefathers shall look after him and bring him back home safely, if not to live out the rest of his days, then at least to rest his bones in their rightful place among his people. Go in peace my son, and may the winds that blow you away also blow you back, if not after a few harvest seasons as you intend, then at least during my lifetime. We are not used to losing our children to another way of life, but your mother and I will have to learn to do so."

"I pity Kamwendo," said Mother, referring to my wife of five years with whom I had a son and a daughter. She had told me only the month before that she was pregnant again.

"She will be fine," I said, trying desperately to banish the guilt I felt at leaving her to trudge on alone. But I hoped she would be well and that I would soon return laden with gifts and money from the mines of the white man.

"So when do you leave for Chitipa Camp, or is it Lilongwe?"

"We are not going to do it that way, Father," I answered. "We have decided to go straight to Southern Rhodesia rather than through the Wenela scheme because from what we have heard so far, the *mzungu* might not accept us if he thinks we are not as strong as he would prefer us to be. If he does not turn us away he might decide to keep us at the labour camp and feed us until he feels we are strong enough for the long journey, and the stay could last several months, a period of time that we cannot afford to spend there in idleness."

Indeed the other young men and I had decided to cross into the land of much promise without going first to the labour recruitment offices around the country where the Native Commissioner was in charge of recruiting young men for work in the mines and on the farms in Southern Rhodesia and South Africa. The decision to go to the former was influenced by our fear of the big Wenela flying machines that were said to fly those labourers who opted for the mines in South Africa, a country much further away than Southern Rhodesia.

Leaving with me was a group of other young men from our village. We hoped to set off before the beginning of the rainy season. We had to choose our time well. Once the rains began to fall, we would have to stay and start preparing the land for the cultivation of crops. Setting off during the rainy season presented many problems. We knew our lives would be at the mercy of the forces of nature out there. In the vast forests we would pass the nights in the open or in caves if we deemed them safe. There would be nowhere to take shelter during heavy thunderstorms or torrential rains. Most rivers were likely to be in full spate and the banks flooded, a situation that would further delay our progress as we would have to wait for days for the water to subside.

On our last night in the village, our fathers, who wanted to bestow their blessings upon us, organised a gathering of singing and dancing for us. It was a farewell that could easily have been mistaken for a funeral, for there were wives who tearfully declared their undying love for their husbands while voicing their fears that perhaps they would never see them again. It was a sad occasion, but a decision had been taken and promises made. In any case there had been other such farewells before and we knew that before we had made our first fire out in the jungles, those tears would be dry and soon replaced by cackles of laughter again as the womenfolk gossiped about village life.

On my last night at home, I lay awake in the dark wondering how soon I would be back to spend the nights in my hut, in my village, and with my family. I listened for the regular breathing of my wife that had always been such a comfort to me but I heard nothing. The silence was eerie, until one small sob escaped her lips. Gradually, the low moans seeped into the space between our chests, cutting through the dark silence. Lying quietly beside her, I wanted to reach out to her and give her words of comfort but I hesitated. I buried myself instead in my own anxieties of the uncertain journey ahead. There was no doubt that the journey had its perils. There was no guarantee we would make it to Southern Rhodesia alive, yet all this did not shake my resolve. I must have drifted off to sleep at some point, for I woke up to feel my wife's hand on my arm, shaking me gently. The cock had just crowed, she told me. I lay still in the dark hut, listening for the last time to the comforting familiar sounds of the village at sleep; cicadas shrieking from treetops and the owls hooting to frighten those who dared walk when the rest of the world was asleep.

"I will wait for you for as long as it takes you to come back," Kamwendo whispered hoarsely in my ear.

"Do not say that. I have already said I shall be back before long, certainly not longer than two harvest seasons," I said, stroking the small bump in which a new life was growing.

"I do not know, but I hope so. The children need you. I cannot ask you not to go, but I can ask you to please come back to us."

"I will, I promise you," I whispered back. We lay in the semi-darkness with Kamwendo's moist breath on my chest, my anxieties buried in my heart, her fears in hers. Anxiety filled the space between us, a fact our lips found too heavy to acknowledge. I let my hand rest on Kamwendo's stomach for a while, and then my fingers carefully traced the base of the raised mound which pulsated in response to my light kneading. Kamwendo brought her hand down there too, and our fingers lay interlaced until it was time for me to leave.

Before I stepped out of the hut I took a lingering look at my sleeping children. Then clutching my bundle of meagre belongings and whatever food we would need on the way, I joined the five other young men under the big tree by the village meeting place. The food was enough to last only a few weeks, but we had traps with which we hoped to snare small animals along the way. That way, we would have endless supplies of fresh or dried meat. Kamwendo huddled together with the other women to see us off to the edge of the village. About a dozen men escorted us far into the forest and spent the first night with us before journeying back home as we proceeded. It was a dangerous journey. We got to the railway line as planned, but we had enormous setbacks. Within a week we had lost Tatani to a snake-bite. The reptiles were swift and vicious. A few weeks later, Pezani fell to his death as we crossed a deep gorge. A short while later, Mpamvu found the strife too much for him and he lost his mind. At first we did our

best to restrain him, but watching over him at night required a lot of effort and deprived us of much needed sleep. When we began to struggle to stay awake and alert during the day, the decision was made to let Mpamvu wander off alone than for all of us to risk losing our bearings in pursuit of him. It was not an easy decision, and it threatened to split the group, but with just one person in disagreement with the other two, there was not much he could do unless he wanted to go after Mpamvu on his own. After this sad deliberation, Mpamvu was left to wander off into the dense forest on his own.

Soon after we left our clansman behind, I came face to face with danger myself. I thought I was being punished for treating Mpamvu the way we had done. We had stopped for the night and lit a fire near a cave. Darkness had not yet fully claimed the forest, and one could still make out the faint outlines of hills, anthills and treetops in the distance. Our food supplies were running low so it was decided that one of us should crawl into the cave and hunt a couple of rabbits that had darted down there. Because I was the thinnest, I was expected to carry out the task. I was not keen on crawling into strange dark caves, yet I could not find a way out of it without appearing like a coward, so I took a deep breath and felt my way into the cave. I had only gone a short distance when the space became narrower. I lowered myself flat on the hard uneven ground and slowly felt my way forward with my hands. So engrossed was I on creeping soundlessly that I did not immediately sense the danger ahead of me. It was probably that which saved my life. I raised my eyes to find myself looking into the bright eyes of a reptile. All of a sudden, the hairs at the back of my neck stood on end. The reptile stared at me with an unwavering gaze, as if assessing how much of a threat I posed to it. The events of that day still unfold in my mind today as if they happened

to someone else, and I can still see man and reptile locked in a bitter war of will.

The reptile stared at me with unblinking eyes. Fear and horror mingled to create a numbing effect on my brain. Clearly, the reptile felt cornered, and was desperate. We both lay sprawled on the floor of the cave. The reptile rose slowly and its neck extended as it did so. My position had swiftly changed from that of the hunter to that of the hunted. I was face to face with a hooded cobra, an angry snake challenged in its domain. My blood went cold. This is the end, I thought. So this is how it ends for me, just a few months after leaving my village. The cobra reared its head backwards, preparing to strike. Bravery, desperation, instinct or whatever it was, made me roll over quickly to the left. Because the cave was narrow and had a low roof, no other movement was possible other than to either crawl or roll. The snake had plenty of room to move any way it wished. When it pulled back and attempted to strike again, I rolled sideways. Left-right-left-right-left-right, I went, as did the head of the increasingly desperate reptile. I knew that so long as I kept moving, the snake would keep trying to take aim before attacking. In that frenzied moment I thought of all the gods of my father's people, and threw in even those of my mother's and I implored them to have mercy on me and save my life. I also remembered the gods of the white man. Surely some god or other would hear my plea? Just then, a rabbit darted out of nowhere and dashed between us. The cobra struck the hapless little rodent, and I scrambled out of there as fast as I could before the reptile realised there was another threat lingering about. After the near-death incident I knew I would arrive at my destination regardless of whatever obstacles lay in the path of my quest.

We stayed as close to the railway line as we could because its trail led to the mines that we desperately wished to reach. Marizani, Chinai and I trudged on until

we came to a place where the locals spoke the Sena tongue. They told us that we were in a country called Mocambique, and that to get to Southern Rhodesia we had to either board the steam engine or make our way to the boarder town of Umtali on foot. A large number of the Sena men had also left their villages to work in the mines in South Africa and Southern Rhodesia, so we were told. Needless to say, we were so emaciated we could not proceed with the journey on foot, so for a while we lived on the generosity of the local people who offered us shelter and food. Unfortunately for Marizani, he caught malaria and was too weak to survive. We laid him to rest in the land of the Sena people. When Chinai and I regained our strength, we found temporary jobs on nearby commercial farms where we worked until we had earned enough money for food and for the train fares to our destination. Our target was the mines, and we were determined to get there however long it took. We had come too far already and we were determined to proceed to Southern Rhodesia.

After a few months, Chinai and I decided that we were fit enough to set off. We were advised to take the steamer_ as the locals called it_ and cross into Umtali, from where we were to board another steam engine to Salisbury, and then another to Bulawayo. Jobs were said to be plentiful in most places along the railway line, from Hartley, Gatooma, Que Que, Shangani, Bulawayo and all the way to Wankie. When we boarded the steam engine in Umtali, we had agreed on Que Que as our destination because we were told there was a big iron smelting company, RHOMAT. However, upon arriving in Gatooma I declared that I had had enough of travelling and wanted to get off and remain behind. Chinai said he would stick to our original plan. It was a sad parting for both of us, but we acknowledged that as grown up men our lives had to take

different paths at some stage. Though six of us had left the village together, only the two of us had made it to Southern Rhodesia. We had buried the remains of three of our kinsmen in two different countries and we had no idea what had become of Mpamvu.

It was easy enough to get to the mines and within a week I had got a job as a labourer at Patchway Valley, a mine owned by John Mack and Company. The first week was a shock. The work was very hard and the conditions were terrible. It was the hardest job I had ever done. The glory of the mines was nothing but a myth. It was not until later that I realised that people often tend to speak of life in faraway lands in glowing terms. I wished I could go back home, yet to do so at that point and empty handed would have been to admit defeat. I would have been the first migrant labourer to return within a short time and with nothing to show for the period I had been away. Besides that, the outward journey had been hard even in the company of my fellow villagers and without them I knew I was never going to make it back to Nyasaland alive. I felt trapped in a land where I was not happy.

At Patchway Valley Mine those of us who had no families were made to share three to a room. The rooms were hardly big enough for one person and we managed only because two of the occupants worked opposite shifts, while the third worked away all day. Mpezewa and I worked in the mine and Yanganani, who worked as a cook for one of the bosses, left in the morning and came back in the evening. All in all, the conditions were appalling, the work was very hard, the bosses were brutish, the locals condescending, and the rewards next to nothing. By the time our employers had deducted money for compulsory rations of mealie-meal and beans from our meagre wages, there was hardly any money left to put aside for when we

would return home. Despite our discomfort, the three of us got along well. We found time to chat whenever one of us was given a day off work, and it was during such occasions that we got to know each other better. We knew of no one who was going back to the motherlands and even if there was, we had nothing to send. We earned just enough money to buy food from one payday to the next. We got no news from home and we were completely cut off from our old life and our clansmen. However, my resolve to go back in the near future remained unshaken, and I said as much to my roommate Yanganani who surprised me when he burst out laughing.

"*A*Bhaureni, do not make me laugh on such a lousy Sunday. Surely by now you realise that you can no longer go back?" It was my turn to laugh, but all I could manage was a mirthless cackle.

"Yanganani my kinsman, I Bhaureni," I thumped my chest with my fist to emphasize my determination, "have every intention of going back home. I cannot lead such a hard life as if I am a bandit sentenced to life in prison with hard labour. It is impossible! Besides, I left my wife, my young children and my elderly parents back there. They need me to look after them all. No, Yanganani. I cannot stay here forever, definitely not me."

"So you still dream of going back laden with gifts and lots of money, to be welcomed as a hero, envied by other men and admired by the womenfolk as they ululate and sing praises to your name? Oh, Bhaureni, did we not all have the same dream when we came over here? But where are we now, all these years later?" Yanganani asked, shaking his head sadly.

"*Mubale wanga*[36], I do not know and, I certainly do not care how many other people before me failed to make their wishes come true. As for me Bhaureni, the only son

36 My kinsman

of Nyirenda of Nuhono village, I will go back home no matter what,' I jabbed the air with my finger with each word I uttered.

'I admire your determination, but I have seen it all before in others who had more determination than what I see in you. We all dreamt of going back at first, but with time it just becomes easier to stay where one is. The longer you remain here the less you dream of those back home. In the ten years I have been here I know of no one who has gone back."

"I will be the first person you shall see going back. I will throw my overalls onto the fire and dance on the ashes to celebrate my departure from this hell, but my helmet and the gumboots will be the trophies that I shall take with me back to my village, so I have to return no matter what it takes."

"Tell me, Bhaureni. What is stopping you from going back now, or next month? You have been here eight months already."

"I do not have enough money to pay my fare on the steam engine."

"So far how much have you saved?"

"I have not been able to save anything yet."

"And when do you hope to have saved enough for your ticket and for the parcels for your family, the money for taxes and other things?"

Silence.

"You see Bhaureni, it is simply impossible, and you cannot take only the helmet and gumboots back there. *Ha ha ha!* Imagine a hunter bringing home only the horns and the hide of a buffalo, *he he he!* No meat, eh?" I was getting annoyed with my roommate, but there was truth in what he was saying.

"You see Bhaureni, *bwana*[37] is not stupid. The moment you accept a job from him you surrender all control of your life to him. He pays you just enough to last from one payday to the next_"

"If we are lucky to make the meagre wages last that long. Mine certainly do not stretch that far. During the last three or four days before payday, I get bread and milk on credit from the store. That debt is the first I pay when I get paid, which leaves me short once more and as a result I have to borrow again before the next payday. It is an impossible situation. That's why I have not saved any money towards my fare so far," I grumbled.

"I know, my kinsman. That is why I advise you to forget about Nyasaland and concentrate on your life out here."

I looked around me to see the life out here that my roommate was talking about. It was dark and gloomy in the small room we shared. I could walk from one side to the other in just five strides. The roof was flat and made of some thick material. The only light came in through the small opening on the wall opposite the door. It was meant to be a window but there was wood instead of a glass pane. So small was this window that the biggest shadow it made in the time between sunrise and sunset was the size of a big plate. Because it was gloomy in the room, like most people, we spent more time outdoors than indoors during the day, but during the night and when it rained, we were forced indoors and had to endure the cold damp rooms because the walls were built of limestone bricks which tended to hold rainwater in them and rendered the rooms cold. On a wire that ran from one wall to the other, cutting across the corner, we hung the few clothes we owned which were mostly shirts, shorts and vests. We draped the work overalls there as well. Beneath the clothes

37 The boss

we neatly laid out pairs of gumboots and other worn out footwear. Each of us had a cardboard box or a wooden crate on which we arranged personal items such as combs, mirrors, razors, jars of Vaseline and handkerchiefs. A pile of blankets and canvas tents, carefully folded, summed up our lives. In the corner to the far right were spoons, knives and an assortment of green, blue and white aluminium cups and plates, most of which had black scars from where the paint had chipped off. There were two black pots, one of which had a handle that had once broken off and was then soldered back on again, leaving a gold-coloured band like a rough-edged ring pushed along the handle. On the base of the pots, a silvery line ran along the edge, a result of years of heavy scouring with course sand. Next to the cooking utensils, in plastics papers were beans, mealie-meal, sugar, salt and dried matemba fish. In one cardboard box we stored a bottle of cooking oil, a tin of powdered milk or condensed milk and peanut butter. In a separate box we had tinned Sun jam and margarine, with the latter immersed in water to keep away ants and also to keep it cool. The margarine could be kept cool and solid in the cold months with no problem, but in the hot dry months it was a futile exercise because it melted and attracted large numbers of ants that ended up swarming all over our salt, sugar and mealie-meal. That was our life. That, loneliness, and thoughts of our loved ones, was the life here. That was what my friend was urging me to settle down to.

"Yanganani, do you have any idea how hard the life of a mine labourer is? Obviously your job in the kitchen of *abwana* is a lot easier."

"Is that what you believe? Do you really think it is fun when *adona* snaps her fingers for you to hurry up and *abwana* kicks you in the backside to get you moving faster? Whenever *adona* clicks her fingers and shouts *'kom'iya!'* I never know whether she means the dog or me, so at times we both end up running towards her. I do not know which

is more bearable, working where there are fewer perils but more insults, or down the mine shaft with its potential hazards but with no one calling me names."

"Whatever job one does, it is still very hard. That is why I have to be gone before my feet grow roots in this place."

"We shall see."

"Tell me honestly, Yanganani. Don't you ever long for your homeland? Do you not ever dream of going back to your village to see all those people you left behind?'"

"'Of course I do. I mean I did, at first. During the first two years I was terribly homesick. I went to sleep thinking of those I left behind. I missed the smell of cowdung. I especially missed the smell of the damp rich black soils of my homeland that wafted up my nostrils everytime it rained. I used to go to sleep with a heavy heart and wake up in the morning unwilling to face the new day. But with time you soon realise that there is no point in yearning for that which is not possible. Though coming to work in these foreign lands was supposed to be a dream, in reality it is a nightmare, one I must endure. I advise that you do the same.'"

"We shall see," I answered. But my head was screaming, 'never, never, never!'

One month passed, then another and another, until a whole year had gone by. Slowly the years began to pile up one upon the other. I tried to convince myself that each coming year would be my last, but it became harder with each passing year. The memories I had of my loved ones began to fade gradually. Back then, photography had yet to enter our lives. I had no pictures to remind me what my people looked like, so all recollection of them evaporated from my mind, to be buried firmly in the past that I had left behind. Time gradually drew a line between Nyasaland and Southern Rhodesia, between the past and

the present, and between those left behind and those of us who were out here. The line, faint at first, became more distinct as the years went by and we slowly came to accept that as pieces of wood cast adrift, we could not hope to go back where we had started off. Just as Yanganani had said, I became one of the many migrants who would never see their homelands again. Ours was a new life and what we had left behind was in the past. I felt deflated just thinking of the journey I had made, one so hard it had claimed more than half the group. I had no wish to embark on it again. If I worked and saved a bit of money, maybe I would go back by rail, but as things were, the gold we had all thought glittered underground belonged not to us, but to the white man, so to him it all went straight from our shovels. All we did was dig it out.

Patchway Valley Mine was, like most other mining communities, a melting pot of various cultures of migrants. We learned to speak each other's languages and we adopted alien customs. The Chewa people learned to speak other languages, as did the Ngoni, the Sena, the Chawa and the Tonga. We learned too to give up a part of ourselves while adopting a few alien habits. We became related by virtue of being from the same tribe, the same village, or by merely answering to the same totem or by being fellow migrants... outsiders. We found our own uncles, cousins and brothers, creating a kinship stronger than blood ties and based on our life of hardship. Within the migrant mining communities was a desperate need in us to belong and to feel like family. We identified ourselves by totem and were quick to clutch at threads of kinship, however flimsy. The Phiri totem has the same origin, whether one is from Nyasaland, Mocambique or Northern Rhodesia, so we are related, we argued. Soon enough we had clans and tribes. I gradually regained my soul and my family and I began to feel that I belonged.

The migrant labourers from Northern Rhodesia had not had far to travel as we had, so it had been possible for some of them to bring their families, or to send for them to come by steam engine once the men were settled. Some labourers died in the mines and others from natural causes, leaving their widows to re-marry, and their daughters to grow up and marry too.

Within a few years of settling at Patchway Valley Mine, the memory of my wife and my children had receded into the distant past. The memory of my father begging me not to go haunted me on some occasions and left me feeling sad and guilty. I thought too of poor Kamwendo who had sobbed the night before I left. The promise I had made to my family was blown into the wind as their fears turned out to be well founded. With each passing year the bonds that tied me to them gradually slackened as I sought to make another life in a different land altogether. I thought of the hope that probably kept them smiling, and also of the sorrow and tears that I knew were sure to flow once they finally accepted that I was lost to them forever. No doubt the worst thing for my family was in never knowing whether I was alive and well, or already dead and buried. There must have been times when they thought I had chosen to forget all about them and that I did not care about their anxieties. If ever they thought I was dead, they must have agonised over whether my death had been swift and painless or horrific, painful and lingering. I knew that anguish ate away at their hearts and would continue to do so until the day each of them was finally laid to rest. I tried my best to banish these thoughts from my mind but it was difficult. I felt guilty as I thought of the wife and the children I would never see again. As my heart gradually turned away from Kamwendo, I sought to fill the void with someone else. It was regrettable and sad but so many things had changed and life had to go on. She

was there, and I was here. I stopped deluding myself into believing that I would one day go back. After all only a few people were known to have ever done so. This was achieved only at the end of one's contract, for those who had come under the Wenela scheme, or upon retirement when the one-way ticket was bought by the Mine Management as part of the miner's pension.

I got on with my life and married a girl called Mwanaicha. I paid two cocks to her father as bride price. Her family had been at the Mine for quite some time, having arrived from Northen Rhodesia years before I did. Mwanaicha was born a few years after her family settled down at the Mine. I felt complete with my wife and my parents-in-law. Mwanaicha was my wife even though our masters did not acknowledge our traditional marriages, referring to them as mere co-habitation. My people had always recognised and honoured our traditional marriages. These ceremonies that united couples in matrimony were conducted the same way since the beginning of time, and we saw no reason to change them. Mwanaicha and I had an asbestos-roofed three-roomed house allocated to us. With its cracked cement floors and soot-covered walls, it was much bigger, much brighter and more pleasing than the single room I had shared with two other men. Within a year, Mwanaicha and I were blessed with of a baby boy whom I named after my father. I had no way of knowing what year that was, but I later learned that it was several harvest periods before what came to be known as the terrible war of the white man, *Nkhonto yaHitila.*I was happy with my young family and I lived happily with Mwanaicha. She was another Kamwendo in many ways. The only difference between them was that Kamwendo was betrothed to me in an arrangement agreed upon by our parents as we grew up. I was raised with the knowledge that as soon as she and I were old enough to have children, we would settle down to married

life together, bear children and get on with our lives in much the same way that our parents had lived theirs.

Neither Kamwendo nor I had been involved in the decision that led to our betrothal. We had only been children then, and we had no say in serious issues such as betrothal and marriage. I just grew up knowing that one day I would set up home with a girl promised to me in an arrangement that saw my family rescue hers from starvation during one terrible period of famine. This arrangement secured a whole year's worth of grain for her family. It also established a bond between our two families, binding together the future of Kamwendo and myself. Throughout our childhood, my family continued to offer assistance to hers whenever they were in need, which seemed to be almost always, further indebting them to us. Although not a very wealthy man by Nuhono village standards, Father had enough livestock and granaries to be in a position to help others. The relationship of the two families was to be finally cemented by marriage as soon as my betrothed and I each had undergone the necessary initiation rites that would catapult us from childhood to adulthood. Though there was no courtship for my betrothed and I, there were, however, heart-stopping moments of stolen glimpses from across the river or the meadowlands. I liked the girl and I could not see any sign that she detested me. I was intrigued by her shyness and I never ceased to be amused by the way she refused to meet my gaze, keeping her eyes firmly glued to her feet whenever our paths happened to cross unexpectedly.

Kamwendo was a lovely girl whose shyness had endeared her to me from the moment I first saw her. I took delight in teasing her whenever I got the chance, which was not often. Her paternal aunts watched over her like hawks and made sure she was never in my company or that of any

man without a grown up woman to watch over her and guard her chastity. Betrothed as she was to my family, it would have been scandalous if she were to fall in love with someone else then elope with him. The preservation of the girl's dignity and chastity were of utmost importance to her family, until she was finally delivered from their care to that of my family as my wife. Failure to remain chaste on her part would have brought disgrace to her family while incurring the wrath of mine. It would have resulted in bad blood between the two families that would have seen future generations feuding indefinitely with one another. So much was at stake and Kamwendo's family had a debt to honour, hence her aunts' eyes on her at all times. Kamwendo herself was aware of the obligation she had towards her family and she took it seriously. On the few occasions I crept upon her while she was alone, she bolted like a mad woman towards the village, desperate to avoid dishonour. As I grew up, I knew about my betrothed but I did not really know her as a person. I only got to do so when she was escorted to our homestead as my wife. I felt nothing deeper than just liking for her, but I was told that I would grow to love her once I got to know her better. When she became my wife I cherished her and I was happy with her. Although we never mentioned love, I think Kamwendo came to love me as the years went by.

With Mwanaicha however, our courtship was the other way round. With my first marriage, my parents had arranged everything so I had no idea how to go about it on my own. As I prepared to take a wife in a land where I was still a relatively new migrant worker, I felt unsure of myself. I was afraid to offend those whose customs were different from mine. With the boldness I initially found shocking in a young girl, but which I soon came to admire in her, Mwanaicha relentlessly sought to attract my attention and my company. I had misgivings about taking

for a wife a woman whose behaviour appeared to be unrestrained, but I soon realised that although she was brazen, she was just like Kamwendo and she would not let me behave towards her in a way that was improper. It was with Mwanaicha that I got to know that hearts have a way of singing to each other, and with that came the realisation that I had merely been fond of Kamwendo. My love for Mwanaicha grew as we enjoyed the process of courtship. I had a choice whether or not to marry her and I chose to. I loved her beyond anything else.

My wife was my whole family. While Kamwendo, whom I had grown more and more fond of each year, was my mother's daughter-in-law first before she was my wife_ careful always not to offend her, striving to do the right thing at the right time_ Mwanaicha was my wife and she sought to please me first and foremost. She was free and unrestrained in our marriage. Like the wife I had before her, she was hardworking and she respected me. She cooked for me and kept the house clean. Within a year she had given birth to a healthy lovely son and I wished for nothing more. Life went on calmly. My world was complete and my life fulfilled once again. In just over ten years my wife had given me two children and a third was on the way. I had indeed got my family back again.

I had been in Southern Rhodesia for many years when the white man went to war. He was said to be fighting his kinsmen somewhere beneath the vast skies but we did not lose sleep over that. It was not our war and it had nothing to do with us. It was just so far away we did not bother thinking about it… until the day we were taken to it. Once again I was compelled to leave behind a wife, two young children and an unborn baby. For the second time in my adult life I had to leave the security of my home life. I was going to a foreign land to fight for a cause I did not understand. I was not even sure why I had to fight for one

white man against another. All my life I had known kinsmen to stick together and fight as one against a common enemy, so my amazement and confusion were great at this disunity of a race that had appeared organized and superior to mine. Among my people, though we were divided within our own tribes, languages and totems, we still banded together as one brotherhood in our black skin. The supposedly superior white race was fighting its brothers, and even enlisting our help to shed the blood of their kinsmen. Only our masters knew their reason for fighting, we were not told why, even though it was also our lives that were at risk. We never asked the bosses anything because it never occurred to us to question their actions or decisions. How could we? After all they were like gods. They knew everything and they had every right to do with us whatever they wished. So off to war we were carted with no explanation given.

* * *

We never saw people of my race in the villages and towns where we fought. The only people of my skin colour were the ones helping the white man fight his war, and they spoke different languages. They referred to this war as the big war of the whole world, but I did not think it was. It was nowhere near Gatooma and we had never seen any flying machines hovering above the skies. Also, it took us a whole day to reach the war zone even when travelling in the big machines that flew faster than the birds of the sky. The horrors I saw in those faraway lands were like nothing I had ever seen before. When the white soldiers killed their enemies, they did so in large numbers, at times wiping out

whole armies. It was nothing like the killing we did back in my village whereby we used spears and burned down huts. Theirs was a bloody war of a magnitude I had never known before. Just witnessing it made me almost lose my mind. I had never got to a stage where I was so terrified except for the times we lost our friends on the journey to Southern Rhodesia and on the day we were marched into the big flying machine to go to the war zone. I thought a lot about Mwanaicha and the children; my son who had just started school when I left and my lovely daughter. I wondered how my wife had fared giving birth to the unborn baby she was carrying when I left.

On many nights I lay awake wondering if I would ever see my family again. There were many things I wanted to do for, and with my children. I wanted to teach my son how to make a catapult and shoot birds. I wanted to be there when he went for his *jando*[38], a custom many migrants had adopted even though they were not of the Chawa tribe. I wanted to be there to take pride in receiving the bride price for Nchesa, that special token due to every man with a daughter. I wondered whether my new baby had survived at birth, and if so, if it was a boy or a girl, and who it resembled. Although I knew that complications could occur while giving birth, at times resulting in the death of the mother or the infant or both, I did not even wish to contemplate that as a possibility in the case of my wife. My heart desired to be by Mwanaicha's side as we tottered towards the end of our lives. In all the time I was away, I never stopped worrying about them all. I was anxious about what would happen to them if I died at war since Mwanaicha's father had died a few years back and her mother had moved to the farms.

38Circumcision rite marking the beginning of adulthood in male children of the Chawa tribe of the Islamic religion

Before I was taken away to go and fight, I was first recruited as a Bantu soldier into what was called the African Regiment of the Territorial Army back in the Federation. The Mine Management, as part of their contribution to the war effort, had sent a group of us for consideration in joining the army. The Rhodesian Native Regiment (made up largely of the Askari Unit of the British South Africa Police, BSAP), the Rhodesian Police and civilians like me, trained at Borrowdale Camp in Salisbury. For several weeks, we were taught how to engage in physical combat as well as in long and short range shooting, which was both exciting and frightening. During training our targets were dummies but we knew that on the battlefield we would be firing at real people. It was unnerving but it was one duty we had to do. Among the recruits was Mupezeni Tsogolani, the man who was to become almost like a brother to me.

After training, we were flown to a country in North Africa. A year later the war took us to another country that looked very much like the land of my fathers. The undulating hills, the rolling valleys, and the climate reminded me so much of Nyasaland. There were large rubber plantations that we had to guard with our lives. During the day the weather would often range from warm to hot, becoming cooler when torrents of rain fell. Night time brought a cool, calming breeze. The serenity, however, would often be shattered by heavy gunfire and fierce fighting. We did not leave our posts, but we became involved in the fighting when it came to us. On these occasions we fought first to protect the plantations, then our lives, in that order. On calm nights my thoughts often wandered to my kinsmen back in Nyasaland and to my family in Southern Rhodesia. I wondered if they could see the same moon, the same stars and the same skyline that we saw out there. At times I failed to link the native son of Nyasaland to the white-skin-saluting-migrant labourer in

Rhodesia, and to the soldier now fighting alongside white men in Burma. I was like three men in one body.

One tranquil night, Tsogolani and I lay on our camp beds after a rather uneventful day.

"*Mubale wanga*, do you think we shall ever see our families again?" Tsogolani asked.

"Only *Mulungu*[39] knows."

"Did you say only *muzungu* or only *Mulungu* knows?"

"What difference is there, Tsogolani? *Muzungu, Mulungu,* it is all the same. *Muzungu* is *Mulungu* in every way. You know that we rely on these *vazungu*[40] to take us back to our homelands and to our families."

"I miss my daughter Chimwemwe, my only child. At times I wonder if I shall ever see her again. If there is one thing I desperately wish for, it is that I get to see my little girl again."

"I hope to see my family too. I miss my children and their mother." For some moments we lay silent in the dark, each lost in his thoughts until I said, "Do you know what I have been thinking, Tsogolani?"

"What?"

"My job as a mine labourer back home is risky, but my life is more at risk out here."

"Of course it is not as bad back home as it is here. At least no one in the mines tries to shoot at you or to blow you up everyday. Tell me Bhaureni, what exactly are we doing in this foreign land?"

"Fighting of course?" I answered, baffled.

"Yes of course, that much I know, but why are we fighting? I have asked myself that question many times, but the answer eludes me, always."

39God

40 Plural of *muzungu (white men)*

"We are fighting a war, Tsogolani. We are here because *abwana* brought us here to guard the rubber plantations, surely you know that?"

"With our lives if it comes to that, yes I know all that drill, but why exactly do we need to guard rubber plantations in a country so far away from our own?"

"Tsogolani, you ask too many questions. It is enough for me to know that we are fighting dutifully for our country."

"Our country? Which country, Bhaureni?"

"As I said before, you ask too many questions. Only *muzungu* knows the answers to these questions. As for the reason we are fighting, if I were you I would not crack my head thinking about it. Everything that requires thinking is best left to *abwana* to deal with. We must just concentrate on carrying out his orders as he constantly reminds us to do," I said. I was becoming exasperated with his incessant questions to which he knew none of us had the answers. Since when has a lowly paid labourer known anything, a black one for that matter?

"Well, I suppose we will never know the answer. We just know that we are here to guard the rubber trees. Trees, Bhaureni! For these trees we should be prepared to lay down our lives, hey! The way the brain of the white man works never ceases to amaze me. Trees indeed! He he he."

"This is a war in which plants are prized above livestock. Ha ha ha, who would believe me were I to tell that to the people back home? No one. They would think I have gone mad. But I have since ceased to be amazed by the strange ways of *abwana*. Are they not the same people who cherish their dogs more than humans? Have we not seen the men love their drink more than their women, and do they not risk their lives_ and ours too_ to go down the mine shafts looking for stones? Stones, *mubale wanga*,

stones! What for, when we could all live an easier life tilling the land above and growing food?"

"The brain of a white man is a puzzle. If you want to go mad, then start cracking your head pondering over the mysteries of his strangeness. All I want to worry about now is when we are going to be taken back home."

"Me too, Tsogolani. Hopefully by the end of this year we will be back with our families. My wife was carrying our third baby when I left. I think about that child all the time, wondering if he or she looks like me or the mother. I hope to see him or her soon, God willing."

"Amen. You will, if *Mulungu* wills it. I would not be surprised though if we should end up in some other country again from here. Remember how we used to think that from North Africa we would go straight back to Rhodesia? Yet here we are, still fighting."

"All through my life there have been only a few things I have had control over. One of them was my marriage to Mwanaicha, the other was the decision to go and work in the mines. But even then I had to fight to convince my parents that it was a good idea."

"Do you still think it was?"

"It is difficult to say. I do not regret my attempt to do something different, but I feel bad about failing in what I set out to achieve."

"And your parents, what did they think?"

That was a painful subject to think about. Since joining the army, I had begun to think more frequently about my village back in Nyasaland. I thought deeply about my father and wondered too about Mother, and whether she thought of me everyday. In my mind I could almost see her offering prayers to the gods of her fathers for my safe return. I wondered whether my departure and my failure to go back had deepened the wrinkles on my parents' sad faces, or whether their souls had shrivelled. I wondered if

they still lived in the hope that one day they would look through the bushes behind their homestead and get a wonderful surprise at seeing me emerge from there in the twilight. Maybe they had given me up for dead and decided to get on with their lives, and their memories of me had gradually receded as time went on. For me, Kamwendo and the children had long become a faded memory as the years rolled by, but I hoped their lives had been enriched in some way. I hoped Kamwendo had found a kind and hardworking man to take her and provide her with the stability and loving care she had expected from me and failed to get. If she had, she would have become wife to a man with several wives already. No single young man would ever marry a woman who was divorced, or a widow with children from another man. While I wished my first wife happiness with another man, any thoughts that I could perhaps find Mwanaicha living with another man as her husband almost drove me mad. I hoped she would wait regardless of how long it took.

In the war of the white man, there was no guarantee that I would go back to Southern Rhodesia alive. A good number of the soldiers were dead. Some had died in combat, others from dysentry, malaria or dehydration. It was hard living in a foreign land whose people were strangers and whose language we did not understand. It was not that easy either amongst ourselves because of the different languages we spoke. At times our very survival depended on our ability to understand advice, warning or orders. The situation for all the soldiers was difficult, but it was more so for us Africans. Though I knew life to be hard at the mines, it was certainly harder in the war zone. Back in Gatooma, migrant labourers were considered to be inferior by both the locals and the whites. It was cruel, but it was an attitude we had lived with for so long that it had become normal for us. The locals shunned the jobs we did and considered them to be back breaking and fit to be

done only by people who were homeless, rootless, desperate, and were therefore compelled to take whatever came their way. Years later, I was to watch with fascination as some of the native men began trooping all the way to the mines in South Africa. Upon their return_ if they remembered to come back, which most of them did_ they were addressed as *Mujubheki.*[41] Strangely, the term did not sound as derogatory as *Mubhurandaya* or *Munyasarande*, despite the fact that all terms referred to places where one originated from, or where they had gone to seek their fortunes. Our white masters at Patchway Valley considered black workers to be dirty and smelly. They called us *kaffir_* whatever that meant_ and we knew it was an insult because it was a word uttered with contempt. We had to address the men as *'baas'* or *bwana* even if they were not our bosses or were complete strangers to us. We showed reverence to their children by addressing them as *pikinini baas*[42] and their womenfolk as madam or *dona.*

That was the state of things back in the mines, but out in the war zone the dangers we faced made us equal. As my mind turns misty at times, there are events I completely forget. At times my thoughts get muddled up but one thing that is forever vivid in my mind is the period I served in the army, first in Egypt then in Burma, and back to Egypt again where I remained until I was wounded. There were people of my skin colour who spoke in tongues I had never heard of. And from others I could make out a few words here and there that sounded vaguely like those of my language. I was lucky in that I met a few people from some mining areas in Southern

41 A term by which those who worked in South African mines were known. The word is a corruption of Jo'burg, short for Johannesburg

42 Little boss

Rhodesia who spoke my language. The greatest joy though, was having Tsogolani in the same regiment. Both of us had come from Patchway Valley Mine. We had not known each other before our training in Salisbury but we immediately became like brothers. Our situation bound us more closely than the community we came from. In the army we were treated like brothers by people whose kinsmen shunned me back home because of the colour of my skin. We were baffled at first at having to sleep in the same pitch tents as the *baas*, side by side on our camp beds and eating the same food. I soon realised that at war, if your very survival depends on how closely you all work together, everybody becomes colour blind and the barriers tumble down. You become brothers-in-arms first before you become black or white, English speaking or Pidgin speaking. In Egypt and in Burma, everything else became insignificant except for the colour of blood that flowed in our veins. Preventing it from being shed became our main priority. I discovered at that point that war brings out the worst in people but it can also bring out the best in them. Black or white, we all shed tears when those closest to us perished and our hearts hurt in much the same way. That realisation strengthened the bonds of brotherhood and increased tolerance of differences in background, tribe and race. Out there I ceased being Bhaureni, the illiterate smelly kaffir.

On the battlefields, we served our masters loyally. Years later, we were to learn that the service of the African Regiment was hailed as the best ever by non-British forces, equalled only by that of the Ghurkas of Nepal. In the beginning I thought the war would last only a short while and that it would be won or lost in a matter of days at least and, at most, over several weeks. I expected it to be like the wars fought by my fathers back in Africa where the warriors pounced upon a village, burned it down, killed or

took the men as prisoners before rounding off the women and their children as the spoils of war, together with their livestock and grain. In the war of the white man, however, the only target were soldiers who, if they were not killed in battle, were taken as prisoners-of-war. This further confused us, the African soldiers. It was as if the soldiers were on a senseless blood-spilling spree that saw them move from one battlefield to another, and from town to town, fighting all the way yet seemingly gaining nothing of value.

In the evenings, we often sat around the campfire singing and at times wallowing in our shared sorrow. In our united brotherhood we sang to keep morale high whenever we felt homesick and despondent. Though singing made us nostalgic, it also filled us with hope. It was not so much what the songs meant as the ambiance with which we sang them. I happily joined in the morale-boosting song Sweet Banana which went like this:

Sweet Banana

A, B, C, D, E Headquarters I will buy you a sweet banana
A, B, C, D, E Headquarters I will buy you a sweet banana

Banana, Banana, Banana, I will buy you a sweet banana

Shield spear and knobkerrie, soldiers in war and peace
In war she fights with bravery, I will buy you a sweet banana

One Two and the Depot RAR-O, I will buy you a sweet banana
One Two and the Depot RAR-O, I will buy you a sweet banana

Banana, Banana, Banana, I will buy you a sweet banana

Shield spear and knobkerrie, soldiers in war and peace
In war she fights with bravery, I will buy you a sweet banana

Rhodesia, Burma, Egypt ne Malaya ticharwa tika kunda
Rhodesia, Burma, Egypt ne Malaya ticharwa tika kunda

Muhondo, Muhondo, Muhondo Inorwa no kushinga
Nhowo pfumo netsvimbo ndiyo RAR-O
Muhondo ne runyararo ndichakutengera sweet banana

A, B, C, D Support Headquarters ndidzo ndichapedza hondo dzoze
A, B, C, D Support Headquarters ndidzo ndichapedza hondo dzoze

Banana, Banana, Banana ndichakutengera sweet banana

Nhowo pfumo netsvimbo ndiyo RAR-O
Muhondo ne runyararo ndichakutengera sweet banana

We sang this song in two languages, both of which were alien to me and the meaning of words was therefore lost to me. However, that did not diminish the spirit of togetherness we all felt as we sat and sang around the camp fire. The war went on for months, then years. Three years after we left home, many of those in the African Regiment and I were still away fighting. As the years went by, some of us gave up hope of ever going back home. I did not blame them. From my own experience I knew that if one stayed away too long, the chances of ever returning diminished with each passing day. It had happened before and I knew it could happen again, but it was one thing I desperately wished would not happen. Tsogolani constantly voiced his fears that we would never leave the war front alive.

"I can feel it in my bones, Bhaureni. We are not going to see our families ever again," he declared in the fatalistic

tone he adopted the moment shells started raining around us. "There is no way we are going to come out of this war alive. We shall all perish out here, far away from our loved ones, hey! The whims of the white man compelled us to leave our people and the land of eternal sunshine to come and die in this strange land, how cruel."

In the cold weather, we suffered from frostbite in spite of the thick army issue gumboots we wore. It was not so bad in the barracks, but the nights we spent in trenches guarding the rubber plantations had us shivering and our teeth chattering. In Burma the cold season gave way to the warm summer months. The heat, though intolerable at times, was preferable to the bone-numbing cold, the blizzards and the torrents of rain we sometimes endured. At times the weather could be so unpredictable we never knew what to expect from one day to the next. On some days we lived through all the seasons in just one day. I longed at times for the warm African nights and sunny days.

Mupezeni Tsogolani failed to make it back to the land of perpetual sunshine. He perished at war just as he had feared and his remains were buried in foreign soils one cold day. The end for him came suddenly and when it was least expected. A group of us was patrolling around the plantation at the time that the orange glow of the fading sun was slowly gliding over the distant hills. Tsogolani was in front and I was a few paces behind him. Behind me were the rest of the soldiers, our rifles slung over our shoulders. We kept our eyes glued to the ground, watching where we put our feet, and careful to avoid ground that looked as if it had been recently disturbed. This patrol was no different from the others. It was routine but what happened as we turned a corner was not expected. The ground did not explode beneath the feet of the man in the lead, as we would have expected. The

bullet that struck Tsogolani lifted him off the ground and the force flung him onto a tree. The burst of gunfire shattered the tranquillity of the golden sunset. It all happened within the blink of an eyelid. I looked with shock as blood gushed from a hole on Tsogolani's chest and onto his naked torso. For what appeared like eternity, his body looked as if it had been nailed to the tree, his arms outstretched. The head was at an awkward angle and it rested on his right shoulder. He could have been a black saviour, his life sacrificed for a cause, except there was no crown of thorns on his head. A black Christ-like figure, was the thought that came to my mind then. So numbing was the shock that I remained rooted to the spot as the other soldiers panted and melted away into the thick foliage around. I vaguely remember being dragged into the bushes but not before I had seen Tsogolani's bloodied corpse begin to slide slowly down the trunk of the tree. I had seen death before, in many different forms, but none so violent.

Up until that day, I had not shed tears for fallen fellow combatants, black or white, but I did for Tsogolani. He had a young daughter whom he adored very much. I said a little prayer for my friend and placed the drawing he had made of his little daughter next to his body in the soils of a foreign land. That was the end of Tsogolani in Burma. I stayed on fighting and each day was very much the same as the one before. It was another battle, another lost brother-in-arms, another shed tear… and altogether another lost dream. I went on doing what I had to do but I was no longer the same man. Tsogolani had been my best friend in the Regiment, and our time at war had strengthened our closeness, making it more like kinship than friendship. In him I had not only lost a fellow combatant but a good friend, brother and countryman. During the night I grieved for him alone in my sleeping

bag. Though I was shattered, outwardly I put on a brave face and continued to march on with my fellow combatants.

A few months after Tsogolani was killed, I was wounded in battle. By then my regiment had moved to Egypt where we guarded the Suez Canal. I had often wondered how it would feel to be shot. I imagined the pain to be excruciating yet when it happened, I felt nothing. My leg just gave way under me and I stared in amazement at the gushing blood that spewed out of it. Strong hands grabbed me by the arms and pulled me to the ground. Of what happened later, I remember nothing. I must have fainted, more from shock than anything. When I regained consciousness, I found myself in the army hospital. That was when the worst and terrible pain hit me. I was later to know that a bullet had shattered my kneecap, and the injury put an end to active service for me. It took a while for me to get better and I was in hospital for some time, which I hated. To make matters worse I did not enjoy being looked after by the Red Cross nurses in a foreign land. I longed to go home and I nearly lost my mind from idleness. A terrible sense of hopelessness depressed me further. When I was finally declared fit enough to leave hospital, I was flown back to Southern Rhodesia.

Upon my return everything that was once familiar seemed strange. People went about their daily lives in a carefree manner. No one stopped to inspect the ground beneath their feet and no one cared what objects flew above their heads or what sounds rang out in the distance. The war out there did not seem to affect the people at Patchway Valley Mine, and they did not know or seem to care that on the other side of the world blood was being shed every day. The war out there had nothing to do with them, and they did not want to know about it. I thought about the risks I had taken with my life and felt bitter that

it had all been for nothing. Even after my return I still did not know why I had gone to fight in that war.

Those of us who managed to get out of the war alive were rewarded with medals for service to our country and to the king who, it was claimed, ruled us from England. We also brought home trench coats and heavy metal storage trunks, items that were to be a constant reminder of the time we spent dodging bullets and offering our lives to defend the empire of the white man. Our masters had given us new names when we joined the Regiment. They claimed it was easier to call us by English names because our own native ones were too long and they found it difficult to twist their tongues around them. So Kondwelani, a fellow labourer from Empress Mine, became James and I was John. Some veterans kept those names after the war, and handed them down to future generations as the family name. Upon going back, Kondwelani would keep his English name and his daughter would be known as Amina James, and his son Andireya James. I chose to revert to the name by which I had been known since birth. I had no desire to carry a name foisted upon me by foreigners. I had more than enough to remind me of the lost years of my life, a period that I wished to thrust firmly to the back of my mind. The Patchway Valley Mine I had left behind did not welcome me back as warmly as I had expected. I returned a stranger to find myself in a strange land. The peace I had eagerly rushed back to regain was elusive. I did not come back to a happy home as I had envisioned. It turned out to be just another lost dream. Only the memory of my homeland in Nyasaland appeared clearer and more distinct as the bygone years of childhood innocence filled my thoughts whenever my mind retreated further into the past. With time, even those memories gradually began to turn into foggy confusion.

I went back in time in search of my lost dream but got lost myself instead as I failed to find my way back. I wandered in the wilderness of my thoughts, moving backwards and forwards, round and round in circles until I gave up and abandoned all efforts at refocusing on my original dream. I had come back to a wife I had missed greatly only to discover that she was no longer there for me. Mwanaicha had raised the children on her own and they did not seem to need me. My son got up to go to work and came back to sleep all day or to talk to his siblings. His mother got on with the housework while Wezi, the child born after I left to go to war, trailed around her. They chatted to each other and went on with their lives in which I played no role. It was as if they were in their own private world where I had no place. I could only stand on the outside, looking in. I hated it when the family I had missed so much carried on as if my return had no significance in their lives. They had seemed overjoyed to see me during the first few days, but once the excitement wore off they settled back to their ordinary lives.

I could not help feeling that had I never returned or if I had died at war like Tsogolani, I would hardly have been missed. My existence would have just fleeted across this life and gone like a breeze, never to be remembered or cherished. So much had changed, not only at Patchway Valley itself as a place, but in the people I once thought I knew well. The open smiles whose sincerity I had previously never doubted were gone and in their place were furtive glances and knowing looks whose meaning I could not understand. I gradually found myself shut out of everybody's life. I was further pushed to the periphery of their world as the home situation gradually turned out to be colder and more unfriendly than the battlefields I had left behind. Mine was a desolate world, one worse than a war zone as I appeared to be shut up with the enemy. I was enmeshed in an invisible war, one in which

I was the sole casualty in a battle I had no idea how to fight and win. The people who had rushed to embrace me upon my return slowly retreated to their own different worlds into which I could not gain entry. Thereafter, they acknowledged my existence with only a curt nod or a quizzical look. A few friends from the past paid me occasional visits during which they would donate a few joints of rolled cigarettes or a small pouch of Shamrock. They were generous, but they always left me behind while they went away to puff on their gold-tipped Players cigarettes whose advertisement shrilled now and again from that tireless wireless of Masauso; 'People Say, Players Please!' whatever that meant. Many things had changed in the few years I had been away. I had nothing much to say to my fellow mine dwellers and with time even their visits dwindled. I could not talk about my war experiences because they were too painful to re-live. Even the happy memories of the times I had had with my fellow combatants I could not share because no one at Patchway Valley understood the world out there. That was a life too far removed from theirs, and I would have bored them with my numerous accounts of a war that meant nothing to them, and one whose significance even I did not understand, and which had mostly been blood, sweat and tears. It was those horrors that I yearned to share, but since I did not know how to make their minds visualise the horrors my eyes had seen, I did not bother to try. I shut myself in my world where those horrors visited me again and again. My friends knew nothing about that world and I knew little about theirs, having lost touch with the everyday issues they talked about.

The son I had longed to groom into adulthood had already grown into a man in my absence. There was nothing I could teach him that he did not know already. Four and a half years might not seem like a long time in the life of an adult but in that of a child it can mean the

difference between childhood and puberty, or late teenage years and early adulthood. In Masauso's case, it was the whole of his puberty years, at the end of which he emerged as an adult. Nchesa was still the lovely girl I knew, but she was no longer my little girl. She was past the age where a girl rides on the shoulders of her father. She was approaching the stage where she preferred the company of other women around her. As for the boy Wezi, he was never mine and never would be. An unborn baby when I left, he did not know me. To him I was some stranger who had invaded his home and threatened to disrupt the life he was familiar with. The boy peered at me warily from behind the hems of his mother's skirts. In his eyes I saw suspicion and resentment. In the early days of my return I had eagerly tried to cajole him to come to me, promising to show him how to make catapults or traps for rabbits, but it was hopeless. Each time I tried to get close to him, Wezi would pull away and scream so loudly even I was alarmed.

"Do not worry about it, *Ababa,*" said my wife. "Wezi is like that with everyone he is not familiar with. He will soon get used to you. He needs time. You just have to be patient, please."

But patience was one thing I did not have. I had lived in the shadow of death for so long there were times when I wondered if I would ever see my family again. I therefore lacked the patience to wait any longer. I wanted to pull my son towards me even as he protested and kicked. I wished to drum it into his ears that there was nothing to be scared of, that I was his father who, for years, had longed to see him, more so since I had no image of him in my mind upon which to base my longing. I wanted to take him in my strong arms and give him a comforting fatherly hug as I wiped tears off his cheeks. I wished to tell him how much I cherished him. Instead he wanted nothing to do with me

and his mother urged me to be patient. I had been away almost five years, *sha*!

I was easily irritated by minor things, but what exasperated me most was the tendency by the children to defer to their mother first before responding to me. I had ceased to be the man of the house, the head of the family. I was not a father, not a husband or the one who brought a wage at the end of the month. I meant nothing in the lives of those whose existence meant everything to me. There was no point to my life any more. *Abwana* and their war had killed me just as surely as they had killed Tsogolani. They could not even give me back my old job, citing the problem with my knee as the reason. "The pit is no place for a hobbling *blati*[43] kaffir, good for nothing. Just slows down the pace. We want sound minds and muscle down there. *Stamina!"* And saying this, the Operations Manager had turned his back to me, dismissing any further pleas from the black overseer to whom I had presented my request. Nobody anywhere needed me anymore. Not my family, the memory of which had kept me sane during the war, not the army for which I had sacrificed my life, nor the Mine for which I had risked a lot to get to. I was wanted nowhere by no one. *Abwana* had stripped me of everything. No longer could I stand among other men and thump my chest with pride. The son I had left a mere boy now walked in my footprints, claiming my path as his own. It was his wages that sustained the family and everybody knew who to go to with their requests for money. Even outsiders who wished to borrow money to see them through to their next pay day brought their requests to my son. On the other hand, my wife looked after everything else. She cooked for the family, washed and ironed all our clothes and went to buy food and provisions. I was like an appendage to their orderly

---

43Bloody

existence. The only way to get their respect was by going back to work and taking care of the family but the Mine Management was not willing to take me back as a labourer. I could not limp from one rock to another with a pick-axe and a shovel. At times the leg hurt so much that it felt as if the bullet was still embedded in my knee. On cloudy days the pain got worse and this made my limp even more obvious.

Months after my return from the war front, I was told that a ceremony was to be held in Gatooma to mark the end of the war. It was also an occasion to pay tribute to our contribution and the distinguished service rendered to the king of the white man and to his country. The service was touted as being of great importance, and more so because the Allied Forces had won the war. Praise was heaped upon the forces of all colour and creed, fallen or surviving who had fought gallantly against the vanquished monster, Hitler. For our blood, sweat and tears, the Empire of the British people sought to reward us. For a brief period I became some kind of hero, although most people did not quite understand why. It was enough for them to know that *abwana* thought highly of those who had fought in the war of the white man. Our rewards were to be presented to us in a ceremony conducted by the Colonial Army. For weeks leading up to the great day, I felt important once again. The old army uniform and trench coat I had kept were washed and ironed, and my boots waxed with ox-blood shoe polish and spittle until they shone so brightly I could see my reflection on them. I attended the ceremony knowing that I was to receive a medal. I was not quite sure what this object was. I had never seen or heard of one before, but that did nothing to diminish the sense of achievement, excitement and expectation that I felt then. Beaming with pride, I saluted as the shiny piece of metal was pinned on my tunic. I had expected more and when

nothing else followed, my disappointment was immense though I did not show it. How could I, when everybody else around me was so excited? There, hanging dapperly on the breast of my tunic was a shiny medal whose real value I did not quite comprehend yet in whose glory I was supposed to revel. I smiled alongside everybody else, my stomach rumbling and my wounded leg throbbing. Years later, I was to endure the taunts of the compound dwellers who ridiculed my war efforts as producing nothing more worthy than a useless piece of metal.

The African Regiment had no job for me, so the Territorial Army discharged me. They had only needed me to be the barrier between the enemy and the properties they sought to protect. My place therefore was with John Mack and Co. at Patchway Valley Mine. Eventually, a job was found for me to go around the Mine compound in the middle of the night, rousing the men who were going underground at the first cock crow. I did this by going round knocking on the windows of their bedrooms. The job isolated me from everybody as I became the owl that was up all night while others slept. My days became my nights, and vice versa. Disorientated, my head turned and I was confused half the time, but grateful for the job though it was far from challenging. It required no stamina, only the ability to work in all kinds of weather and a high degree of punctuality, upon which the smooth-running of the Mine routine depended. The routine was monotonous, especially after my years at war. I did not enjoy the job but I had no skill at anything else except digging and shovelling underground. I was prepared to learn something new. I was sure I could learn any task that required muscle, in the same way I had learned to blast rocks underground and fire a rifle but the opportunity was denied me. I had already been labelled a *blati* hobbling kaffir. I accepted the job of night crier because it gave me something to do and I also hoped it would please my wife.

I needed to be cherished and respected. Altough the job gave me back something, the sniggering continued behind my back. My only solace was the time I headed for the beer hall to drown my sorrows in Chibuku beer.

Before I started work and could contribute to the cost of beer_ no one drank their beer alone for the occasion was a pastime to be shared_ I had relied on the generosity of friends who were willing to share theirs. I sat down with a group of labourers as the beer mug was passed round and each of us took a swig before passing it on to the next person. At times they offered me only the dregs, but in my situation I could not afford to choose. The job therefore meant I could finally afford to buy beer with my own money, so whenever I was not working or sleeping, I went to the beer hall. With the beer dregs sitting snuggly in my stomach, I became a man again. I ceased to care what people thought, said or insinuated. I was happy once more even though no one else seemed to share my joy. Gradually, I began to enjoy my situation and my job which I stopped despising.

Most of my evenings were spent at the beer hall, drinking and drowning my sorrows. I went home at closing time and promptly fell into a slumber from which I never wanted to wake up. I believe I was happiest then. In that state I did not feel the scratchy blankets on my skin nor did I hear the noisy, creaking mattress springs each time either my wife or I turned on the narrow bed. So long as there was beer in my stomach, warmth in my bones and a feeling of contentment in my heart, I was a happy man. It did not matter anymore what food I was served so long as it was well seasoned. With this increased feeling of fulfilment that had eluded me for some time, bliss soon came back, through my stomach and right through to my head.

I should have known that this kind of bliss would not last forever. Nothing good lasted in my life. I was just

unfortunate that way. Things changed. Just like that. On certain days I woke up to find a strange woman lying by my side in bed. We had no black female soldiers fighting alongside us, so her presence puzzled me. Surely she had no right to be there? We were constantly reminded to be vigilant at all times. I certainly did not wish to be held responsible for allowing the group to be infiltrated by the enemy. We had to watch out especially for women, because the enemy comes in the guise of a helpless and pitiable female. Honeytraps was what they called such women. Whenever one of them appeared by my side in bed, I would shout, 'Fire, Fire,' to alert the whole group. To my amazement, none of the other soldiers would react to this threat. Maybe the person sleeping by my side was the comfort woman of the Major. Such women were known to exist in the lives of those who faced death on a daily basis in distant lands, never sure whether each new day would be their last.

On bright sunny days I woke up with a strong urge to go out into the field beyond my father's kraal and put seed in the ground before the start of the rainy season. But I needed to till the land first. For some reason, I could never find the bullocks we harnessed onto the yoke, or the donkeys we used to carry bags of seed or maize from one place to another. Probably stolen by Hitler's soldiers as they swept through our village, driving all the livestock away, I mused. With no livestock to yoke and harness to a plough, I would resort to digging the hard, drought-stricken earth using a hoe. Now if that is not laborious, I do not know what is, apart from digging for gold, of course. When you break your back to do the best you can under difficult circumstances, the last thing you want is to be wrongly accused of digging up the neighbour's vegetable patch. Such an accusation coming from the lips of a woman you call your wife is a sign of ingratitude and disloyalty on her part. A woman should know that she has

to side with her husband, not the villagers. I did not need an enemy in my camp, yet the woman in my life was turning out to be exactly that. Sometimes I despaired at the confusion in Kamwendo's mind and I told her so. Instead of seeing my point, she would angrily deny that her name was Kamwendo. Then she would shrill out a long list of her resentments, none of which I paid attention to. While at war, I had regarded with contempt those of my African brothers-in-arms who eagerly discarded their native names and replaced them with English ones which they proceeded to wear like badges of honour pinned onto their foreheads. I could not understand why even my own wife would despise the name she had been known by all her life. She would not tell me though what she wished to be called. In a voice tinged with sarcasm, I would sometimes call her Little Leg, which is what her name meant in the tongue of *abwana.* She did not like to be called that either, for she would sulk and flounce away.

'That is not my name,' she screamed one morning. The woman had never screamed at me before. 'My parents did not give me *that* name. That-is-not-my-name!'

'But it *is*, only in a different language,' I continued to taunt her, taking delight in the confrontation that sent my blood tingling with the anticipation of a pre-destined victory. Here at least was one fight from which I could come out unscathed. In the time I had been back, my wife and her children had done nothing but make my life unbearable. Nobody would begrudge me just one small victory on the home front, surely. To my huge disappointment the fight was over before it had even flared. The woman just turned her back and flounced off, her eyes telling me what her lips did not even bother to utter; I was not worth the effort. The effort! The effort of what? The unvoiced insult was what made my blood boil. The rage in my veins urged me to haul her back in front of me, push her down to her knees and demand that she

utter the words. The effort of what? Talking to me, explaining, loving, caring, arguing with, hating even, or the effort of trying to make me feel appreciated? I wanted to grip her by those stiff, proud shoulders of hers and shake her. I wanted to rip the words from her tongue and rinse out her mouth with soap until there were no more defiant words left in her. In the end I thought it was *she* who was not worth the effort. After all she was no longer the Kamwendo I knew, the mother of my children. It is not clear when exactly it started but she had changed from the shy, obedient woman I married, to a critical and embittered old woman. A hag, and now a nag! I did not despise my wife for getting old because we all do, eventually. It was the change in her behaviour that I found hard to tolerate. Is it surprising then that I got cross most of the time? As a result, I preferred my own company. So long as I had the precious land of my father to till, I was contented. *Vazungu* could keep their jobs and fight their wars without me. What they did with their gold or to each other did not concern me.

MASAUSO'S STORY
(1929-1985)
Patchway Valley Mine- Gatooma

Our existence at the Mine was distinctly structured. Whites had, by far, a superior existence to that of blacks. The tarred road from Gatooma town to Chakari Mine cut across Patchway Valley, separating the offices, the golf course and the dwellings of African labourers from the houses of the white bosses. The area inhabited by the whites was fenced off. The high diamond-shaped fence, with rows of barbed wire at the top kept the whites separate and safe from the black labourers who used the road to get to the shops half a mile away. From this road we were able to peep into the privileged world of the whites, one we would never inhabit, as decreed by the colour of our skin. I remember how, as children not yet of school-going age, my friends and I would often walk down the road to get to the main shops. We always referred to the white man's privileged premises as *Makamera,* or *Mayadhi,* so called due to the big yards on which the houses were built. It was only years later that we got to know the word Camera was in fact a corruption of Camelot. I suppose Africa was the white man's Camelot. Anyway, the knowledge would not have made any difference to us. So we continued to call the place *Makamera.* We never ceased to feel intimidated yet awed by the grandeur within. Red and green roofed dwellings that were typical of most colonial settlements lay sprawled over a large area. At the main entrance to *Mayadhi,* a black security guard manned the gate, watching out for trespassers in general and Africans in particular. We would not have dared enter the premises anyway, given the aggression of the Rhodesian Ridgebacks so loved by the whites. The beasts were always ready to pounce on

anyone with a dark skin. They were, after all, familiar with the likes and dislikes of their masters. From the road could be seen the green bougainvillea shrubs that bordered each property, their ever blooming red and purple flowers adding a beauty that was also typical of colonial settlements. Each property lay on an area so large the orchard alone was big enough for six houses of the size of those built for African labourers. Exotic trees bore fruit that, upon ripening, looked succulent and inviting. From the other side of the fence, saliva filled our mouths at the thought of sinking our teeth into the ripe peaches, apples, oranges and naartjies that lay on the ground, some of which were rotting. If we happened to pass by when the servants were outside, we would plead with them to throw some fruits over the fence. Most of the time they were happy to oblige, but only furtively or they found themselves being reprimanded by their masters for their act of kindness.

Jacaranda trees lined the wide tarred roads in the white neighbourhood and at the beginning of the warm season, beautiful flowers blossomed on these trees. As light winds blew, the petals were gently blown into the air where, for a few minutes they floated like butterflies before spreading themselves on the ground. That transformed the roads into long stretches of lilac carpets, the beauty of which made us gasp with awe. *Abwana* drove nice cars on these roads, their beloved dogs sitting in front, side by side with the master, the best of friends, friends forever. On these same roads also walked those of our kinsmen allowed into the world of the white man, even though it might only have been to wipe snot off the noses of the *picanini bwana*. The maids, the cooks and the nannies told us with the superior airs of the lucky ones, about the pipes that brought water into each house. The taps never ran dry, they said. The pipes, which were regularly cleaned_ and the water treated to make it easy on the tongue and kind

to the skin_ stretched all the way from the tanks in Gatooma. As with the water, the houses had a constant supply of electricity too. They also had windows with glass panes that let in plenty of light while keeping out dust. Gauze wire was fitted on the inside of the windows to let in fresh air while keeping out buzzing flies and mosquitoes whenever the windows were opened. Garden 'boys', some of whom were fathers and grandfathers, were employed to tend the beautiful gardens at the front and back of the properties. They looked after the grass, watered it, made sure it did not wilt and dry in the scorching heat of the African sun, and kept the weeds in a straight line..... no, *not* weeds, you stupid kaffir! Herbs...! Basil, parsley, thyme, dill... what ignorant, uncivilised savages, *ha,* no brain!

Further down the road was the Sports Club where the blue-hued swimming pool waters shimmered in the blazing heat like the folds of an invisible blanket. We marvelled at the ease with which the young daughters of *abwana* hit little balls over a net, their white almost-not-there skirts riding over their almost-not-there bottoms. '*Misisi, misisi!*' we would call out to them, the purpose of which was to later boast about our 'conversations' with *picanini bwana* to those of our friends who had never in their lives had an occasion to 'talk' to *abwana.* On some days we got a limp wave back but on others we were hissed at as they barked '*voetsek*' and shooed us away like dogs whose attention one finds annoying and disruptive. Further down, water sprinklers kept the grass on the golf course lush and green, regardless of whether or not everything else around was withering and dying. The world of *abwana* was one of abundance. It was their birth right by virtue of the lightness of the colour of their skin, our elders constantly reminded us. After all it was God who had created them with such a light colour and such long hair, was it not? We saw it as their due because they

were clever, and it was they who owned the gold that our parents risked their lives and broke their backs for in the tunnels.

On our side of the road were the Mine offices and noisy workshops. These buildings on their part were separated from the Mine compound by a railway track built on a raised ridge that was about two meters high. The mile long track stretched from the Mine shafts where the gold was mined, to the mill on the other side, where the ore was taken in small wagons that we called *ngorovhani,* to be crushed and smelted. On their way to work the miners crossed this track on the two underpasses designed for this purpose. Because the main shops_ the butcheries and the grocers' shop_ were on the other side of the track, past the dwellings of *abwana,* we had occasion to use the under passes from time to time. The labourers reported for duty at the offices first before proceeding as a group to the mine pits. Those who did not want to walk the long distance to the underpasses climbed over the ridge to the other side. Women crossed on the farthest end to collect fine alluvial dust with which to scour the pots caked with thick black soot from hours of cooking on open fires. In the beginning, nobody objected to crossings on the wagon tracks, but we were eventually forbidden from doing so. The Mine Management said climbing on the ridges set off landslides of stones which, though harmless on a single occasion, could become a hazard over time.

Clusters of grass and weeds grew anywhere and everywhere on our part of the Mine, which was commonly known as the compound, or *komboni.* During the rainy season the red soils soaked up water and formed puddles in which we, as children, found delight in splashing about on bare feet. We stubbornly ignored the warnings of our mothers to stay away from stagnant waters which they claimed were breeding grounds for mosquitos. Now and

again we suffered from bilharzia, we caught malaria and we had ringworms crawling beneath the surface of our skins but it was nothing the nurse at the local clinic could not take care of. During the month of August, gusts of strong winds lifted the loose top soils and the alluvial deposits of Patchway Valley Mine into the air and sprinkled them over our homes, coating everything with a thin layer of dust. The Compound Manager, the *bwana* who was responsible for the upkeep of the compound and the welfare of its inhabitants, made few and irregular forays into our midst. On the rare occasions he did, we all knew about it for he thundered down the only road into the compound, raising the red dust with the huge wheels of his jeep and adding to the dirt in our homes which resulted in bouts of coughing that lasted for a while after the dust had long settled.

During the hot months the ground became dry and cracked. Long and deep lines criss-crossed the ground and it looked as if some invisible hand had crafted giant honeycombs on it. The grass turned first yellow, then brown. The trees shed their leaves and the compound gradually began to take the appearance of an abandoned village in the early stages of dilapidation. The few vegetables grown in the small spaces available in our yards wilted, leaving only the stalks of the *covo* vegetable to withstand the drought and ready to sprout again with the coming of the rains. Almost every house was bordered by either a spikey hedge or cassava shrubs which we called *mujumbura*. The yards were so small that one risked stepping into the neighbours' yard just by taking a few strides. In a few of these yards were paw-paw and mango trees which did not do very well because they were never watered. The only time they received any water was when it rained. The mulberry trees, however, thrived and there was one in every yard, without exception. The shade they

provided made life bearable in the suffocating heat. Our parents did not grow and tend grass like *abwana.* Mother said that was because our lives were about necessities, and that the luxury of growing what could not be eaten was best left to *abwana* who had both the space and the water. Mother and her fellow women often stood in a queue to get water from one of the three taps that served the whole compound. It was necessary always to have several buckets full of water on stand-by because water was not always available. Sometimes the water was turned off altogether at the main supply. At other times the flow was controlled and it trickled slowly and lazily into the five gallon containers the women brought to the taps. The trickle was such a slow process that the women often left their buckets in a queue after asking us to watch them while they went back to cook for their husbands due from, or about to go to work. We did not mind doing this, for it was another opportunity to play with friends. Whatever the weather, we still found games to play and make childhood a pleasure, how could it not be? We knew no other life. The only thing that scared us was the possibility of illness and hunger. For our parents however, these were issues that were common enough.

We played football in the dust, with our tattered shorts showing the dirt-streaked chaffed skin of our bottoms. Screaming at defeats and rejoicing at triumphs, we glimpsed our fathers trudging past us looking exhausted, dragging their feet in gumboots, and covered all over in dust from the mine shafts. Unconcerned about their fatigue, we played on, and they in turn, oblivious to the perils of our games shuffled on, leaving to our mothers the task of warning us about the dangers of taking dust into our lungs. It was after I started school that I began to notice the differences between the lives of the families of labourers and those of other black families. We spoke different languages, lived in separate quarters and our

parents did different jobs. Most of the Shona pupils in my class wore shoes every day to school while we left ours at home, to be worn only on 'special' occasions. They were never without books and pens, and always returned home for tea at break time. Their parents were teachers, mine clerks or security guards, but never labourers. They employed maids to clean their houses and to look after their children. Although not on the same level as *abwana,* the locals were treated better than we were by *abwana,* which placed us below everyone else. On their part, the locals shunned us and referred to us with contempt. *Vabvakure, Mabhurandaya* and *Manyasarande* were words I grew up hearing. The children of the native people of Rhodesia pursued education to the highest levels they could afford. Even illiterate villagers seemed to know the benefits of sending their children to school. Fathers were known to sell an entire herd of cattle to raise money for their children to attend the expensive boarding schools established mainly by Missionaries. Mothers on their part were said to kneel for hours by their grinding stones, crushing peanuts into butter to sell for the same purpose. They valued education and did whatever they could to ensure their children got it. But that was what we heard from rumours. What we actually saw was the interest the teachers and the other employees of the Mine showed in the work of their children.

My Shona classmates were scared of getting punished lest their parents got to know about it, and their parents encouraged teachers to mete out even more severe punishment. On the other hand, our parents did not take kindly to teachers who beat up their children, regardless of whether the punishment was deserved or not. Their position, however, made it difficult for them to confront the teachers whom they held in high esteem. They were regarded as being almost god-like, their word taken as the undisputed truth on any subject, ranging from whether

Dynamos was a better team than Highlanders, or if George Shaya could make a better captain for the national football team. No one thought these luminaries in our midst could be challenged in any way. Unlike our parents, they could write, read news in the papers and they had knowledge. The locals could curl their tongues and string out words of the language spoken by *abwana* with a dexterity and fluency we could only marvel at.

Our dwellings were three-roomed, semi-detached buildings with arched roofs. The air in these structures chilled our bones in the cold months but during the hot season we perspired like pigs in the suffocating heat. One room was reserved for the private use of the parents while another was where the family took their meals and received visitors. The third room was used for storing utensils such as spoons, knives, plates and pots, most of which were soldered over several times to patch up holes resulting from many years of constant use over hot fires. These same rooms were used as sleeping quarters by the children. Every night, my sister and I lay in the sitting room with a thin blanket or two on top and a mine- issue canvas tent beneath our bodies to lessen the severity of the chill seeping from the cement floor and into our bones. That was our life and we regarded it as normal because we knew no other. We were over-crowded but we saw nothing wrong in that. Instead, we marvelled at the comfort of *abwana* and took it for granted that it was their birth right to live like kings. Quite often I heard adults talk about how grateful they were to the white man for their jobs.

"Were it not for John Mack and Company, where would we be today? On the farms no doubt, that's where we would be. We would get up at the time when the witches are said to ride their hyenas and the *baas boys* would hurry us up with whips raining down on our bare

backs. I could never survive such a life," I once overheard *a*Banda tell Father.

"How could our people journey all the way from Nyasarande to come and work in the fields here as if there is no land in our villages back there?" mused Father. "Those farm masters whip their workers as if they are baboons and they work them like donkeys while starving them at the same time. I hear they do not allow them to cut grass with which to thatch their miserable looking huts that leak whenever it rains. The unfortunate souls often spend half the night shifting their miserable looking reed mats, jute sacks and tattered blankets from one spot to the other in an effort to dodge raindrops. Meanwhile, their masters tell them not to cut grass because it is for the cows to graze on. *Sha*!"

"No doubt the farmers treat their labourers worse than animals, but then we too get the same treatment from our masters who pinch their bloodless noses and frown from disgust when they come near us. Our blackness stinks, they say. The mixture of our body odour and the almost suffocating stench of sweat offend their sensitive, pointed noses. But who wouldn't stink after hours of labouring underground the way we do? They would too if they worked that hard. The ungrateful *abwana* shun us so much they will not let us ride in their cars. If they do, they make us sit in the back of an open truck in the blazing heat or in the rain. Meanwhile where are their dogs? On the seat right next to their masters, grinning into their colourless faces. As for those piercing blue eyes of the *bwana mubale wanga,* if they stare at you, you'd be lucky not to have nightmares all night," said *a*Banda.

"I think it's the water they drink that makes their eyes so blue and clear. They scare me at times you know, those piercing eyes. They bring to my mind the image of what ghosts are said to look like. Do you know that the water

abwana drink comes from Gatooma where it is stored in huge clean tanks?"

"Of course they do not drink the same water as us. I cannot imagine *Baas* John drinking hard water. Ours is tasteless and full of lime scale, and those huge tanks it comes from are never cleaned. *ABhaureni, wosayangana mukati mamatangi amadzi*[44]. If you do you will never again drink water without feeling like all the food in your stomach is struggling to come out the way it went in."

"I do not have to look inside the tanks to know how dirty the water is. Sometimes slimy green stuff comes through the tap with the water. If you do not look before you drink you could end up like *a*Bhauti who felt something slimy slide past his tongue and down his throat. When he hawked and spat it out, he was disgusted to find that it was algae," said Father, hawking and spitting in disgust as if he too had just swallowed algae.

"*Hahaha, hehehe*! How hilarious that must have been. *Mazerere*[45] sliding down his throat! I know it's not funny but honestly, it could have been worse. Think of *vhirombo,*[46] *aBhaureni*! It could have been a dead toad, or tapeworms, or any number of badly decomposed birds that had been unfortunate enough to fall into the tank. *Muzungu* is very lucky in that he does not have to drink the water here, but I cannot say I envy him defecating inside the house. Umph!" shrugged *a*Banda at what he deemed an unthinkable act.

"Human waste should be kept out of the house and confined to *chimbuzi* like we do with ours," snorted Father, wrinkling his face in disgust.

44Mr Bhaureni, do not look inside the water tanks

45 algae

46 Creatures

"*A-a, woenda kuchimbuzi munyumba awa anunkisa nyumba yonse*[47]," laughed *a*Banda. "*Akuki*[48] tells me that the windows on the houses of *abwana* have gauze wire to let in fresh air, so that obviously takes care of the problem. The cook himself, however, is not allowed to use the toilet in the house. There is a pit latrine outside for him, the garden boy and the nanny. The servants have to go out in all kinds of weather to relieve themselves should they need to. If the rain is pelting down, they must go out all the same but then that is all right because that is what we do as well. I can well understand that. I do not suppose *bwana* would like it if *akuki* were to put his bare black bottom on the same seat on which *adona* puts hers. It is somehow indecent and it is not right."

"I do not mind the rain, *a*Nyirenda. It is the snakes that I dread. The slithering creatures make my blood go cold and my hair stand on end. I am so petrified of them that I avoid going to the latrine at night. I always imagine there is a cobra, a mamba or an adder waiting in the dark to bite my bottom the moment I go on my haunches over the hole. I shudder just to imagine it happening to me or to anyone."

"It is a miracle that so far no one has been bitten, considering the numerous times snakes are seen in those pit latrines. Only last week *achimbangu*[49] killed a black mamba in the latrine by the beer hall, and the week before that he had seen a cobra slithering down the pit of the latrine for *akazi*[50]."

---

47 These people who relieve themselves inside the house make the whole house stink

48 The cook

49 The latrine cleaner

50 Women

"Maybe it is not such a bad idea to relieve oneself in the house after all," laughed *a*Banda who seemed to find the whole idea absurd. "But I could never do that myself, *iyayi, a*Nyirenda. I do not know how anyone can relax enough to do so. Just imagine the whole family moving about in the house, maybe listening to the sound of urine trickling down the toilet like a tiny waterfall, ah *iyayi!* Me, I want the freedom to enjoy the satisfaction of releasing wind while emptying my bowels. I want to be able to sigh with relief after a job well-done, just like we do in our latrines out there, away from people and houses. Talking of our toilets, I wonder though how *achimbango* manages to do that job of his. There can be no worse job than that. Just imagine having to tug along a bucket of water and a broom to clean up other people's human waste, day after day! Then he has to sprinkle that foul-smelling white powder that is supposed to get rid of the horrible smell of the decaying stools! Umph! I wonder why the man bothers. The terrible stench of tons of faeces of several days by the whole population of the *komboni* hits you before you even enter the latrine. The powder itself smells equally bad, if not worse, and a combination of both is overpowering."

"*Ya,* you need to take a deep breath of fresh air before going in there lest you fill your lungs with poisonous gases and suffocate. Mind you, *achimbango* probably considers himself lucky not to be risking his life going underground everyday like the rest of us. If you give him a pick axe and a shovel, and send him down the shaft one day, he is likely to emerge from there thanking his gods that he does not have to work so hard for a living. It is a hard job you know, breaking rocks with pick axes underground."

"Yes it is," agreed Father's friend. "I would not be surprised if he goes straight to embrace his bucket and

---

broom while whistling cheerfully as he goes about his rounds." At that, both men fell silent, each lost in his thoughts.

"I suppose we are all just born to suffer. Look at the lives of farm workers..., miserable. Ours... depressing. Only those who work in the houses of white people seem to suffer less than the rest of us," Father resumed the conversation after a while.

"Except for the times they get beaten up by their masters and are spat at by the master's children. Wasn't it only last month that *a*Zuze was beaten senseless by *bwana* Simisi for taking food for his children that was meant for the dog?"

"*Ya,* some masters can indeed be very cruel. Not all are like *baas* Beaton whose workers will tell you that they are treated with nothing but kindness. They get second hand clothes for their children as well as leftover food, and they are treated with compassion if they fall ill. The only thing with *bwana* Beaton is that you have to be very hard working. He hates lazy workers. He does not hesitate to fire and evict anyone who shows signs of laziness. But those like Zuze's master will whip you and have their children spit at you. If they give Zuze any second hand clothes at all, they deduct the money for them from Zuze's meagre wages. He can only eat after the family and their dog have all eaten. He says the family makes him use the plate used by the dog. Ah! I would not stay in a job like that. Never."

"Our lives are hard. I really do not understand why our people left their kinsmen and their lands to come and do these lowly paid jobs. For what? We were free back home before we came here to surrender our lives to slavery. I would not have risked my life for such an existence had I known about the hardships beforehand, never," Father and *a*Banda began to move away as they talked.

* * *

There were only three lamp-posts in the whole compound, each of which was a landmark of some significance. Sparsely positioned as they were, these lamps gave only minimal light, like some gloomy halo. That was as far as electricity came into our lives. Only a few people owned wirelesses which were run on batteries. I could not understand the obsession of these people with contraptions that did nothing but crackle and hiss incoherently, and needed an awful lot of patience in tuning and twisting of knobs before they could produce some semblance of recognisable sounds. Those who owned them explained that the reception was bad... whatever that meant. They claimed the static was due to the closeness of the pylons that brought electricity from Gatooma town to the Mine and to the houses of our bosses. These pylons were very close to the compound, on the edge in fact, well away from the homes of the bosses.

Without father's wages, life was hard. The food rations could barely keep us alive and the mouldy bread was not available everyday. Mother had to go cotton picking on neighbouring farms for meagre wages. Although the money was not much, it helped sustain our livelihood. Mother joined the women and children who were collected and ferried in tractor-trailers to the various farms dotted on the outskirts of the Mine.

If there was one thing I resolved to do from eavesdropping on the conversations of adults, it was to try my best to learn to speak *chilapalapa*[51] so that I could work in the homes of *abwana* or in the local store. We lived a

51 Pidgin

miserable existence, one only made bearable by the fact that we were able to laugh at the jokes made at our expense. A favourite joke that was told repeatedly as I grew up was about the cook who, on returning from the butchery, put his packet of meat on the carrier of his bicycle. The parcel fell off as he turned a sharp corner and one of the locals called out to him in Shona, "*Iwe, nyama yadona!*" Which means, hey you, the meat has fallen off. *Dona* also means madam in Chichewa, therefore the statement could also be taken to mean 'hey you, the meat belongs to the boss' wife. The cook, who continued to pedal furiously without even glancing back, answered, "*Iyayi, siya dona. Niyanga!*[52]" It was a hilarious example of how the complexities of language could lead to total misunderstanding, all because of one shared word whose meaning was completely different in another language. If I learned to speak *chilapalapa,* I could work in the local store and escape the hard life of the mines. The compound store was not entirely better as a work place though. It was owned by an ageing *bwana* whose fiery temper was legendary. He was a vile, ugly old man with a nose resembling that of a hawk. He was nicknamed Chimuromo because of the permanent sneer the scar on his upper lip gave him. He was not part of the Mine Management but he was allowed to run the local store for the benefit of the Mine workers and their families.

I never saw any of the Mine bosses beat up their workers in public but Chimuromo did jusyt that. His employee, *a*Mazizi the storekeeper, was the victim of his violent temper on several occasions. It saddened everybody in the community that this humiliation should befall such a kind, quiet and mild natured man as he. His name was not really Mazizi but it was one he was known by for as long

52No, it does not belong to the madam, it is mine

as I could remember. Those who were in a position to know said his real name was Moses, but due to the difficulties in twisting our tongues around a foreign name, people just resorted to a corrupted form of the name. So Mazizi he was to everybody in the compound. Kind though he was, the storekeeper often showed impatience with children who went into the store. If we were slow to put our money onto the counter he would grab our clenched fists and knock our knuckles onto the cement slab that served as a counter, at which we immediately released the money in the hand. There was one distinguishing feature about the storekeeper which intrigued me throughout the years of my childhood. No one could quite explain how he came to have the permanent protuberance on his forehead that made him look like he had, glued to his forehead, one of those torches worn by miners when they went down the shafts. In spite of this, no one ever made fun of him because of it. *A*Mazizi was well respected and liked in the community.

Long after Father had left to fight in the war of the white man, it was *a*Mazizi who helped keep us from starving. He gave us dry or stale bread that was supposed to be thrown away as no longer fit for sale. I helped Mother remove the black-greenish fungi from the bread and broke it into pieces that we dipped in *mahewu* to soften it before giving it to my siblings to eat. It was lucky that even four years after Father's departure, we were still looked after by the Mine Management. Though Mother did not get any wages, she still got the family's rations of food; weevil-infested maize-meal, beans and black-eyed peas. On Fridays the children used to go and collect the family's rations of *mahewu*, a nourishing drink brewed with grain and yeast. We also got buns to take home. The provision of food was part of the wages.

While most men preferred to have all the wages as cash, their wives were perfectly happy with the

arrangement. It suited and pleased mostly those whose husbands would have been irresponsible enough to spend most of their wages on beer while their children starved. That way, even if the workers spent most of their wages on beer or on gambling, the family at least had food. While the motives of *abwana* were not always honourable, they did at least serve a purpose. There was no doubt that John Mack and Company did not care whether or not we ate well. It was the good health of the miners that concerned the management. We did not know then that they wanted their workers fit for the back breaking work of the mines, hence the rations of food though it was of the type they would not give to their dogs. Yet we were grateful for it. We thought the generosity of *abwana* was an indication of the extent to which they cared about our welfare. We were their workers and therefore belonged to them. That was the way we saw our existence. *Abwana* gave us jobs, they gave us accommodation, they gave us wages and they gave jobs to the children and descendants of their workers.

We saw nothing but security and continuity in our lives and for most of us, the fact that the locals did not get rations of food filled us with glee. At that time we thought we were favoured over them. The implications of that did not dawn on us until much later. Despite our impoverished lives we were not unhappy because we knew no other life. Patchway Valley was a world unto itself. My people were born and raised there, and they settled down to married life, then patiently waited for the end of their lives there while working their bodies to the ground. Beneath its red soils, they knew their remains would be laid to rest.

Indeed Patchway Valley was our whole life, and one family's life generally mirrored that of the next, with only a few minor variations. Our parents slept on sagging beds with sisal sacks stuffed with feathers for mattresses. The windows to our houses were of metal panes that had only

one glass pane on top to let in just a little bit of light during the day. The latches on most of these windows were broken and the asbestos sheets on the roof rattled in the wind especially at night, which made sleep difficult. During the dry summer months, the shimmering folds of heat could be seen rising above the asbestos sheets. We had either to open the windows and at the same time let in swarms of flies escaping the heat, or shut ourselves indoors and squirm. The same roofs leaked during heavy rainstorms and we would sit indoors with the windows tightly shut. Needless to say, we blamed our discomfort on nature.

The best years of my life were those of my childhood, despite the fact that for part of it I lived with only a vague recollection of the man who was my father. I never really missed him even though Mother did. She talked about him during the day and prayed for him at night. On warm evenings, my brother and my sister_ both of whom were younger than me_ and I often left Mother alone in the dreary looking house to go and play with other children under the halo of a full moon. She must have felt even more lonely then. I knew of no other child whose mother was left to fend for the family while her husband fought in the war of the white man. The little I remembered of Father was his kindness and his high-pitched laughter. He never raised his voice like other fathers did. My parents did not fight on pay days as did some husbands and wives. I never heard them argue either. If they did, it was never in our presence. I could understand why Mother missed Father that much. His departure meant Mother had to shoulder the burden of supporting the family.

Like most other women who went cotton picking, Mother used to boil sweet potatoes and maize the night before and take them to work. She would eat the food in-

between periods of bending down to hoe, weed or pick cotton, depending on what season it was. Working in the cotton fields was hard and the daily grind of soul-destroying drudgery slowly but steadily drained Mother of her exuberance. It was harder still working with Wezi, my baby brother, strapped to her back. I felt guilty about continuing with school when I could have left and gone to work full time on the farms where the age at which one could start work was not restricted, but I wanted to stay on in school and get educated. Maybe that could lead to a good job, and hopefully, a better life. Mother would then leave her life of poverty behind forever. On the other hand, if I insisted on continuing with school, Mother had to work even harder. I was worried that my dream would destroy her yet it was a dream I was reluctant to give up.

While Mother was out working I cooked the evening meal, a chore I learned to do at the age of eleven. I had to because Mother did not always return from the farms until twilight. At times she came back complaining of a backache and barely able to walk upright. On some days when the tractors came back Mother would not be on them, having got off somewhere along the way to gather firewood before sunset. It was not an easy life for Mother, but she probably got some comfort from the message on the only picture that hung on the walls of our living room. It was done in embroidery and cross-stitch, the result of many weeks of squinting and working painstakingly in the hot summer months. It was a picture of man sitting on a throne, and with a glittering gold crown perched on his head from which long, curly blonde locks protruded. Underneath were the words, 'TO LIVE LIKE A KING YOU MUST WORK LIKE A SLAVE'.

The room in which the cooking utensils were kept was not ideal for cooking as smoke tended to filter into the whole house, making it unbearable to be in. Furthermore, during the hot months, cooking indoors made the heat

intolerable as the entire house simply turned into a furnace. We therefore had a fireplace outside which served us well in good weather but whenever it was raining we had to make a fire in the house. We did not have a make-shift outdoors kitchen. Rain meant wet logs for firewood, and wet firewood meant blowing in vain for hours onto the barely glowing embers to get flames for cooking. Smoking wood meant a smoke-filled house, smarting eyes and frayed tempers. On numerous occasions we used candle wax to help kindle the fire, which meant plenty of smoke first before the fire eventually got going. Even then it was erratic and needed stoking regularly. Mother and I took turns to do this, which left us exhausted and gasping for air, our eyes red and tears running down our cheeks. At some point these tears turned to tears of frustration on my part. Just when we needed it most, we got to eat our evening meal quite late. There was not always enough food and Mother often gave most of hers to the young ones whenever they asked for more, which was almost always. I too wanted more at times but I did not say so because I knew mother would give hers to me. She would pretend not to be hungry but, I knew otherwise.

Late at night, while lying next to my sister Nchesa on the cold hard floor of the sitting room, I would hear her teeth chattering from the cold. Mother too would go to her room with Wezi, their eyes sore from the smoke, their lungs congested and their chests heaving. Long after the whole family had gone to sleep I would often lie awake and listen to the sounds of laboured breathing and blocked noses. The wheezing usually went on into the early hours of the morning, in unison with the shrill cries of cicadas outside. In the early morning light I would wake up to the sight of soot-coated rafters with sooty cobwebs suspended over our heads. Above the rafters, the asbestos sheets creaked in the wind and thunderstorm. It was not unusual to wake up with lizards sprawled on our blankets. These

were merely one of several kinds of creatures that occasionally invaded our homes. On very cold mornings, despite a strong urge to wrap my blanket tight around me, I would get up and go to fetch water from the communal water tap. The water was for Nchesa and me to wash our faces, hands and legs, and also for other uses at home. It was my duty to fill the drum with clean water every morning. Meanwhile, mother would make a fire outside and heat the water for our wash in an enamel tin. Two holes were bored on opposite sides at the rim of the tin and a strong wire was inserted through these holes to make a handle. Once the water was hot I would lift the tin off the fireplace with great difficulty because the wire was very hot and tended to scald my fingers. I would carry the tin to the washing place by the side of the house and pour the water into an enamel dish that leaked. We used to plug the holes with mud to stop the water running out before we finished washing.

Next to the wall was a big stone on which Mother rubbed those clothes with stubborn stains that could not be removed just by rubbing hard between the hands. She washed the clothes for the whole family at this place. During our morning wash, Nchesa and I would sit on the stone and rub the cracked soles of our feet against its rough surface. Regular rubbing meant the cracks never got deep to the point of bleeding. At times this resulted in smooth soles and heels. We had to be careful though not to make them too smooth because that made it painful to walk on the gravel and stony roads on bare feet. After the wash we would dry ourselves, tip over whatever water was left and place the dish upside down, against the stone. The washing place always had a white residue from the foam of the Sunlight soap that reacted badly with the hard water. Small featherlike lumps formed when the soap came into contact with water, and these floated on the surface. Mother told us that the soap and the water

refused to mix, which made it harder to remove the dirt from the clothes. Those who could afford it used washing powder, either Surf or Cold Power. The detergent in powder form softened the hardness of the water, so Mother said. The water also made the skin rough and look ashen, so we had to rub on oil or Vaseline to moisturise it and give it a smooth feel.

The big mulberry tree in our yard played an important part in our morning routine. From it we got saplings and stripped the thin bark off them. We then chewed them on one end until they became soft, fluffy and supple. We brushed our teeth using the fluffy ends then rinsed our mouths with plain water. At sunset every other day, we used the communal bathrooms for a full body wash because the wash place by the wall was for washing the face and limbs only. Before we set off for school, Mother gave us whatever food was available, which was mostly boiled sweet potatoes or pumpkins and tea with so little sugar it melted on the lips before it touched the tongue. Long after the harvest season, when there were no fresh crops, Mother cooked the crops she had dried out earlier, such as black-eyed peas, groundnuts and maize. Boiled together for hours and lightly salted, this made a tasty meal of *mutakura*.

After the morning meal, Nchesa and would I set off for school, our scrubbed bare feet pounding the dusty ground. During the hot dry months, by the time we got to school our legs were often covered in a thin coat of red dust that stuck to the Vaseline wed rubbed onto the skin. During the cold months, the chilly air whipped our cheeks and numbed our toes and fingers. Through the numbness we still felt the sharp pain as our feet stepped on small jagged stones, some of which got stuck in the spaces between the toes where they grazed the delicate skin and made it bleed. We limped on to school, our teeth chattering from a combination of pain, cold and the fear of

punishment for arriving late. During the rainy season it was not only stones that got stuck onto our feet. Mud also squashed and squished between the toes and under the soles of our feet. When the feet touched the wet ground, they gripped the lumpy mud and squashed it. In its struggle to escape, the mud was squeezed out between the toes and came out smooth like toothpaste being squeezed out of a tube. Sometimes the mud struggled quietly but at times it sploshed and hissed. We went to school regardless of the weather because it was only a short distance away.

Nchesa and I clutched plastic bags emptied of the five kilograms of roller meal originally packaged within, which then contained exercise books, text books, biros and pencils. As school bags, they served us well because the books were protected from dust, dampness and rain. With the other hand, we held up the hems of our uniforms that were too big for us. Mother always bought them in big sizes so that they would last several years. At the ages of six and eleven years, we had a long way to go. Our everyday clothes were also just as big for the same reasons. A garment that got torn was patched with a piece of cloth. It was not unusual for a green shirt made of thin material to have a red patch of heavy material held together with blue thread. For some reason, my shorts always got torn on my bottom, with a hole on each side. I continued to wear them as they were if Mother was too busy to mend them right away, or if she did not have the cloth for the patches. The nakedness did not worry me that much since most of the children were dressed as I was. I had no elder brother from whom to receive some hand-me-down clothes, but I saw many of my playmates wear oversized shorts that were kept tight around their waists with large safety pins. Covering our nakedness was the most important thing and fitness and fashion did not even come into our minds. After all, we did not get clothes regularly. Most parents tried their best to buy new clothes

for their children at Christmas, which was a more important period during which to get new clothes than at any other time. New clothes, rice and chicken were necessities at Christmas. Fanta Orange and Coca Cola were the ultimate luxuries that set you apart from those grinding their noses in poverty. We were all poor, but we had varying degrees of poverty. A family of eight fared far worse than a family half that size on the same wages.

Coca Cola.
Bubbles of luxury in a bottle!
I remember the delight Nchesa and I used to derive from watching bubbles of Coca Cola rushing furiously from the bottle and shooting upwards upon their release from a cramped space. This agitation always took place whenever the bottle was shaken just before the bottle top was removed. We soon learned to make our own bubbles whose fury we could control. On the rare occasions Mother bought us cold drinks, she would remove the bottle tops before leaving us to sit alone and enjoy our drinks on the veranda. We savoured the moment so much that we strove to make it last as long as we could stretch it. Nchesa and I would each drop a small pebble into the bottle and watch as it descended to the very bottom. Bubbles would rise from beneath the pebble, race to the top and spill over the sides in a swooshing sound. At this point, either Nchesa or I would bring one's small mouth onto the rim of the bottle and suck in the fizzy liquid. Mother used to admonish us for dropping what she called dirty things in our drinks. She said the stones were dirty and we could end up contracting all kinds of diseases, but we did not share her concerns and we did not care about them either. Although Mother kept buying us the drink of our choice despite her disapproval, she adamantly refused to buy us chewing gum. She said the problems caused by the gum after it had been sucked of all the sweetness and

discarded were enough to make her go mad. She hated finding the sticky stuff on our clothes, our books, on the plates, on doors and on chairs. She hated it even more if it stuck to her shoes. The sight of people chewing for hours like cows chewing cud disgusted her, she told us.

Whenever the need for money was great, Mother kept me from school and took me to work on the farms with her. I was not the only child who missed school on occasions for that reason. A number of other migrant children did so from time to time, some more often than me. Others dropped out of school altogether at different stages and for various reasons, which resulted in a sizeable number of children accompanying their parents to work on the farms. We rode on the tractor trailer with our legs dangling over the edge, and to the chagrin of the adults who could not bear loud noises that early in the day, we screamed, yelled or sang. For us children that ride was an event to look forward to since, for the majority of us, it was the only experience we had of travelling in a vehicle. The few lucky ones amongst us rode on the Mine bus to take part in sporting activities at various schools.

Although we enjoyed the tractor rides, the adults embarked on the trip with an air of resignation. Those trips were the best part of the working day. The rest was arduous and exhausting. By sunset I would sit down to nurse my bleeding shins, my back aching from bending over the thorny cotton plants. Even as I lay on the tent at night, I could still feel the sharp, stinging thorns of the cotton plant pricking and scratching my bare legs and hands. With time, the continued hardships numbed my body and the hard work paid off. The few items of clothing we owned were bought from those earnings. The second-hand clothes were sold by cooks, nannies or gardeners who in turn got them as cast offs from the children of their employers. If we were lucky Mother

would take my sister and me to the store run by the vile Chimuromo and buy us new pairs of canvas shoes.

We never bought clothes from the store though, mainly because they were too expensive, and also because they looked awful. Suspended from the beams on the roof, the clothes seemed to have been there since time immemorial. Flies landed with filthy legs on the hems and left dirty marks on them. The red dust did not improve the appearance of these miserable garments that, with time, gradually began to fall to pieces. Only then would Chimuromo ask the shopkeeper to take them down. Whenever Mother made me miss a day of school to go to work, my teachers got furious. My class teacher in particular, said I was a very good pupil and he believed that if I worked hard I could proceed all the way to Standard Six, after which I could qualify to go and train to be a teacher like him. I rejoiced at the praise but Mother said we had to be realistic and not waste time on unattainable dreams.

"In the first place, Masauso," she said, "we do not have the money to pay your fees up to Standard Six. Then there are the uniforms, books and pens you have to buy. It is impossible. If we have to work in cotton and maize fields to buy food, I do not see how we can manage to pay for your education. And another thing, that kind of job is not for migrants like us. Teachers and policemen raise their children to take up those jobs and we raise you to go down the mine shafts as your fathers do. So forget about any big ideas."

"*ATicha* Moyo says he can buy me books and provide pens if you pay my school fees and buy me a uniform," I said, hoping this would sway Mother's stance.

"Where would we get the two shillings, six pence and a tickey for your fees and uniform? If your father were here maybe that would be possible. As things are, in order to afford your fees you would have to come to the cotton

fields with me all winter, but then if working that much keeps you away from school for a whole term, then there is no point in the whole thing. You can only do one thing or the other, but certainly not both."

"For what reason do I go to school then, *Amayo*?" I cried with exasperation.

"You go to school because it is there, because everybody else does, and mainly because you need to be able to count, read and write. Your father says that if you can at least do that, the Mine bosses might make you *foromani* or *ovhasiya,*[53] which would save you from the back breaking job of your father. For that, you only need three or four years of schooling, not the Standard Six you are aspiring towards. If your father were here, who knows, perhaps things would be different."

"But *Amayo,* I can work in the fields for our teachers, or in their houses. Some of my classmates do."

"I know, Masauso, but for how much? I have never supported what your teachers do. They exploit you. How can they make you work in their gardens and in their houses for a mere *susipenzi nitiki?*[54] They regard you as nothing but cheap labour. I would rather see you work for *abwana* instead of them."

"I beg you, *Amayo,* I want a good job in life. *Aticha* Moyo says I can be a teacher because I always come first in class. He says my brain is quick to grasp knowledge, and I do not forget easily what I learn."

"Your teacher could very well be right but your fathers' masters expect you to take up the shovels underground after your fathers become too old for the job. You are not expected to change the order of things, so just

---

53 Overseer

54 Six pence and a tickey

forget those dreams and let us trudge on as we have always done."

There was no point in arguing with Mother, so I went to school only to pass time and stayed away occasionally to go cotton-picking, depending on how badly we needed the money.

The school was fenced with barbed wire, parallel to which ran a hedge on the inside. This hedge was not the leafy type that bordered the yards of the white people's homes but was the same as the type we had in our yards, which grew to not more than a meter upwards, and had spikes that grew off the thick stem, spreading sideways and upwards. From these spikes sprouted yet more spikes and it went on like that, creating a thick wall of spikes. When the hedge was cut, or if one of the spikes broke off, a creamy substance oozed out and dripped lazily onto the ground where it seeped into the soil, thin and warm at first until the air cooled it. It congealed and thickened as it cooled, and resisted the sucking motion of the soil. The resulting gooey, sticky substance was often used to trap wild birds. Once their feet came into contact with it, the unfortunate birds were not able to fly away. The creamy gum was dangerous when swallowed or if it got into the eyes, so we did our best to steer clear of the hedge altogether. But this substance was not the only danger that lurked there. Sometimes snakes could be found stretched languidly or coiled on the spikes as they basked in the sun. Green mambas were the hardest to spot because they blended well with the spikes. The evergreen hedge provided shade for all kinds of creatures during the hot dry months. Lizards darted about or fought each other, racing from one end of the hedge to the other, up the stems and down the spikes.

Our school consisted of two blocks built from burnt bricks with grass thatch for roofing. Each block was

divided into four big rooms. As one entered the gate, with a frangipani tree on either side, the two blocks stood on either side and ran parallel to each other. The block on the right accommodated classrooms for the junior classes, most of which were taught by female teachers. Behind that block was the school vegetable garden. The other block accommodated three senior classrooms, at the furthest end of which was the Headmaster's office. The Headmaster, a man as feared as he was respected, was very much a part of the school buildings. Behind the senior block were the toilets and the fields where sporting activities took place. The space between the blocks was big and divided into four equal squares. In these squares grew lawn that looked like it could not quite decide whether it wanted to be green, yellow or brown. There were patches of naked brown soil in some areas and in the centre of each lawn was a bougainvillea shrub, and along the edges were beautiful orange-coloured rosemaries, yellow marigolds, white daisies and some purple and pink asters that exploded into a profusion of brilliance in summer and caught the eye as one approached the gate. The squares which held the lawn were separated by gravelled pathways that led from one block to the other. We were not allowed to cut across the lawns, or to pluck the flowers. The punishment for doing so was caning by the headmaster during Friday assembly.

Every Friday morning we had assembly, the purpose of which was to sing the national anthem, sing a hymn or two, listen to a moral lecture and to the announcements of the week, capped by the public canning of the mid-week offenders. We were made to stand in lines according to our classes, with a school prefect on either end to make sure we behaved ourselves. The prefect wrote down the names of those who misbehaved during assembly, and the offences ranged from anything such as whispering, giggling to fidgeting or not knowing the words to the

national anthem and mumbling through it. The Sub A class stood in the front line, the Sub B in the one behind it and it went on like that in order of class and right up to the Standard Six class at the very back. The lines were tidy, a feat achieved because we stood on rows of bricks that were embedded into the ground. These lines of bricks curved inwards at both ends, making the rows look like the moon in its dying phase. This helped bring us all within range of the Headmaster's eye as he addressed us. Assembly started off with a hymn followed by a prayer. Announcements were made about the events of the following week such as football and netball matches, athletics, music practice, and any other activities. It was also here that offenders were canned for misdemeanour such as turning up late for school during the week, not combing one's hair or anything the prefects deemed an offence.

I remember one frenzied term during which Lever Brothers was giving free soccer balls to schools that managed to collect a certain number of Reward Soap wrappers. We were ordered to bring a wrapper per school child once a month. The only way we could get them was if our parents bought the soap. What the teachers did not know, or rather chose to disregard, was that our parents could not afford such luxuries. It was a struggle to buy even the cheap long bars of Sunlight or the red Lifebuoy whose scent was an onslaught on the nasal sensibilities. Mother said Sunlight soap served our purposes better because of its multi-purpose use. A bar could be cut into several pieces that were then used separately for bathing, washing clothes and washing the dishes. One bar went far, especially if it was dried in the sun first before use. We knew that our parents could not afford Reward soap, but neither could we afford to get canned every month. Most school children, like me, threatened to go hungry for days, or to leave school altogether if their parents did not buy

Reward soap. In the end our parents stretched their wages and bought the soap. I felt sorry for classmates who had several siblings in school because regardless of how many tantrums they threw, their parents just could not afford to buy more than two in a single month. Once the campaign was over, the school children and their parents rejoiced. The teachers rejoiced too, for they had collected three soccer balls.

In my final year in school, I got into serious trouble with my class teacher, the music master and the soccer coach. The three of them were firm believers in the use of the cane when enforcing discipline. Mr Zvidzai, my class teacher, used to quote, with rather too much glee, the adage that goes, "Spare the rod and spoil the child." He believed that the only way to teach truants a lesson was to hit their knuckles hard with a thick wooden ruler or with the wooden part of a blackboard duster. I took this punishment with hardly a whimper. Most of us did not dare withdraw the hand as the duster descended on our knuckles because we knew that doing so further incensed Mr Zvidzai, who would then swear and double the number of blows. I do not think he understood that one would withdraw one's hand instinctively out of the fear of excruciating pain.

The soccer coach made us bend down until we could touch our toes with our fingertips. Most of us often screamed before the whip descended on our bottoms. Mr Moyo raised his hand high in the air, swung it back as far as it could go and brought the cane down on the bottom of the offender. The pain was agonising and crippling and it nearly drove us mad. It did not matter what excuses we had, our teachers did not care and simply wanted us where we had to be at any given time. The music teacher gave the worst beating which often left our hands bruised and black. We were caught in a very difficult situation. We could either go to school every day without pens or

uniforms, for which the teachers beat us up, or we could miss school to go and earn money for pens and we would still be punished for what they insisted was truancy. There was always something we needed, after all pens ran out over time or went missing. As time went by, we filled our exercise books and rulers and pencils got broken; so ours was an on-going nightmare.

School was hard for mine children, but it seemed even harder for those from the farms. At the Mine, migrants and their families were the least educated and therefore the least respected. They were at the very bottom of everything but in the classroom, we considered ourselves to be above the children from the farms who walked a long way to get to school. For those who had longer distances to walk, it meant getting up and setting off at the first cockcrow. The forests were dark and wild. The children from the farms said they watched the sun glow and rise over the horizon as they sprinted on bare feet all the way to Patchway Valley Mine. I can never forget the sight of my friend Chinai standing in a queue at the school gate, his head bowed, his eyes staring at his feet and cowering behind the older boys and girls as the prefect on duty wrote down the names of all late comers.

On Fridays, the farm children were caned for arriving late nearly every morning. Later in the day when school broke up for lunch, I used to take Chinai home with me where we shared with my siblings the boiled plain maize Mother always cooked the night before. It was the poorest food one could eat, but seasoned with a generous amount of salt and washed down with water, it filled empty stomachs and stilled the rumblings within. Tired and sleepy as a result of a combination of getting up at dawn and sprinting long distances, Chinai often slept for a while on a sack under the mulberry tree. I would sit by his side and keep the fat green flies from settling on the scabies he seemed to get on his legs and arms every summer. No

matter how often I saw the dried blood on the raw cracks on his feet, I never got used to the awful sight. How Chinai managed to run to school and back to the farm everyday was hard to comprehend. Though the majority of the Mine children did not go around wearing shoes, except maybe on Sundays and on some special occasions such as Christmas, if we were lucky to own a pair, we did not have to walk through thorny bush areas. I could not understand why the children from the farms used the paths in the forest and I suggested that my friend use the roads used by the farmers.

"Have you ever tried walking barefoot on grit or loose gravel for a long distance?" he asked.

"Yes, I have," I answered. "Do you forget that the area around the underpass is sprinkled with quarry stones? I know the pain of walking on them."

"Now try to imagine three or four miles of it. It is unbearable. If you cut through the forest paths you can avoid the grit. But the forests have their own problems. Most of the time, thorny bushes scratch and graze my feet, legs and thighs, leaving them itching and bleeding. It is not so bad on the way back home because with the last few rays of sunlight we are able to pick our way through and avoid the brush. I envy the fortunate children of the *bwana* who do not have to endure the hardships we go through and are driven to their good schools for 'Whites Only' in their lovely warm cars. There are times I wish I were born white. They have everything. And us, what do we have?"

"Hardly anything," I said.

"Very true, Masauso. We have so little it isn't worth noting. We do not even own our very lives. Van der Byl is king at March Hare farm. John Brown is master of Montana. Susipenzi is lord at Potters Farm. Their children are little bosses just waiting to step into the big shoes of their fathers. They rule the land with might, believe me.

Each time I pass by the homestead of the *bwana* I tremble with fear. The beasts they keep as pets come growling after me, ready to sink their bare teeth into my flesh.

"*Akuki* repeatedly warns us never to run or the dogs would tear us to shreds. This is easier said than done, especially with those beasts growling fiercely and sniffing right next to me. I keep imagining that anytime they will jump onto me. I shake uncontrollably and I can hear my teeth gnashing. And what do the miserable *pikinini bwana*[55] do? They find the whole thing amusing, something with which to brighten their otherwise dull lives on isolated farm homesteads. Above the noise of the dogs growling, you can hear their masters' voices shrill with laughter. It takes a lot of effort and willpower to remain motionless. *Akuki* advises that no matter what happens, one should never bend down low and let the dogs tower over them. He says once you do that your life is as good as over. The dogs, according to him, are the type that can sink their teeth into your throat and kill you there and then. *Ratiwera,*[56] I think he calls them."

"*He-eyi, vinango azungu niwoyipa mutima nditu*[57]. I don't suppose that at this stage they can continue to laugh, surely, Chinai?" I asked, shocked.

"I suppose not, but the dogs are so vicious they can maul you and be done with it before their masters can come to your rescue. Some of those beasts are trained to challenge and harass black people. *Vazungu* believe that we cannot be trusted. They suspect *akuki* of always looking for an opportunity to steal sugar, salt, and soap as soon as the back of *bwana* is turned. But then again, my father says

55 The young bosses

56 Rottweiler

57 Some white people are cruel, honestly.

with the little he is paid_ which is hardly enough to buy a month's worth of food_ very few of us can blame the man. Once in a while the cook helps himself to some of the meat meant for the master's pets, especially if his own children are starving. As far as *abwana* are concerned, anyone loitering around the farm must be looking for a chance to steal crops. We are all regarded with suspicion. Whenever they come across you, the dogs corner you until their masters call them away, but only after sniffing you all over and making sure you have no stolen goods on you. Should you panic and run away, that could very easily be the end of your life. I understand it happened once at Potters Farm. The young son of a*dhiraivha* was going up to the homestead to take a message to his father when he saw the master's ferocious beast charging silently towards him. Ignoring his father's pleas urging him to stand still, the young boy bent down to pick up a stone with which to shoo the dog away. He never stood a chance. It was over within minutes. They say it was a horrific death. As if that was not enough, the owners of the dog blamed the boy for the tragedy. They accused him of teasing the dog, thereby provoking it to attack. They claimed he worsened the situation when he reached down to pick up a stone with which to challenge it. They said their normally gentle pet had no choice but to defend itself in its territory. Mother says the dead boy's mother died of a broken heart soon after. He was her only child."

The unfortunate woman, I thought, although I could not find anything to say. There are times when words are simply not enough to express one's shock or sympathy. The family was unknown to me yet the nature of their tragedy was nothing new. We had watched often enough as injustices unfolded in our midst. My disillusionment with our supposedly fair God who did nothing to level the injustices of our lives left me questioning a whole lot of what I had been taught in Sunday school. But then again

Sunday school had not deluded us. The Word had stated very clearly that we, the poor, were the blessed ones, for we would one day inherit the earth and not just for a lifetime like the cursed rich, but for all of eternity. We the poor were the long term winners, and that surely appealed to me.

"How sad," I finally said, bringing my thoughts back. "It reminds me of Yotamu, our deceased schoolmate. You remember him don't you, Chinai?"

"How can I not? And who can possibly forget Yotamu, given the manner of his death?"

"Ya, that was a big shock to many, including even those who did not know him. He was very quiet. It would have been hard to notice him had he not been the fastest athlete ever at Patchway Valley Primary School. They say his mother could not bear to wake up every morning and be confronted with the sight of those lime deposit dumps. In spite of that, John Mack and Company refused to give her family another house away from within sight of the tragic place."

"I hear the poor woman went and swallowed the *saineti*[58] that had eaten the mouth, throat and insides of her son. What nobody could understand was why Yotamu went and drank from the rivulet he knew to be well contaminated with the poison. Maybe he was not aware of the danger," said my friend.

"Impossible. Chinai, the dangers of *saineti*, whatever it is, is the one thing our parents have always warned us about. None of us can claim to have seen it, but the horrors of ingesting it are forever ringing in our ears. If one swallows it, the poison burns its way down the insides and one experiences the worst possible pain. Death comes in a matter of a few heartbeats. It is a horrific way to go, so we are constantly reminded. Father always said he could

58 cyanide

not imagine a more painful way of dying. Those little rivulets and lime dumps have always been a no-go area for all children because of the *saineti*. Everybody knows that. Because of the toxic nature of the waste, the bosses do not want it dumped anywhere near where they live, so they bring it around here."

"Yet Yotamu drank straight from there!"

"I cannot imagine what drove him to do that. Father said his mother was at first advised not to view his body before burial, but she insisted on one final look at his face."

It had only been a year since Yotamu died and no one knew whether his death was an accident or not. At almost every home at Patchway Valley Mine there were big enamel drums that were only given to miners for use at home after they had been thoroughly washed and rinsed. The words DANGER- SIKELEMU! were written on them to warn everybody of the poison within. For the benefit of those who could not read, a picture of two bones crossing over a skull conveyed a message clear enough to be understood by all. That the poison flowed in a rivulet at an unprotected mine dump did not make it any less hazardous.

Long after my friend had gone back to the farm, my thoughts kept drifting back to the death of the cook's son and to that of the boy's mother. I thought too of his poor father who, on his way to work, still had to pass by the place that was a constant reminder of his loss. While most white farmers ill-treated their workers, this could not be said to be true of all of them. The *bwana* at Montana Farm allowed school children to ride on his tractor on its way to Patchway Valley Mine to collect cotton pickers. The children also got a ride back to the farm after the driver had returned the casual labourers. The kind *bwana* allowed his farm labourers to cut grass with which they thatched the leaking roofs of their huts, and he gave them rations of

food. However, *bwana* John Brown had one big weakness. He continually chased after the womenfolk amongst his workers. It did not matter to him whether or not they had husbands. He did not even bother to hide his interest in them and he tried very hard to find reasons to be alone with a woman he liked before disappearing altogether with her for a while. Her husband would fume at first, then pretend not to notice until the day his wife gave birth to a baby of mixed race. The family would then be unceremoniously evicted from the farm and left to wander, homeless, with their meagre belongings until the husband got another job at another farm. Though John Brown was the *bwana* most notorious for his wandering eye, he was by no means the only one. Quite a number of farmers fooled around with black women, mostly in the maize fields. Their sons did the same too and a sizeable number of children of mixed race were born as a result of such activities.

When Mother said she was no longer going cotton picking at Montana farm, I suspected her decision had something to do with *bwana* John Brown and his reputation. We did not have enough to live on, but I did not think Mother was the kind of woman to accept a few cheap favours at any cost. She would not do it even if our very survival depended on it, of that I was certain. Also, she loved Father and believed he would one day come back. Just the year before, Mother had spurned her friend's advice that she marry again since Father had been gone a long time.

"I cannot do that. *Ababa a*Masauso is still my husband and I shall wait for him until he comes back," Mother had protested.

"He may never come back, and here you are, wasting your life. You are still young and attractive, yet you wish to devote the rest of your life to the shadow of a man who's been gone these many years," said *ana*Phiri, raising

her hand with three fingers extended. "He could be dead by now, you know. A certain woman I know whose husband went to war long after yours is already married and has children. Look at Siteriya_"

"*Ana*Phiri, I do not care what Siteriya chooses to do with her life. *I* want to wait for my husband. If he is dead, then I shall devote the rest of my life to bringing up our children and treasuring his memory."

"I do not understand you at all. ABhaureni has been gone for quite a few years and not a single letter has he sent in all that time, yet you say he will come back. I do not understand this pointless devotion of yours. If it were you who had been gone that long, he would be twice married and divorced already, with several other women in-between_"

"Well, such is the nature of men but as a woman, I cannot possibly behave in the same manner."

"So it would have been perfectly all right for your husband to just father children and move on?" demanded *ana*Phiri with indignation.

"*A-a, imwe anaPhiri, wosanitsutsa ine!*[59] I know what I want to do with my life. In any case it is common knowledge that men cannot live without women to look after them. Anyway, A*baba a*Masauso would not do that. He is very responsible towards his family. When he comes back I shall be here waiting for him. If he is dead, then like I said, I shall devote the rest of my life to his_"

"_memory, oh yes," interjected *ana*Phiri, her voice thick with sarcasim. "I suppose his first wife back in Nkhotakota is busy devoting her life to his memory too, believing his poor soul to be wandering in the savannah lands of Central Africa, while his body has long since gone back to the dust from which it was created! How blind, how totally blind can you be, *Amake* Masauso? You are a

59 Hey you, *ana*Phiri, do not argue with me.

very tough woman, I have to admit, but you are trapped in the past, with misguided loyalties to a man lost in the past and who therefore has no room for you in his future. What you feel is nothing more than just blind devotion which has no place in the real and practical world, my friend. That husband of yours is probably married with ten children by now. Tell me, my friend,' said *ana*Phiri clearing her throat. "If *a*Bhaureni were to return to Nyasaland today, do you think he would leave you and the children behind?"

"Of course not!"

"There you are! He would definitely take you, his current family, back to his village to meet and live with the family he left behind. I can almost hear him say to his first wife, '*Amake mwana,*[60] meet my new wife, the one I married while you were here pining after me. To which his first wife would ululate and declare that an increase in the size of the family is welcome, and that only a witch would condemn the idea. Wake up, *mubale wanga,* and use your brain or you could actually find yourself experiencing this situation in reverse, with you as the wife to whom a new wife is introduced. In these few years that your *husband-who-is-no-longer-really-a-husband-but-a-shadow* has been away, he could have married and started another family. So it should not come as a surprise if he should one day turn up and say to you, '*Amake mwana,* while you were here pining after_"

"*Heyi!*" screamed Mother, "how can you even consider such a fate for me? Surely, *Ababa a*Masauso cannot just forget about us and start his life all over again?"

"He can, and you know it. *Mubale wanga,* that is what I have been trying to tell you all along. Leave the past behind and get on with your life. Enough time has passed

60 Mother of the child

to enable you to put a barrier between the past and the present, eh?"

"What past, *ana*Phiri? My past is very much a part of my present. These two phases are much too intertwined to ever be regarded as separate. When I became the wife of Bhaureni Nyirenda, I did not intend to discard that role at some stage in the future. I committed myself to loving the father of my children for as long as *I* myself lived, and up to now I still do. As for being trapped in the past, yes I am indeed and I feel quite tired spiritually, like I've been there a really long time and simply lack the energy to drag myself into the bleak future, but that is my decision, and I do not regret it at all."

"*A-a, kaya,*[61]" said *ana*Phiri raising her hands in a gesture indicating she was leaving Mother to get on with her stubbornness. "Do as you wish, *Amake* Masauso, but I personally think that waiting for *a*Bhaureni is taking loyalty and sainthood too far. It is a waste of time. However, it is entirely up to you whether or not to devote your whole life to a man who is probably dead by now, but just remember that the dead cannot love you back. You have the whole of your future to think about, to make plans for, and to live through, yet here you are wasting your precious time and clinging to a sentimental past whose magic you cannot recapture. You cherish a past that keeps you trapped in time and you wallow in misery and shed tears of sorrow and frustration when you can be shedding tears of happiness at the joy of living. Who can blame you should you move on with your life?"

"What type of friendship is this, *ana*Phiri, is this your way of showing support? You, the very person who should allay my fears and encourage my hopes! How little I know you! Anyway I cannot accept_"

---

61 Whatever

"What you ought not to accept is that your life should be over at your age. I am being a true friend in trying to get you to open these eyes of yours that only roll inwards and look backwards. When you turned down *a*Pikicha from Coronation Farm I thought it was because of his age, though he cannot be older than the age your father would have been had he been alive. So I thought *a*Buruzi the tractor driver at March Hare farm would be acceptable but you shunned him too. And now even *abhasibhoyi* at Mayor's Farm you turn down, all for the memory of a man who has not been heard from for many years." Shaking her head and wringing her hands in exasperation, *ana*Phiri got up to go, still mumbling. "A *baas* boy, she turns down a *baas* boy, the favourite employee of the *bwana. Baas boy,* a man in charge of the farm, the one who gets all the unwanted food and clothes from his masters. Beyond belief! Utter foolishness…!"

* * *

The following year, I started work in the mines and our life improved. I was almost fifteen years of age, not yet old enough to work underground, but I looked older than my age and fit enough to do a man's job. I had hoped to get educated and get a job that paid well, but that was not to be. It was with great reluctance that I watched my dream slip away. If Father had been there maybe my life would have turned out differently. I got a job, as Mother wished, as a mine labourer, a *malaicha.* She started to smile again, though the smile did not always reach her eyes or brighten her face. She urged me to be contented with my good health and my strength. I took the job with a mixture of trepidation and excitement. My first trip down the mine

shaft is still very vivid in my mind, and it was nothing like I had imagined.

In my childhood I often accompanied Mother to bring Father his tea at the mine shaft where I saw men troop out of the cage that brought them up from underground. I thought it quite an enjoyable experience, until the day I went down. As I stood by the shaft entrance, I watched with fascination as big pulleys went up and down slowly right above the gaping mine shaft. From this big yawning hole a big steel cage came up and disgorged sweaty, dusty, exhausted and hungry looking men. Ten of us stood by the entrance of Shaft number Three, lanterns in our hands and bottles of water tied to the belts tied around our waists. Our helmets had built-in torches that gave out a dim light. I trooped with my work mates into the cage and its heavy steel doors clanged shut and were bolted. The sound was like a death knell. Just for that moment it felt as if I was in a death machine in which I was trapped.

The trip down was a nightmare. It gave me the feeling of being sucked into a dark, bottomless void. None of us talked, including those who had made the trip for several years before me. The cage slowly went down and a darkness I had never thought possible enveloped us. My eyes gradually adjusted to the dark and with the faint light from our torches, I was able to see the faces of those around me. We travelled down for so long that I wondered whether we would ever be able to come back up again. I was filled with dread just knowing I would be working so far away from the surface and from everything that was familiar to me. There was no doubt that if the cable lowering the cage snapped, we would crash to the bottom and die on impact, if not before. I voiced my thoughts to no one in particular but an inner voice admonished me. 'Hazards of the job young man, but better not put such dark thoughts into the devil's mind.'

"It does not matter how many times you go down the shafts, Masauso. The feeling of dread still envelops you each time the cage takes you deeper into the dark, lifeless bowels of the earth. For a moment, you feel detached from the real world," Chemasi my friend had warned me before my first day. Watching the solemn faces around me that refused to acknowledge the fears I had voiced, I remembered those words.

Going down into so dark a place was a frightening experience but working in a tunnel alone was even more so. After we got onto the landing, or what we called the platform, the foreman dispatched us all into various tunnels that branched off, like veins, in different directions. The miners worked in twos, threes and on rare occasions, alone. We used pick axes to break rocks, carefully working along gold veins that twisted and turned, determining the direction the tunnels went. We shovelled the ore into buckets that we carried to the platform, and from where they were loaded into the cage and taken up to the surface. The Mine Management gave us industrial gloves to prevent blisters on our thumbs, though the gloves made it difficult to get a firm grip on the mining tools. The work was hard. It was not only back-breaking but it broke our spirits as well though we took care to bottle up these feelings and leave them behind in the tunnels, to be buried with shovels in the dust. To the people outside, we emerged from the shafts as hardworking miners who were simply hungry and tired but very brave and strong. What they did not know was that a man is as strong as he is driven. For me the driving force was poverty and survival. Simply put, the job had to be done. That was our life.

After several hours of digging and shovelling, the miners went home to bathe, eat and sleep… in that order. Those of us who had time off the following day went out to

drown our sorrows in *masese,* some kind of opaque beer, in the sweltering heat of the asbestos-roofed dwelling that served as a beer hall. On the other side of the compound, John Mack and his kinsmen sipped ice-cold beer and clinked glasses of wine in the air-conditioned coolness of Patchway Valley Country Club. After a bit of relaxation, they exercised and kept their bodies toned and strong by playing tennis. They also played golf on the lush green plains that were regularly watered with sprinklers. At times I acted as a caddie for one of the bosses when he and his colleagues played. I sprinted after stray balls as *bwana,* pristine in his whites, strolled at a leisurely pace to the next hole. I got a few bobs and a curt nod at the end of the game for my efforts, the only time my presence was acknowledged. On the large veranda of the cool, grass-thatched Sports Club, the men's wives cradled glasses of wine in one hand and in the other they held dainty hand fans with which they swatted flies away from their beautiful faces. In the swimming pool a few feet away, their children cooled themselves off under the ever-watchful eyes of the sweaty nannies in crisp, starched uniforms.

Back in the tunnels, we continued to labour as the world above us either slept or went about their daily lives, oblivious to the blood, sweat and tears flowing miles below their feet. Life for us labourers went on like that for a long time; labour and sweat... then five shillings, sixpence and a tickey at the end of the month, with rations of beans and maize meal thrown in every Friday. Life was not easy and the work was not without danger. We were always aware when we went down the shafts that we were taking risks with each trip but when disaster strikes, it is shocking all the same. One afternoon during my shift, one like any other, my lantern went off, leaving me in darkness so thick that I could not see my hand in front of

me. I thought I was getting a glimpse of what death must be like; total darkness, complete silence, not a sound or any form of activity… no life. The atmosphere was eerie, scary and funereal. I put my tools down and tried to light my lantern, without success. Although I knew it was hopeless to shout and call out for help, I did so all the same. I was amazed and thrilled when, with the first attempt, I heard sounds. My excitement soon turned to dismay when I realised that the sound coming to me was my own voice bouncing back on the tunnel walls and filling up the vacuum. The echoes made the darkness even more eerie. I decided to try and grope my way out of there but, after bumping into rock outcroppings a few times, I abandoned the idea. I was putting my life at risk. It was possible to hit my head on over-hanging rocks and be knocked out flat, or I could bleed to death. Terrible things could happen to a miner trapped underground in the dark. We were not supposed to try and find our way out anyway, in the evernt of an accident. At the end of each shift, the supervisor blew his whistle, which summoned all the miners to the meeting point. We had about half an hour to get there. If anyone was missing, a rescue team would be dispatched mmediately into the tunnel. I therefore resolved to wait until my absence was noticed and a team was sent out to rescue me.

The hardest part was the waiting. Unable to see the dials on my wristwatch, I had no way of telling how much time had elapsed since my lantern failed. I had no way of knowing if the other labourers were still shovelling away, totally oblivious to my predicament, or whether they had finished work and had somehow failed to notice my absence, which was impossible anyway as the foreman did a roll call and a head count as well. If you are in a desperate situation however, you imagine the impossible and the worst. My thoughts wandered to incidents of miners who had lain in tunnels for days waiting for rescue

after a tunnel had collapsed, trapping them inside. I thought too of miners who had got injured and bled to death before anyone even knew rocks had collapsed on top of them.

On one occasion, a rescue mission failed after dynamite ignited prematurely and blew up rocks, completely blocking the tunnel entrance and trapping miners who could at first be heard pleading for help, then for food and water until all they desperately wanted was just a drop of water to quench their thirst and wet their parched throats. I had a feeling that my situation was not that bad, but I also knew that no situation could be considered light as long as one was stranded underground.

After sitting for what seemed like hours, I decided to take the risk and find my way out. It was better for me to die trying to save myself than to wait meekly for a slow, agonising death. I felt suffocated by the dust and the darkness, and I had to move. I was sweating from fear and the air was becoming stuffy and hotter. I decided to crawl out of the tunnel on my hands and knees. It would normally take about half an hour to walk back to the meeting point, but without a lamp to see my way out, it was impossible to make it within that time. I dreaded banging my head on protruding rocks, or tripping and getting myself in worse jeopardy than I was in already. It turned out to be one of the most unnerving experiences of my life. About halfway down the tunnel, the rescue team found me. They later told me that I was exhausted and delirious. My knees and feet looked as if I had been nailed to a cross. My stomach was badly bruised and had horrible cuts that criss-crossed over it. I was taken straight out and to the clinic where I was treated. Mother pleaded with me not to go down the mine again. Though the experience had scared me, I did not wish to be mocked by other men as a coward, so I was back at work within

weeks, going down the shafts, shovelling the ore into buckets and delivering it to John Mack and Company for smelting. After all, as the saying went, you can only have one accident underground. More than that is personal bad luck and one cannot blame it on the bosses. Either you survive or you do not. I had survived mine and I had nothing more to fear.

* * *

Paydays were a major event in the compound. One group of workers got their wages mid-month and the other at the end of the month. As the money was not enough to last the whole month, we lent each other a bit of the little we got. On paydays some workers refused to surrender their wages to their wives, others drank themselves senseless. Some took a few swigs of the intoxicating opaque Chibuku beer before going home to sleep like the dead, hoping for just one day to banish their hardships to the back of their minds. But then hardships were not always banished to the back of people's minds on paydays. Trouble brewed even in the most stable homes. I can remember an incident that took place during my childhood one hot afternoon, the day after one group of mine labourers had received their wages. Father was dozing in one of the two cane chairs we had in the sitting room and I lay sprawled near his feet, savouring the coolness of the cement floor as I tried to concentrate on my school work in the smothering heat. Mother was somewhere outside with my sister, getting the afternoon meal ready.

Suddenly, from out there an ear piercing scream shattered the calm of the afternoon. At first I thought it was Mother, but when a limping figure burst into the sitting room I recognised our neighbour, Ronika. She and her husband lived with their three year old daughter in the house directly in front of ours. Ronika was the only woman at Patchway Valley Mine who was addressed by her given name, despite the fact that she was married and had children. Her eyes darted about the room like a cornered rabbit. Before Father could react, Jemiya, Ronika's husband, pushed past the main door of the house and strode into the kitchen, roaring like a wounded beast. His terrified wife ducked into my parents' bedroom just as her husband was entering the living room.

The moment it occurred to Father that Jemiya and his wife were having a fight he instantly shot out of his chair, now fully awake, waving his arms about and shouting. I dreaded a fight between Father and the much younger Jemiya, but I had no doubt that Father would beat Jemiya senseless. Father's skill with his fists was legendary, though I had never seen him engage in a fight at home or elsewhere. I hastily scrambled to my feet just as he bellowed, "Get out of that bedroom this instant, Ronika! You and your husband get out right now and take your stupid fight back to your house. Out, out!"

I was shocked, and so was Mother who, by now, was standing in the doorway between the kitchen and the sitting room, just a few feet behind Jemiya. Emboldened by Father's rant, Ronika's husband took several more steps into the sitting room and was heading towards the bedroom from where his wife could be heard whimpering. Just then, Mother shot past Jemiya and planted her feet firmly in the doorway, between the terrified woman and her aggressive husband who stopped in his tracks. Mother started hurling abuse not only at Jemiya, but also

at Father and all men in general, calling them cowards and bullies. Her arms flailing in front of her, Mother challenged Jemiya to dare take just one step towards her bedroom.

"You miserable son-of-a-no-good father! Dare you take a single step towards my bedroom and I will teach you a lesson your mother neglected to teach you," she growled, her face contorted and her teeth gleaming white against the curling lips. I had never seen Mother in such a state before. Jemiya was momentarily shocked by the unexpected challenge, coming as it did just a few seconds after gaining what appeared to be support from the head-of-the-house himself. Assuming that Father's word had more authority than Mother's, Jemiya looked straight at her and raised his fist. Alarmed, I quickly got off the floor from where I had been observing everything. Mother did not flinch. With deliberate slowness, Jemiya brought his fist down on his chest and thumped it hard with each word to emphasize his point.

"I, Jemiya," thump, thump! "go down dangerous mine shafts, risking *my* life while this greedy, useless cripple remains snug in bed, yet she dares demand my wages as if she has a right to them. Tell that woman in there that if she wants money, she had better go and slave for it as I do. I, Jemiya," thump thump, "have every right to spend my hard earned money in any way I wish!" Then wagging his finger at Mother he said, "*You*, tell that woman in there that if she is not out of there by the time I count to five_"

"Hey, you! Don't you dare point that ugly finger at me, you ill-mannered brute. And if your wife is not out by the count of five what will you do then, Jemiya? Tell me, what will you do? Shove me out of the way and drag Ronika from the room where I sleep? Dare you try it, and today you will get to know why a dog is not able to laugh despite its ability to grin, as the Shona people say. You are nothing but a pathetic bully, Jemiya." Mother did not

generally shout, and even then she was not shouting but she could barely control her rage. Then turning to look at Father, she sneered, "And you there, how can you turn away a helpless woman who seeks refuge in your house when it is obvious that she will instantly be pounced upon by this snarling animal? Does a stone sit in your chest, *Ababa a*Masauso?"

"I do not know who is at fault and_" began Father before he was abruptly cut off.

"This is not about who is right or wrong, but who is in danger of being maimed or worse. Have you never heard Jemiya bellowing in the middle of the night like a wounded beast while his poor wife and child_"

"*Heyi, heyi!*" fumed Jemiya. "The way I choose to discipline my family is nobody else's business but mine. *Sha!* Who are you to_"

"And you there," shouted Father, pointing his finger at Jemiya. "You can shout at your own wife in any manner you want but__"

"Not in this house!" Mother's shrill voice pitched in. "Jemiya *cannot* shout at Ronika in this house_"

"But don't you dare, I repeat, don't you dare shout at my wife, especially in her own house, you ill-bred layabout!" boomed Father's angry voice.

"You people, just give me back my wife and I will leave this instant,"said Jemiya, his voice no longer threatening but pleading.

"*Blati furu!* Did you leave your wife with me that you should come here and ask me to hand her back? *Nxi,*" snarled Father.

"What is she running away from in the first place?" Mother asked.

"He beats me up if I do not serve him meat with every meal, yet he squanders all his wages on beer and women," shouted Ronika, suddenly sounding very bold from behind the safety of Mother's body in the doorway.

"You shut up over there or I will break your one good leg, then you will know who is boss in this marriage. You have a very big mouth. Now you listen very carefully: *I* spend my wages any way I want and nothing is going to change, now or ever, so you had better get used to that fact, you stupid useless piece of garbage! If you know what is good for you, you will come out of there this instant. These people are not going to protect you forever. I will get you. Just you wait and see."

"And you, *Ababa a*Masauso, how can you call yourself a man when another man has the audacity to force his way into your house, flaring his nostrils and flexing his muscles as if he owns the place?" Mother scolded Father.

"You are a beast, a dog without a tail! I want you to kill me today. Yes, you have to kill me today. You coward, come and kill me now!" screamed Ronika as she made half-hearted attempts to push past Mother while at the same time aiming spittle at her husband. Without turning around, Mother effortlessly shoved Ronika with one hand and she staggered back inside the bedroom where she crashed to the floor with a thud. Jemiya looked at the two women in amazement before shifting his gaze to Father who was struggling to suppress the laughter bubbling in his chest. He opened his mouth to say something but snapped it shut wordlessly. Jemiya shook his head and laughed as he walked away, and Father's pealing laughter rolled out after him. Mother turned to Father with disapproval, then she told him to leave the house while she comforted Ronika. The two men caught up with each other outside. They could be seen waving their hands and shaking their heads all the way to the beer hall. Ronika too could be heard giggling as she emerged from the bedroom.

"Love and war are brewed in the same calabash,' observed Mother. "The only difference is in the way they are served."

Not all disputes between husbands and wives were solved amicably. One domestic incident involved a labourer who beat his pregnant wife to death and, with the help of a workmate, tried to make it look like she had taken her own life. There was a lot of gossip, speculation and whispers about the death. The Mine Management would normally have reported the incident to the police in Gatooma but in this case they did not. Whether an incident was reported or not depended on whether there was a shortage of manpower at the time. The bosses did not always regard it as necessary to have a useful labourer locked up in the *stoeks* when they could make use of him in the pits. As far as they were concerned it was just the death of yet another migrant. The incident was merely one among many that occurred at the Mine once in a while, so the Management did their bit in assisting with the burying of the body. They got the Mine carpenter to knock together planks of wood for a coffin and they provided a tractor to transport the body to the graveyard.

By sunset it was all over and as good as yesterday's event. What else was one to do, they argued. After all, the savagery in the labourers reared its ugly head now and again, and it was nothing to destabilise the calm of the workforce about. At the same time, one could steal a bar of soap from their employer and go to prison for months. Nothing was ever certain at Patchway Valley Mine. It all depended on the mood of the bosses. Fortunately, violent deaths happened only rarely.

Pay days made us all forget, if only temporarily, the hard work that was our daily grind of drudgery. I could not contain my excitement when my first wages were handed to me at the Mine offices where we queued to receive them from the Mine clerk. I gave my wages to Mother who put them in a tin under her bed for safekeeping. I saved a little at a time for three months before I had saved enough to go

shopping in town. At the first opportunity, my friend Chemasi and I boarded Ruredzo Bus Service to Gatooma. It was my first trip to town and was therefore full of revelations. No one had told me back at the Mine that in Gatooma there were places that, as black people, we were not allowed to go, places reserved for whites only. We were stared at with contempt and even open hostility as we walked down Cecil Street towards Cameroon Square. I had gone into town with a heart full of hope but left with only a handful of goods and disillusionment. On my wages I was only able to buy a tiny wireless, not because it was a necessity in my life but because it was something to boast about.

I bought Mother a pair of *mariposa* and Nchesa and Wezi each got a pair of tender-foot canvas shoes. I made sure they got the best brand, Super-Pro. In my enthusiasm at going shopping for the first time ever, I spent my money recklessly. By the time I had bought what I wanted_ and also what I had not planned to buy but which had enticed me from shop windows_ I had only enough money for my fare back to Patchway Valley. It did not take long before I started regretting buying the useless wireless. I cursed my folly in buying a contraption I hardly had time for. If I was not working underground, I was sleeping off the fatigue of the previous shift, or I was out at the beer hall with my friends, playing a game we called 'slug'. On the few occasions I found time for the wireless, I had trouble tuning it to clarity, and succeeded only in getting garbled sounds or ear-splitting shrieks that exasperated me until I felt like flinging the annoying object down a mine shaft. I cursed myself again and again for spending my hard earned wages on an object that failed to give its money's worth. The next few months were easier as I became more prudent with my wages, a big portion of which went towards our food. Mother stopped working till every bone in her body ached. On some days she not

only smiled but laughed as well. It was at that stage that I realised just how difficult our lives were as poor, uneducated black migrants. Like us, *abwana* were migrants yet they were not looked down upon. The locals were black Africans like us, yet they shunned us. We did not seem to be appreciated by either group and we made excuses for their behaviour. We were not educated, we were labourers, we were black, and we were only migrants who had no claim to either the land or the jobs.

Though we did not have much in the way of possessions, we considered our lives to be enriched in many other ways. We had each other, we were bound by the traditions of our people and we did not need blood relations to find closeness with each other. A child to one was a child to the other. The whole community was one big family. A shameful deed brought disgrace to the whole clan just as good deeds were a source of pride to all.

Then one day, Father came back. His return was a joyous occasion marked with ululating, drinking and dancing. Mother said over and over again that she had always known deep in her heart that Father would come back. She cried and laughed, and cried and laughed again until we could not tell anymore whether she was crying or laughing. Father's return filled her with so much joy it was touching to see stars shine once again in her eyes. Sadly, unbeknown to Mother, the husband she knew went away and never came back. In his place was a stranger who bore little resemblance to Bhaureni the man she had lived with for more than ten years.

Although I was by then employed and entitled to my own single quarters, I still lived at home. Mother worried that the walls of the so-called *mudhadhadha* were damp and therefore likely to make me ill. These *mudhadhadha* dwellings were single room dwellings attached to each

other to make long rows of accommodation for those who were not married. The walls of the hideous rooms were very thick, which made the interior hot and uncomfortable in the hot weather and cold in winter. But then these dwellings were not built for comfort, but to serve a purpose. Mother did not want me to go and live there but for most young men like me who had never had a room all to themselves, these dwellings were a kind of haven. She wanted to wash my dirty and sweaty overalls and to cook my meals. She said that to be able to bear the work I did, I needed to eat well. In other words, Mother meant that I needed her, but I stayed because I thought *she* needed me. After all, there was only herself, my brother and my sister at home. I wanted to live by myself like my friend Chemasi, but I understood Mother's need.

The unexpected return of Father meant I could now ask for my own accommodation. I was promised one within a few months, and I did not mind waiting. Father was back and I wanted to spend some time with him. The few years he was away had left me with only a hazy picture of a kind and loving man with a voice full of laughter. However, within weeks of his return it became obvious that the man we had all sorely missed and whose return we had eagerly awaited for so long had become a different man altogether. It was hard to comprehend that this was the man whose absence over the years had created a huge void in our lives and made Mother miserable. In his place was a foul-mouthed, impatient and loud stranger who was never satisfied with anything. He complained about the food being unfit for humans to eat, and that the portions were meagre, he said the bed was too hard and uncomfortable and it made his back ache, the children were noisy and an irritant to his tormented soul. Gradually, the excitement with which we had welcomed him back slowly began to wane.

My siblings and I walked nervously around Father for we never knew when he would explode. If we could, we avoided being in the same room with him altogether. His moods were unpredictable and he had no patience with whoever got in his way. Gone were the cosy evenings around the fire when we all chatted as a family while roasting green mealies. The slightest thing could set the old man off and the aftermath was always a sad, tearful and sorry situation. The laughter faded from Mother's life and her eyes welled with tears more often now with Father back than they did with him away. It saddened me to see her like that because I knew how much she had missed him.

I remembered the nights when she would sob quietly alone in her room, usually after a hard day picking cotton on the farms. I thought too of the years of hardship, loneliness and anxiety on her part. Despite all that, Mother urged us to be patient with Father and try to understand him and give him time to settle down. Mother's concerns went deeper than she let anyone see. One day I overheard her talk in whispers to her friend *ana*Phiri, the same woman who had urged her to remarry and get on with her life.

"He has changed, *ana*Phiri. He is certainly not the same man I used to know."

"That is to be expected, *Amake* Masauso. Three and a half years_ or is it four_ is a long time to be away. Surely the man cannot be expected to just come back and fit into your lives effortlessly. Allow him time to adjust."

"I know the war is bound to have changed him but not to that extent, surely?" said Mother with sadness in her voice. "The father who used to love his children so much now thinks they are a nuisance. The calmness in his nature that used to balance my exuberance has been replaced by a turbulence of mind that goes deep into his soul, burrowing further into his sleep."

"Meaning what?"

"*Ana*Phiri, *Ababa a*Masauso screams words that are not fit to come out of the mouth of a respectable man. His lips are like the rectum spewing out what the gut cannot bear to keep within it. Words I have never heard of, and whose meanings I can only guess, spew out of his mouth with such venom it scares me. Last night he leapt off the bed, crouched in a corner and started shouting, 'Fire! Fire!' You should have seen his eyes, *ana*Phiri. They were terror-stricken and absolutely terrifying! It was as if he was confronted with a horror he was trying to fight and get away from at the same time. I had never seen him like that before. It filled my heart with dread. As he shouted, *Ababa a*Masauso leapt from one corner of the bedroom, to hide under the bed just as I jumped off it. We almost collided in mid air. It would be hilarious were it not so pathetic. I looked nervously under the bed as I thought that was where he had seen the fire, but there was no sign of it, not even smoke."

"That is strange indeed. Where would the fire come from? He has not taken up smoking now, has he?"

"Yes he has, though he never smokes inside the house. He always goes outside to light up and he comes back only when he has discarded his cigarette butt. He complains though that the *chimonera*[62] he gets from friends is inferior to the cigarettes he is used to. *Ababa a*Masauso has become a difficult man to live with…" Mother's voice trailed off as her eyes took a far away look.

"*Amake* Masauso_"

"*Ana*Phiri, if it were only his nightmares, I could learn to live with them. I can live with him like that but I cannot… I cannot bear him touching me any more. That man is no longer human. To make matters worse he calls me Kamwendo."

62 rolled up cigarettes

"*Amake* Masauso_"

"The man has turned into a beast. I do not know what the war did to him but I know for sure that he is now a beast. I do not want him near me." Mother started sobbing softly and quietly, as if resigned to her misery. With Father away, Mother had suffered loneliness and hardship, but she never once lost hope. She lived for the day her husband would come back. The woman whose voice I was listening to was one without hope, and was bewildered by the unexpected turn of events.

"Be patient *Amake* Masauso, and give him time to adjust. I am sure he will get settled eventually," urged *ana*Phiri.

"You just do not know how hurtful he has become. You have no idea, *ana*Phiri. The man who used to love me tenderly, and whom I missed sorely for all those years came back to hurt me terribly. Things can never be the same again, ever."

"But he has only been back one month, *Amake* Masauso."

"Yes, but it has been one of unimagined brutality. The children cower behind me when he is around. I am scared for them and for myself. I wish I could leave him, but where would I go? I have neither a father nor a mother to take me back. You know they are both deceased. The thought of going through a lifetime of these horrors fills me with dread."

"You have to be strong, *Amake* Masauso. The greatest challenge for a woman is to be strong enough to bear the burden that marriage is."

"I would rather die than live the rest of my life like that, *mubale wanga*. I know I just can't do that. I know I can't. I just can't. *Iyayi!*" sobbed Mother. "Isn't the life of a woman so unfair? Life is really hard, *ana*Phiri. When my husband was away my life was hard, but with his return, it has turned out to be even harder! While he was away I

knew what to expect; loneliness, hardship and self-pity. With him in the house, I do not know what to expect. I am forever apprehensive, expecting him to lash out even when there is no provocation at all. I cry most of the time and my heart is filled with fear. With the return of my husband, I ceased being the wife of a man *who-is-not-really-a-husband-but-a-shadow*, to become the wife of a *husband-who-is-not-really-a-husband-but-a-ghost*. Though one is not much better than the other, I would rather live with shadows than ghosts."

At that point, I moved away. It hurt to hear Mother lament her woes and at that moment I hated Father. I could not understand the change in him, but I could not bear to see him hurting Mother. The lovely person that he once was had been replaced by some monster whose demons we did not know how to deal with. I too had often heard him stamping in the bedroom, shouting and swearing late at night. I decided then and there to leave and share Chemasi's room while I waited to be allocated my own. Mother's misery made me feel bad about my decision. I did not wish to leave her with a man she was scared of but I had to go. It appeared she had finally accepted that the man she loved got lost at war. Everybody at Patchway Valley Mine knew that Father had changed. The friends who had been eager to welcome him back gradually stopped visiting. The Mine Management would not give him back his old job and they made him the 'night crier', a job he hated at first but which he soon went about with zeal. Instead of going round in the early hours of the morning and knocking only on the bedroom windows on the houses of those workers due on the four o'clock shift, Father simply roused the whole compound with his loud singing, military style. At the top of his voice and often off-key, Father sang any song that came to his mind, but he had two favourites he never failed to sing;

Ndofamba munzira yakaoma
Ine misha yekuDenga
Tichiti aleluya, aleluya
Aleluya, aleluya, wokuden

At his most unabashed he would go;

"Heyi, heyi aBhaureni
Siya mukazi pamubhedha apo,
Uyende kunchito, aBhaureni."

Whenever Father sang the last song, I wished I could just bury myself deeper in my blanket and never wake up to face the compound dwellers the next day. However, we all soon got used to it. His job was a blessing in that it got him out of the house in the middle of the night, and when he got back he was too sleepy to stay awake all day. Mother made sure she cooked him some food very early in the morning so he could go straight to sleep and leave everybody else to have a peaceful day. That way, she managed to live side by side with the ghost without the threat of it haunting her. She stopped crying so much but she never regained her smile. I moved away from home to go and live with Chemasi. It was time for me to grow up.

KERESIYA'S STORY
(1934-1974)
Patchway Valley Mine, Gatooma

Had I known how much grief I would experience in the last few years of my life, I would have treasured my earlier years even more. My children filled my life with joy and I had a good marriage. I was far happier than most women I knew. My husband did not take all his wages and gamble them away at a game of *njuga,* nor did he spend them all on beer and other women. He did not drink to excess and he did not get alcohol on credit at the local beer hall as some of the miners did. The father of my children never beat me up nor did he ever refuse to give me his wages throughout our entire married life. I was not like some of our neighbours who occasionally woke up with swollen faces and broken teeth the night after their husbands got their wages. My husband was indeed a considerate man and I was forever grateful to him for that.

I lost my parents when I was very young. Father went away to fight in the war of the white man and Mother died sometime after that, leaving me orphaned and alone among strangers in a foreign land. No one had any idea where, in Livingstone, my father's people could be found. So with no blood relatives to take me in, it was eventually decided by the elders of my tribe that I be raised by *a*Mpinganjira and his wife, an elderly couple who had no children of their own. I had been in school for only a year when they took me in. They looked after me well but it is never easy to feel a mother's love for one who did not suckle at your breast. I found my new mother rather distant, which made me feel like an outsider at times. Now and then I felt like a burden to them though they never said so, at least not when I was within earshot. At times my new mother showed me tenderness but I never stopped wishing I still had my own parents with whom I

had been very happy and whom I missed a lot. I cannot say that I had an unhappy childhood with my new parents, after all they gave me a home when there was no one to take me in. *A*Mpinganjira was easier to talk to than his wife though. He was a good storyteller who often had me and his wife enthralled with the ever-fascinating tales of the clever *Kalulu*[63] and his extremely stupid uncle *aNyane*[64] which he told in the evenings as we sat around the fire and roasted mealies and ground nuts. I was happy at home and I was equally happy at school. I started school later than other children of my age. Father_ my real father who later went away to war_ had tried twice in the past to get me enrolled in school but each year the teachers had declared me too young and sent me back home.

"Sorry *a*Tsogolani," said the Head Teacher to Father when he took me to school in the year he went away. "Your daughter is too young to start school yet. Next year, perhaps."

"AHedhi Tichara,[65] how can you say Chimwemwe is too young to start school this year? Our neighbour's daughter, Shupikani over there, born two full moons after my daughter, is already in Sub B. You accepted her last year yet you want my Chimwemwe here to wait yet another year, how can that be fair?" asked Father in a voice that was more of a plea than a demand for fairness. In the queue with us were other parents and their children. At the beginning of each year, those children who wished to enrol for the Sub A class queued with their parents for enrolment on the first day of school.

63Hare

64Mr Baboon

65Mr Head Teacher

I had stood in the queue with Mother the year before, but we had been sent home and advised to try again the following year. The next time around, Father decided to take me there himself. He had no doubt that he would be able to convince the head of the school about my maturity and have me accepted.

"But your daughter is still too young," the Head Teacher's voice had boomed in the quiet morning.

"I heard you, *aHedhi Tichara,* but if I, the father, cannot tell you what year my daughter was born, how can you possibly know that she is not old enough to start school?"

"Simple! Come here, er... what is your name?" asked the Head Teacher, beckoning me over with his finger. I looked at Father and then at the man in front of me. I was undecided and confused. But because I desperately wanted to start school so that I could proudly wear the lovely maroon school uniform, after only a moment of hesitation I stepped forward, eager to demonstrate that I was clever and old enough for Sub A.

"My name is Chimwemwe," I said as clearly as I could. After all, getting admitted into the first class depended on just how clever one was, so I thought.

"All right, Chimwemwe. Put your right arm over your head and touch your ear on the other side," said the Head Teacher. I attempted to do as instructed but my right hand failed to reach the left ear.

"See? I told you so. Not old enough to touch the ear with the hand on the opposite side, definitely too young to start school!" said the Head Teacher without malice but obviously very pleased with the logic of his method.

"But she was born before Shupikani over there. Even Marizani who was born in the same month as my daughter is already in Sub B."

"That may be so but since you people do not have birth certificates, there is no way we can prove who is

older than whom. We have to use one consistent method in order to be fair to everyone."

"*Bhesefesiketi, bhesefesiketi*, of what use is that piece of paper to anyone when *I* the father am here *in the flesh and blood* to tell you when my daughter was born? How can *mabharani* who is miles away in Gatoma know when Chimwemwe was born unless I tell him? Do I really have to travel *a-a-all the way to Gatoma* just to tell some clerk how many summers ago my daughter was born so he can give me a piece of paper to bring back to you before you will believe me? Are you telling me that you will not accept what I say unless I tell it to the clerk in Gatooma first?" asked Father, unable to hide his exasperation.

"I am sorry, *a*Tsogolani, but there is not much I can do about it. Rules are rules. Try again next year."

"Chimwemwe may be short but she is as old as_"

"Next year, *a*Tsogolani. Bring your daughter back next year," emphasised the Head Teacher, cutting off Father's pleas and dismissing us with a wave of his hand. "Who's next there? Stand in a straight line or I shall send you all back home with your parents. Your right hand above your head. Touch your left ear. Good boy. Write down his name, Madam Chimuti. Very good, should be in the junior soccer team in a few years. Next *apo*!"

Father was disappointed and so was I, but he did his best to comfort me on the way back home.

"Do not worry too much about it, Chimwemwe. Next year or even the one after, you should be able to start school. There is no great hurry. In any case who needs education anyway? After all you are merely a female child. One day you will get married and settle down with a husband and have children. School is just to help you pass time as you grow up. You only need to learn how to read, write and count money while you wait to get married. Even if you do a year or two of school, that should be all you need, really."

"But I wanted to start school this year, *Ababa,*" I grumbled petulantly.

"I know, but you heard what *aHedhi Tichara* said, 'too short'. Maybe by the beginning of next year you will be tall enough to be accepted but if you are like my mother back in *Vhingisitoni*[66], then you shall wait until your hair turns white before you reach the acceptable height. Anyway, *aHedhi Tichara* says you have to wait until you are tall enough to touch your ear."

"But why, *Ababa?*"

"Why what?"

"Why must I touch my ear?"

"Because, Chimwemwe my girl, *aHedhi Tichara* says so."

"And why does *aHedhi Tichara* say so?"

"Because... because... ah, you ask too many questions, you. Will you be satisfied only when you see my hair turn white from your pestering?"

"But I need to know why. Please, *Ababa.*"

"Sometimes I do not know the answers to these never-ending questions of yours, Chimwemwe."

"But you do, *Ababa*. You know the answers. You just don't want to tell me. How can a big person not know the answer to a simple question? *Amayo* says children must never argue with adults because adults know better. You are supposed to know everything, so tell me, *Ababa,* why *aHedhiTichara* says I must touch my ear__"

"I do not know, believe me," said Father, barely concealing his exasperation. "You know that I never went to school. I am not like these educated teachers who know everything. After all it is to them that our people take their letters to be read. As soon as you start school and can read and write, we will not need to do that anymore. That is the

---

66Livingstone

main reason I want you to go to school, so that you can be able to read letters from home."

At that stage I did not care about the reading and writing part of education. My sole interest in school lay in my yearning to wear the maroon uniform with the pink stripes on the sleeves and on the collar. I hoped Father would be able to afford it when I started school. I did not want to be like Shupikani who, although she had been in school for a whole year, still did not have one. Her father could not afford it, and the two dresses she owned had patches all over them. I was lucky that I did not have to wear clothes handed down from elder sisters like she did because I had no sisters, or brothers for that matter. I liked our life like that but I envied Shupikani and her seven brothers and sisters whenever there was work to be done.

"Oh, so you receive *karata kuchokera kumuzi*[67]?" I asked, hoping to convince Father that my eagerness to start school was because I too was interested in the reading and writing of letters.

"*Iyayi,* not yet. I am waiting for you to learn how to write on my behalf. There is one problem though. I do not know the address of the village where I come from."

I did not understand what an address was but I decided not to pester Father about it because I knew that being asked about things to which he did not have an answer annoyed him. Only a moment before, he had shown irritation when I asked him why the Head Teacher insisted that I be big enough to touch my ear. The address, whatever it was, surely was not that important, or else Father would have found a way of borrowing one or looking for his own until he found it if he was really determined to send and receive letters from people in

---

67letters from home

Northern Rhodesia. Then I decided he must know of a way and dismissed the thought from my mind.

"You should be able to read, write and count after a few months or so in school, so it doesn't really matter how late you start school. Hopefully, it will be before you are old enough to get married," said Father, clearing his throat before aiming and shooting the phlegm onto the side of the path along which we were walking. Married! The idea appalled me.

"Get married, *Ababa*?"

"Of course yes, Chimwemwe. Every woman gets married, just as every man goes to work."

"But I want to go to school!" I mumbled, petulantly flapping my arms against my sides.

"Yes, and after that?"

"Then I will get married."

"That is exactly what I am saying, my girl. When the time comes I shall find a good man who will look after you very well. I know the tribes whose men look after their women well. I do not want some lazy *muchuwere*[68] to ill-treat my little angel. You are the very image of my mother and I want only the best for you."

That made me happy indeed. I wanted my life to follow that of my mother's; marry a good man, have children and look after the home. That was what I desired most, even that early in life. I knew Father would marry me off to a good man from a good family of a good tribe. Sadly, that never happened.

Father never came back. He was not there to see me finally get accepted in school the following year. Mother died several months after Father's departure. I was never told

68 a person considered to be inferior, hopeless and insignificant

the details of her death. In fact, at first I was simply told that she had gone away. I assumed she had gone on a journey somewhere faraway, maybe to visit Father, but it turned out that she had travelled towards the direction of heaven. For months afterwards I would gaze wistfully at the clouds in the sky hoping to catch a glimpse of Mother. On numerous nights I went to sleep crying quietly because I missed her very much. Regardless of how closely I scrutinised the clouds, Mother was nowhere to be seen, at least not easily or regularly. There were a few times though when I could have sworn that I saw her smiling face on the moon, gliding slowly past the clouds. On such nights I experienced a mixture of sadness and elation; sadness because she was visible yet not reachable, elation because after numerous nights of disappointment at not seeing her, Mother had finally made an appearance.

The school I had yearned to attend for so long was not all bliss. Our lessons did not always take place indoors because there were not enough classrooms. For a week, we would have our lessons indoors then have them outdoors the following week in order to give the other Sub A class a chance to learn indoors. It was not too bad during the hot, dry months but it was a nightmare during the cold season. Mercifully, the sun broke through the grey clouds on some mornings, taking the chill out of the air a bit. Whenever this happened, our teacher would bring out her chair and sit basking in the sun, leaving us to get on with our work. On those cold, sunless mornings the mood of the sky was adopted by the teacher as well. Mrs Muropa made us do our writing in the sand while we either sat or squatted on the ground. Using either sticks or fingers, we wrote down whatever she dictated. At first I did not understand what she said when she spoke in Shona and since she could not speak my language, she had no way of explaining anything to me in a way I could understand. The English lessons were even worse, but not as bad as learning Sums.

How I hated the subject! "Ten take away three. Write that down and the answer to it in the sand. I will come round and see who has got the answer right and who hasn't." At first I used to struggle to do those numbers in my mind. In the end I resorted to using my fingers, and toes too if the situation demanded it. Mrs Muropa went round from pupil to pupil looking at their work, the cane in her hand ready to come down hard on the back of whoever got the sums wrong. Sometimes the cane came down with rather too much eagerness. The closer the teacher came towards me, the more nervous I became.

I was not bright, but I did not need the teacher to call me 'dunderhead' before I could acknowledge the fact. As far as I was concerned the Sums were some squiggles in the dust and try hard as I might, I could never make sense of them. The longer I looked at them, trying to work out an answer, the more they made my head spin. My teacher called me 'dunderhead' or '*sadza rekurasa*'[69], as her cane descended upon my back nearly every day. School was a nightmare I could not wait to get away from. Things did not get better as I moved to higher classes. I envied those who found school work easy because I had no doubt that education had its benefits, somehow.

I had been living with my new family for several years when I had a very frightening experience, one that was to transform my whole life. I ran screaming to 'Mother' to show her that I was afflicted with an illness whose exact nature I did not know. I was due to go to school, but I was told to stay indoors while the elderly women of our tribe were summoned to come as soon as they got the message. I knew that something terrible was happening, but the panic that immediately followed alarmed me even more and I started crying. I pleaded with God not to take my life just yet. I cowered in a corner of the living room as the

69 A waste of sadza or food

women who had arrived went on to converse in low tones in the other room. There was no doubt they were talking about my illness. I was scared. I was able to identify the voices of *ana*Phiri, *Ambuya a*Baidati and *Ambuya a*Ifaresi who were in our house together with 'Mother'. The three other women were considered to be among the oldest women of the Chewa tribe in the community. Their wrinkled and lined faces were an indication of not only their age, but of their wisdom as well, so we had always been told. They were also the traditional tribal midwives through whose hands most of us had made our entry into the world. That they should be summoned to our house because of my condition was no doubt due to the seriousness of the illness. I cringed as I watched them approach me with solemn faces.

"*Tiyeni,*" said *Ambuya a*Ifaresi, reaching for my hand and beckoning that I get up and come with her. Her voice showed neither sympathy nor concern.

"Where are we going?" I asked, pulling away.

"Do not worry my child, everything will be explained to you soon," said *ana*Phiri, her voice tuned to the right tone designed to elicit the opposite response to what I had given to *Ambuya a*Ifaresi. "It will be over in a few days' time and you will soon be back home." I started sobbing out of fear and confusion. I was going to be taken away from home during that period and I had no idea what was wrong with me, or where the women were taking me, or how long for. It would be over in a few days, one of the women had said, but what length of time is a few days, I remember wondering. Five days in a month or a year are few indeed but in a week they are almost the entire week itself. That was indeed a long time. A few days in one period, an eternity in another!

"When you come out you will be a child no more, but a woman. You will have a new name and a whole new life

starting for you. That is what *chinamwali* is all about," explained *ana*Phiri.

The relief I felt was immense at the mention of that often whispered about ritual. I was not seriously ill after all and I was not in danger of dying. I was going for initiation instead, the performance of which required that I be confined in the house of one of the elderly women. That meant being isolated from the whole community while I underwent training, to emerge only when the wise women were satisfied with the results of my transformation from girl to woman. My relief was soon replaced by anxiety over the secretive ritual that saw girls step swiftly and instantly into womanhood. *Chinamwali* was shrouded in a high level of secrecy that was observed and respected by all, from the elders in the community to the initiated themselves. It was a closely-guarded secret that was kept from children and from males of all ages. It was taboo for those initiated to discuss it with anyone other than women who had already undergone it. As I and other girls grew up, we had always thought of initiation with awe, anticipation and dread as well. The occasion marked a turning point in the life of every girl. I was therefore excited about the whole thing. My isolation lasted a week, a period during which my life was transformed from childhood to womanhood. I went in innocent and came out wise beyond my years. The training I received included being a good subservient wife, among other things. I was to exercise tolerance to the demands of my husband and to put his needs before my own. I was instructed on the proper way to make my husband happy at all times, and I was never to be the source of his troubles. Instead, I was to be the refuge upon which he rested his weary heart. I was always to remember that a good wife never got tired and had food ready as soon as her man got back from work.

Most important of all though, a really good wife never suffered a headache. Being a wife sounded very easy and I looked forward to the role. I understood that a lot of things would change. I was no longer to bathe with the uninitiated in the communal baths and I would get pregnant if I let a man get too close to me. I no longer went out unescorted and I was careful how I conducted myself in public, especially in the presence of males. On coming out, I was presented with a lovely string of multi-coloured *mukanda* that I wore around my waist. These beads caressed my waist when rolled against the hips. The length of time one spent in isolation depended on how soon one mastered the teachings and showed obedience. Within a week I was ready to leave. I had had enough of the early morning cold baths. I went in as Chimwemwe and came out as Keresiya, a person with new knowledge and a new name.

I was considered to be a new person with new opportunities ahead of me. Everyone in the compound was obliged, by tradition, to acknowledge my new status as an initiant. I was supposed to be presented with a gift by those who greeted me in the first few days of completing the initiation. Money was usually offered and if one did not have anything to give they were not supposed to greet me. If they did I was to shun them. From the day I came out I began preparing for the major role of my life. At the age of thirteen years I was ready to start life as a mature woman.

According to our custom, I was expected to get betrothed or married off immediately or within months but that did not happen in my case, which relieved me and made me slightly anxious at the same time. I hoped to get a man and settle down. After all that was the whole purpose of the ritual, to prepare girls for both the rigours and the joys of married life. Unlike most initiated girls, I was not compelled to leave school immediately. I

appreciated the decision because I had come to enjoy spending time with friends in school though the acquisition of book knowledge was still a big problem for my small head. What I came to enjoy most was playing netball. Whether one played in the junior or senior team was determined by one's height. Because of my small stature I played in the junior team with and against girls who were far younger than I was.

Though I was not very bright in class I was at least able to read and write in cursive, an achievement I was proud of. It was a pity that Father had gone away before I could write letters to his relatives on his behalf. Not many people wrote to relatives from our homelands. Only those who arrived in later years were able to keep in touch because by the time they left their countries of origin, the Missionaries had established mission schools and telegraph posts in rural areas, making communication possible. As for those of my father's time who had left long before, there was no contact with the relatives whose addresses we did not know. We knew about them, but we did not know them. To us they were those people left behind with whom our only bond was by way of the remembered stories told with nostalgia by the elders of our community, and through the fading and often unreliable memories of others. The people in our homelands lived in our past, not in our present.

With the loss of my parents, all links with any kind of family, however remote, were severed. That meant I had no one and the people who mattered in my life were at Patchway Valley and they were not many. For most of us, the Mine was a world unto itself. Throughout my childhood migrant labourers had continued to cross the borders into Southern Rhodesia by train. The few who had managed to keep some kind of irregular contact with the relatives back home did so through letters, the receipt of

which was a big event. The recipients were informed of significant events in the lives of those back home; illness, deaths and marriages. That the news got to their destination several months later did not matter. Of greater importance was the arrival of these letters, for some were known to disappear altogether after many months on the steam trains and coal wagons.

For most of the Mine children school was just a passing event in our passive lives. We saw no reason to widen our horizons, therefore education did not have any real purpose to serve in our closed lives. The white man spoke to us in *chilapalapa,* a mixture of several *bastardised* languages devised to make communication easier on both sides. This rendered it unnecessary for us to learn to speak proper English. We only needed to be able to count money and make sure that *a*Mazizi, the local storekeeper, gave us the correct change. We had full trust in him though and we knew he would not cheat us, so there really was not much point in learning anything else beyond the basics in reading, writing and counting. Our men continued to go down the mines, one generation after the other. Nothing had changed in almost half a century and it did not look as if anything was set to change in the near future. For us women life went on just as it had for as long as anyone could remember. We grew up well versed in the traditions of our people and we observed rituals with the seriousness with which we observed our roles in the lives of our men.

A year after my initiation, a husband was finally found for me. His name was Domingo and his country of origin was Mocambique. Domingo's people were from a village not too far from Lorenco Marques and he spoke Sena, a language that was so different from mine it was a struggle to understand what he said. Domingo worked as a farm labourer at March Hare farm. He would visit every two weeks and bring watermelons, mealies, sour milk, chickens and on one occasion he brought a live goat for his

prospective parents-in-law. He left them in no doubt that he was capable of looking after me. I too had no doubt that he would be a responsible husband and son-in-law, but I wished he were not as old as *a*Mpinganjira. I hated his bad breath, the crooked and gaped yellow teeth and his sweaty body odour, but I dared not show it. I would have preferred a husband who lived at Patchway Valley Mine so that I would not have to leave my friends and family, but I had to make a home wherever my husband took me. The decision had been made for my own good. That point was made clear to me, and emphasised upon. Initiated as I was, I understood the importance of obeying one's elders and submitting to one's husband.

"Always remember, Keresiya, that it is the man who leads. The woman merely follows. His people become your people and his home your home," advised *Amake* Mpinganjira. I was prepared to take her advice even though I felt rather sad about my impending marriage. There was nothing exciting about it and I was not looking forward to it. However, it was a role I was prepared for.

On the weekend *a*Domingo was expected to bring the bride price agreed between him and my 'parents'_ two live chickens and a few bobs_ after waiting all day, word eventually reached us that he had been 'arrested' by his master for stealing farm produce and livestock. 'Father' cursed his ill luck while I was greatly relieved. Only 'Mother' did not appear to be concerned one way or the other. Not long afterwards, a search was begun to find me another husband. It took only eight weeks and the shy, migrant labourer of the Chewa tribe came to give my father the two chickens he wanted. Marriage was the destination of my life and on that day, I knew I had finally arrived. I had seen the man around the compound_ Patchway Valley Mine being a small place_ but I could not remember ever talking to him. Besides being far younger than the previous would-be husband, this one spoke my

language and seemed shy and kind. I had nothing against him though I found very little to say to him at first. Marriage to him meant I would not have to leave the only place I knew, the place where I was born and raised and where I wished to spend all of my life.

Two weeks after the bride price was paid, *Ambuya a*lfaresi escorted me to my husband's place, and thus began my new life as the wife of Masauso Nyirenda. I was fortunate in that my husband was a kind and understanding man who did not make many demands on me. All he wanted was a tidy home, a good meal at the end of a hard day's work and a hot bath in which to soak his weary limbs and soothe his aching muscles. I was not bubbling with joy but I was not miserable either. I was just playing my role and did not have strong feelings either way. I was contented, knowing that it could have been a lot worse with someone like *a*Domingo, for instance. My new husband had no family that we knew of. His mother was said to have left his father and taken her children with her to go and live at Milverton Farm, quite a distance from Patchway Valley. Masauso had at first kept in touch with them, so he said, visiting at least once every few months to take them groceries after his payday.

As time went on, their worlds drifted apart and gradually, the bonds that tied them loosened. By the time 'Father' arranged for me to become Masauso's wife, there was no contact between them anymore. Soon after I became his wife, Masauso went to Milverton Farm, only to be told that his mother had left the place a while back. It was rumoured that she had gone to live with the widowed supervisor of a dairy farm a long distance away. I settled down to the respectability of married life with Masauso without the mother-in-law versus daughter-in-law problems that beset many couples in the early stages of marriage. Married life was just as I had imagined. It was calm and I was contented. Though I had no choice in the

man I had married, I was not forced into it. It was my duty and I had no reason not to oblige.

Not long after I was escorted to my husband's place, I discovered that I was expecting a baby. The mornings were difficult as I felt dizzy when getting out of bed. The smell of certain foods made me feel nauseous. Then on the other hand I had absurd cravings for stuff that had never before passed through my lips. I went to the outskirts of the compound looking for anthills from which I carefully scrapped soil that I took home to eat whenever the craving for it gripped me. I started drinking rye brewed beer that I had never drunk before. Masauso was a wonderful husband who did his best to get me the paw-paws that I craved during the early days of the pregnancy. However, as the stomach got bigger, the mere sight of the fruit made my stomach turn. My husband teased me about how spoilt I was becoming, staying in bed as late as I wanted and having him fetch water for our chores. A few months into the pregnancy, my stomach stopped being just a bump. It moved, first to one side then to the other, slowly and gently. Then came the kicks. Masauso was fascinated by the movements, but they made me feel embarrassed. While Masauso was at work I sought the company of other young mothers who offered all sorts of advice, and this differed from person to person. What they all agreed on though was that childbirth was the most excruciating pain each of them had ever experienced. They said it was an ordeal to be survived. I dreaded the day obviously but since it was an experience almost every woman went through, I did not think I needed to dread it very much. Some women I knew had as many as eight children, not counting the occasional miscarriages here and there.

With three months to go, my pregnancy was beset with problems. I experienced terrible pain in the back, and

at times the pain tore across my stomach from side to side. One morning I waddled over to my mother's house. The moment she set eyes on me she knew something was wrong. She panicked and sent for one of the three traditional midwives in the community. While we waited in the house, I explained what form the pain was taking. 'Mother' sat there wringing her hands helplessly and sighing heavily. "Keresiya my girl," she addressed me, breathlessly. "If I had any advice to give, I would help you but having failed to conceive myself, I wouldn't even know where to begin. *Ambuya a*lfaresi whom you know well from your days in *chinamwali,* will tell you all you need to know about your condition."

When *Ambuya a*lfaresi arrived she did not waste time before examining my heavy bump. I watched anxiously as her cheeks twitched now and again. She prodded my stomach, pressed harder in some places and, without raising her head, asked no one in particular, "Who is responsible for the herbs?"

"Herbs?" 'Mother' and I chorused as if with one voice. *Ambuya a*lfaresi looked from one of us to the other with narrowed eyes. We both stared at her, our own eyes showing total lack of comprehension.

"I see," the old woman said at last. She turned to my 'mother' and said, "Do not worry about your girl here. She will be fine. All first pregnancies are beset with problems."

"Thank you very much, *Ambuya a*lfaresi. I didn't know what to do," my 'mother' thanked her.

"You do not need to thank me, *Amake* Mpinganjira. That is what we the old women are there for. But like I said, there is nothing to worry about. First time expectant mothers worry at the slightest ache and pain. I shall take Keresiya back to her house and explain to her what she needs to do as the pregnancy progresses."

The old woman proceeded to do just that. She led me back to my house and over a cup of tea she explained a few things.

"Some pregnancies are calm and trouble free, but not so others. You just happen to have one that needs a bit of extra attention. The baby is not stable in your womb so I shall make it my duty to make sure it is."

"Not stable, how?" I asked, worry and fear creeping into my voice.

"Your womb could spit the seed that nestles within it_"

"No!"

"I said it could, but that is not to say it will, Keresiya. What you need now are herbs to stabilise your womb."

"But I do not have any knowledge of herbs," I wailed in despair.

"I have already told you that I shall take care of all that, from this moment till your baby is due."

The relief and gratitude that I felt then made my eyes well with unshed tears. I thanked her profusely.

"Have you decided yet who is going to deliver your baby?" asked the old woman. I stammered that I did not know that I needed to ask someone. She chuckled.

"You need to prepare clothes for your new born. You shall need to buy a new dish in which your baby will be bathed, and you will also need new razor blades with which to cut the umbilical cord. I will tell you more of what you need as the weeks go by. I shall come back later today with those herbs I told you about."

By the time *Ambuya a*lfaresi left, I had made up my mind that she would be the one to bring my baby into this world. For some reason I felt safer with her. When I mentioned this fact to other mothers, they all agreed it was a good decision.

"That old woman can rightly claim to have heard the first screech of about half the young people in this

community," said *ana*Phiri, a statement that was obviously not true. She was both a friend from my childhood and also one of my neighbours. Her advice meant a lot to me. In the next few weeks, *Ambuya a*lfaresi did as she had promised and I was given concoction after concoction of herbs. Though the pain did not go entirely, its intensity diminished greatly. I was told that was to be expected. I often felt so hot at night that we had to open the window, which was all right if Masauso home, but I could not sleep with the window open whenever he was on night shift. I sweated and itched all night and by morning my skin was raw from scratching. I had headaches most afternoons and struggled to wash our clothes, do the cooking and the general tidying up of the house.

Early one morning, I woke up and felt a sticky kind of wetness down my leg. My husband was snoring softly by my side. My first thought was that I had wet myself in my sleep, so I sought to get up and out of bed as quietly as possible. I did not want Masauso to see my shameful mishap. Furthermore, he had gone to sleep after an exhausting evening shift in the pit, so he needed the rest. When I tried to sit up, a searing pain shot from my navel downwards and I screamed, all the caution not to wake Masauso cast aside. He woke up in a daze and rubbed his eyes as he tried to shield them against the early morning rays of the sun criss-crossing on the one pillow that we shared. I was still trying to stifle the first scream when another sharp pain tugged at the sides of my stomach. By the third scream I was gasping for breath like a fish hauled out of water. I had one hand on my stomach while the other was at the base of my bent back. I thought I was getting cramps. Later, I would vaguely remember my husband shouting my name in a panic-stricken voice.

The next thing I knew, *Ambuya a*lfaresi was leaning over me. I was confused. I could not understand why she was present. My baby was not due for at least another two

weeks. The searing pain continued to come at brief intervals. *Ambuya a*lfaresi told me that the baby was coming and I was in labour. She and a companion were going to deliver my baby. I did not think I was in labour. My mind told me that I was dying. The pain was far too much for anything beautiful to result from it.

After what seemed like a very long struggle between me and my womb, everything went quiet. I could feel myself slowly drifting off. When my eyes focused again, the first thing I saw was *Ambuya a*lfaresi's face swimming towards mine. Her eyes looked everywhere but at me. In the dish beside her was a bundle swathed in a small blanket. *Ambuya a*lfaresi went on gathering together the rags and the other things she had used for the birth.

"I am sorry, Keresiya. The baby had no heartbeat," she said, her eyes focused somewhere below my chin.

"What? What are you saying?" I heard myself ask feebly.

"The baby was born without a heartbeat. I am sorry."

"You mean my baby is… is, handicapped?"

"I am very sorry Keresiya, there is no easier way of saying it. I have asked *Amake* Mpinganjira and a few of the elderly women in the community to come and help."

The ordeal I had just experienced had left me rather dazed. In my mind was the image of a baby that was somehow deformed, maybe with a leg that was shorter than the other, a crooked arm or six fingers on each hand. I looked at the old woman with little comprehension of what she was saying.

"As soon as the women arrive, they shall go out and look for an anthill somewhere out there," continued *Ambuya a*lfaresi. "That anthill shall embrace deep within its womb what has been ejected from yours."

My mind struggled to come out of the fog surrounding it. Many thoughts and images crowded my

mind; the afterbirth, the umbilical cord, burying that lot and many other thoughts.

"I do not know why it happened," continued the old woman's voice in the darkness of my mind. "You still had two more weeks or so to go. The little boy was not ready yet for this world and he has refused to stay."

It was then that I screamed. At least I tried to but only tortured sounds of groaning escaped my lips. I was told firmly but kindly to keep quiet. From then on, everything was foggy. Later, all I could recall were muffled sounds and fleeting odours. I remembered the thoughts too, and the herbs whose smell assaulted my nose, food that refused to go down my throat without a struggle, tears that I was forbidden to shed, an infant that my arms could never cuddle nor one that would suckle from my breast, breasts that would swell to the size of giant paw-paws in expectation of nourishing a life, but that would give up for lack of stimulation, a baby whose loss I could not mourn, and for whom no one could shed a tear, and for whom condolences could not be offered, ground that held a life so precious yet too insignificant to merit a resting place with a lasting mark. Tradition dictated this, and it dictated that... By sunset there was no sign that I had ever expected a baby, except for the stomach that was still to realise it had let go of its bundle. The baby's clothes were removed, as was the dish. Masauso and I did not know what to say to each other, or how to say it. So we said nothing.

We were both relieved when I found myself expecting again a few months later. This resulted in yet another baby without a heartbeat, as did the third and the fourth. By the time I turned twenty years old, the remains of four of my babies lay buried somewhere on the outskirts of the compound. I had no idea where exactly since it was taboo that I should know. Babies who died at birth were not buried in the same graveyard as the adults. The loss of my

babies hurt badly at first, but I soon got used to it. The pain was gradually replaced by sadness and a sense of hopelessness when I realised that I was being labelled a witch because of my misfortune. '*Ali kuzid'yera vana vake,*[70]' it was maliciously whispered behind my back. It was fortunate that I had a caring and understanding husband who turned out to be a big comfort. I cherished Masauso greatly for his kindness, but I was sure the feeling had nothing to do with love. I did not feel a deep sense of longing for him or an aching emptiness when he was away, neither did my heart beat rapidly in excitement at the sound of his voice or in anticipation of his arrival. But because of his kindness, I slowly grew fond of him as the years rolled by. As a married woman, it was considered disrespectful for anyone to call me by my actual name. Because I had no child and could therefore not be called Mother of so-and so, the community addressed me as *ana*Banda, my totem. The longing for a child to hold and cradle in my arms grew stronger with each baby I laid to rest. The desperation grew with each pregnancy. That my husband understood my pain was a blessing, but that did not lessen it. Late one night, during the later months of my fifth pregnancy, I lay awake in bed, engrossed in my thoughts. I assumed Masauso was fast asleep, so I was quite surprised when his voice cut through my thoughts.

"Worrying is not going to help in any way, Keresiya. Let us just hope everything goes well for us this time."

"What are you talking about, and why are you still awake at this late hour?" I asked.

"How can I fall asleep when you toss and turn with every breath you take? I know what is on your mind, *mukazi wanga.*[71] But why torture yourself worrying about

70 She is devouring her own children

71 My wife

something you have no control over? What will be, will be. Only God knows what His plans for us are this time."

"Masauso, how can you honestly tell me not to worry? It is now more than six years since I became your wife, a period during which I have been nothing but a big disappointment to you. Most women would have filled the house with children by now."

"Keresiya! Have I ever complained, or told you that I am disappointed in y__"

"You may not have uttered the words but that is only because your heart is big and kind. You do not wish to hurt my feelings. I am certain that deep in your heart you long for a child."

"I am not going to lie and say I do not wish for children, because I do. I know you do as well."

"Of course I want a baby that I do not have to bury alongside its umbilical cord. Why, of all the women in this whole community, has it got to be me that go through the whole of my life suffering? Why, Masauso?"

"But distressing yourself is not going to help, *mukazi wanga*. Stop weeping, please."

"How can I not cry when I have let you down so badly? You have no family, nor have I, what better way is there to enrich our lives if not by having children of our own, as many of them as we want? Sooner or later you will tire of this situation and you will eventually get rid of me. Oh, I feel so hopeless and useless. Maybe you would be better off sending me away."

"How can you even think of such a thing? If you were not crying I would really have had a good laugh. What an idea! If we are not meant to have children together then so be it."

"No, you can get another wife."

"Who, me?" Masauso was appalled. "Can you honestly imagine me with two wives? Me, Masauso, a polygamist? Never! While polygamy may be an

indulgence for those back home, or the locals who are well settled, it is definitely not for a struggling migrant labourer like myself."

"But you need a woman who can give you living children, something that I have failed to do__"

"Keresiya, you of all people should understand that a man and his wife can live together and be very happy even though they may not have any children. You were raised by such a couple yourself, and you say they were so fond of each other it made you feel like an intruder at times."

"Well, there was something special about those two."

"Shush, Keresiya. Wipe your tears and try to get some sleep."

"AMasauso, do you think the reason I cannot have a child is because I do not pray?"

"What a question! But I do pray."

"I know you go to church but it is more like a club than anything. I have never heard you pray here at home."

"Oh well, I do not need to. I pray whenever I go to church."

"Which is once a month, roughly."

"I work some Sundays. Better one Sunday a month than not at all. Would you like to come to church with me the next time I go?"

"Um, no. I am not ready yet. I will let you know when I am."

"What are you waiting for?"

"For a better understanding."

"Of what?" asked Masauso, baffled.

"Of who we worship, and why."

"It is God, of course!"

"Which god, that of the white man or one of the various gods of the Shona people? I understand none of them. The Shona people worship various ancestral gods, so how can I, a foreigner, also worship them? They are not

my ancestors so they will not listen to my prayers. From what I hear, these spiritual gods live in the soil. The living quench the thirst of their gods by routinely pouring beer on the ground. At times goats or cattle are slaughtered to feed the hungry ancestors who are said to possess the living through whose lips they speak. The god of the white man lives between the pages of a holy book, or in the heavens above. He is fed from the money collected in church."

"Keresiya! Where do you get these wild tales from?"

"So you think poor Keresiya does not know what goes on in this community? I do know, you know. Sleep well, *amuna vanga,*[72]" I said and turned over.

When the pregnancy resulted in a living baby boy, I could not get over the shock and happiness. I kept expecting him to stop breathing at any moment. After many years of hoping in vain, shedding endless tears of frustration and enduring endless pain, my husband and I were finally blessed with a healthy baby boy who was perfect in every way. When I heard him cry for the first time, I wept. Four times in the past I had listened anxiously for that sound, but my babies had remained mute. Now one had sung into my ears a joyful noise. I was thrilled at having finally given birth to a baby that cried and breathed and did the normal things other mothers took for granted because their babies seemed to do them without any effort. *Ambuya a*lfaresi and her helper delivered my baby as she had done the others before. She ululated and shouted, "It's a boy, a healthy son to dry his mother's tears and end his father's despair. Congratulations!"

Much fuss was made over the fact that not only had I finally given birth to a baby that was going to live, but also that it was a boy. As far as I was concerned it did not

---

72 My husband

matter whether the baby was male or female, so long as he or she was alive, I was a fulfilled mother. My joy knew no bounds and I wanted to go right to the top of the highest alluvial deposit dump at the Mine and proclaim to the whole world that I was a mother, at long last. I wanted the howling wind to carry my voice to lands far and near. I wished the baby to have a name that reflected our joy, but I knew that I would not have much say on the matter. However, there was no doubt that the names of our children would be from our tribal languages, but my people were gradually shifting from the deep-rooted, traditional names of long ago. We tended to give names that were a reflection of the situations we found ourselves in. As immigrants, we had the whole history of our lives to tell and we did so in the names of our children as a reminder of our experiences, past and present. Those names were a testament of our resilience, our fears, joys, hopes and our aspirations. Ganizani, Mavhuto, Madalitso and Kondwelani summarised all there was to say about where my people had come from, where they were and where they hoped to go. It was only natural that as a young mother finally blessed with a baby after many years of mourning, I should wish to give him a name that reflected my happiness.

The sound of my baby crying was not a matter of course but a miracle and a blessing in my life. That is why I wanted him named Madalitso, not Kumbukani, because I did not wish to dwell on the pain of previous experiences. I did not want my son to be called Mavhuto either, because with his arrival our troubles were finally over. The birth of our son was to mark the beginning of happy times, yet I was apprehensive even as I cradled him in my arms. I knew from past disappointments that miracles tended to disappear when one blinked, leaving one doubting either one's sight or one's sanity, if not both. I knew my husband felt the same as I did, but I only got to

know how deep-rooted his fears were when he decided to name the infant Chakumanda.

"*A*Masauso," I gasped, "why do you want to place such a heavy name around the child's neck? Let us name him Madalitso," I pleaded. "After all the pain we have been through is it not proper that we regard him as *madalitso aMulungu*[73] in our lives? You are the one who encouraged me to worship the God of the white man, yet you refrain from acknowledging Him over this miracle. Why?"

"I know, but who knows for how long we are to remain this blessed? To tell the truth, Keresiya *mukazi wanga,* I have come to a point where I dare not hope for that which I have no control over. We may be this boy's parents but we do not have control over his fate, and it is still too early to presume he will be ours for long. So, Chakumanda he will be. Then should anything happen to him, my heart is prepared."

"My husband, you are condemning your own son to walk in the shadow of death. You are setting his tiny feet on the path of death, the very one we have been praying to be steered clear of since the moment we realised I was carrying the seed of life in my womb. Must you point his life towards the grave so soon, even though he protested at birth? Apart from screaming his lungs out, how else was he supposed to show his determination not to take the path taken by his siblings before him? Don't you have any faith, or hope in your God, and at a time when I thought I was convinced! For the little happiness we feel now why don't we, at least, call him Kondwelani? To condemn one's own son to the grave, honestly..."

"Mother-of-the-child, who amongst us can steer clear of the path of death? I live in its shadow every day, and so do you, and so does everybody else. Who among us can

---

73 The blessings of God

claim to be able to dodge it, and ascend to heaven in a chariot of fire like Elijah, tell me?'

'While it is true that no one can run away from it, is it wise though to tempt death?' I begged, almost in tears, but my husband was not moved.

'This boy shall be called Chakumanda and that he shall remain until the day we take him *kumanda* and lay him in his grave."

After that there was no point in arguing further. I was going to have to get used to calling my son by the death-evoking name. It was a name I had never heard before. No one at Patchway Valley had either, and needless to say, everybody expressed shock at Masauso's choice of name. With time, I got used to being called *Amake* Chakumanda. Motherhood suited me and it was a role that fulfilled me and gave me immense satisfaction. I think I became a better wife too. I raised our son with tenderness and care, taking him to be vaccinated against childhood diseases such as small pox and measles.

Together with the other miners' wives, I went to receive the family's rations of beans and mealie-meal every Friday. I joined other wives to take food to our husbands, with our babies strapped to our backs. I dutifully heated water for *Ababa a*Chakumanda to have a hot, soothing bath after a hard day's work. I got used to the sweaty smell of his clothes that I washed every three days, but I could not stand the pungent smell of his sweaty gumboots. Several months after the birth of Chakumanda, that smell was replaced by an offensive one that seemed to cling to my skin no matter how thoroughly I bathed. I could never quite work out its source. One day I took Chakumanda to the clinic with teething problems and happened to mention it in conversation to *Amai* Tino, the community nurse with whom I was friends. "*Amai* Chakumanda, I think you have the disease of the men," she said, averting her gaze. I was dumbfounded.

"*Siki*?" I shrieked, "Me, *siki chaiyo*? No, never!"

"It is possible. People get these diseases now and again."

"But not to people like me, they do not! I am not a whore."

"I am not implying that you are, but there are two people in a marriage."

"Not *Ababa a*Chakumanda! No, he is not that kind of man. Masauso would never do what you seem to be implying. He never has and he never will," I protested, eyes brimming with tears. I knew my husband and I knew his virtues. I recognised too that he was not without vices but taking women outside our marriage was not one of them. Patchway Valley was a small community and I would know if he did. We always heard sooner or later how father of so-and-so had been caught red-handed with the wife of such and such a man, but there had never been any scandal linked to my husband. It was humiliating for those involved and it debased their spouses. The shame of *chigororo*[74] was the worst thing one could put their spouse through, and I knew my husband was far too responsible, considerate and much too kind to ever put me through that.

"Tell me more about this smell, *Amai* Chakumanda," said the nurse who treated me like a sister and a friend. I told her about the stench. I must have convinced her that it could not be what she thought it was because she sent me home with a packet of long, colourful tablets for me and my husband. She explained that Masauso needed to take them too since we lived in the same house and shared everything. The tablets would work best if the smell was not given the chance to shift from one of us to the other. Nothing more was said about the infectious disease, and the odours soon disappeared.

74 adultery

Life went back to normal. Normal for us was getting live chickens on credit from the teachers who reared them, and giving almost half the wages to our creditors at the end of the month. By the second week of the following month, the balance of the wages would be gone, and off to the teachers we would go again to get yet more chickens on credit. So the circle continued. Most families lived on *sadza, mujumbura_* boiled cassava tubers_ wild okra and vegetables. Chicken was therefore a delicacy that most families could afford only once in a while. There was *a*Wayani however, who boasted of eating meat at every meal even though he did not have the cash to buy it with. In the whole of Patchway Valley no couple was as devoted to each other as *a*Wayani and his wife were. The husband would ride his prized bicycle after work, with his wife riding side-saddle, and go to get some chickens on credit from whoever was selling them at the time.

Wayani was not his real name but a nickname he got for always saying, *wayani mwana wody'era terere nkuku ziri mbwe-e kwaMabhachi*? Which meant; whose son eats okra when there are plenty of chickens at Mr. Mabhachi's? Indeed *a*Wayani detested okra and preferred to get chicken on credit, of which there were plenty at Mr Mabhachi's. At the end of the month, when the miners got their wages, all those who were owed money waited by the only gate that led into the compound from the payments office. There, the debtors were relieved of some of their wages before they even got home. Also waiting resolutely by the same gates were women whose husbands were deemed irresponsible enough to visit the beer hall with all their wages in their pockets.

Only those debtors who were notorious for always trying to avoid paying their debts for one reason or another were accosted at the gate. The creditors stood in a queue with their hands extended towards those who owed

money. If the amount owed was disputed, the creditors swiftly whipped out their books with one hand and with the other, pointed to the figure written in black and white.

A story was told with hilarity of one labourer, *a*Mutombo, who stopped by every single one of the creditors and by the time he got to the last one, he had nothing left of his hard earned wages. The next day, when *Mabhuruwayo* turned up at his house to collect the money owed for the clothes that his wife had bought for their little child, there was nothing to give them. Having come a long way, the vendors were obviously not amused. It was always very difficult for them to know when exactly payday was for the miners. It could be anything from one to three days before the very last day of the month. If they were fortunate to arrive on the actual day, they stood a good chance of being paid, but one day too late could mean getting nothing at all, in which case they would have to make another trip the following month. It was therefore to be expected that *ma*Sibanda from Gwanda would be cross when Mutombo's wife said she could not pay her.

"You should have come yesterday," she shrilled. "We paid all our other debts."

"Well, I am here now, so give me what you owe me."

"Too late, the money is all gone now."

"But you knew that I would be back to collect the money this month end, surely?"

"I completely forgot, *mubale wanga,* but do come again next month. I promise you that I will have your money ready then."

"How interesting. If you paid your other debts, no doubt next month you will be saying, '*mwezi siwatu,*'[75] won't you?"

---

75 it is not our month

"Oh yes,' exclaimed Mutombo's wife, smacking her forehead with the palm of her hand. "My head is full of holes this morning. This is what happens when *abwana* do not pay your husband enough money to buy food, then you go to sleep on a stomach full of nothing but water. It muddles your head. Now I can't think straight. What was I saying? Oh yes, indeed it will not be our month. So make it the month after and please, bring more clothes for my baby, eh?"

It was not uncommon to hear those who owed money say *'mwezi siwatu'* upon being asked to settle debts. There was nothing one could do after that except wait for the end of the following month, only to be given the same excuse again and again. If the creditors were a bit lucky the next time around, their efforts were rewarded with a small fraction of the money owed them, even after many fruitless visits in the past. Those who were notorious for evading settling debts rarely did so with the teachers from whom they got chickens, but they repeatedly did it to *Mabhuruwayo.* Sometimes they hid from them and told their children to inform them that they had gone to such and such a farm to attend a funeral, and would not be back till the end of the week.

The early seventies saw a flood of foreign vendors coming into the compound. We called these traders *Mabhuruwayo* because they were all thought to come from Bulawayo since most of them spoke the language of the Ndebele people, iSindebele. By the time it was known that some of them were from Sipolilo, Belingwe, Fort Victoria and Gwanda, the name had stuck already and it was too late to call them anything else. That applied even to those who came from Fort Victoria and spoke a dialect that was commonly known as *chi*Vhitori. We never got to know what their dialect was called in their language because

*chi*Vhitori was not a Shona word, but a corruption of Victoria which was derived from the name of their town, Fort Victoria.

The vendors sold clothes made from different pieces of leftover cloth. That their yellow and red dresses had hems sewn with black or blue thread did not bother us because they were good value for money. We still took them because we considered ourselves lucky to get the goods on credit at the beginning of the month, with the promise to settle the debts in instalments each month-end until all the money owed was paid up.

On paydays, these vendors walked around the compound with their small note books in which were written the names of the debtors and, against each name, the amount of money owed. The women we greeted eagerly and with excitement as we perused their goods were not so warmly received upon their return to collect their money. '*Mwezi siwatu*' was an excuse they were to hear so many times, often driving them to exasperation as they could never work out how the turn to benefit from the coffers never seemed to be anyone else's in the whole compound. Despite these frustrations, the vendors and the teachers had found an easy way of making money out of our needs and they took full advantage of it.

Although traders poured into Patchway Valley to do brisk business, there were some amongst us whose skills served us well over the years. Apart from their jobs on the Mine, their skills were beneficial to the rest of the community. Operating from a makeshift grass-thatched structure, *a*Bhuraki_ so called because of his very black complexion_ cut the children's hair and the men's. He used the only pair of scissors he had from one person to the next. He also shaved the beards of most men, inserting into his prized shaver the same razor for every customer until, with continued use, the blade gradually became blunt and had to be discarded and replaced.

*A*Zuzeya mended our clothes on his ancient foot-pedalled Singer sewing machine that an emigrating former employer had given him to show her gratitude for long service. Operating from the veranda of the local store for many years was *a*Mbewe who repaired our worn out shoes. We called him the shoemaker although he only repaired them, working on heels that got repeatedly worn out on the sides because of the rickets most of us had. I had often watched *a*Mbewe examine a shoe with squinted eyes and pursed lips before cutting off a piece of rubber from an old vehicle tyre. He would shape the rubber into what his mind envisioned as the correct size and shape then smear some glue onto the heel of the shoe and some on the piece of rubber. He would position the rubber patch onto the heel and press the two together, hard. That done, *a*Mbewe often selected a few nails, turned the shoe upside down and hammered the nails into the four sides of the heel. If he deemed it necessary, he would turn the shoe right side up and hammer a few more nails inside the shoe. I hated it whenever that was done to my shoes because the nails were uncomfortable and tended to dig into my heels and cause blisters. We took the same pairs to be repaired over and over again. It was said that *a*Mbewe had only to look at a pair of shoes to know who was standing before him before he even raised his head to acknowledge the person's presence. That was how familiar he was with the shoes, the ability to recognise them anywhere; stolen, discarded, borrowed or mislaid. *A*Mbewe was skilled at his craft but in the end, even he had to advise some people to discard shoes that were beyond repair. By the time the owner grudgingly agreed, the original heels of the shoes were gone, as was the twine or string that had held the hide together in the first place.

* * *

Normal life also meant strapping Chakumanda onto my back and walking to the alluvial deposit dumps where the other women and I collected the fine alluvial soil, called *motoro*, with which we scoured our pots and pans. To get there, we had to go up the rail track on which travelled *ngorovhani,* the small wagons on wheels that transported the ore to the mill. As we picked our way through the crashed stones, we often saw glittering yellow stones. This was the gold Kamupaundi was after.

Kamupaundi was the Compound Manager but we just called him Kamupaundi, which was easier on the tongue. We did not care about gold so we left the ore where it had fallen from the over-filled wagons on the way from he mine shafts to the mills where it was smelted and made into gold ingots. Our people had no use for the useless glittering stones, and though we picked them up to admire, we threw them away because we had no use for them. As far as we were concerned, there was more value in the fine alluvial grains of sand than in the granite grit with bits of gold that was far too coarse for scouring the pots with.

Normal also meant being good, obedient wives, which we achieved by getting pregnant as often as we could. I did my part by giving birth to another child, a girl whom we called Dhairesi. We attended funerals and played *chiware,* a game that was a favourite mid-week hobby for most women. Up to about five women would play *chiware* with many multi-coloured beads, winning some and losing others. It was a gambling game so addictive that the women often neglected house chores and children as they went about satisfying the burning urge to play, to the chagrin of their long-suffering husbands who considered *chiware* to be a vice they were better off

without in life. So engrossed in it did gamblers become that many lost track of time and forgot about the meals they were cooking until they got burnt and the children left to watch over them could be heard shouting, '*Amayo, ndiwo zanyeka.*[76]'

A great number of women became compulsive gamblers. Numerous fights between the men and their wives resulted from that but we could not give up the game. We strung together the beads we won and wore them around the waist as *mukanda.* They were the treasure of every woman. The more layers of beads a woman had, the better she was able to dance to the muted sound of the beads rolling in unison. They were also said to accentuate the waist, making a woman more shapely and admirable. We felt beautiful with the beads, hence the need to win as many as we possibly could. We showed off our waist beads to other women at the communal bath. The more strings of beads a woman had, and the more colourful they were, the more she was envied by her fellow women. They formed part of the few possessions we women could claim as totally ours. For that reason we strove to amass as many of them as we possibly could, and nothing could keep us from playing *chiware* in the hot summer months when there was not much else to do. I can remember in those days a song that derided women who let *chiware* destabilise their marriages.

'Anopenga, ane waya, anopenga
Siyana naye. Akaramba murume
Nekuda chiware saka shamwari
Siyana naye!

(She's crazy, keep away from her
She dumped her husband for the love

---

76 mother, the stew is burnt

Of *chiware* therefore have nothing
to do with her.)

Despite the song and its lampooning of the one game we relished playing, we could not give it up. The thrill of winning took the monotony out of our otherwise dull lives. The beads made us feel beautiful in a way that was unique. To further enhance our beauty, we pierced our earlobes using long, firm thorns and made holes that, upon healing, made it possible for us to wear earrings. Mishaps happened at times, though rarely. If we did not clean our earlobes properly, they became infected and discharged foul-smelling pus. In some cases, the earlobes swelled and became disfigured if they did not heal properly but that did nothing to deter us for we were convinced that the enhancement of our beauty was a far greater reward that outweighed the risk of disfigurement. We just had to choose our time with caution and consideration for the weather.

The cold season was the best time to have the piercing done. The women of the Tonga tribe had the holes on their lobes made so big they needed twigs the size of a cigarette to adorn their ears. *Nyora* too added to our beauty but it was not just anyone who could be entrusted with the delicate task of making the permanent incisions on the skin. Only certain women were experienced to do it, as was the delivering of babies. I had my beauty marks carved by a friend of my late mother when I was a very young girl. On that day Mother had wedged my head between her knees to stop me from breaking free and running away while *Ambuya a*Cheusinje cut into my skin with a sharp razor blade. Four quick sharp strokes on each cheek, and it was over. By the end of the session I had double crosses on each cheek and on my forehead. To make the markings more permanent and visible, *Ambuya*

*a*Cheusinje rubbed ground charcoal powder mixed with snuff onto the incisions, the result of which was a permanent tattoo. Against my light skin colour, the contrast was remarkable and beautiful. Although it had hurt at the time, I was pleased with the result and I was proud of my beauty marks.

Marital strife was part of life in our community but it did not necessarily lead to drastic measures such as divorces. When conflict between a husband and a wife became intense, the tribal chiefs were called upon to resolve the differences and try to save the marriage. These kangaroo courts were held in a makeshift courtroom that we referred to as *sipeshari* since it was a building usually reserved for 'special' events such as the yearly meetings of the tribal chiefs. It was in that building that Isaki accused his wife of committing adultery with *a*Buruzi of Chimusokoma Farm. Ronika did not deny the allegation with the said farm labourer, but she refused though to take any blame for it, insisting that it was entirely her husband's fault.

"How can *he,* of all people, blame me for *chigororo*?" demanded Ronika. "Everyday, Isaki here only gets up to go to work, comes right back to have his food before going to sleep, too tired at times to even take a bath. On his days off he goes beer drinking and comes home either in a querulous mood to provoke me into a fight, or too drunk to help himself into bed. *That,* my kinsmen, is the kind of man I have for a husband, a man who does not and cannot show me either appreciation or affection, in whatever form.

"All I am to him is a cleaner and a cook, nothing else. I prepare his meals, heat his water, wash his clothes and keep the house tidy, but not once are my own needs considered. Anyone would think that after all I do, I deserve to be cherished but it just never happens. I feel useless, hopeless and used. I am nothing in this marriage

but a useful shadow he got in exchange for two or three lousy cockerels. My husband's whole life consists of nothing but *chipani, kugona, kud'ya nimowa,*[77]" panted Ronika, ticking off the fingers of her raised hand, the preoccupations of her husband. "Nothing else exists outside of that, nothing! Absolutely nothing!"

"Our ears are open, *Amake* Dhori, but surely you exaggerate?"

"Oh, is that what you think? In this *komboni,* who does not know how tolerant I have been with Isaki over his drunkenness? Well, if his eyes stray to something that causes them soreness he should have the self respect and the decency to avert his gaze. He should focus his eyes on something that he appreciates more, such as his beer, for example. Ask Isaki here if it is not true that he does not have time for me."

The tribal leaders, the family members, the friends and those presiding over the case conversed in hushed tones in reverence to the solemnity of the occasion. After a while, *a*Kobe, the man leading the proceedings, asked Isaki if what his wife had said was true.

"It is true indeed," answered Isaki slowly, keeping his eyes glued to the floor.

"What have you got to say then?"

"About what?"

"About your wife's complaint that you do not pay her any attention!"said *a*Kobe with exasperation, at which sniggers were heard around the room.

"It is she who is here to be questioned, not the other way round. I lodged the complaint, remember?"

"We are coming to that, Isaki, but you need to confirm or deny what she just said."

"Well, if as she says, I am not a husband to her, how then can she consider herself to be my wife?" asked the

---

77shift work, sleeping, eating and beer

complainant in what appeared to be genuine bafflement, then indignantly went on to say, "If she says I am no husband to her then I suppose *ndili garu,*[78] a proper dog with four paws and a tail." There was more laughter from the audience.

"*You,* Isaki, brought this matter to our attention. We put your allegation to your wife here who has explained why your marriage is in this sad state. Of great concern is failure on your part to recognise your responsibilities towards your wife who today, you accuse of *chigororo.* What have you got to say about that?"

"Palibe!"

"How can you have nothing to say, Isaki? Do-you-or-do-you-not acknowledge the needs of this woman as your wife?"

"A-a imwe, wosanishupa ine[79]*. Vhimata gazi!* Her demands are a blood draining exercise."

It took a long while before the peals of laughter finally died down all around. Nobody bothered to wait for the outcome of the case. We filed out of the building shaking our heads at the hopelessness of the case. There were many more such hilarious cases just as there were many more serious ones. It was definitely more hilarious than the case of *a*Banda who was summoned to court after his wife reported him for beating her up. Her crime was daring to serve their visitor the head of the fish *a*Banda had purchased on credit that day.

"I buy fish mainly for its head. My wife knows quite well that *musoro wansomba* is what I find most delicious. Besides, fish is a delicacy and therefore expensive. It should not be dished out to whoever decides to pass by our house."

---

78 I am a dog

79 *hey you people, do not bother me*

It was agreed that *a*Banda's wife had erred in giving her husband's brother the part of fish she knew her husband to be fond of. Other women had been divorced for less serious failings, she was warned. Those who did not agree with the verdict called the husband a glutton, and nicknamed him *Musorowansomba*. He was called by that name for many years afterwards until nobody could remember his real name anymore. At first he would not answer, but with time he ceased to care and even seemed to enjoy his notoriety. Such incidents were a normal part of our lives.

Births and deaths were normal too, but not the nature of some. When *a*Chetaimu of the Chawa tribe died of diarrhoea, he was buried with haste. He fell ill one day, vomited for four days and four nights and died on the fifth morning. Barely a few hours after his death, people of different tribes had gathered at his house to mourn his passing. His tribesmen washed his body and prepared it for a twilight burial that same day in accordance with their Islamic religion and culture.

Secrecy is maintained about how the body is washed and the tribe does not divulge their customs to outsiders. The rest of us were allowed inside the house only to view the body before it was taken away to the graveyard. We filed into the house slowly and quietly. It was not a funeral like others I had attended before. Unlike other body viewing sessions I had been to where women wailed and tore at their hair as soon as they laid their eyes on the deceased, the Chawa womenfolk filed past the coffin with solemn faces and pursed lips. There was no singing either. Only their red eyes showed the extent of their grief.

I was later to know that according to their customs and religion, weeping for the deceased indicates lack of faith in Allah and His promise of paradise. One does not weep for someone who has departed for a better place, surely, unless one is not sure about the existence of such a

place. After the last of the mourners had bidden farewell to the deceased, the body was laid out on a flat board they called *geneza.* It was this very same *geneza* and not a coffin that carried the corpses of all the Chawa people out of the compound to their resting place at the cemetery. When it was not in use, it was suspended from the rafters of the roof of the mosque on the outside, to be used again for the next dead body and other future burials.

The womenfolk stayed behind as the funeral procession, made up of males only, took away the body of *a*Chetaimu on this stretcher-like contraption which they carried by its four corners. Women were not allowed at burial sites during the actual burial. *Ababa* Chakumanda later explained to me what went on during the burial, and I thought it was a good thing the presence of women was forbidden. I could not imagine myself watching the whole process and not having nightmares later.

Within the main grave was a small chamber carved into the right side of the wall. It was in this chamber that the body of *a*Chetaimu was placed in a sitting position and with his legs bent at the knees. That explained why the burial had to take place within hours, before the body became too stiff to be placed into the desired position. The inner grave was then sealed off and the outer one was refilled with sand and marked as the resting place of the deceased. Mothers, wives and all other female relatives could only get to see the resting place of their loved one the following day. I imagined *a*Chetaimu's widow standing by the side of his grave, muttering a little prayer while a few feet directly below her feet sat the body of her dead husband.

Two days after the death of *a*Chetaimu, *a*Sondo had the same symptoms of the disease that had killed *a*Chetaimu. Five days later, he too was dead and buried. Another four days and *a*Banda died, and then *anaBanda* and *Amake* Tifurani and *a*Mpakha and *a*Marizani. The

whole community was shaken. Never before had death roamed so freely amongst us.

At its most rampant, death claimed three or four victims each week. It was not selective about its victims. Men and women, children and adults, it plucked them all. Then it got so bad that there were two or three funeral gatherings at a time in the compound, with burials taking place one after the other. Fear gripped the inhabitants of Patchway Valley Mine and many fingers were pointed at various old men and women about whom it was said they practised witchcraft. What puzzled everybody was that all the deceased showed the same symptoms of the illness and all of them perished.

Prior to these mysterious deaths, Patchway Valley had been a place where death was a rare and sacred occurrence. The dying of infants was nothing unusual but that of adults happened mostly in old age or as a result of an accident or, from the cough-and-spit-blood disease of the mines. Whenever the mines killed the men, their widows died of misery and despair or from working too hard to support the families. These deaths were expected and therefore deemed normal, but they did not happen all the time. People talked about the ill and the dying in hushed tones. It was an event that happened maybe just once a year, until the mysterious string of deaths began. I could not understand it and I was scared. I knew we were all set to be trapped in this net of death, but I thought Chakumanda was more at risk. I confided in my husband about my fears for our son.

"It scares me too, *Amake* Chakumanda," admitted my husband. "I wish we had never named our son Chakumanda."

"It seems to me like throwing death a challenge," I agreed. I was almost tempted to remind him that the decision to give our son such an ill-fated name had been

his alone and that I had no say in it, but I decided to bite my tongue and concern myself with the issue at hand.

"A meeting was called yesterday by the tribal chiefs. They are concerned about these deaths."

"What can they do? What can *anyone* do? Nothing!" I said, exasperated.

"I hear they are determined to get to the bottom of it. They seem to think that this misfortune is the work of the mischievous hand of man. Someone must have sown the seed of the plant-of-death."

"*The plant-of-death!* What is that?" I asked, perplexed.

"It is a small shrub that, when planted next to a homestead or just outside the compound, grows then wilts and starts shedding its leaves one at a time. For each leaf that falls, someone dies. People will continue to die indiscriminately until the plant has shed the last of its leaves, or until somebody finds it and uproots it." I was dumbfounded. I had never heard of the death plant before, and could not understand why anybody would want to grow such a plant. It seemed a senselessly cruel thing to do. The very idea paralysed me with fear. The bodies of four stillborn babies of mine were buried on some anthills out there and the memory of their loss was still fresh in my mind. Because death had stalked me mercilessly for years, I was gripped with fear whenever I heard it mentioned. I had no reason not to believe in the existence of this evil plant. I was, after all, part of the community that was steeped so deep in superstition it was almost like a religion. We believed in the supernatural, even in the absence of evidence. We whispered and wondered about the mysterious and the supernatural in awe and fear in equal measure.

The mysterious fascinated us more than the obvious. One morning, the men went round the compound looking for the so-called plant of death but they never found it. It would have been a miracle if they had as almost all of

them had no idea what it looked like. A few more people died. The local clinic gave out large quantities of tablets they said were for cholera, whatever that was. We were not ill and most of us did not see why we should take tablets that were said to cure a disease we did not have, but we took them all the same because we were told that Kamupaundi had insisted that we do. The water tanks were cleaned and we were advised to boil our drinking water at all times.

We never questioned the wisdom of the Mine bosses or their word. They feared death enough to tell their house boys, cooks and nannies to stay away until they were called back to work. On its part, death recognised the superiority of the whites and left them alone. After some time, the mysterious illness stopped as suddenly as it had started. We could only assume the plant had finally shed all its leaves. Life went back to normal… but not for long.

Our lives were thrown into upheaval by the arrival of Chikanga in the compound. The presence of this mysterious man in our midst was announced to the whole community through our tribal chiefs, *vamfumu*[80]. Each *mfumu* then went back and sent the elders of his tribe to individual homes to explain the practices and intentions of the diviner. He was there to sniff out witches and witchcraft practices. We all trembled at the things he was said to be able to do, but there were some who trembled more than others.

The tribal chief of the Tonga, *a*Mfitizarimba, told us that Chikanga had been invited to perform certain rituals because Patchway Valley Mine was full of witches who were becoming more and more daring and claiming the lives of many. The witchdoctor was said to possess super human powers that enabled him to see into the dark souls of those who dabbled in black magic. No one quite knew

80 Chiefs

where he came from and various versions of the source of his supernatural powers were whispered about from ear to ear, each of them more intriguing than the previous one. The most captivating was the one about his having risen from the grave.

"It is whispered that once upon a time in a certain land, Chikanga lived as a wizard who possessed evil powers. He brought misfortune to those he cast a spell on. After years of causing misery, he died of some strange disease. He had been dead a few days when he arose from the grave, with instructions from God to repent and go back into the world and help destroy evil," explained *a*Mfitizarimba.

"The name Chikanga struck fear in the hearts of many people, so the rumour goes. Once he cast a death spell, his victim would not live to see the sun rise the following morning. That was how evil the man was. Now he comes back into the world as a changed man and working against the very forces he once represented." The tale intrigued us as much as it filled us with fear. We were not used to coming face to face with the living dead, however noble their mission in our midst might be.

"What if he wrongly accuses someone of practising witchcraft, *amfumu*?" I asked anxiously because Chikanga was said to sniff out even the smallest *mankwara*[81]. I was worried because I had *chipfungaidzo* that I burned in the house whenever I could not sleep well. Apart from that, I also had a few herbs given to me for wind, and some bits to chew and spit into the children's faces whenever they had nightmares.

"It is not possible, *Amake* Chakumanda, for the witchdoctor to mistake someone for a witch."

"And if one has a few herbs that are not harmful…?"

"Like what exactly?"

---

81 herbal medicine

"Like the black concoction that some mothers rub onto the fontanelles of their babies, you know, er, when the skin sags into the grove on the top of the baby's head?"

"There is no need to worry about that, *Amake* Chakumanda. Who doesn't know that now and again our people resort to our own traditional methods of healing? Herbs have been known to cure aches and pains, as well as other invisible ailments. It is common knowledge that since the time of our forefathers, the boiled leaves of certain trees ensure that a cold does not get worse. Burning dry ginger or the leaves of certain plants will ward off evil spirits and negative forces. It is herbs that are used for evil purposes_ black magic_ that concern Chikanga. However, you need to bring all the herbs you have in your house when you go before him. *Kamupaundi* has allowed us the use of the women's clinic."

Male and female patients went for treatment at separate clinics. Men were attended to by a male orderly, and women by a female nurse.

"As you know, the building has two entrances, one on either end. Chikanga will be in one of the middle rooms. Every adult will have to go before him, through the door facing the west. The way he wants it is like this; you walk towards him, with his aides on either side of you. He will look into your heart, search it then wave you away to go back the same way you came, if you are declared clean but if you are a witch he will let you come right up to him. He will proceed to tell you the form your witchcraft takes, and then arrange to cleanse you. You will be required to leave through a different door on the opposite side. That way, the whole compound will know you have been denounced," explained *a*Mfitizarimba.

I was still not convinced that it was not possible to make a mistake and see evil where there was none. I had often heard it said that witchcraft was an evil supernatural

power passed on from one generation to another within the family. It was generally believed that witches could also recruit other people without their consent or their knowledge by rubbing some kind of finely ground herbs into small incisions made on the skin. The initiated, it was said, would become witches and start practising the craft without being aware of it. It bothered me that anyone could be a witch and not know it. I imagined myself denounced in the eyes of the whole of Patchway Valley Mine for something I was not aware of and had not gone into willingly.

After all it had been maliciously rumoured in the past that I caused the deaths of my unborn babies through witchcraft. The presence of Chikanga filled me with fear and made me miserable. I was reluctant to go before him but I had to. The tribal chiefs had gone to great lengths to explain to us that it was not a matter in which we had any choice. Refusing to go before Chikanga would cast suspicion on the particular individual. The first day of witch hunting went without incident, as did the second and the third. Everyone who went in there was declared clean and waved away to come out using the same entrance they had gone in. They emerged to be congratulated by a crowd of women ululating and tribal chiefs who shook their hands. It was beginning to look as if all the talk about the man's supernatural powers had been nothing but myth after all.

I went in on the fourth day, feeling slightly emboldened by the fact that no one so far had been denounced. Once inside, my knees began to knock against each other. With Chikanga's aides on either side of me, I somehow managed to place one foot in front of the other, gazing ahead where the omnipotent stranger who was about to decide my fate sat on a reed mat. He took one look at me before averting his eyes and looking at the wall on the

other side. I almost fainted then. He had not waved me away and with each slow step I took towards him, I willed him to raise his hand and signal for me to go back.

My heart started pounding very fast. I was sure that Chikanga could see with his once-evil-now-good-eye that years back, when I feared that my husband would leave me because of my failure to give him children, I had sprinkled some herbs into his food in order to strengthen his love for me. It was not my idea, honestly, I wanted to confess, but my tongue felt like heavy lead. The whole idea had been my friend's, never mine. She had assured me that it was not bad magic, but good love potions that would bind our hearts together forever. Surely that was not a sin?

I willed my tongue to utter those words in a bid to convince the great man of magic that my intentions were pure. My mouth, however, was dry and I could not say anything to save myself, so my fate lay in the hands of some stranger in our midst. Three more slow heavy steps, then he raised his hand, looked at me and without uttering a single word, the traditional healer waved me away. The aides let go of me and the legs that had felt heavy and reluctant to move only moments before suddenly felt springy and catapulted me back to the door through which I had entered. The relief I felt was immense, beyond description! I wanted to shout to the whole world at the top of my voice that I WAS CLEAN! I opened my mouth to scream but no words would come. When I finally regained my senses and was able to talk, my voice was drowned by thunderous applause. Numerous high-pitched voices of women ululating and children screaming filled the air. Men shook my hand and congratulated me. The beating of the drum echoed in rhythm with the beating of my joyous heart. At long last I was finally vindicated. I had lived for years with the shadow of those stillbirths casting a sombre gloom in my life. I was happy

that at last all of Patchway Valley Mine would know that I did not practise witchcraft.

The next three people to go in after me were the first to emerge from the door opposite. Their denunciation was heralded by a chorus of jeers from school children who were standing by the door just for that purpose. *A*Nkhata and his wife emerged with their heads bowed. They were booed and followed all the way to their house. Some adults even joined in, my husband among them. *A*Mutombo and *a*Musorowansomba were also denounced and booed. Those condemned were required to bring all their crafts to Chikanga who, in the presence of the tribal chiefs, burned them before proceeding to cleanse the witches. Once cleansed, one was not supposed to take up witchcraft again.

Within two weeks, Chikanga had finished casting out evil. He had seen every adult in the community, except the teachers. The Headmaster, a man of God, denounced Chikanga's deeds as unChristian. A devout Christian said to know the Bible from the book of Genesis to the book of Revelation, Mr Rwizi challenged the myth that Chikanga had come from God, sent back from the dead to do good deeds to atone for his past evil ways. During the cleansing process, nothing was said about God, nor were verses quoted from the Bible. No one was encouraged to confess their sins, repent and give their lives to God, so the man of mystery could not be His messenger, argued the Headmaster. He refused to have his teachers subjected to what he called the pagan practices sweeping through the Mine community. Some of the Mine dwellers were disgruntled about the Headmaster's decision but the majority of us did not really care what the teachers did. While others argued that teachers were mortals just like anyone else and could be evil and practise witchcraft in much the same way as everyone else, for some of us they were not really part of our lives. They existed as a slightly

superior minority among us, yet made no effort to learn our language while forcing our children to learn theirs at school.

Altogether four couples, including *a*Nkhata and his wife, were denounced. Three women were accused of witchcraft, among them my neighbour, *Amake* Evherina. The day after *a*Mutombo was denounced, his body was found hanging from the roof beams in his bedroom. He left behind a widow and three grown up children. Chikanga left Patchway Valley and was never heard of again. No one knew where he went. Long after his departure the legend of the witch hunting Chikanga remained the talk of the Mine community. The man with the paranormal powers had not spoken much to people but those to whom he spoke claimed he had a red piece of cloth in his mouth, patched onto the right cheek. This, so went the legend, was to keep hidden the part that had begun to decay before he was raised from the dead. What truth there was in the legend of his life and death and his supernatural powers, I did not know, but I did see Chikanga with my own eyes. I was brought before him for witch hunting and was declared clean. Years later we heard about two or three more witch hunters, but none of them was Chikanga, and they were sooner or later unmasked as charlatans. Chikanga was real. He had come into out lives from nowhere and he left to go back wherever he had come from like a breeze that comes all of a sudden, and is soon gone, leaving no trace of its having ever been there.

Life went back to normal after the cleansing. Normal sometimes meant the not-so-normal. At Patchway Valley Mine, as in every other place, whenever somebody died, we laid them to rest with the other dead in the graveyard. Their place of rest was on the outskirts of our compound, an eerie place where not even the sound of birds singing

could be heard. The only time we dared venture back there was either to bury another body or clear the place of weeds and grass. We placed cups, plates or dishes on the graves to mark the resting places of loved ones, after first boring holes on these utensils to make sure they would be of no use to the living.

Whenever the tribal chiefs felt the graveyard was overgrown with weeds, they organised groups of people to go and clear the place of weeds. It was unheard of that anyone would go there alone. So scary was the place that nobody dared contemplate it, which is why the whole community was alarmed when little Chinai and his friends were found playing among the graves a few months after his twin was buried there. *Ambuya a*Siteriya, who had gone to her field some distance beyond the graveyard, brought the boy back to his mother, holding him by the hand as the two friends with him_ one of them Chakumanda_ followed meekly behind. Their house was two houses away so I dashed over there to get my son. I had been calling him for some time and he had not responded. I got there as Chinai's mother was answering *Ambuya a*Siteriya's '*hodhi!*[82]'

"*Amake* Chinai, strange things are happening, *mubale wanga*. My heart is close to bursting," said *Ambuya a*Siteriya, out of breath. "You will not believe where I found your son playing with his friends." Without waiting to be asked, she sat down on the reed mat on the veranda, bent her legs and crossed them at the knees before tucking them beneath her. Making a gesture of exaggerated exhaustion, the old woman slumped back against the wall of the house. She folded her right arm at the elbow and rested it on her thigh, opened the palm, tilted her head sideways and rested her right cheek in the open palm. I sat down opposite her and folded my legs beneath me.

82 hello

"I have been looking for him all over the compound since his father came back from *chipani chakuseni*[83]," said Chinai's mother as she knelt by the side of the old woman. "Where did you find him?"

"Give me something to drink, I beg you. I need to wet my parched throat first." Chinai's mother went into the house and came back with some water.

"Hard water! What awful taste!" complained *Ambuya a*Siteriya as her dry lips touched the green rim of the yellow enamel cup. The ball of flesh just below her jaw bobbed up and down with each gulp she took. After swallowing the last few drops she handed the cup back and said, "It tastes like rubber. Even soap coagulates in this water, ha! The hardships we face in this miserable life."

"Where did you say you found…?"

"*Kumanda.* There, where our departed find their rest, is where I found your little boy. These children of today amaze me. They have no fear of, or respect for the things we consider sacred. What our own fathers feared, they laugh in the face of. I was coming from that piece of land where I grow mealies, the one beyond the graveyard, when my eyes met a sight that almost caused my heart to stop. I do not want to till that field but with nothing else available, what choice do I have? Anyway, as I was saying, not daring to look in the direction of the graveyard, I braced myself to walk hastily past. As you know, *Amake* Chinai, the place of the dead is always deathly quiet, except that on this occasion there were tiny voices squealing from within those eerie graves. I stood rooted where I was, all energy seeping into the ground. How I mastered the courage to look in that direction still baffles me. I almost fainted when I saw these small figures darting among the graves."

83morning shift

"Small figures? Do you mean to me tell that…?"

"*Amake* Chinai, I thought I would not live to see the sun rise again after setting eyes on a ghost. Not just one but three of them. Then I realised that the three little ones were your son here and his two friends there." *Ambuya a*Siteriya pointed a gnarled forefinger first at Chinai, then at Chakumanda and his friend. Chinai's mother screamed. I froze. Chinai appeared unfazed by the furore around him and stared defiantly at his mother. Chakumanda and the other boy stood by the edge of the veranda. My son cocked his head to one side and poked at the dry ground with his right toe. The other boy, whom I had never seen before, stared at the ground, twiddling his fingers.

"Where have you been, Chinai?" his mother asked, looking at her son as if he were a ghost that had come to haunt the living.

"Playing. Kumanda," answered Chinai with a nonchalant shrug and pointing in the direction of the said place. Without warning, his mother slumped and fell in a heap at *Ambuya a*Siteriya's feet. I just sat there feeling numb from the top of my head right down to the toes tucked beneath me. In that moment I saw every single crack that ran across the cement floor of the veranda. My mind registered the ants that streamed in a single file following the sugary scent of spilled tea. I saw too the cracks on the soles of *Ambuya a*Siteriya's small feet. When I finally roused myself from this stupor, I got up and threw a see-you-later glance over my shoulder that was aimed at no one in particular. I grabbed my son by the ear and he squealed and pulled away. I lunged at his shoulder and got a firm grip. I was not angry with the boy, but I was filled with a terrible fear. I half picked him up and half dragged him the short distance to our house as his piercing screams filled the hot afternoon. Chakumanda kicked and struggled to free himself, only to end up

sweeping the ground with his feet as I held him by the scruff of his collar.

Later, when we were both calm, I asked Chakumanda how he and the other boys had ended up at the graveyard. He told me that Chinai had led them there to go and play.

"What exactly where you doing there, Chakumanda?" I tried to hide the panic in my voice, but I was close to tears.

"We only went out to play, *Amayo.* And what a good time we had, jumping onto heaps of sand, collecting the cups, dishes and plates lying there. I wanted to collect some of them for you *Amayo,* but they had holes on them. I will look for good ones tomorrow."

"You must promise me that you will never go back there again, my son, eh? I beg you!" Chakumanda nodded, rather puzzled by my obvious distress. I decided to watch over him more closely in future. Children that young never ventured beyond the boundaries of the Mine compound alone. Worse still, it was unheard of that they would cross the tarred road that ran from Gatooma to Chakari Mine. The road was not busy, but it was precisely for that reason that it was dangerous. The white farmers and the Mine bosses who used it drove their vehicles recklessly because there was hardly any other traffic to worry about. Apart from that, tractors often came rambling down the road. I also made sure Chakumanda steered clear of Chinai whom I suspected of putting strange ideas into his head.

Strange tales were being whispered about Chinai in the compound. Some people said that he missed his late twin brother, that was why he visited the graveyard everyday. Some claimed that he played only on the grave of his brother, even though it had not been pointed out to him.

And this was a boy aged only six years, the same age as my son Chakumanda.

"The parents of that boy did not cleanse him with medicinal herbs," said *Ambuya a*Siteriya when we met at the water tap one morning a few days later. The old woman was known to possess knowledge about the customs and traditions of her people. "When one twin dies, the surviving one should be cleansed of the spirit of death. Babies whose lives are formed together in the same space are bonded by the umbilical cord. But that is not all. Their flesh, the blood that flows in their veins and their souls are one person. They are tied together forever, and not even death can separate them. Should one of them leave this world, the other soon follows. The spirit of the departed sibling lures him or her from beyond the grave. The surviving twin has no place among the living, unless the proper ritual is performed to cleanse him of the spirit of death. That is why, until not so long ago, the Mashona people were said to kill the surviving twin. It was to despatch him or her to the spirit world where he or she was said to belong."

The words made my blood run cold. The hair on my head stood on end and it felt as if there were maggots crawling under my scalp. The idea that the boy was being lured to the land of the dead while in the company of my son frightened me. Chakumanda. My son Chakumanda was already as good as sacrificed to the grave.

"So you mean, you mean that the boy will die?" I stammered, barely able to get the words heard above the hoarse whisper.

"Not if the appropriate ritual is performed," replied *Ambuya a*Siteriya. "In order to separate the spirit of the boy from that of his deceased twin, the ritual should have been done before the burial. That is the way our peole have always separated children whose souls are joined while they are still in the womb. They are difficult to separate

because twins do not usually want to be separated, which is why, when death claims one of them, the ritual has to be performed before burial. If that is not done the surviving twin soon joins the dead one. It is not too late for the ritual to be performed, though. It is only six months since Chinai's twin died." Whether Chinai's parents heeded *Ambuya a*Siteriya's advice or not, I never got to know, but after several days during which Chinai sneaked off to the cemetery on his own, the sojourns abruptly stopped. He must have simply got tired of going there to play on his own, I thought.

Such happenings made the blood in my veins go cold, but superstition was part of our lives. After years of burying the dead, we were bound to have our own compound ghosts. We got up in the night to go and ease ourselves, but not before rousing one or two family members for company. On dark nights no one, no matter how brave, dared venture out alone for fear of coming across the phantom miner and his lantern. His footsteps were said to be steady and unhurried. No one could swear that they had actually seen the ghost, but everybody claimed to know of his existence.

It was part of the story of our lives. Only ghosts dared venture out on dark nights, but the man who walked into *a*Mumba's house one very dark night was not a ghost. That was a very long time ago when I was still young and living with my real family. My parents were woken up one late night by the rapid and urgent sound of heavy pounding on the door. Father immediately feared the worst, for I heard him mutter under his breath, 'God, I beg you, don't let it be another disaster in the shafts'. I remember feeling scared, young as I was. I was sleeping on the floor next to my parents' bed. As an only child I was too scared to sleep in the other room on my own. Whenever Father was on night shift I shared the bed with Mother.

"Who is there?" shouted Father.

"Open the door, *a*Tsogolani. It is me, *a*Mumba."

"Is everything all right? Has there been an accident underground? Has somebody died?"

"Thank God nobody has died, at least not yet. You have to come with me to my house before I kill someone."

"*A*Mumba, try and calm down. I am getting dressed and coming out right now."

As soon as our night visitor was gone, Mother begged Father not to go.

"Why not, *Amake* Chimwemwe? The man was clearly angry. What if he beats his wife to death?"

"He should call the Mine security officer, not you. What if you get hurt? If you insist on going, then I have to come with you. Besides, we did not really see his face, did we? What if it is the disguised voice of a witch luring you out there?"

Father hesitated briefly, as if considering the possibility of what Mother had just said. "You could be right, *Amake* Chimwemwe, but I really have no choice. I promised to go, so I have to. What kind of a man lets his kinsman down by hiding behind his fears?"

"In that case I shall come with you, *Ababa a*Chimwemwe."

"No, you stay here. We cannot leave the girl here alone."

"I will strap her onto my back and come with you."

"What? She is too big for that, surely? If you insist on coming then I will carry her on my shoulders but we have to wake her up so she can hold onto my head. All this trouble for nothing really, *Amake* Chimwemwe," protested Father. Mother paid no attention to his protests and set about hoisting me off the floor and onto her back effortlessly as if I were a rag doll. I held on tightly as she tied a big piece of cloth around the two of us. We immediately set off for *a*Mumba's house, a short distance

from ours. It was a very dark night, not that I could see much from behind Mother's back. On the way there Father kept mumbling over and over again that he hoped *a*Mumba would not do anything he would later regret. All was quiet when we arrived, but the door was ajar. My parents went right in without knocking, through the kitchen and into the room that served as a sitting room.

Mother, who by now had realised that I was awake, untied the cloth and let me slide down her back and onto the floor. I moved to stand by her side, my right hand in hers, with Father to my left. From the doorway where we stood, I could see *a*Mumba sitting on a chair in the far left corner. Next to him sat his wife and at their feet were their three children. Huddled in the middle of the room was a figure covered with the kind of cloth women wrapped around their waists as part of their attire. It was not possible to say whether the person in the middle of the room was male or female, since they had their head in their hands. *A*Mumba seemed surprised to see Mother and me. He then waved his wife and children, Mother and me into the kitchen. We all sat huddled there, feeling anxious and sleepy at the same time. Three more men arrived and they were shown into the inner room by *a*Mumba's wife. For a long time Father, *a*Mumba, the three men and the figure huddled on the floor were engaged in heated discussions and arguments. *A*Mumba's threatening voice could occasionally be head raised above everybody else's. I must have fallen asleep at some point because the next thing I remember was Mother laying me down on the floor back at our house.

"This looks very bad, *Ababa a*Chimwemwe," Mother's voice whispered in the dark after a brief silence. They must have thought I had fallen asleep.

"It is awful indeed, really shocking. I never thought I would one day witness such a thing," answered Father. The bed creaked as he turned. "The man was caught right

there, unashamedly casting spells in the middle of *a*Mumba's sitting room."

"It is indeed bad," agreed Mother. "Poor Magaba, how will he face the mine dwellers tomorrow? Anyway, how does he explain his actions?"

"He claims to be puzzled by the whole incident."

"Hmm! Does his wife know, and what has she got to say?"

"*A*Mumba says she seemed unaware of what was happening at the house opposite, until he knocked on their door asking her to hand him Magaba's clothes. When he asked her where she thought her husband was, she replied that he had gone outside to relieve himself." Mother gasped. "He was naked then?"

"Completely," answered Father. "It was *a*Mumba's wife who covered his nakedness with a piece of cloth when her husband called her to come and see the intruder in their home."

"Do you think Magaba wandered into their house while walking in his sleep or could he have mistaken the *a*Mumba's house for his own in the dark?" asked Mother.

"He claims not to remember leaving his house. As for going in there by mistake, that depends on whether he normally goes out at night to relieve himself with no clothes on. Even if you want to believe that, it would still be hard to explain how he gained entry into a house that was securely bolted from inside."

Mother sighed before saying, "That complicates matters for him, yet I still find it hard to believe it of Magaba. His mother, poor soul, was very honourable and well respected in this community."

"I do not see him capable of practising witchcraft either, but *a*Mumba saw him with his own eyes walking in his house. Who knows, maybe Magaba was casting his spells. *A*Mumba went and woke up several men to come and bear witness to the deed. Mind you, the man has

warned evil doers for a long time to steer clear of his place or face the consequences. Tonight I have seen it with my own eyes," said Father. Although I could not see him from my position on the floor, I could imagine him pulling down his lower eyelids with the forefingers of both hands.

"For some reason, this whole incident has put a chill in my bones. What an unfortunate thing to happen to Magaba!"

"*Amake* Chimwemwe, the man should thank his gods that it was not in the house of one of the Mashona people that he got caught. Those *Mashambadovi* do not waste their time parading a wizard or a witch caught in their homes. They use a hammer to drive a nail deep into the skull of the culprit before setting him free to totter slowly back to his home, and eventually to his grave a few days later."

"*Amake* Chimwemwe!" I screamed for Mother.

"Are you awake? I thought you were asleep. What is it?" she asked.

"I am scared," I whimpered.

"What of?"

"Of... of... of *amfiti*[84] and, and a hammer, and...." Mother comforted me by trying to convince me that I had just had a bad dream. I pretended that it was indeed the case even though I knew otherwise. It was easier to keep up the pretence because it also meant there was nothing to be afraid of. I eventually drifted off to sleep, safe in the knowledge that my parents were there to protect me. No one was going to wander naked into our house, and no one was going to drive a nail into my head either. In the morning, Mother made me swear that I would never repeat the bad dream to anyone. I gave her my promise, which I found imppossible to keep since the incident became the number one topic of discussion everywhere for

84 witches

months afterwards. That was decades before the incident when Chinai took my son to the graveyard.

Like everything else, life got back to normal again. Each week we looked forward to the bioscopes that were screened as entertainment on Thursdays, courtesy of the Mine Management. Normal also meant food rations and communal baths and Chimuromo and cotton picking and teacher Mabhachi and *chiware* and births and marriages and *vhigororo* and *mujumbura* and Kamupaundi and measles and small pox and paydays and creditors. It was simply everything that we had grown up with and which was routine as far as we were concerned. Retrenchment, which we called *chigumura,* was normal as well.

All the mine labourers of advanced years lived with the threat of retrenchment and retirement hanging over their heads. In the beginning, those affected were ferried in the Mine truck together with their meagre belongings, to the railway station in Gatooma. From there, they were put on board trains that took them back to Nyasaland, Northern Rhodesia, Tanganyika or wherever it was they originated from. Although there were a few who were happy to go back, the majority dreaded it.

It was generally believed that those who went back did not live long and their deaths were blamed on their relatives back there. For this reason, most miners and their families lived with the fear of being laid off. I was one of them. I feared that my husband would one day be made redundant due to the cough-and-spit-blood disease of the mines.

My family and I had nowhere to go and we had no one. We never heard from my mother-in-law again after she moved from the farm where Masauso had last visited her. All we heard were rumours of her living in one place or the other. Each time my husband sought more information on her whereabouts, nobody ever claimed to have personally seen her or her son and daughter. My

father-in-law died the year before I became Masauso's wife. By the time of his death he and Masauso rarely acknowledged each other's existence. Some people claimed that old Bhaureni Nyirenda lost his mind when his wife left him. Others argued that it was already lost when he came back from the white man's war. His death and the disappearance of his wife and the other children meant we had no known relatives. I had no ties with Northern Rhodesia and my husband had none with Nyasaland either, both of us having been born here. The bonds that had once tied us to our homelands snapped a long time ago. Northern Rhodesia existed merely as a fading memory of a place that my parents had remembered and talked about with fondness and longing but it meant nothing to me. It was just a place I could point out on a map.

I was born at Patchway Valley Mine, and was therefore a child of the Mine. My life was shaped by the culture of the migrant community and the place was my whole world. I had only ever left the Mine to go and work on neighbouring farms as a casual labourer. Once or twice, I had boarded Ruredzo Bus Service to go to Bherina African Township in Gatooma. Everything the old people felt nostalgic about, I felt nothing for. I was sure a lot had changed back in their homelands. Had Father been alive and tried to go back there, he might not have been able to find his way without difficulty. The country he had left behind as Northern Rhodesia was no longer part of the Federation.

My son Chakumanda, though more keen on sport than the reading and writing part of school, enjoyed learning about other places. He listened eagerly when his teachers talked about the history of our countries, and came home to share his knowledge about the disintegration of the Federation states. It was he who came

home and told us that the Prime Minister of Southern Rhodesia, one Ian Smith and his Minister of Justice, Clifford Dupont, had wrestled control of the country from the British government on 11 November 1965. Smith called it the Unilateral Declaration of Independence, UDI… whatever that meant. Chakumanda's teachers told him that when Northern Rhodesians were granted self rule by Britain, they renamed their country Zambia. The same thing happened to Nyasaland and the country became Malawi.

These changes meant nothing to me but to the ears of the old people, the new names made the former homelands sound like some foreign countries they had no connection with. It was therefore not surprising that in later years, those miners who were retired and pensioned off opted to stay in their adopted land. By then most of then had grown up children who were married and had families of their own, and from whom they did not wish to be parted. Quite a number of them went on to settle on the farms where they worked as seasonal farm labourers. At least on the farms *abwana* needed as much labour as they could get. They never had enough, hence the despatching of tractors to collect cotton pickers and harvesters from the mining communities. There, at least one was never too old or too young to work, or too ill for that matter. Unlike on the mines where the workers were evicted from the houses as soon as the men got their pensions_ about three months' wages or so_ farm workers were allowed to stay for as long as they wanted. All they did was erect their huts and work seasonally for the farmers who would pay only for the work done by an individual.

Although life was harder on the farms, one felt more appreciated there than on the mines where the Management took only young and healthy men who went down mine shafts to blast rocks with sticks of dynamite

before working with a pick axe and a shovel. With time, the eyes of these young men became red, watery and could only see things that were close. They had to squint their eyes in order to see things that were far away. Over a long period of time, they developed pain in the back and they became hard of hearing, as what happened to *a*Bhiriyati.

As soon as it became clear that the job had become too heavy for him, the Management laid him off with three months' wages and a bicycle as his reward for a service spanning over twenty-five years. He was given a week or two to vacate the Mine house. In his place the bosses installed the son. The whole community was relieved and grateful that though the father had been laid off, *abwana* had been kind enough to give the son a job. Meanwhile, *a*Bhiriyati went away smiling with his new bicycle to start a new life at Hoffman Farm. When he came back to Patchway Valley a few months later, his bicycle was a sight to marvel at. We all gathered around to look at it. The proud owner was happy enough to show us what he had done to it and how. He had painted it in very bright colours; red handlebars, yellow bell, blue pedals, white spokes, and a green carrier. He had also added to it a few extra attachments for decoration. *A*Bhiriyati was proud of his most prized possession. His happiness and the pride he took in his *njinga* made others think that maybe *chigumura* was not such a bad idea after all. Happy though *a*Bhiriyati looked, I still dreaded the idea of retiring to the farms, and yet we did not have much choice. The situation was as sad as it was exasperating.

Our fathers had left their homelands and given up their lives, their families and their countries for the mines in Southern Rhodesia, yet despite the difficult choices they had had to make, they were not allowed to spend the rest of their lives in the places they had given up so much for. Some of the chiefs had pleaded with the Compound

Manager to take their case to the Mine Management, but he did not even bother to do so.

"If we let you stay in your houses after retirement, we would need to keep building more houses year after year, which of course we can't. We are no *blati* communists," he said. The request was never made again. At times I woke up with a headache from worrying about becoming homeless. Quite a good number of mine widows whose husbands had died in the shafts or from mine related diseases had gone and settled on nearby farms after burying the deceased in the Mine graveyard. My greatest fear was that I would one day end up as one of them.

Some migrant labourers who had married divorced or widowed local women escaped life on the farms by settling in the villages of their wives. However, not all inter-marriages survived retrenchment or retirement. Most local women, though happy enough to stay with their migrant husbands while they still held a job, refused to go with them back to the husbands' countries of origin, or to settle on nearby farms.

Our men took in these women together with their children from previous marriages, which was a cause for many heated debates among our people. They provoked different feelings in various people, especially those who were not directly involved.

"Have you heard, *Amake* Chakumanda, that *a*Nkhoma has taken a new woman?" asked my friend *Amake* Chisoni one afternoon when she came by my house so that we could go and collect some alluvial dust.

"Well, that does not surprise me. What surprises me is that it has taken him this long to do so. Is it not three years now since he lost his wife?" I remarked.

"Almost, yes. Almost three years, but have you heard who he has taken for a wife?"

"No. Don't tell me it's some young girl just out of *chinamwali*?" I asked in despair. More and more widowed

or divorced elderly men were marrying girls young enough to be their daughters. The fathers of these unfortunate girls practically forced them into mismatched marriages in the belief that they would be better looked after by responsible elderly husbands. I had narrowly escaped such a fate myself.

"No-o, it is nothing like *that*. Do you know the dark-skinned woman who comes here monthly to vend dried fish and other wares?" she asked, leaning towards my ear with a conspiratorial air. I wondered why she bothered because everybody knew that once a rumour started in the community, it would spread faster than a wild fire.

"Ehe!?"

"*A*Nkhoma has moved *her* into his house! Can you believe such stupidity? Do our men never learn from the mistakes of others?"

"I do not understand."

"*Amake* Chakumanda, how can these bright eyes of yours fail to see what is so obvious to everybody else? Have you not seen how all these native husbandless women are flocking into our community and targeting those of our kinsmen who are divorced or widowed? Have you forgotten that these are the very same people who shun us? What is suddenly so appealing about our men?"

"When two people decide to set up home together, who is to say it is not appropriate because of tribal differences? We are not talking of some young girl forced into marrying a man of her father's choice here but two adults who decide, of their own free will, to settle down together regardless of tribal differences. After all the migrants do it all the time, those from Malawi are inter-marrying with the Zambians and Mocambicans."

"Your innocence never ceases to amaze me, my friend. We outsiders are fine amongst ourselves. These native women are after only one thing."

"Which is?"

"School fees for their children, after which our naïve kinsmen will get discarded like soiled rags."

"You ought to have some faith, *mubale wanga*."

"I did once, oh yes, until I saw what was done to *a*Kondanani. Everybody here knows the unfortunate story of his life. You know it too *Amake* Chakumanda, surely?"

"Only the wild rumours. I am not sure I ever got to know the details."

"That man worked hard underground and looked after that Shona widow from Murambinda and her three children. Most people at Patchway Valley admonished *a*Kondanani for failing to buy himself new clothes as his meagre wages were all spent on his wife's children for whom he bought clothes and paid fees at boarding school. *Boarding school, Amake* Chakumanda! Do I need to spell out to you how high boarding school fees are? Isn't that the reason we can never afford to educate our own children to the standards of the locals? But *a*Kondanani broke his back to do it for *ma*Moyo and her children."

"He was a generous man then," I said.

"Foolish is the word you want here, not generous," retorted Chisoni's mother, clicking her tongue against protruding front teeth.

"It depends on which side you are looking at it from."

"Ha, you and your nonsense! Which other side is there to look at it from except that of our people? Can you not see that our men are being used?"

"Which men? You mean the very ones seeking out these local widows? Surely they need each other, can't you see that? Which of our young girls would willingly agree to settle down with the widowers and divorced men from our community when there are desirable young men around? The young people of nowadays are rebelling against our customs now."

"That may be so, but I still maintain that our men give more than they get. Ask anybody who knows what

happened to *a*Kondanani. His kinsmen chided him years later when he gave most of his wages to his wife every month. He said she was paying for the building of a homestead in the village where they hoped to retire to at some point in the future. Some say he was a victim of the strong Mashona type of love potions that can cook a man's heart and his mind till he can't think straight anymore. Whatever the woman says he will only ask, 'When, where or how soon,' and never 'why'. She demands and gives orders, and he obeys." At this, Chisoni's mother snorted with exaggerated contempt. It was too funny not to laugh, and I did. In no time we were both giggling and clutching at our stomachs.

"Ya, you see, *Amake* Chakumanda, how one sometimes finds humour even in the sad situations of our lives? At times it is better to just laugh than cry. I tell you *mubale wanga,* these women are dangerous. How else would you explain an otherwise sensible man's blind devotion to a local woman with the morals of a female dog at the height of the mating season? How do you explain his failure to heed the well-meaning advice his people were trying to drum into that already-muddled-up-head of his? No self-respecting man settles down with a woman that a few of his kinsmen claim to have lain with. It is the love potions that turn their heads, *nxi*!

"When *a*Kondanani was pensioned off, his fellow labourers called him *chitsiru*[85] when his wife took half his retirement package to go and buy a bed for their new home. He waited for her during the two weeks he was given to vacate the house. She never came back. He died a broken and bitter man. His remains lie as nothing more than dry bones in a foreign land, beneath a miserable looking mound of earth no one bothers to tend at Montana Farm. If that is not a lesson worth learning, I do not know

85 A fool, an idiot

what is," declared my friend smugly. "Our men need to open their eyes and refuse to be used. I thought they had all learned a lesson for the future from the misfortune of the poor man."

"I believe they learn various lessons all the time. Maybe *a*Nkhoma has decided to learn from the experience of *a*Kaunda whom we all know took in a local woman and did for her and her sons exactly what *a*Kondanani did for *ma*Moyo. *A*Kaunda recently retired to Mhondoro where he is said to be very happy. Why shouldn't he be, indeed? He has a caring wife and step-children that adore him and do everything they can to make him happy. It is their way of showing appreciation for a man who sacrificed a lot to give them a good future. So one can never tell how these marriages will turn out," I explained.

"Maybe, but most of them collapse, and it is too risky to simply plunge into them without giving much thought to what might happen in a few years' time. Nobody's future can be said to be secure, whatever one does. Most of these local women refuse to go to their husbands' homelands when the men retire or are retrenched. What sort of marriage is that which stands only while the husband has a job? When are our men going to open their eyes?"

With the fear of retrenchment forever on my mind, I instilled in my children, Chakumanda and Dhairesi, the need to work hard at school. Apart from the inevitable eventuality of the mines becoming exhausted and the labourers getting laid off, things were changing for us migrants. And the change was for the better. We soon realised that education held the key to a better life. We did not need to focus our future on the Mine or the surrounding farms.

One needed to work hard at school and aim higher than being a labourer or domestic servant. Still, you can

only do what you can for your children and the rest is up to them. Chakumanda was very good at soccer and by the time he was twelve years old he was already playing for the senior team. His height turned out to be an advantage. He had no interest in schoolwork and only ever dreamed of playing football and working in the mine. When he left school, he started playing for the Mine team.

The Chamber of Mines organised tournaments where teams from Eiffel Flats, Venice, Brompton, Commoner and Chakari Mines competed for the Chamber of Mines trophy. Our team was so good that one of the players, Seleta Banda, played in the national team alongside George Shaya and Shaky Tauro. I suppose it was he, and other very good players such as Teddy and teacher Mabhachi_ the only teacher to ever play for the Mine team_ who inspired my son. Those were heady days. My son was popular, he was a good son and I was proud to be his mother. His father was even more proud. I remember him once saying, "I am sure if we had not offered him to the spirit of death and named him Chakumanda, we would have lost him a long time ago."

"Yes, I think so too," I agreed. "I suppose that which is offered with no protest is less appealing than that which is snatched out of spite."

There were other major events in our lives, such as births and deaths, marriages, and very rarely, divorces. There was also *chinamwali* for girls and *jando* for young boys of the Chawa tribe who practised the Islamic religion. The boys were taken out in groups for circumcision in the forest, a ritual that lasted several days. This was the traditional initiation of boys into manhood. Mothers worried for their sons then, but fathers took pride in them. Chakumanda did not attend *jando* because his father and I were not Moslems.

During the hot summer months when there was no work for which our services were needed on the neighbouring farms, we often found ourselves idle. Most women therefore sought to amuse themselves in various ways. After the house work was done and the children were back from school, they brought their beads and reed mats to the huge tree next to *a*Mazizi's store and played *chiware* in the cool shade. On the other side of the local store, next to the only beer hall in the Mine compound, the women's husbands and their grown up sons played *tsoro* or *njuga* for hours. Their games were as absorbing as *chiware,* and they lost themselves in them. Once they started playing, most of the men only went home to eat their evening meal. It was their only pastime of the mid-week, one of the few things that helped break the monotony of going down the pits and coming home to wait for the next shift. On weekends however, it was a different matter altogether.

Each weekend, the various tribes that made up the community of Patchway Valley took turns to provide entertainment for the miners and their families with their ethnic traditional dances. The men of the Tonga tribe delighted us with *muganda,* a kind of laid back dance that did not require fast and energetic body movements. The *beni* of the Chawa males was equally graceful. The women of the Chewa tribe entertained the community with the *chihoda* dance, while those of my tribe performed the *chimutale* dance. The former was a dance that required movement of the shoulders while the latter required movement of the waist, hips and backside. I remember as a child going with my friends to watch the dances. The *chihoda* dance appealed to me. It was always fascinating to watch the women swing and move their waists with seemingly effortless grace. Their songs too had a calmness about them that matched the rhythm of the drumbeat.

The dance that enthralled me the most though was *chimutale*. The first time I watched it is still etched in my mind. That was a few months after the incident of witchcraft at our neighbour's house. Mother had held my hand as we set off to the entertainment area next to the grocery shop. Under the huge flamboyant tree was a bench on which two men sat, each of whom had a drum clutched between the knees. A third man stood behind a drum so big it came up to his waist. A fourth man stood a few footsteps away, a small drum tucked under his armpit. These drums, with varying degrees of tautness, produced different tones, Mother explained.

As the men started beating the drums with their palms or with the base of their fists, spectators slowly gathered. We stood in a circle, with many people standing behind or in front of others. Mother, who was not a tall woman, made sure we were in the front row. As the drumbeat increased in fury, two women moved to part the crowd and create a gap for the dancers to get into the ring. Mother and I were standing to the right of the dancers as they began to come through. They were so close that I could have touched them by stretching out my hand. One moment the ground was a patch of brown earth, and the next it exploded into blue and white colours. The dancers wore white blouses and wrapped long blue cloths around the waists. These cloths were embroidered with white thread and had matching head scarves. The leader of the dancers blew a whistle, at which the drumming rose in pitch. The crowds went wild with excitement. Men whistled and women clapped their hands and ululated.

When she was sure the crowd was ready for them, the leader of the dancers walked backwards into the ring, her whistle glued to her lips while beckoning the dancers to follow her. The dancers, with their shoulders hunched forward, their backs bent at the waist and bottoms stuck out as if they were being barred from following the rest of

the bodies, moved forward. And like a millipede with its numerous legs moving in one motion, the feet of the dancers moved as one. They placed the left feet forward, wiggled obliging waists, brought the right feet level, straightened their backs, shook their bottoms vigorously, placed the right feet forward and wiggled their waists again. As the line reached the open space, the line of dancers moved towards the right. They went round the open space and continued with the routine until the dancer at the rear had completed the ring. By then the dancers had formed a complete circle at the centre of which stood their leader.

Once they had made their entrance, the real dance was about to begin. Silence fell all around. We held our breaths while the dancers let out theirs in short spurts, their chests heaving. The drummers remained outside the circle. When the leader blew her whistle, one of the dancers let out a high-pitched sound that was soon joined by other voices. A song took shape, fast and sharp. The drums responded with an intensity that commanded everything else to stop and pay attention and the whistle whipped the dancers into a frenzy. Flexible hips swayed first to the left, then to the right, followed by the vigorous shaking of bottoms up and down. The feet detached themselves from the ground at one point, landed a pace away and shoulders shook as bosoms heaved up and down. The picture was enchanting. It was like watching the image of one person reflected in a row of mirrors. The *chimutale* dance not only required agility and stamina, but also the ability to vigorously shake one's ample bottom in rhythm with the furious drumbeat. Different dance styles were performed in tune with different rhythms. As each dance reached frenzied heights, the leader would blow her whistle and egg the dancers on. Each danced to the best of their ability. The drummers, their brows bathed in sweat, pounded on the taut hide with fury and determination. Columns of dust

rose, red and thick, and swirled into the air above the ring. The dancers danced on, oblivious to the pushing and shoving of spectators as they fought to maintain their positions in the front rows.

Coins were flung above the heads of the dancers and landed in the ring. A woman pushed her way forward and collected them. The money would buy Fanta and Coca-Cola for the dancers and the drummers when they stopped to rest. That day I went home with only one thing in mind. When I grew up I wanted to join the dancers of the Chewa tribe. I did not care that my tribe did a different dance. I wanted to stick out my behind, thrust forward my chest and shake my hips the way I had seen the dancers do. And I wanted a bottle of Fanta too.

Years later, my dream was realised. I joined the Chewa women for the traditional dances. Since the woman who raised me was of the Chewa tribe, I was regarded as one of them. By then I understood much more about *chihoda.* We tied scarves across our ample bottoms to make them more compact and less liable to wobble in all directions. The drumbeat excited us and fuelled our vigour as we sang;

AKamuzu Banda iye-e
Ali kupita kundege!

We did not know much about the man we eulogised in song, except that he had liberated Nyasaland from white rule. We sang over and over again about his trips here and there but we did not seek to know why he was always flying to other places. We just sang the song and danced as vigorously as the pace of the drumbeat dictated. Apart from that song, there were a lot more, among them the all-time favourites, *Kanganirume Kambeva* and *Amuna Vanga Anagura Wachi.* We wore to these dances, two-piece outfits

which were made of a special kind of material that had the approved portrait of the president of Malawi printed on it. As we energetically shook our bodies in rhythm with the drum, the chin of the Ngwazi would bob up and down our bottoms as if in approval of the praises we sang to his name. He was His Excellency The Life President of Malawi and we had a daily reminder of that in our songs, in our dances and in the clothes we wore.

Of all the Sunday entertainment, I enjoyed watching the *nyao*[86] performances best. The *nyao* dancers were known as *vhinyao*. Covered entirely from head to toe in scary masks and costumes, they looked like phantoms from the land of the dead. *Vhinyao* had an air of mystery about them and were said to come from another realm altogether. Their intrigue lay in their anonymity and when they entered the compound, their approach was heralded by a fore-runner playing an eerie kind of drumbeat that made children scream and rush to hide indoors. From the safety of their homes the mine dwellers, with a mixture of awe and fear, peeped at *vhinyao* as they advanced towards the flamboyant tree. Although we were afraid of them, we could not draw ourselves away. It was like being drawn by some magical and magnetic force towards what one fears yet finds intriguing. As the drumbeat increased in tempo, many would leave their houses and flock to the entertainment arena.

To further strengthen the myth of their immortality, *vhinyao* were said to come from the cemetery, and it was indeed from that direction that they emerged. So revered and feared were they that their true identities were not supposed to be revealed. If, by some rare accident their masks fell, spectators were supposed to avert their eyes and walk away without a backward glance. To dare stare a *chinyao* in the eye was to court untold misfortune whose

86 Mask dancers

exact nature remained forever a mystery because no one, as far as I can remember, ever dared challenge the myth by looking. Pregnant women were advised not to watch the dancers because if they did, they either miscarried or risked giving birth to a monster, so we were told.

The masks of vhinyao were designed to instil fear and a sense of mystery. *Vhinyao* also made terrifying guttural sounds. The adults knew that the dancers were mine dwellers who lived amongst us, but they were also regarded as great dabblers in magic and rituals that gave them supernatural powers.

In spite of all this, most people still found the dances to be the most entertaining of them all. Jakopo, one of the *nyao* dancers at Patchway Valley Mine was the only one whose identity we ever got to know. To watch him perform was the height of entertainment as he was undisputedly the greatest *chinyao* of all time at the Mine. It was never known who exactly it was that identified Jakopo among *vhinyao,* but in no time the whole community knew, which led most people to treat him as no ordinary person. He was feared and mocked at the same time; feared for the rituals he supposedly took part in and derided because the term *chinyao* was used derogatively to mean a hopeless, useless and ugly, scary person. So it was that Jakopo, the man who sought to entertain mine workers and their families on Sundays, was not allowed to swiftly revert to the role of a fellow worker and mine dweller during the rest of the week.

It was unfortunate for Jakopo that the community stubbornly refused to separate the Sunday entertainer from the Monday to Saturday labourer that he was. His name became one with which most mothers used to scare their children into silence when they would not stop crying. It was not unusual to hear mothers say, "Stop crying or Jakopo will hear you and come and take you with him to the graveyard." The children would promptly

shut up. Even as a child, I too had trembled at the mention of that name.

Unfortunately for him, even out of his mask Jakopo was still feared and derided, and his looks did not help matters much. People often joked that he was a natural looking *chinyao* that needed no scary mask. He never wore shoes, footwear being a luxury for most mine dwellers. Since he was only a gardener, he could not benefit from the standard gumboots that were issued for other jobs. The cracks on his heels were legendary. It was a joke among mine dwellers that if you slipped a small tickey into them it would get lodged somewhere in his heels, never to re-emerge. The grit all over the compound must have made his life intolerable especially during the cold winter mornings when he had to rush to work, pounding away on the ground with his large flat feet. Many thought it was through the distinct cracks on his heels that Jakopo was recognised in his dance outfit and had his identity exposed which made him a target for taunts and insults. Yet despite the way he looked and his weird choice of hobby, he was a kind person with a simple mind. He would grin in the face of taunts, like the idiot that most people took him to be.

Jakopo was jeered by men and shunned by women. He had no interest in women, but then no sane woman would have accepted a proposal from him for fear of being ridiculed, and for that reason, Jakopo remained unmarried all his life, a hitherto unheard of thing in a society where every man got married at some point in his life. Jakopo was associated with all that was unnatural, an image quite essential if one was to be a success at *nyao* dancing. His life was a masquerade but I would not be surprised if deep down he was the happiest man around. Nobody knew if he had any hopes or dreams. If he did, no one knew what they were because he was not known to share his thoughts. He was a quiet person who expressed himself

only through dance and the sound of the drumbeat. Jakopo lived his life forever hidden behind his dance, and he was destined to bring joy and laughter into the lives of others. To most of us he was a man with a perpetual grin painted on his face, a man without dreams or desires.

Nobody thought of Jakopo as capable of feeling hurt or offended, so the taunting went on unabated. From behind the mask he made guttural sounds that nobody understood, and he looked at the world through the eyes of a clown. We enjoyed watching him dance but we did not accept him as an equal. It is possible though that Jakopo enjoyed the dance so much that nothing else mattered to him so long as he got to dance regularly. Everything else around him blurred until it ceased to exist altogether, and the only life he felt was in the strong muscular legs that pounded the ground in rhythm with the beat of the drum as it spoke to his soul. He was there for the whole community yet there never was anyone for him. Nobody claimed to understand him, and I doubt that anyone ever did, except perhaps, his mother.

DHAIRESI'S STORY

(1958- to date)

Patchway Valley Mine/Chestnut Farm, Gatooma

My life…
So short, yet so full of events both sad and happy. I am two people, sometimes three in one. Who I am on any given day depends on who the mirror says I am. At times it shows the smiling face of a young woman, her skin taut across the cheekbones, robust and smooth. On another day this same mirror throws back a drooping face. The skin on the face sags and folds over the jaws. This always reminds me of the face of the bulldog kept by Twoboy's bosses at the farm. I need not tell you how menacing that dog looks even without baring its teeth. The skin of the woman in the mirror also looks as if it has been washed and rinsed out, then left to gather mould over a period of time. These are the images that the mirror has been reflecting of late. And they are supposed to be images of me. One mirror, one person, two reflections. They depict who I am, depending on the position of the moon in the sky, and on the shape of the moon, and on the stars too, and their brightness. What I am depends also on the clouds; whether they are dark or clear, and whether they are high up or hang down low. It depends too on whether the sun rises with a smile or with a frown, or not at all. On the evenings when the sun sets with a warm glow against the

horizon, my nights are peaceful, but not so when the day is swallowed by menacing shadows and eerie sounds.

When the sun glides slowly across the green pastures and over the rolling hills at Chestnut Farm, my thoughts drift to a dream not deferred but derailed, a dream from the days of my youth, crushed to fine particles of dust that were left to fritter in the wind, one that is impossible to gather together again and remould. But I sleep better knowing that at one stage I dared dream. In the serene hours after a glorious sunset, the nightmares and the demons that plague my reality are laid to rest, even though it is merely temporary reprieve. I still nurse hope, not of that which might have been, but of the realities the mirror throws back at me.

On the mornings when the rain pelts down the thatch on our hut, and little rivulets race like maggots wriggling towards an alluring object in the distance, I see not the impoverished state of my existence, but the possibility of a new life. It is the promise of a new beginning that changes the reflection in the mirror. In the rain I see the beginning of one season and the end of another. I see too, the life and the non-life in-between. A small seed bursts through the warm, moist earth and the life within embraces the warm caress of the rays of the sun, and reaches out with promise. Hope is born. It is the turning of the seasons. In the bush and in the fields, the earth yields new life. In the distance too, smoke from cooking fires signals the heights to which our dreams can take us.

On bad days though, hope disappears beyond the shimmering hills where it gets buried with the sun, but fails to rise with it. The sun rises and spreads its tentacles over the already parched earth. The flowering crops and the budding plants wilt, droop and die. The new life clutched in their bossom dies with them. The clouds, clear and high up above, flap their feathers but refuse to yield

the moisture trapped beneath their wings. Below, those who have reason to leave the shade of their huts cup hands with dry skin over the eyes and stare into the bleak distance which soon draws them out. Mothers and wives poke at bushes and plants looking for tubers and leaves that cling to whatever life is still in them. They scratch the dry earth, pick up a tuber or two and move on. Men sling catapults and traps over slopping shoulders and, shielding their eyes from the heat, they peer into the naked branches of trees for signs of life. On some days the men get lucky but on other days it is the birds and animals that do. Then in the far distance, thick black blankets of smoke billow into the skies, signalling the death of hope. But that is what our life is like on the farms. The promise of life and the death of hope exist side by side.

But today hope has died with the stopping of a heartbeat. Right now the mirror throws back images that run one upon the other. Backwards, forwards, up and down. Everything is jumbled like a hazy dream. Father has died. That is no dream, but the reality around me. This death worsens the wretchedness of a life whose destruction began many years ago. I have often heard people argue that we are responsible for the way our lives turn out. Maybe, but it is hard to see how mine could have gone any other way. If, at seventeen years of age I was already a mother, maybe it is only natural that though still only in my early thirties, I should feel like a grandmother.

The miserable conditions Twoboy and I live in drain me of energy. I am almost always tired. The pregnancies I am compelled to carry one after the other drain me, leaving me shrivelled inside and outside. Twoboy, the man I live with, would not pay *lobola* to my father until I bore him a child and for that reason he has never been regarded as my husband. Since we can no longer be regarded as boyfriend and girlfriend after more than ten

years of living together, Twoboy is referred to as the *husband-who-is-not –really-a-husband.*

My life has been different in many ways from that of other women in my community due to a decision I made years ago, and one that I have never once regretted. Had I not dared try, I would have become a dissatisfied and embittered woman full of regrets. I only wish I had caused Father less heartache in my quest to find myself. I should have made more effort to soothe his anxieties over what he took to be a stubborn streak in me. I should have patiently explained that he and I looked at the world through different eyes. I feel guilty that I never tried, making it seem as if I did not care what he thought or how he felt. As far as Father was concerned, I rebelled out of a stubborn desire to challenge his authority and add to his misery. His love for me was boundless and without conditions but the community could not, and did not wish to forgive what they saw as my rebellion against their way of life. People said I was immoral and unmannered, and they behaved as if they feared that I would contaminate those touched even by my shadow, no matter how lightly. This stemmed from my refusal to be initiated into womanhood. They said I could never be a good woman without undergoing *chinamwali.* The whole community shunned me. It took some time before I realised that to the men at Patchway Valley, I could only be a girl they spend time with but never take for a wife.

It was for this reason that I turned my attention to the people from outside our community, but that was after a pointless relationship with Giribhati. I can still remember the rage that gripped Father when he got to know about it. He confronted me one morning upon his return from the night shift. I was on my hands and knees in the sitting room. I had finished scrubbing the floor and I was by then applying Cobra, the wax we used to smear on the floors and make them shine and to make the cracks less visible.

"You! You, *you* Dhairesi! My own daughter! My flesh, my blood! How could you put me through this shame?" Father demanded, towering over me and wagging a trembling finger. I stood up, threw the oily rag across the floor and took two steps backwards.

"Now what am I supposed to have done *this* time?" I demanded, throwing my arms up in the air, ready to defend myself. Father was constantly berating me for one reason or the other and this was beginning to wear me down. I could not take it anymore.

"How could you put me through this shame? Tell me it is not true," he demanded as if I knew what he was talking about. He regarded me with squinted eyes before asking in a hoarse voice, "Or is it? Is there any truth in the rumour that you and, and that Giribhati are, are er, well, do you see Giribhati, Dhairesi?"

Eyes averted, I replied meekly, "Yes, Father. I do."

"Of course you do, but not in the sense you mean. Do not pretend that you do not understand what I mean, Dhairesi. Answer me now!"

My tongue became heavy and I could not find the words to tell him the truth that was sure to shock him. Father stormed out of the house and before I could gather my thoughts together I saw him pass by the only window of the sitting room. I looked through the window and saw him walk past the water tap, towards the shop. He was headed somewhere in the compound. His swinging arms spoke of the rage his lips would not voice. I feared he was going to confront Giribhati, a scary thought indeed, but there was nothing I could do about it.

After a while Father stormed back into the yard with *Ambuya a*Firipo in tow. The old woman had to run to keep pace with his brisk step. I was scrubbing the veranda by then. I took a tent and spread it where I had already scrubbed, gesturing towards *Ambuya a*Firipo to sit down. I had barely finished offering her greetings when Father

bellowed, "You ask her, *Ambuya a*Firipo. Talk to this useless girl before I bury an axe in her neck." He then pointed towards the door that led into the house, in a gesture that left no doubt that he wanted me to go indoors. I refused. I was not yet ready to be butchered like a beast. I had never before seen him that angry. It was only after I was assured that no blood would be shed that I agreed to enter the house.

"You ask her, *Ambuya a*Firipo, because if I continue to do so myself, I will lose my temper and surely kill this shameless piece of trash," swore Father. Fear numbed me and I could not utter a word. Later, *Ambuya a*Firipo would accuse me of behaving disrespectfully towards him because of my stubbornness and arrogance. She further said that by remaining resolutely mute I had foolishly shielded a man who had taken advantage of me. What Father did not realise was that I was so shaken by his anger I had become paralysed with fear. After trying in vain to get me to talk, *Ambuya a*Firipo finally said, "Let the rage in your blood subside first, *a*Nyirenda. Give your daughter time to reflect on the shame of her deeds. I am sure that she will soon stop engaging in this disgraceful manner with Giri__"

"That is utter nonsense, *Ambuya a*Firipo, and you know it. Once one starts, does one ever stop, eh? Tell me, does one ever stop? All the men in the neighbourhood need only follow their noses and the scent will lead straight to my daughter. As for that good-for-nothing Giribhati, a man almost old enough to be her father, how could he behave with such disrespect towards my own flesh and blood? Even if my daughter were wanton, couldn't his regard for me prevent him from bringing dishonour to my household? That_ that_ that stupid *muchuwere* clearly has no respect for me, none whatsoever. But how can he, when my own daughter shows none? What kind of misfortune is this that intends to follow me

right to my old age? Have I not endured more than my fair share of the travails of this life? Of all the fathers in this compound, why must it be *me* that suffers so much? This goes to prove my seed was meant for the soil, nothing else. Ah Dhairesi, Dhairesi! "

"This matter ought to be brought to the attention of the tribal chiefs so that Giribhati can be publicly admonished for his behaviour. We cannot have a man of his morals running loose. Who knows how many other girls he has taken advantage of? If you do not report him, he will continue to exploit our innocent daughters and that should not be allowed to happen," the old woman chipped in.

"*Ambuya a*Firipo, I have indulged these stupid ideas of Dhairesi to the point where people whisper and pity me behind my back. Now enough is enough! I am going to accept the bride price from the first man who offers it for her. Mkandawire has offered to take her off my hands year after year since his wife died but the stupid girl refuses him all the time. She can't even be grateful that someone is willing to overlook her stubbornness and have her, uninitiated as she is. Indeed, this time she is going with Mkandawire."

"It might be the best way out of this mess. It will also prevent further trouble which I can foresee coming your way, *mubale wanga*. The way your girl is going about, she will soon start filling up your yard with tots sired by men of various totems. Just disregard her protests and marry her off, otherwise she will push you towards an early grave." With that the old woman got up and left, leaving me staring on the floor as Father glared at me. In one respect, *Ambuya a*Firipo was right. Although I stopped seeing Giribhati, I also started seeing the young men who flocked to the Mine at the weekends. I was determined to find a man of my choice, one that I loved before Father carried out his threat and married me off to the gap-

toothed, bow-legged Mkandawire of the eternally bad breath.

I had not intended to get pregnant but it happened all the same. Father, who was already shattered by my refusal to get married to a man chosen for me, regarded my pregnancy outside marriage as the ultimate act of rebellion. He was angry and disappointed, and I was sad for both of us.

A few years after the birth of my son, I eloped to Twoboy's place. I left Mavhuto behind to go and start a new life. Many people accused me of callously abandoning my little boy for the love of a man. What they did not know was that I had run off to live with Twoboy so that my son could have a father. Back then the man had promised to bring up my son as his own but after living with him for a few months, I was glad that Mavhuto had remained with Father. To the inhabitants of Patchway Valley Mine, I committed the unforgivable sin of putting love for a man before that for my son.

"As well as having no morals, the girl has no heart. What kind of woman abandons her helpless toddler to go chasing after a man?" remarked those who seemed to know everything.

"Her mother neglected to squirt a few drops of milk from her breast over her daughter to cool her fiery blood. *Ha ha ha!*"

"That girl is surely going to shove her father into an early grave. What heart can endure such pain and humiliation?"

"It will be worse when she returns from the farms with more fatherless children for her long suffering father to look after. The poor man!" sighed yet more people.

"Yes, in a few months the silly girl will be back. You mark my words. Her mother's early death mercifully saved the poor woman from shame."

I endured the taunts that reached my ears at the farm. It was hard at first but I found comfort in distance. With time I got used to the insults and they stopped hurting, especially after I got to know that it would have been an ordeal for Mavhuto to grow up with Twoboy's unpredictable moods. I did not find it easy living with him myself in the beginning. The situation is quite different now. I was often asked by friends why I stayed with a man who ill-treated me despite not having paid anything to my father. I had reasons for not abandoning the 'marriage'. I had been condemned as wanton and fickle. I had to show those who criticised my behaviour that I was a courageous woman who did not shy away from problems. What I could not decide on was whether courage lay in my ability to endure the abuse of the man I lived with, or in taking the decision to leave him.

In the end I decided that running away was not an option in my case. I was not sure that Father and his horrible new wife would welcome me back, given the way I had left, so I decided to endure the strife in my marriage in the same way I had seen other wives do. Married couples disagreed now and again and at times the arguments turned into physical fights that ended with the wife getting beaten into submission. I had witnessed this many times as I was growing up. A number of men in my community became crazed animals at month ends after downing large quantities of *masese* at the beer hall. They became incensed over the miserable wages that barely stretched from the first day of the month to the last, after sweating their lives off underground.

I could have left Twoboy as some people suggested but it would have meant moving on to another Twoboy elsewhere, of whom there were plenty in the community. I could have made a life for myself and my son at another farm but I was aware of the attitude of married women who despised unattached women. I understood their fears.

After all, most men regard any unattached woman as one who is readily available. I would have become an object of insults and name-calling, and that would have affected Mavhuto more. It was bad enough that he was referred to as '*mwana alibe ababa,*' a fatherless child, and it would have been harder still for him with '*amai alibe mamuna*', a mother without a husband. Mavhuto was not responsible for the unfortunate circumstances of his birth, and I did not want him to suffer for the folly of my youth. While I was not stuck in that situation, it seemed to be just one of those cases where there were more reasons for staying than there were for leaving. It took me more than ten years to realise that there was always a way out. My misplaced pride had blinded me and prevented me from realising it sooner.

I had tried to live my life according to the expectations of my people, but the strain of trying to be who I was not slowly began to wear me out. All these people gathered here today judge me in one way or the other. They do not understand the conflicts in my life. They wonder how I can continue to live with a man who has no valid claim on me. Had I left Twoboy, they would have called me immoral and lacking the determination to persevere with the trials and strife of marriage as every well brought up woman ought to do. It is unfortunate that whatever I do, I am likely to be shunned and insulted for it. In the early days I was in a dilemma. I had grown up rebelling against the normal. Now for once I wanted to be like everybody else but I was not sure what was expected of me; to leave and get myself a more considerate man, or to endure the consequences of my decision. If I left, the men themselves would have examined my past and counted the number of failed relationships behind me, based on which they would have decided whether to regard me as wanton or not. I have completely failed to understand what is expected of me.

While I do not understand the world out there, my son does not understand me. He resents me for not being around during the early years of his childhood. I hope that as he grows up, one day he shall realise that sometimes mothers make sacrifices that appear not to show consideration for their children. I was not a mother for Mavhuto as he grew up, therefore it is not surprising that he hardly knows me. I stayed away for long periods and as time went by, I was unable to retrace the footprints that led home. I want to talk to my son now but I do not know where to start or what to say since he and I are strangers. I hope that one day he will understand that it is normal to want to protect one's loved ones by keeping away from them so that they are shielded from the painful experiences of one's own life. As far as my son is concerned, I abandoned him to follow the man I worshipped but as far as I am concerned, I left him in the care of Father, in the same house where I was raised with abundant love. Mavhuto could not have had a better substitute parent than my own father whose love I never doubted even during those times when I thought he was being too strict.

Twoboy was the first man I fell in love with after I became a mother, though he was not the first to try and have a relationship with me. The first was a workmate of his who has since moved to another farm. When this workmate approached me I could tell right away that his intentions were not serious. Besides, there was nothing to admire about him, except his navy blue bell bottom trousers that were in fashion at that time. I remember thinking that at least he dressed well for a farm labourer. It was a pity though about the cigarette burn mark at the hem of the trousers. Two months later, Twoboy introduced himself to me at a football match. He was wearing a pair of navy blue bell-bottomed trousers whose hem had a hole from a cigarette burn. Twoboy was kind

and easy to talk to and he spoke with pride about his job and his position as the overseer at Chestnut Farm.

"Some few months ago I met someone who works at the farm where you work." I told him who it was.

"Oh, that one? I know him. He is my friend though I regard him more like a brother. His wife belongs to the Sena tribe like me," he answered. I said nothing about the trousers. Whether they belonged to Twoboy or his brother-friend did not matter. I knew that many young men and women shared clothes. I had done the same in the past, wearing with pride a blouse belonging to Fereti and matched with Mada's skirt before stepping out in my own shoes. That was what we did to keep up with fashion. Twoboy was similarly trying to keep up with the latest trends in fashion on the meagre wages of a farm labourer.

When I eloped with Twoboy, the intention was not to leave my son behind for longer than just a few months. It is unheard of for a woman to elope with her child or children, so I had to leave mine behind. Twoboy assured me that it was only a temporary arrangement until we were settled in married life. I made the decision to start a new life with Twoboy because it was the right thing to do. I could not remain a child forever, especially as I had become a mother myself. I had to wean myself from Father's care and try to be a responsible adult. Father had married again and his wife had brought her daughters along. I am aware that many people think I left home out of resentment for the new woman who had taken my mother's place, and that to spite her, I callously abandoned my son to be raised by her. These malicious allegations hurt as much as they angered me.

The whispers continued, but I soon learnt to ignore them. Father's new wife, *ma*Mpofu and I resented each other right from the start when she and her two young daughters installed themselves in my late mother's house. She was forever trying to tell me how I should live my life,

treating me like a slave that should remain chained to one place when not being ordered to do this or that. My stepmother was an impossible woman who found fault with everything I did so I talked back to her.

By then I was already carrying Mavhuto, a situation I had known about just a few weeks after *ma*Mpofu's arrival. My pregnancy did not cause me any problems. I did not experience any dizzy spells in the morning. I was not fussy about what I ate although I had a few minor cravings that eventually died away. The only change was that I longed to curl up in bed longer, which infuriated my stepmother. She called me all sorts of names, from wanton to lazy, and more in between. When my baby was due he made no effort to come.

"It is as lazy as the mother who carries it, *nxi*!" I once heard *ma*Mpofu tell a neighbour who had asked if I had given birth yet. The more Father's wife tried to make my life miserable, the more I defied her. My baby was overdue by about two weeks. I continued attending the baby clinic for expecting mothers at the local clinic.

One Saturday morning I woke up with a sharp pain slicing down my navel and down my sides. It felt as if my intestines were coiled around huge fingers that clenched into a tight fist and tugged hard at intervals. I ambled over to the clinic. I had just stepped through the door when I was seized by the most excruciating spasm. I doubled up and groaned before gasping for air. One hand clutched my stomach while the other clutched my back. The nurse rushed over to assist me.

"Stay calm, Dhairesi," she urged. "Remember what I told you during the baby clinic sessions?" I nodded while at the same time trying to stifle a scream.

"Amama ine! Amayo!" I murmured through clenched teeth.

"Dhairesi, take a deep breath and keep walking." Nurse was trying to lead me to the maternity room but I was fighting her.

"I can't breathe. I am dying. Do something I beg you, *a*Nurse."

There were a few women and children waiting in the clinic but I behaved as if they did not exist.

"*Amayo, Amama ine*!" I screamed this time.

A few of the women tried to hide their sniggers behind clenched fists, with little success. They obviously regarded my whimpering as the height of cowardice.

"Hahaha, now she calls for her mother. What has her mother got to do with all this business?" sneered one of the sniggering women. Two women who were sympathetic to my plight helped walk me to the bed. By then the pain felt as if the clenched fist was twisting my insides while attempting to rip them out. I remember little of how I was settled onto the bed. I do not know either how I got through it all but after a few more moments of grunting, groaning and panting, the knotted fist of pain shot out of my stomach like an arrow off a bow. The gruelling ordeal was over. The nurse held by the feet a slimy baby with a wrinkled face and turned him upside down. She gave his pink bottom a smack and the little thing scrunched its face and howled with a strength that surprised me.

"You have been blessed with a healthy baby boy." The nurse ululated. The sound carried down the corridor and into the reception area where the women waiting there also took up the ululating. The baby screamed again. I turned my head away and faced the wall. That sound turned my world upside, and it would continue to do so for a long time afterwards.

I took my son home the following day. It was the beginning of a strange and new phase. It was difficult to comprehend how so small a human being could change

my life in such a big way. My nights became days, and the days became part days and part nights. There were baby clothes and napkins to be washed almost all the time, water to boil, food to prepare, always. Always. It was tiresome. Most of the time my baby would open his mouth and expose toothless gums, then yell as if there was a league of demons inside his tiny head. He would not respond to my cooing. He cried even as the whole world slept, which deprived Father of much needed sleep and irritated his wife. Mavhuto would only calm down when I strapped him onto my back. It made me feel like a harnessed and yoked beast and I was failing to cope. No one was offering much of their help. There was no husband to moan to either about the wretchedness of motherhood, a battle I had entered into unprepared and unarmed. I was always tired and irritated by the baby's constant crying. *Ma*Mpofu said my son cried that much because I kept him in wet and soiled nappies most of the time and that the dampness, the coarseness of the nappies and the heat caused a rash which in turn made his skin itch. That irritated him further and made him cry even more, she said. I argued that I had no way of knowing when his nappies were soiled because he never said anything.

"Dhairesi, your problem is that you nurse your young one as if you were a cow. You think sticking your nipple into the infant's mouth takes care of all other problems. Well, it doesn't. That baby needs to be kept warm, dry and well-fed," *ma*Mpofu took to lecturing me on motherhood almost everyday. I retorted that it was not my fault if there were no clean and dry nappies. I was not responsible for turning on the water taps, nor was I in charge of controlling the weather to bring out the sun everyday.

One morning I woke up to find *ma*Mpofu towering over me. I was lying on the reed mat on the floor in the main room. She had my son strapped onto her back and

she was shouting at me. The baby was screaming at no one in particular and for no particular reason that I could see. I was feeling sleepy, confused and tired. *Ma*Mpofu waved her arms about and the baby kicked his puny legs and clenched his fists.

"Get up right now, Dhairesi," shouted my stepmother. "Get up and roll up that mat, I said. Now!"

"*Nxi,*" I snorted in annoyance as I tightened the blanket around my body. I could not believe the woman expected me to be up before sunrise despite knowing that I had had a restless night. Mavhuto had been up most of the night crying non-stop in between periods of suckling. My step-mother bent down to wrench the blanket off me but I resisted and tucked it tighter underneath me.

"Leave me alone, please. Just go away and leave me alone. I am still feeling sleepy," I mumbled.

"No! You are not going back to sleep, Dhairesi. You have more laziness in those bones of yours than all the old women in this compound. I have had enough of your spoilt ways. Other women wake up with the rising sun and do their house chores before the dew dries on the grass, but not you, Dhairesi. You want to sleep until the sun has tucked shadows under your feet. What is so special about you?"

"I have a headache. Please leave me alone."

"A mother has no time to listen to the aches and pains of her body, do you hear?"

"Just go away, please. I have already told you that I have a headache, but you do not care about my pain. You hate me because I am not your daughter," I screamed. At that point Mavhuto screamed even louder.

"This has nothing to do with whether or not you are the fruit of my womb. It is about your laziness and your neglect of the innocent baby your own womb produced. You are lazy, Dhairesi, and that is what I cannot tolerate,"

my stepmother spat furiously. By then she was gasping for breath, having given up the attempt to remove the blanket.

"This is not about anything but the joy you derive from seeing me suffer. You *do* hate me. You think I do not realise that? Where is the harm in my getting some rest before I get up?"

"The harm lies in that by the time you finally choose to get up, the water will be turned off at the main tap, and the water *I* fetch for cooking, drinking and cleaning will all be used up by you within a short time. Get up and fetch the water for washing your baby's clothes and nappies. You need water for your own bath and for his too. The plates from last night need washing up, and the yard must be swept before the sun rises. I will be busy cleaning the house, after which I will prepare food to take to your father at the shaft."

"I cannot do all that," I complained. "My baby needs looking after."

"Ha, just shut your mouth, Dhairesi." *Ma*Mpofu sprang swiftly and this time she caught me unawares and managed to rip the blanket off me. She waddled away with it towards her bedroom with little Mavhuto now sitting quietly and snuggly on her jutting behind.

I sat up and blinked back tears of frustration. I took some time to stretch my limbs, yawn and roll up my bedding and put it away. My mind was racing with all the different ways in which I could drive Father's wife out of our lives, after all she was beginning to cause friction between Father and me. I was not going to watch the situation get worse, I vowed. I had no idea how I would go about getting Father to get rid of her but I was sure something would come to mind sooner or later.

While I was brushing my teeth on the veranda, the woman I had come to regard as my tormentor emerged from the house. Little Mavhuto was still strapped onto her back and she was singing him a lullaby. He contentedly

sucked the thumb stuck in his mouth and his head nestled comfortably between *ma*Mpofu's shoulders. Utter betrayal that was, on my son's part, I thought, fuming inwardly. My first instinct was to rush at my stepmother and grab my boy from her, but another thought came to mind. If *ma*Mpofu wanted to steal my son's affection and turn him against me, then she could have him. I decided that instant to wean my son. *Ma*Mpofu would have her uses after all. She had always said it was time he was weaned and she accused me of keeping him longer on breast milk as an excuse not to do any work and sit instead with my breast stuck in his mouth. In the months that followed, despite the help she had taken to giving me with my son, my relationship with *ma*Mpofu did not improve. She still considered me the laziest person she had ever encountered, a view she shared with anyone who cared to listen, and there were many of them. She told neighbours and those she counted among the women as her friends that in her village, children like Mavhuto were given the name Chenzira, which means he or she-who-was-begotten-by-the-path.

*Ma*Mpofu explained that such children were said to have been conceived when the mother stepped off the path and into the bushes to cavort with some man and the result of the encounter produced baby Chenzira nine months later. Mavhuto was spoilt by *ma*Mpofu's girls but they soon returned to their village. *Ma*Mpofu said she wanted them removed from the bad influence of *komboni* life. Before they went back I had been able to leave my son with them while I visited my friends, both men and women. Father warned me not to bring another totemless baby to his house. He said that while he was fond of Mavhuto, he would prefer it if I got married first before there was another grandchild. I retorted that I was going to spend time with friends, not to make babies.

By the time Mavhuto turned two years old, he had contracted every disease a toddler could possibly get, from measles, mumps, rubella, diarrhoea, stomach cramps to the effects of dehydration. He wailed endlessly. Father, however, was very good with him. He soon became attached to his grandson whom he loved as if he were his own son. He found it easy to tolerate the boy's screams that constantly made my head almost explode. Slowly, *ma*Mpofu also started warming towards my son. She would strap him onto her back and go about doing the house chores and he seemed to settle better on the comfort of her wide back than he did on my thin one. Mavhuto's birth had turned my dreams into a real nightmare. This was not how I had wanted to live my life. I hated the reflection I saw in the mirror. Power pylons, cyanide dumps, ore wagons, perpetually weary-looking gumbooted labourers, miserable-looking fires cooking miserable meals and no hope beyond that! I had to get away from Patchway Valley Mine before it finally swallowed me. When I met Twoboy, I saw a way out of the compound life.

When I told Twoboy about my son, he had assured me that he was willing to have him and raise him as his own. The plan was that I would leave my son and elope to his place and that within a day or so, he would send an emissary to Father stating his intentions, after which he would pay whatever bride price Father charged. After all that was over, Mavhuto would then come and live with us. I clutched at the chance as to a log in a raging storm. I did not need much persuasion. My son would stay behind just for a little while, a period during which I was sure he would not miss me. Anyone could step in and be his mother, and the boy would not notice the difference. Father and *ma*Mpofu would think I had no concern for him but I had to get out while I still could.

By the end of that week I had given Twoboy a bundle of the few clothes that I owned; three skirts, four blouses and a knitted jersey. He took these with him to the farm. A couple of days later, I sneaked out of the house as my son slept. My new life was to start from that point. Unfortunately, things did not go as planned. My dream crumbled shortly after I got to the farm. The life out there was not one of bliss but hardship and I became unhappy and frustrated. To begin with, there was the War. It was raging mainly on farmlands. That was no situation to bring a small child into. Gunfire could be heard in the dead of the night. It was my misfortune that the war we had only heard about from *ma*Mpofu had reached fever pitch at the time I went to live on the farm. Father and his friends had talked about it as if it were some event in a distant land. Up to that point there had been peace on the farms, so Twoboy and the others labourers said.

Then the dogs of the bosses barked ferociously one night. In the morning, the beasts were found lying on their sides on the ground, their tongues hanging out and their eyes bulging. Both were dead. They had been poisoned. The cotton and maize crops were burned to ashes the next day. Telegraph wires were cut in the days that followed, and the bosses' line of communication with the outside world was disconnected. A landmine exploded along the gravel road leading up to and out of the farm. Another exploded where the gravel road from the farm joined the main road from Chakari Mine to Gatooma. The first explosion claimed no lives. The second one did. The car taking the two eldest children of the bosses to Jameson High School hit a landmine, exploded and went up in flames. There were no survivors. Everybody was on edge; the white farmers, the workers and their families.

The weekly sojourns to the mines were abandoned as people preferred to be safe at home. I was effectively cut off from my people at Patchway Valley Mine, and more

importantly, from my son. It was to be nearly three years before I was able to go back again. By then cease fire had been declared by the warring parties. The Patchway Valley I went back to was a completely different place from the one I had left behind. There were party people campaigning for the community to vote for them. It was scary. At times I stayed for a few days with Father and his wife, but I did not move back home. Father's friends still came round to discuss the war. This time they also discussed politics, not that they understood who was who. They mixed up their slogans and party names, which they found hilarious. After all, the war had never really touched their lives.

Mavhuto hardly noticed my presence and he went about playing with other little boys of his age, kicking a ball made of plastic bags. He was not aware of who I was and nobody thought to tell him. There was enough time to get into all that when the time came to take him with me. My situation was a difficult one though. When peace finally returned to the farms and the birds could be heard singing happily again in the forests, I stayed there. I needed to hide my face from Father who would pity me, and from those who delighted in my misery.

The majority of the people at Patchway Valley Mine still shunned me and they did not expect anything good to come out of my life. Those who revelled in my misfortune called me a silly, immoral woman who shamelessly co-habited with a man from the farms. I was therefore determined to stay on with Twoboy no matter what. Initially, I had stayed with Twoboy out of love for him, then it was out of a stubborn desire to prove to myself that I could be in control of my life. I only had to wrestle with, and subdue, the demons that occasionally haunted Twoboy. I was a fighter and this was my war. It was not long before hope died, and from its death emerged the ghost of the woman whose shadow I had tried to escape

from for ages, the one whose reflection often appears in my mirror.

Despite that, I continued to live with Twoboy only to shame those who sniggered behind my back, waiting for me to come back so they could say they knew all along that my life was set on a self-destructive course. Years later, I still live with Twoboy whom I have come to understand well and the demons that drive him. When he would not let me collect my son from Patchway Valley, I was angry and disappointed at first and I accused him of tricking me.

"We will get the boy after I pay *lobola* for you," he would say. "I will then be recognised formally as your husband and will therefore have the right to raise the boy as my own." A few months later he said that he could not pay *lobola* until I bore him a child. He was reneging on his promise, I realised, but I thought he was just like the majority of men who wanted things in a certain order; a woman, children and marriage. I therefore endeavoured to have the baby we both desperately wanted. Having a baby meant Twoboy paying *lobola,* which in turn meant the stability of our relationship. It also meant a change in the way people regarded our relationship but, more importantly, it meant instant redemption in Father's eyes who, over the years, had despaired over my way of life, considering it to be decadent beyond salvation. It also meant that at last my son could come and live with us and we would be one big happy family, together. Unfortunately, war got in the way, and life happened. Twoboy forgot about his promise and I did not get my dream.

* * *

The dream remains unfulfilled with my failure to bear babies who survive. All the ones I had were stillborn, and Twoboy wants us to keep trying. If I do not, he will eventually take another wife. He reminded me of the likelihood of that happening the day I returned from Chakari Mine clinic after the fourth stillbirth.

"The nurse says I should take a break and avoid pregnancy for at least six months," I told Twoboy.

"Take a break from trying to have children?" he barked, straightening up from the bicycle he was fiddling with which he kept in the hut where we slept. Turning around to face me, he demanded, "Who ever heard of such nonsense, a childless woman taking a rest from the chance of becoming a mother? *Nxi*!"

"But I think the nurse is right, Twoboy. My body is now exhausted. It takes me longer to recover after each stillbirth."

"Is that so? Okay then, you go ahead and take a break, a holiday, days off, rest or whatever you wish to call it, but move back to your father's house first. When you have rested enough you can then come back. But let me warn you, Dhairesi. There might be another woman here, in which case there will be no room for you. In fact, I do not see why I need to wait until you remove your useless, wretched self from my house before taking another woman. That decision has been long overdue. On this farm alone, there are many young girls just out of *chinamwali* who are forever throwing themselves at my feet. I could have any of them any day if I wanted. I have no doubt they would be capable of producing strong and healthy children for me. The parents of these women would be proud to have me as a son-in-law. So go have your rest, Dhairesi. Go!"

"The nurse did not say we have to stay apart while I rest my body. She gave me family planning pills to take everyday to stop_"

"What!" shrieked Twoboy, horrified, his hands cupping the back of his head. "The nurse at the clinic gave you pills to prevent pregnancy?"

"Yes, she said_"

"Shut up, Dhairesi. *Shatapu*! That nurse is an idiot. *Dhemeti, blati furu!*[87] Instead of giving you those stupid pills she ought to give you medicine to flush out the rot in your womb that contaminates your unborn babies, making them unfit to survive outside the womb. Then maybe you could finally give birth to healthy babies that will live to suckle at your breasts. I should have known that the cesspit you grew up in is a breeding ground for all kinds of immorality. Pills to stop my seed from coming to life, *eyi!* Who ever heard of such abomination?" All this while Twoboy had been scowling and stamping his feet about, then all of a sudden he stopped and stared at me as if something had just dawned on him. "Aha!" he said, "now I know why your womb is rotten. *Mirandu,*[88] *nxi!* It's those filthy pills. I am sure you have used them before, Dhairesi. Now your womb is rotten, that's why your babies come out dead. They are poisoned by the rot inside your womb. I know now that you do not care about making me a man among men. And once you start taking the seed-destroying pills, what is to stop you from having other men while I am busy chasing rustlers out there, eh?"

I wanted to tell Twoboy that I had given birth to a son who was strong and healthy and that it was most likely his seed that was weak, but he did not give me the chance. He went on ranting and raving, non-stop. "What baffles me is why a childless woman would willingly take pills to stop herself conceiving. Family planning indeed, what family is there to plan when there are no children? This is just an

---

87 Damned, bloody fool

88*sins*

excuse to go fornicating with whoever glances your way. Only immoral women take the stupid things. Do not think I'm stupid, *nxi!*"

"But Twoboy_"

"Oh, shut your mouth, Dhairesi. I knew you were wanton when I met you but I thought you would be grateful that I saved you from a life of eternal wretchedness. How mistaken I was! What is a woman without a man, eh? Who, in your fastidious Chewa tribe would take you for a wife, uninitiated as you are, unless it were some toothless old man who is not fussy, so long as his food is cooked and his soiled trousers washed? Well, Dhairesi, if you want to continue living here as my wife, then you had better hand over those pills to me now. I will throw them down the pit latrine and we can forget you ever brought such things into this home. As for that nurse at the clinic, I forbid you to consult her ever again over anything. I can see she is a bad influence, so no more visits to that clinic, you hear? The next time you are ill, go to Patchway Valley Mine clinic."

"Twoboy, I beg you, listen to me. I too want to have children but my body needs a rest. I have to get strong before carrying another child."

"Rest! What rest are you talking about now? Who ever heard of an elephant needing rest from carrying its tusks, eh? If you feel that way, why should you stay here then? Why did you come here if not to give me children? Do you think you are here just to eat the food I provide with from sweat?"

"Twoboy, do you have any idea how I feel each time I strap the lifeless body of my baby onto my back, covering it and pretending it is living and breathing so that I can bring the body home to bury? Do you think I enjoy carrying on my back that which was once a part of me, kicking away in my stomach not so long ago? Whenever I get off the bus from Gatooma, the women in this

compound now hide from me. From behind the reed walls of their homesteads, they just stare with curious eyes and still lips at the bundle strapped to my back. Who can blame them? They do not know whether to congratulate me or to pay their condolences. Do you think I enjoy that, time after time?"

"In what way is that my fault, Dhairesi? In any case why bother bringing your lifeless bundles back here? From what I hear, there is a big fireplace where they take care of such things. So if you choose to burden yourself unnecessarily, it is your own problem. Now do as I say and give me the pills right now, or pack your things and go. Now! And if you go, do not ever come back again."

I stood facing Twoboy, but not daring to look him in the eye. I was debating on whether to hand over the pills or to pack my things and go. It was not the first time he had ordered me to do as he said or else leave his house. I had always stayed, but only because I had nowhere to go. I did not know how Father would receive me, if at all.

I could visit him for a few days but that was different from moving back in forever. During the first two years of my elopement, I did not go back home because I still believed Twoboy would go through the formalities of paying *lobola* so that I would be free to visit my family. When that did not happen I became ashamed. I could not face the people in my community and I stayed for only a few days at father's house, a period during which I did not venture into the compound. There were whispers already that our relationship was nothing more than mere co-habitation. But shame or no shame, after several years I had finally had enough. My life had not turned out as I had imagined, but that was no reason for me to chain myself to eternal misery. So, for the first time since we started living together, I defiantly looked Twoboy straight in the face and said, "Okay then. I am leaving." I do not know who was more shocked, Twoboy, that I had decided

to leave him, or me that I had actually uttered the words. Like two beasts preparing to lock horns, Twoboy and I glared at each other. Then I turned round to start packing before I lost my nerve. The blow that landed on my cheek was so unexpected it winded me and catapulted me across the room. I hit the floor with a thud. In no time blood started gushing from my mouth. I shook my head to clear my eyes of the stars I was seeing and a bloodied tooth fell onto the floor. As I struggled to rise, a sharp pain shot through me. I could feel the right side of my face swelling, twisting my mouth in the process. Twoboy took a couple of strides towards me. He looked menacing, like a rabid dog. I flinched and braced myself for further attacks.

"Repeat what you just said, Dhairesi," he snarled, towering over me. "You said you are doing *what?*"

"I said, I said I am leaving," I lisped, blood oozing from my rapidly swelling tongue.

"How dare you say that? You want to leave me? After all these years during which I bought you clothes, fed you and spent my hard earned money on you? I toil and sweat for the food you eat and this is what I get in return; ingratitude? I would rather kill you than let you walk away from me. You used me. Do you know that I could kill you right now?"

"Yes, I do. If you do not kill me today you will eventually kill me one day. So why prolong the misery?" I lisped, resigned to whatever lay ahead. "I am going back to my father. I shall ask for his forgiveness. I hope he will forgive me, and help pay you back all the money you spent on me over the years."

What happened next blew the wind out of my chest and left my mouth dry. Right before my eyes, the man who had controlled my life and intimidated me crumpled. The big fierce bulldog turned into a puppy; yapping, blubbering and begging.

"Dhairesi *chikondi,*[89] I am your husband, the only person who really cares for you in this whole world. Please do not leave me. I will be a better husband from today onwards. Please Dhairesi, say you won't go. I will take you to Gatooma and buy you new clothes; shoes and hats and sandals and skirts and blouses and whatever else you want." This Twoboy who acknowledged the importance of my presence in his life was new to me. I pitied him for his weakness, but I decided not to let it move me. My mind was made up. He had made me suffer for so long and I could not take anymore. I had to leave.

"What do you say, huh, Dhairesi?"

"I need to go back home."

"But your home is here with me, your husband. Nobody at Patchway Valley has any respect for you. They snigger at you behind your back. Your father probably doesn't want you to move back and live in his house again."

I did not care what anyone else said anymore, I told Twoboy. I hoped Father would forgive me and even if he did not, I still needed to apologise for all the misery I had caused him. Twoboy went on to tell me over and over again how much he cared, and that he wanted us to stay together. I was not convinced that he would ever change, but I wanted my wounds to heal first before I went back to Father. I did not wish to go back with a swollen face and bleeding gums; proof of a violent 'marriage'. It was bad enough that I was going back to tell him that my so-called marriage was an unhappy one, I did not need to show him the evidence. I told Twoboy that I would stay on condition he never beat me up again, and that he would let me visit Father within the month, and let me heed the advice given by the nurse. He readily agreed to the first two, but eventually agreed, albeit grudgingly to the third after I

89 Beloved

told him I would definitely leave him that day if he refused. For the first time that day, Twoboy told me about his pain, frustration and fears. I realised only then that the man who had demeaned and intimidated me for years was actually a lot weaker than I was in many ways. I pitied him, but I was not going to let sympathy sway me. Twoboy considered his life unfulfilled so long as there was no issue from his loins to carry his name and continue his lineage, even though it was a wretched and miserable long line of labourers.

Independence was supposed to have brought equality, brotherhood and reconciliation between blacks and whites, *abwana* and farm labourers but Twoboy still remains the farm labourer who must see to the smooth running of the whole farm, for which he continues to earn meagre wages. The hours are long, the work is hard and the conditions are terrible. He must still rise with the sun every morning and he hardly returns home before sunset. If there are suspected rustlers in the area, he can be gone for the whole day and the whole night and come back hungry and tired the next morning. In times like these, Twoboy does not have much patience, especially if *bwana* blames him for whatever goes wrong on the farm. I can always tell when he has had a bad day, for he can be heard bellowing long before he gets to the cluster of huts that make up the farm workers' compound. He charges home, his bloodshot eyes darting all over the place, his brow furrowed with fury.

Until just a few years ago when Twoboy changed for the better, I had lived with him in spite of the taunts and insults he hurled at me. He called me names that his masters reserve only for the laziest of slobs. I should have hated him then but I pitied him instead. The *bwana* insulted him and he in turn would insult others. But all that has changed. I suppose the poor man has learned to

return the love of those that love him while bottling up those insults that make him look like a caged wild animal.

Over the years I have learned not to ask Twoboy what is wrong. I quietly step out of his way. All the fury he feels at whatever treatment he gets from the master, my *husband* channels into digging our garden. The black mood lasts until that of the master lifts too. It is a hard life and these are demons that I can live with but which I do not wish Mavhuto to endure. I understand the *husband-who-is-not-really-my-husband* and I learned to live with him a long time ago. It is not an entirely miserable life but on the occasions Twoboy gets angry, I dare not be in his presence. Luckily, these black moods are now rare and we are happy some of the time. Everybody around chooses to close their eyes to the goodness in Twoboy, preferring instead to focus only on the dark side when the demons within him rear their ugly heads. They refuse too to see the person that I have become in their determination to shun me and call me wanton. They hardly acknowledge Twoboy and me as a couple. To them we are co-habiting in sin, and we will remain sinners in their eyes until the day Twoboy pays *lobola*. The story of my life precedes me wherever I go.

During the early years of my son's childhood, I stayed away for long periods not only because of the hurtful comments but also because I did not wish to cast a dark shadow over his innocent life. I do not expect Mavhuto to understand of course but one day he will be grateful that I left him to grow up without my reputation hovering like a shadow over his head.

All these people gathered here today look me up and down before expressing their condolences. I can tell what goes on in their minds when they see the person I have become. Instead of my strength, they see only the weather-beaten skin and the calloused hands as a result of working hard in all kinds of weather. Years ago they had looked at

the same hands and skin and shunned them as too soft and too smooth which, to them, were signs of laziness and proof that I was incapable of doing any real work. If they do not envy me, they despise me. Since I can never please anybody I do not care anymore what people think. I am who I am and that is that. I have come here to mourn Father who was the most sincere man I knew. I will bury him, after which I shall go back to the life I know. At least it is a life that is predictable and steady. The pain I feel at the death of my father is numbing in itself but it is magnified by the guilt that wrecks me for neglecting to maintain regular contact with him over the years. Father was a wonderful man in many ways and I should have been a better daughter to him, especially during the period following the untimely loss of Mother.

There were a lot of things I did not understand then. Through Father's own death, I have now come to understand that grief can grip you and wrap you up to the point of excluding even those people that you love and care for the most. It is only now that I understand the depth of the pain my parents must have felt at the loss of my brother. Their grief must have been total, given the manner of Chakumanda's death. The loss of a child, I now know, is a wound that never heals. No pain compares to it and not even the passing of years diminishes the sense of loss. It lives on as a scar which is a constant reminder of pain buried deep in the heart. At that time, however, I had not understood the depth of my parents' grief.

"*Amayo,* for how long are you going to mourn your son?" I asked Mother one afternoon when I came home from visiting a friend and saw that her eyes were red and moist. It was not the first time I had come home to find her alone, weeping or showing signs of having recently done so.

"My daughter, a mother cannot place a limit on the period the heart aches for her lost child. The pain in my

heart refuses to go away, no matter how hard I try. It is as if a sharp knife is repeatedly plunged into my heart where it twists, the deeper it penetrates. There are no words to describe that kind of pain. It crushes the heart. Right now I just wish to die, *mwana wanga*. I do not see the point in living." I was not surprised that Mother considered her life to be pointless after her son's death. After all, Chakumanda was her favourite child, the one she had longed for with all her heart. It was always my Chakumanda this, my obedient Chakumanda that, whereas I was always the rebellious and stubborn Dhairesi. Maybe my parents would have preferred me dead instead of their precious son, but God had decided otherwise and I wished they would accept His decision.

Chakumanda was my only sibling, but with time I got over his death, and remembered him always with fondness. That did not mean I had not experienced profound grief at his passing. In fact, I never thought death could affect me so deeply again. It was a big shock when he died, mainly because I had never lost anyone so close before. The shock numbed me as I struggled to understand what death meant. For months after it happened, I kept feeling my brother's presence all over the house. I heard his music, I saw his friends, I heard his joyful whistling but more painful were the moments I thought I heard his futile cries for help in the collapsed tunnels. The memory of my brother even invaded my dreams and I woke up drenched in cold sweat, my mind confused, and my heart hurting with an ache I did not know how to soothe.

When Mother died about two years later, I was stunned by the injustice of it all. I was angry with her for dying and I blamed her for it. I clenched my fists in fury, gripped my sides and dug my nails hard to blot out the pain tearing at my heart. I wanted to lash out and hit someone or something. It was then that I understood that

it does not matter how often or how intensely one has experienced grief in the past, it is still painful the next time around. Today I feel crushed by Father's death. Maybe it is that loss which draws me closer to my son whom I intend to make the most important person in my life from today onwards. I will break my back working if I have to so that he continues with his education. At the moment, he and I are like strangers walking warily towards each other. I hope that with time we will finally get to understand each other.

The twists and turns that my life took began sometime back. I can still remember how trusting and innocent I was then. I was born and raised at Patchway Valley, a mining community that was very much a world unto itself. The only contact we had with outsiders was when traders came to do brisk business with miners and their families. Occasionally, we saw the outside world pass by as huge Coley Hall trucks shunted and grunted laboriously down the road on their way to the railway station in Gatooma, filled to the very top with mineral ore from Chakari Mine. The ore was transported from small surrounding mines to places we had only ever heard of but never visited. School also brought us into contact with the outside world when trainee-teachers were posted to the only school that served our community. We listened with amusement as they struggled to understand our language. With school also came the radio lessons that seemed to serve no purpose. We could never understand why we needed a teacher we could not see when we had one that was present in the flesh and blood.

It was hard enough trying to understand the visible teacher who spoke loud and clear through the mouth. The invisible teacher seemed to speak through a pinched nose, her high pitched voice shrieking from the small Marconi wireless that the teacher brought to class once a week. We had difficulties understanding Miss Childs the Radio

Lesson teacher because the radio crackled half the time. We called her Miz Chides because that was what we thought she introduced herself as. Whether the class enjoyed these lessons or not depended on the teacher's mood.

During my first year of school, if Mrs Marewe was in a bad mood she would hover over our heads and wave her menacing cane in readiness to strike whoever she thought was not doing as instructed. If she was in a good mood she would get on with her marking and leave Miss Childs to get on with the business of teaching us.

"Humpty Dumpty sat on a wall. Class, repeat after me..... Humpty Dumpty sat on a wall....." Miss Childs would instruct us. We mumbled something because we knew we were expected to make some sound. Undiscouraged, Miss Child's voice would praise us, even when we were too confused to follow her instructions. At other times she would have better results, as in;

Little Jack Honor
Sat in a Corner
Eating a Christmas pie.
He pulled out a plum
And stuck up a thumb
And said, what a good boy I am."

We never stopped to ask what a Christmas pie was. It was the same with everything else that we learnt in class. It did not matter if we understood it or not, what was important was that we remembered what we had learnt, even if it meant memorising the information with no understanding of it whatsoever. By the time I was in Grade 7, the final year of primary school, we had more to remember for the exam. We sang as if at a contest;

The capital city of Egypt is Cairo.
The capital city of Nigeria is Lagos

The capital city of France is Paris
The capital city of Belgium is Brussels
The capital city of Canada is Ottawa.

The five great lakes of Canada are Lake Superior, Michigan, Huron, Erie and Ontario. My Grade Seven teacher, a male one at this stage_ for some reason female teachers taught lower classes while their male colleagues taught the higher classes_ was always very happy when we correctly recited these facts by heart. He even encouraged us to say, 'Sister Mary Has Eaten Oranges' and use the first letter of each word to remember the names of the five great lakes. For some reason it seemed important that we know by heart who the President of the United States was. We never questioned why that was so, we just made sure we remembered. Failure to do so earned us severe punishment.

Despite that, I liked school and I enjoyed my time there. I took part in most school activities but I detested athletics. During the season for athletics tournaments, promising athletes were made to practice each morning by doing two laps of the football pitch. It was painful to run barefoot on frostbitten grass and it was worse when sharp blades of grass or tiny pebbles embedded themselves in the cracks on our feet. In school we formed friendships, and broke some of them up for various reasons. We fell in love too, but only from a distance, and on paper. With hearts fluttering, we wrote back to the boys who sneaked love letters into our desks.

Greenland of Love
Where love was born
P.O Romance.

We then went on to declare our undying love to boys we barely knew and from whom we ran away coyly the moment they tried to get near us. Our 'suitors' vowed to

swim the deepest ocean and climb the highest mountain to prove their love for us. One of my classmates wanted to show me exactly what that love involved in reality. His name was Isaki, but I preferred to call him Isaac, the English version of his name. He and I expressed our love for each other only through stolen glances for three good months. I was contented with the way things were but Isaac clearly was not. The first time we came into close contact was at the weekly bioscope show, a place where love that was declared elsewhere blossomed. On one particular Thursday evening, we sat next to each other. Under cover of darkness, as the crowds around us shouted enthusiastically at the actors on the screen, Isaac snuggled even closer and embraced me the way we had seen it done in the films. Suddenly, and with a force that almost knocked me over, he thrust his revoltingly slippery tongue into my mouth where it lay limp and cold like a dead frog. It was disgusting but I had to pretend to like it or be regarded as backward by this handsome boy who loved me enough to consider doing the impossible on my account.

This was despite my ignorance about what an ocean was, and it was also despite his inability to swim, which I did not know about until the summer he almost drowned in the shallow waters of the stream beyond the Mine dumps. As far as I knew Isaac had never even been to the Muvuti River nearby. Only a boy deeply in love could perform such an impossible feat, surely. But then love gives one the courage to do the impossible. We saw it all the time in the films we watched; one cowboy wiping out an entire army of Red Indians, all for the love of a woman, or for the defence and preservation of her honour.

The world outside our classrooms had everything that was characteristic of our way of life. I remember clearly the happiness that filled our lives as we grew up. Because the cooking was done outside, the fireplace became the

central part of family life in the evenings. Parents and their children sat out there warming themselves by the fire as mothers prepared the last meal of the day. Age old tales of the animal kingdom were told repeatedly with a slight twist time after time. During the harvest season, mealies and nuts were roasted on hot embers while sweet potatoes or pumpkins were boiled in big pots. Sometimes several families gathered in one place for story telling. At other times we played games while the adults sat gossiping by the fire. One of the games almost ended tragically one dark night. I must have been aged six or seven years when it happened, though I cannot say so for certain. Father, Mother and our neighbour, *a*Zuzeya, were sitting by the fireplace and chatting. My brother Chakumanda and his friends were playing hide and seek, a game they enjoyed on the darkest nights. It was a game best played when there was no moon. There was no shortage of places to hide because of the fruit trees in the yard, the chicken coop and the stack of wood by the side of the house. On these dark nights, wild cats also roamed about in search of scraps of food.

When *a*Zuzeya heard a rustling sound, he signalled for everybody around to keep quiet.

"Shh! A wild cat. *Bonga,*" he whispered, placing a finger on his lips before indicating where the said cat was. He then pulled out one of the bricks that formed the border of the flower bed.

"There is no cat out there, *a*Zuzeya. It is only the children playing," we heard Mother tell him.

"*Iyayi*, it is a cat, I can assure you. I can see its black eyes glittering among those logs."

"It could be the children playing hide and seek. Please be careful," implored Father.

"I tell you, *a*Masauso Nyirenda, it is one of those evil black cats, the type used by witches in the night. I am

going to bash this one to death, or maim it so that it shall never roam this way again."

Slowly and surreptitiously, *a*Zuzeya crept closer towards the shadows with the brick held firmly in his strong muscled right hand. With all his might, he then hurled the brick towards the stack of wood, whereupon a blood curdling scream ripped through the air. For an instant, everybody froze. Then, as if someone had blown a whistle to start a race, everyone came to life and sprinted towards the stack of wood. There was no mistaking that sound. It was definitely not a cat's yelp. The adults got there first, with Mother screaming, Father panting and *a*Zuzeya blabbering incoherently and trembling. Chakumanda lay flat on the ground as blood gushed from his face. Mother fell to the ground in a heap. Father knelt by my brother's side and cradled his head with trembling arms. I screamed. I had never seen so much blood before. It covered his whole face.

"You hit him with a brick in the face," observed Father.

"No, I did not. It was not a *briksi* that hit him. *Ndanhonga briksi, ndatema sticks, sticks ndiyo yazomubaya muziso,*[90]" blubbed *a*Zuzeya. I was scared for my brother and also felt much sympathy for *a*Zuzeya. The brick that had hit Chakumanda was still lying next to him, covered in blood on one corner. Our neighbours from all sides rushed out to our house when they heard Chakumanda scream. Mother was doused with water while Father heaved my brother onto his shoulders and rushed him to the local clinic, almost sprinting. I smelt fear in the air, and saw it in Father's manner. I had no doubt that in that moment he saw his son going to that place where the name given to him at birth had long since condemned him

90I picked up a bricks (sic), and hit a sticks (sic). It was the sticks that hit him in the eye

to. Father was filled with fear so thick you could almost touch it, and cut through it with a blade.

Chakumanda was back home within an hour and he had a white bandage over his left eye.

"The nurse said it is a miracle the boy did not lose his eye. The brick hit him just above the eye, narrowly missing it. Even then it is a wonder his skull is not smashed," I heard Father tell Mother.

"And yet you warned him not to throw that brick. He is lucky my son did not die or get maimed, or else he would have had to kill me too," declared Mother.

"It was a *masteki,*[91] *Amake* Chakumanda. Surely you saw how the man was shaking? It is a miracle that he did not open his bowels there and then. Try and consider how he must be feeling. Just a mistake."

"*Ababa* Chakumanda, have you forgotten so soon how much we suffered before we got that boy? And all it takes to threaten our happiness is the thoughtless act of a man who has never once suffered the pangs of labour. It is fortunate that he did not send my precious son to his grave or else I would have hanged myself at his doorstep."

"Watch what you say, *Amake* Chakumanda. Such words are not for the ears of our little girl here. Now, Dhairesi you go and lie down next to your brother. Make sure you do not thrash about in your sleep or you might end up kicking him in the head. He is still very much in pain," cautioned Father.

The following morning we all showed great consideration to Chakumanda who clearly seemed to enjoy the attention. Mother was even more attentive, treating him like the revered heir to some chieftainship. I thought he looked rather like those one-eyed bandits we saw in western films at the bioscope. It was a sad but comic sight. By evening I was suffering from a headache.

---

91 mistake

Although it was not a real one, it got me the attention I wanted. Mother told Father about my headache when he came back from work. She winked at him as she did so, and I guessed she was trying to remind Father of Chakumanda's pain above the eye.

* * *

In a place where several families were related to one another in one way or another, by totem or by the mere fact that our ancestors could be traced back to the same village, it was easy enough to claim some sort of kinship. So as far as I was concerned, any man who had the same surname as Father's was either *babamukuru* or *babamunini.* Apart from totemic and tribal links, we all socialised on a wider ethnic level and our being patronised migrants gave us greater cause for sticking together. When you are regarded as outsiders, the need to stick to one's kinsmen is even greater. Polite locals called us *'vabvakure,'* meaning those from faraway lands, but in derogatory terms they called us *Mabhurandaya.* Though it was said to be merely a reference to those places we supposedly originated from, I hated to be referred to as such because the word was used in a tone that implied contempt.

I grew up in a community where a large number of the men were my uncles and another sizeable number were my *aramu*. *Aramu* is one's in-law, he or she who is married to one's sister, a paternal aunt or brother. In the case of the husband of one's sister or aunt, one's *aramu* is also one's token husband as far as custom goes. One could indulge in all manner of banter with one's *aramu,* which was considererd normal and acceptable. In a community where the children of the men I called *babamukuru* and *babamunini* were numerous, it also meant that I had lots of *aramu* in their spouses. What should have been explained to me but was not, was that *aramu* is not in practice a husband. Giribhati, husband to one of my numerous 'sisters' was *aramu* to me. He playfully called me his wife from ever since I could remember. Mother often left me in the care of his wife whenever she went to fetch firewood so that I could play with Giribhati's two children, both of whom were younger than me. He would lift us all onto his shoulders, brush his lips against ours, hug us and tickle us under the armpits. We would giggle and tickle him as well. Each time Mother came to pick me up from Giribhati's, she profusely thanked him for being such a kind in-law who never tired of looking after his 'little wife'. So it was that I grew up knowing I was Giribhati's wife and of a few other *aramu* too.

A few years later I started school, which was an enjoyable experience. I made friends and did my best always to get along well with everybody. I became very good friends with Mudanjani who was the teachers' favourite pupil. She was to become my best friend through the years as we progressed from class to class. All of the teachers, without exception, liked her. That was not surprising because Mudanjani was good in class. No subject was too difficult for her. Whoever was our class teacher for the year showed us her work as an example of what we had to emulate. Unmarried male teachers sent her to their houses to wash the previous night's dishes and prepare the midday meal. For these services our classmate got pens, books and a few favours for which we all envied her. It was a privilege and an honour for one of us to be allowed into the homes of the teachers who were held in high esteem by the whole community. Such occasions afforded us the opportunity to glimpse into their lives.

The teachers in our community led comfortable and superior lives compared to us. They dressed well and sent their children away to boarding schools for secondary education. That was the kind of life I wanted for myself as well and there was only one way to get it. I had to work hard at school and pass. Father would have to save hard to pay my fees for boarding school if I passed. I was prepared to work on neighbouring farms weeding and picking cotton to supplement my fees. I had lived long enough with the quarry dust and the alluvial dumps of Patchway Valley Mine and I wanted to leave it all behind and live my life differently. I longed to be well educated and become a nurse like Mrs Tafirenyika or a teacher like Mrs Matsa. Then, like them, I would have a maid to do all the house work. Educated people lived a good life that I envied. The women seemed to stay young forever whereas the wrinkles on Mother's face seemed to increase and deepen as the years went by. The more I got a glimpse of this other kind of life, the stronger a better future beckoned. I wanted to keep on looking into the lives of my teacher frequently but I did not always get the chance, especially with Mudanjani around, providing stiff competition.

Giribhati continued to call me his 'little wife'. What Father and Mother did not realise was that he had since gone beyond just tickling my armpits. I would have told Mother, but Giribhati cautioned me against divulging such things to other people. He swore me to secrecy and said that whatever went on between us was a secret that should never be told to anyone, no matter what. He said that everybody else did it but did not tell it to anyone else. I believed Giribhati. I had no reason not to. After all I was brought up to believe that adults never lied. My parents trusted him with me just as his wife did, so I had nothing to fear. I was baffled though that Giribhati seemed to be the only one of my *aramu* who went further than engaging in mere verbal banter. He repeatedly warned me never to talk about such things or else something terrible would befall me. I kept our secret well, both out of respect for Giribhati and also out of fear of the terrible consequences, whatever they were. I kept the secret from even my best friend, Mudanjani

One day Mudanjani did not come to school. No one was surprised at first but after three days, our teacher became concerned that she was probably ill. She had never missed school without a good reason before.

"Let him worry," whispered Chisoni. "The favourite pupil is not coming back ever again."

"Why not? What is the matter with her?" I whispered back during a Nature Study lesson.

"She has gone for initiation."

"What are you talking about, Chisoni?" I asked, aghast.

"I said Mudanjani has gone for *chinamwali!"*

"Impossible. She's only twelve, the same age as us."

"So? She's ready for it. Some go even earlier. Nobody chooses when to go. It just happens when the time is right."

"Of course, I know that," I said impatiently. "I mean about her not coming back. She must come back to school and proceed all the way to Standard 6, surely?"

"She does not have to now, does she? Playtime is over and serious business beckons, as *Ambuya aFiripo* is fond of saying. It is being whispered that her father has already found her a suitable husband, so from the hands of the wise old women she goes straight into those of her new husband, *kumudhadhadha,*" explained Chisoni. I was appalled. I did not want to leave school and get married, or even get betrothed.

I liked none of the boys I went to school with who were much too young for marriage anyway. I also did not like any of the young men who worked in the mines. They were too old for me. I wanted the path of my life to be very different from that which Mudanjani's was destined to take, I vowed. I did not wish to give up my dreams and the books that enabled me to lose myself in new places and different experiences from the community I lived in. I read far into the night, at times enraging Mother when I fell asleep with the candle burning. She said my carelessness was not only a waste of our meagre resources but it could put our lives at peril. At times the candle burned out until the melting wax flowed onto the shiny floor where it cooled and hardened.

We did not have candle stands since they were considererd to be luxuries and therefore beyond our means. We sprinkled a few drops of hot candle wax onto the bare floor and placed the candle over the hardening wax to make it stick. At times we used discarded tins to stand the candle in. Mother used to scrap the wax off the floor and keep it in an old jar and when she had collected enough of it, she would melt it in a tin on the fire. When it was all liquid, she would remove the tin from the fire and add paraffin to the hot liquid and mix the two thoroughly. The mixture cooled after a while and the result was a kind

of mushy polish that we smeared over our cement floors. We had found ways of keeping our homes looking smart and the floors shiny.

We had uses for food that was left over from previous meals. Nothing was ever wasted, from bits of material, buttons, candle wax, scraps of metal and wood. We did not have the luxury of throwing away something merely because we did not like it. Someone in the compound was sure to need it. When we ran out of candles, which happened often, Father would bring out the home made paraffin lamp he said was unsafe and should only be used if we were very desperate and had nothing else. This lamp was made from a tin with an air-tight lid. A hole was bored in the centre of the lid and from it, a twisted cord was pushed through and immersed in the half full tin of paraffin. A short length of the wick was left showing above the lid and tied into a knot to prevent it from slipping into the tin. The knotted bit was then lit. It burned slowly, providing a dim smoky glow. Though the light was only a faint one, it enabled us to do our homework.

This makeshift lamp at times emitted thick black smoke that stung our eyes. Mother repeatedly warned Chakumanda and me not to use it too close to our eyes lest it affected our eyesight. Indeed our eyes watered and turned red, but we had little choice. The blindness would come sometime in the future but a thorough beating from our teachers would be sure to occur the very next day if we did not do our homework. I decided to worry about today and leave tomorrow for later. We painstakingly did our homework by lamp light, wiping away teary fluid from our eyes. Apart from the smoke, there was the pungent smell that almost choked us, but that was the least harm that could befall us. The worst and the most catastrophic was that the burning wick could slip into the tin and set off what our teachers mockingly called a Molotov cocktail type of bomb that could easily incinerate

everything, including people and property, to ashes within a short space of time. A family of six was said to have perished years back in a house fire that started when such a lamp exploded. It was a danger in whose shadows we lived but we got used to it and did our best to exercise caution. Ours was a life where we learned from the tragedies of others.

My fondness for reading continued even after I completed primary school and failed to get fees for secondary education. I filled my time with reading to banish from my mind the thought of the imminent and crucial issue of *chinamwali.* To me the ritual was still just a whispered secret, one that I would sooner or later be compelled to undergo. It was supposed to mark the beginning of a new phase of life for girls. I was not sure about the ritual but I certainly did not want to grow up, at least not just yet. I was not ready to step into the role of my mother, whose world I had lived in long enough to know that there was nothing much to make me yearn to rush into it.

Marriage would mean the beginning of an indefinite round of washing, cooking, making babies, fetching firewood, ironing clothes, making more babies and heating water, with very little variation, if any, so I buried myself in reading books, most of which I borrowed from friends in boarding school when they came home on holiday. It was through my fondness for reading that I got to know Tatenda who was the nephew of the Mine clerk, Mr Moyo. His family lived in Mrewa where his father was the village kraal head and his mother was a school teacher. Tatenda's life was very different from mine. In his world time was demarcated into distinct phases; *chirimo, zvizha, masutso, chando,* whereas in mine it was one long monotonous stretch, with each day just the same as the one before. Tatenda talked of vast forests, wild and domestic animals, fields of plentiful harvests and moonlit

nights. His description of the rolling hills and the shimmering mountains of his village, the meadowlands as well as the beautiful, slow flowing rivers that meandered down the valley was a captivating image. His was a world I did not know but one I yearned to venture into. I found it alluring in many ways.

When I fell in love with Tatenda, it was a steady and gradual progression from mere friendship based on a shared passion for reading, to a passion for each other that neither of us was capable of comprehending at that stage. I was flying into territories unknown, with the wind beneath my wings and I loved the feeling. Soon, everybody knew about Tatenda and me but I was in love and I did not care who knew about it. Father was alarmed and Mother dismayed. One of her friends, *Amake* Chisoni, warned me about the foolishness of getting involved with outsiders. I did not think she had any role to play in my life and I told her so.

"*Uyu mwana ali nimwano, Amake* Chakumanda," remarked Mother's friend. "She will surely languish in confinement when she goes for *chinamwali,* and I will personally see to that. She is so stubborn it would be a disgrace should she be left to go into marriage like that. What man would tolerate a wife whose unfettered lips spew whatever rubbish collects on her tongue? If you can talk back to your elders, you are bound to talk back to your husband."

"You have to be very strict with her, *Amake* Chisoni," agreed Mother. "Indeed, who would willingly share his home with the shrew that she is? She needs taming. As a daughter-in-law she is sure to be an embarrassment, answering her mother-in-law back. As a wife she would be utterly impossible; lacking in submissiveness and neglecting to look after her husband while spending the

whole day with her nose buried in those useless books she reads."

"Must you read all the time, Dhairesi?"asked the friend. I ignored her and kept on reading.

"What kind of books are those that you have to read all the time?" she persisted. "Read, read, and read! All day long! 'Benny and Betty, Benny and Betty.' Of what use is that Benny to anyone? So you think you have become some kind of superior being to all of us, and we are no longer good enough for you just because of your book knowledge? Those stupid books do nothing but fill your head with nonsense and ideas of a life well beyond what you or any migrant should hope for. If your father had any sense he would bethroth you now and marry you off as soon as you undergo *chinamwali.* This nonsense with that Shona boy has to stop, as should the pointless reading that turns your head."

"I enjoy reading and I shall continue to do so," I said, adamantly.

"What I fail to understand is why one should keep on reading even after learning how to read and write those useless squiggles of *abwana.* Dhairesi here can read letters and write them as well. And she is forever receiving letters and *masinepi* from people, some of whom she has never met. She can count and she knows her change, yet all day long and well into the night she sits with a book on her lap, her eyes glued to those tiny squiggles on paper. I fail to understand her fascination with all this," complained Mother. I could scarcely believe that she was the same woman who had urged me to work hard at school. Her new attitude towards my reading was astonishing.

"These people she writes to and whom you say she has never met, who are they?" asked *Amake* Chisoni.

"Penpals," I said, aware that I was showing off and displaying a bit of arrogance. I knew that neither Mother nor her friend knew what I was talking about but I

refrained from elaborating further. The two women both looked at me but upon realising that no explanation was coming, they gave up and went back to lecturing me on the evils of corresponding with total strangers.

* * *

I took my time to grow up and distanced myself further from the life around me, one that I did not understand. The more I detached myself from it the more I sought to understand the world beyond the boundaries of my community. The dust-coated gumboots of the miners did not appeal to me, nor did the echoes of their footsteps on the ground as they hurried off to work move me in any way. The sight of heavily pregnant young women carrying buckets of water on their heads did not fill me with envy either, nor did the sight of breastfeeding mothers who thrust shrivelled breasts under their armpits for the tots strapped to their backs to suckle while they got on with the house chores. The sight of new brides plaiting each other's hair after vigorously scratching dandruff off dry, flaky scalps did not appeal to me. I had no desire to slowly progress to the stage where I would sit under a tree with other elderly women and crotchet doilies while we waited anxiously for *Mabhurawayo* to come and pay a few cents for the goods they would sell in Jo'burg at a huge profit.

Whenever I gazed in the mirror, it was a different Dhairesi with a different future that stared back at me. I was at the point where the one thing with any real meaning in my life was my relationship with Tatenda and the burning desire to explore the world beyond the horizon. I was fond of my parents but their lives were deeply rooted in a world I wished to leave behind. Tatenda was the future. His was the world I hoped to inhabit but that was a long time in the future though.

I was only fourteen years of age and in no particular hurry to grow up, but that did not stop me from dreaming. I had visions of myself as a married woman and living somewhere far away from Patchway Valley Mine. Although Tatenda's home was in Mrewa Tribal Trust Lands, he was attending a boarding school near Marandellas; Waddilove Secondary School. My parents and Mother's friend, *Amake* Chisoni, could not understand how I, a simple girl from a mine compound, the daughter of an migrant labourer, could get involved with someone from a completely different background, someone they derogatorily referred to as *Musambadovi.*

"That boy is wasting your time, Dhairesi. Just because he sees you whenever he is here on school holidays, you think you fit into his world? What can he possibly see in you? He will soon dump you and go back to his own people," said Mother's friend.

"You judge him unfairly," I vehemently defended Tatenda's sincerity. "I know him very well, whereas you do not. He loves me and he has promised to marry me when we are both old enough."

"What rubbish!" screeched *Amake* Chisoni. "Whoever heard of such nonsense? You must get some very strange ideas from those books of yours out of which you never withdraw your nose."

"Tell her, *mubale wanga!*[92] I have grown weary of telling her the same thing all the time," Mother urged her friend.

"You must be more foolish than I thought if you imagine that any of these natives can even consider marrying you. You should know by now that they shun us and prefer to marry their own kind, and not just anyone for that matter. Have you not heard how they preach

---

92Tell her, my kinswoman

about *kuroorana vematongo?*[93] You are a Chewa girl Dhairesi, so it is with the Chewa people that you should stick. Our kinsmen understand our culture. Why do you want to get married to that *Musambadovi,* eh? Is it because you truly love him, or is it because he is one more step away from this culture of ours that you seem to despise so much? In a place swarming with various men of our own tribe, both young and old, you have to choose this one!" retorted *Amake* Chisoni, shaking her head. "And you are not even educated!" she spat.

"So-o?" I asked indignantly. I had gone to school up to the highest level in primary school, which was not much and did not lead to any training but that was the best I could do, considering the circumstances of my family where money was concerned. Most secondary schools were boarding schools and the fees were beyond us. Some locals were known to sell their livestock or part of their harvest to raise fees for their children but my people had neither of those to sell, so secondary education remained unattainable for most of us.

"*So-o* Dhairesi, let me tell you this now, and if you know what is good for you, you shall open your ears and listen carefully. You are not good enough to be the wife of an educated young man, who happens to be of the Shona tribe for that matter. He would never dream of presenting you to his family as his intended bride, never!" repeated *Amake* Chisoni.

"What is so special about these people that you have to worship them as if they are Mulungu?" I burst out, exasperated by the tendency of my kinsmen to regard the locals as if they were superior. "I am disgusted by the way you people grovel at their feet whenever you encounter them. When two men, a Mushona and a Muchewa pass each other on a narrow path, you can be sure it is the

93 Marrying from within one's community

Muchewa who will give way. He meekly steps aside, even onto thorny bushes or muddy soils so that the Mushona does not get inconvenienced. And you, *Amayo,* do not think I have not noticed how ready you are to genuflect and clap your hands whenever *aHedhi Tichara* passes by. What is so special about them, eh, are they not people just like you and me? Must you really scrape before their wives and treat them as if they do not breathe the same *komboni* air as us? Your behaviour disgusts me."

"*Heyi* Dhairesi, that is no way to talk to your mother!" screamed *Amake* Chisoni. "At least her behaviour shows how well brought up she is, unlike you whose mouth needs harnessing. What is wrong with being polite, especially to those one holds in esteem? Who says showing someone respect is akin to worshipping them? We show respect according to our traditions. It is you who considers the locals superior, to the point of discarding your own traditions. *Ha*! There is no brain in this head of yours despite the time you spent at school. *Nxi, chitsiru*! And you think these Mashona people regard you as an equal? Just you wait and see. That Mashona boy is not going to marry you and by the time you realise your foolish dream has become a nightmare, you will be stiff and hardened like over-ripe okra that's no longer fit for cooking. Girls should get married while they are still young and nubile, the way men like them. Otherwise only bald and gap-toothed old men will stoop low enough to marry you. *Sha*!"

"Leave me alone, I beg you. Tatenda is going to put you all to shame by marrying me, just you wait and see. I, Dhairesi, shall be the first young woman to escape the never-ending whiff of poverty that clings to all of you here like a second skin. I shall have a proper wedding with a beautiful white dress decorated with lace, ribbons and flowers. I trust my Tatenda. I am the woman whose heart

is joined to his. Our hearts beat in rhythm," I boasted and flounced off, before either woman could respond.

Even as I protested about the sincerity of Tatenda's intentions, I began to worry about obstacles that could stand in our way. I knew he loved me with all his heart as he repeatedly professed in his letters. I could already picture myself in the role of bride and daughter-in-law but I knew that in accordance with the Shona tradition, questions would inevitably be asked by my prospective in-laws about my parentage and my ethnic origins.

Where does she come from?
Whose daughter is she?
Who is her village headman?
Of what tribe is she?
What is her totem?

Although I could state that I was Dhairesi, the daughter of Masauso Nyirenda of the Chewa tribe, I would get stuck on the other questions. It was one's parentage, one's rural home background and totem that gave one an identity and respectability according to the Shona people. Without that one was labelled *'bhonirukisheni*[94]' to emphasize lack of village roots. Tatenda did his best to reassure me that we would get married with or without his people's approval. Part of me felt emboldened by that but there was another part of me that viewed marriage as more than just two people getting together. I saw it as a union of two people, one that spread its tentacles deep into the extended family, touching everyone from the young to the elderly and embracing the whole clan. In my mind I could already hear myself singing praises to Tatenda's totem;

Murehwa, Uzumba

---

94 Those born in the towns

Nyakudirwa, Kache
Mhofu yomukono
Vakapfura zuva rigere
Nenhopi yaTaidza.

I envisioned myself on my knees in reverence to my in-laws, a headscarf covering my hair and a wrapper cloth covering my legs, right down to my ankles. I was convinced that I was as good as any other girl and therefore suitable as a bride for Tatenda, despite being a barely educated descendant of a line of poor migrant labourers.

I was aware even in my anticipation of marriage that it would not be easy at first. I knew from the experiences of others that a new marriage was often put under immense pressure with the embracing of the entire clan and by striving to meet the expectations of one's in-laws and upholding them at the same time. Adapting to a new way of life would be hard, but I was determined to try. I had to give myself a chance and in order to do so, I had to disregard the crucial issue of initiation because it meant instant betrothal and marriage eventually if I was lucky not to have both at the same time. I had my life mapped out and I had vowed not to allow myself to be dragged into a future I was not ready for. It was because of this that I refused to go for *chinamwali.* The entire community was shocked. I had done what nobody else had done before. I adamantly refused to be initiated and no amount of cajoling or threats would make me change my mind. Father was horrified, and Mother was distraught. Mother's friend was asked to try and knock some sense into me but she found herself knocking her own head against a wall instead.

"I really do not know what is so wrong with you Dhairesi," said *Amake* Chisoni after another session with me. "Do you find joy in doing things that exasperate and

embarrass your parents? Why can't you be like other normal girls in our community, eh?"

"For what reason anyway must I take part in a ceremony aimed at thrusting me into marriage when I know that I am not yet ready to get married?" I sulked.

"You do not have to get married just yet, Dhairesi."

"So why do it then?"

"Because that is our tradition," Amake Chisoni stressed each word in a loud and clear voice as if I had said I had not heard her rather than that I did not understand the significance of the ceremony.

"You do it *not* when you are about to get married but when the first sign of maturity appears. These customs have been observed and passed down generations since time immemorial." When I did not comment, *Amake* Chisoni continued, "Must you Dhairesi have a 'why' for everything that you are told to do? Traditions are meant to be observed, that's all."

"That does not explain anything. Moreover, why must I go through initiation? The Shona girls do not. My Shona classmates are not subjected to such backward rituals, yet I can bet you now they will go on to lead good lives and get married to good men who will pay numerous heads of cattle for them and huge sums of money at that."

"These Shona people whom you want to emulate do observe their own traditions. In those villages they call home, they pay homage to their ancestors and pour libation to the gods of their fathers. They are said to beat drums far into the night, dancing and ululating as the spirits of their dead forefathers speak through the tongues of the living. Do you hear that, Dhairesi? Just because they do it away from the eyes of us immigrants does not mean they shun their age-old customs. Wake up, girl!"

"What do you know about what the Mashonas do in their villages, *Amake* Chisoni, you who cannot speak a word of Chishona, and you do not associate with the

locals at any level and are always ready to think they consider you inferior? How would you know about their way of life, cocconed as you are in your backward world? Besides, you are not telling me why a girl needs to undergo *chinamwali*. That is what I want to know. It's as simple as that," I retorted.

"That information is only disclosed to the initiants, but if it will make you understand the importance of this custom and give your mother some peace, then I will tell you but you are never to tell anyone that I told you beforehand."

"I haven't said I will go for *chinamwali*__"

"Now you close that never-still-mouth of yours that continuously churns out filth in the presence of adults, *sha*! Now listen; a woman needs to make her husband happy in every way, eh? That way he will not find a reason to ever look at other women. Unless you get initiated in the ways of__"

"Oh, is that what all that secretive nonsense is about? But why would I need to learn that at my age? I am not getting married just yet, not for many years to come. If it is as important as you want me to believe, then I will learn when I feel ready."

"But the timing is very important, Dhairesi. A woman's body is considered to be supple only until a certain age, after which it becomes rather inflexible. You cannot decide when you want to__"

"Forget it, *Amake* Chisoni. I shall not do it."

I felt sorry for my parents but I hoped that with time they would accept that I needed to make my own decisions in life. I was a child of an era different from theirs and they could neither understand nor accept that times were changing. They wanted to cling to the past and were content to remain there forever, but I was not. The issue of *chinamwali* was eventually dropped, but I knew I had

gained immense disapproval from many in the community. They said no one would marry me, uninitiated as I was. I was not duly worried as it pertained to a period far into the future. In any case I was on my way out of there, so it did not matter much what people thought.

Tatenda loved me and he showed it in various ways. I remember him as the only person who ever picked flowers for me, but never more than one at a time. The fact that the Flame Lily grew all over the place and I could have picked hundreds of them for myself did not make the gesture any less special. After all it was the national flower of Rhodesia. The flower looked like the flames of a raging fire, or the rays of a glowing sun at sunrise. Later at night, I would pluck the long yellow and red petals until I was left holding only the stem and I would smile to myself as I remembered the memory of a love recently shared. I loved Tatenda even more for the romance he brought into my life. In that kind of romance there was no room for outdated rituals. I was convinced that I had made the right decision about *chinamwali.*

From then onwards I was referred to as the-stubborn-girl-who-read-far-too-much-and-had-her-head-turned-by-books. Most people predicted that I would end up like Rameki the compound idiot. *Saskamu* is what they called him because, although his body continued to grow and mature into adulthood, his mind remained trapped in the early years of childhood. Rameki grinned at everybody, talked to himself and laughed for no apparent reason. Spittle dribbled unchecked from the sides of his mouth as he stared blankly into space.

Although most people poked fun at Rameki, everybody cared about him. Housewives gave him scraps of food whenever he passed by their homes. He spent most of his time at Chimuromo's store where *a*Mazizi would speak to him as if to a four year old. Even in his

twenties, Rameki was still an infant in mind and he spoke and behaved like one. Something must have happened to him in his mother's womb, declared those people who claimed to know everything. His poor mother would have been better off with a miscarriage, so said others. His mother did not share the same view though. She loved her son and cared for him with tenderness. She always said she was happy to have him, and often quoted the Shona adage which goes, *'Midzimu yakupa chironda yati nhunzi dzikudye*[95]*."* She quietly endured whatever taunts came her way, including insinuations that her plight must be some kind of punishment from God for evil deeds on her part. My parents, who did not share these views, argued that Rameki came from an honourable family that was well known for their good deeds.

"Rumour mongering is malicious and hurtful," Father used to say. "Gossip travels faster than the truth and it is more appealing despite being evil. It is not only hurtful, but it can be extremely damaging as well. Never be the bearer of unproven allegations if you can help it." It was one lesson I learned from my parents from a very early age. Apart from Rameki, there was also Manuwere whose left hand was withered and deformed, and Ronika, an old woman whose right leg was shorter than the other. I never took part whenever cruel jokes were told about their conditions but like everybody else I did wonder what had caused their deformity. We had never seen anybody else like them, and Patchway Valley was a world unto itself. It was a stigma to be different from the rest of the people in the community.

My refusal to undergo initiation caused me to be regarded as a freak. In other words, Rameki, Manuwere, Ronika and I were abnormal and could never fit into the

---

95The gods that give you wounds intend to have flies nibble at your flesh and feed off you

community and be accepted on the same level as everyone else. That did not worry me much, especially as the winds of change were breezing into the compound. A bus service had recently started operating from Gatooma to Chakari Mine and since Patchway Valley was along the route, the inhabitants benefitted from the service. On board the buses came young men who made endless journeys into our compound as it became much easier and faster to cover distances that were previously dreaded as being too long and too far to walk. Ruredzo and Matambanadzo buses opened up the mining communities and we socialised with each other on a broader scale.

This change, while welcomed with joy by the younger generation, was viewed sceptically as a bad wind by those of the older generation. I understood that for them, life had gone on in exactly the same way as it had done for decades. As far as they were concerned, nothing was supposed to change, having settled contentedly into a comfortable and close community as they had. My parents too were content with things as they were, and were understandably upset when their only son decided to leave Patchway Valley to go and work first, at Shabanie Mine, then on to Wankie Colliery Mine, a whole world away from home. I was happy for my brother and with time my parents accepted his decision, though grudgingly. Chakumanda was one of a growing number of young men who decided to move away and start life in other mining communities that promised better opportunities. Shabanie, Selukwe and Wankie Colliery in particular were said to offer better housing and better standards of living than Patchway Valley.

One day we woke up to a bright, sunny day but by midday a blanket of smoke billowed over our heads, thick and black. It was the fateful day Father was called to the Mine office and informed of my brother's demise. There had been an accident at Wankie Mine. My brother was

among hundreds of the workers trapped underground. Waiting for news from Wankie Colliery Mine and over the radio was torture. It mattered not that the tragedy had happened elsewhere, the mining fraternity was one huge migrant family. What happened at one mine could easily happen at ours. The tragedy was felt even more keenly because of my brother who was popular at Patchway Valley. Fear and sadness gripped the whole community. It was a terrible time for us all. My parents left me in the care of neighbours while they travelled by train to Wankie the same day on what was their first journey away from our community. The farthest either of them had been to was Gatooma, a mere fifteen kilometres away. By the time they returned several days later, we all knew that the fate of my brother and that of his fellow workers had been sealed as surely as the collapsed mine shaft had been sealed. What happened at Wankie Colliery Mine was the dread of every miner and his family. Everyone lived in the hope that it would never happen to them. Many people came to our house to pay their condolences and they talked to Father and Mother about their sadness at the loss of a much-loved son. My heart ached too, but to the rest of the community I was just on the fringes of this tragedy. I was told to be good to my parents and to be careful not to add to their misery. The deeper Father and Mother immersed themselves in their grief, the more I turned to reading and writing, and the more I lost myself in my own sorrow.

It was the concern Tatenda had towards me that eventually helped ease the pain of loss. He was the only person to recognise that I too was deeply affected by the death of my only sibling. He gave me the platform to share my grief, examine it and try to find a way of dealing with it. With his help, I began to smile again even when everything else around me looked gloomy. More than a year after we lost Chakumanda, I still thought of him, but

with diminishing clarity and less frequency with each passing day.

As the months went by, the lost brother gradually became a memory in the past though the pain of his absence resurfaced occasionally. Just when I thought my relationship with Tatenda was solid and would only end in marriage, my dream lay in tatters. I was never going to marry the young man that I had loved so intensely for two whole years. His aunt, *Amai* Moyo confronted me one morning at the communal water tap. She looked me up and down, contempt dripping from her eyes for what seemed like eternity. With an upturned nose she finally asked, "So *you* are the Dhairesi Nyirenda that I have heard so much about?" I nodded, not quite sure how to respond.

"O-o, I see. *Va*Moyo and I have heard about your meetings with Tatenda, our nephew," she continued, rolling her eyes as she pronounced the word 'meetings' with exaggerated emphasis, leaving me in no doubt of her insinuations.

"We wanted to see this *Mubhurandaya* who dares dream beyond her own position, but we thought it not worth our time and effort. So long as Tatenda keeps you in the bushes where he meets you then we would not worry about it. I know the reputation that you daughters of *Mabhurandaya* have. You take up with anyone who comes along. Maybe it is not your fault but that of your mothers who neglect to cool your fiery blood with their breast milk when you are newly born. Let me give you a piece of advice though; get yourself a nice man from the compound and settle down with him. Tatenda's parents will not accept an migrant labourer's daughter, an uneducated one for that matter, for a daughter-in-law. As Tatenda's guardians while he is here, we take full responsibility for what he does, and that is a duty we take seriously."

I stood rooted to the ground as my dreams disintegrated at my feet. For once I was unable to utter a word. *Amake* Chisoni would have been impressed beyond speech by what she would have undoubtedly regarded as self-restraint on my part. The truth though was that I was shocked into numbness of both thought and tongue. The mere presence of the self-assured woman standing in front of me intimidated me so much that I could only gape at her like an idiot. I had seen Tatenda's uncle from a distance but I had never seen his aunt. Our paths hardly crossed because they lived in an area reserved for blacks with better jobs than ordinary mine labourers.

"I hope you are wise enough to take my advice. There will be no *muroora* in the family who has neither a village home nor acceptable roots. We do not cement relations with people who have no known villages and whose ancestors one cannot pay homage to," said *Amai* Moyo as she turned to go. My hands trembled as I carried my bucket of water on my head and walked slowly back home. For a while I felt despondent, but later a surge of hope returned when I remembered that Tatenda himself had said we would elope together if we encountered resistance to our plans. I decided to ignore *Amai* Moyo's warning and keep my love for Tatenda burning. I wrote him several letters and waited eagerly for his replies but he did not write back. It took a couple of months before my heart could accept that my beloved boyfriend had jilted me. The pain that followed was terrible. The days were empty and I spent sleepless nights tossing and turning, often crying into my pillow until it was drenched with tears. Tatenda had gone out of my life with no warning. I was shattered by his deception and his callous rejection which I found hard to bear.

The whole of Patchway Valley seemed to know about my heartache and that made me even more miserable. The pain gradually gave way to anger, which in turn was

replaced by numbness and hopelessness. I lost interest in everything and immersed myself in my dull, grey world where no sun shone. Tatenda did not come back to Patchway Valley on holiday for some time, not even for the short Rhodes and Founders national holiday. When he eventually did, enough time had passed to heal my wounds and I did not wish to reopen them by talking to him. He too behaved as if he had never known me or made me promises that once filled my heart with joy. We behaved towards each other as two strangers who had no wish to make each other's acquaintance. By then I had ceased caring which way my life went. I passively watched events around me drift by. Life went by slowly as there was no particular hurry to get anywhere in a community where, after birth, the one sure event we all waited for with resignation was death.

* * *

After my brother's death, Mother became an entirely different person altogether. She stopped laughing and whenever she smiled, on the rare occasions she did, her smile did not reach her eyes. I could not talk to her and she did not talk much to me. She no longer urged any of her friends to caution me over my behaviour as she had done in the past. Father went about like a man lost in time. Though living under the same roof, Father, Mother and I each lived in our own different, isolated worlds, emerging only occasionally to make brief contact with each other. Though my parents were lost to me, they were not entirely lost to each other. They occasionally found time to wallow jointly in their misery. I lost interest in reading and spent more time with friends, of whom I had plenty. Giribhati continued to pay me some attention whenever he could. I

plunged into various relationships and resolved to put the pain of the past behind me. I met my boyfriends at the bioscope on Thursday nights and elsewhere on other days. This went on for almost two years. Then one morning Mother complained of breathing difficulties.

A few days later, she started spitting blood. By the end of that week she was frothing at the mouth and she was dead within a week. I was in a state of shock. Father was inconsolable for months afterwards but between the two of us we struggled to carry on. We had no one else but each other to find comfort from. We grew close out of fear and out of our shared grief. My fear stemmed from the fact that death seemed to be on the rampage in my family. First to fall victim to it was my brother, followed by Mother. I did not want to be its next victim, but I did not want it to take Father either because I would be left all alone. But for how long before I too died? Mother's death catapulted me into instant maturity in a way not even *chinamwali* would have done. At fourteen years of age I took on the responsibility of looking after Father by washing his heavily soiled work over-alls, cooking his meals and heating water for his baths. It was not easy but I did the best I could.

With Tatenda no longer in my life to help me pull through that dark period, I went back to reading and found solace in the make-believe world of books. My love for reading was to be of great benefit when, a month after Mother's burial, a group of happy-clapping, Bible-toting missionaries descended on Patchway Valley Mine and set up camp. They introduced themselves as Christians from Dorothea Mission who had come to spread the Word of God to heathens. They distributed brand new Bibles, the Gideons International, for free.

All of a sudden, our slumbering community rose like a serpent awakening from a lengthy period of hibernation. Here at last was a religion I could take delight in. Church

goers did not need to be solemn in order to be considered pious, I thought. The Dorothea Mission preachers brought liveliness to their sermons through song and dance. They played guitars and tambourines before going into what they called praise and worship sessions. I could feel the pulse of the Mine throbbing in the air we breathed. There was excitement as the passive community came to life with the clapping of hands and stamping of feet. Most of the elderly people did not understand this new form of worship that was alien to them. Some chose to have nothing to do with it, my own father among them and others condemned it outright as ungodly. There was far too much excitement for it to be holy, they argued.

The preachers encouraged us to confess our sins, which we did, some of us with rather too much fervour, I thought. We were baptised and given new Christian names that were chosen from the Bible, after which we were declared born again, sin-free new creations. The new converts were urged to discard names that condemned them to eternal misery, and also to desist from taking part in pagan rituals. They singled out in particular paying homage to one's ancestors, worshipping idols and initiation rites in whatever form. They condemned these practices as the most demonic of them of all. I was glad that I had resisted my parents' efforts to get me initiated and I felt vindicated. One girl convert I knew got a new name for the third time in her life. Her father disowned her outright, declaring that if she wanted to be born again then she had to be dead to him first. As far as he was concerned, his daughter was born only once. If she insisted on the miracle of being born a second time like the so-called Son of God, then like Him she had to die first. From then onwards, the man considered his daughter to be dead and wanted nothing more to do with her.

The Missionaries said there was nothing about my names that condemned me to evil or misfortune, so I

remained Dhairesi and Fadzai. The former was the name given to me at birth and the latter was the one I chose to be known by among my friends. Nobody really called me Fadzai though. My friends insisted that by refusing to be initiated I had given up the right to change my name.

Bible tracts with fascinating tales were distributed at the end of each service. In them we read about the promise of a better world that could be inherited only by the meek. What a relief for us poor immigrants! At last here was a place where we could be considered special. We did not care anymore about retrenchment packages or pensions since the Word promised an inheritance from none other than God our Father in heaven. I found the whole idea of paradise appealing even if it could only be attained after death. Gradually, I began to accept the will of God in my life, especially where the deaths of Mother and Chakumanda were concerned. When the missionaries finally moved on to another place, our elders were relieved, but we the young were left yearning for more.

The weeks after their departure were like the blandness of okra boiled without soda. With time, my lovely, still-new Gideons International Bible steadily began to gather dust on the window sill in the living room. I put it out of sight a few months later and life went back to normal. The winds of change continued to blow across Rhodesia and we interacted more with people from other mining areas through soccer tournaments as our horizons broadened. With *simane-manje* also wafted into our lives, the sounds of music and the modern jive that accompanied it. Most miners bought the Marconi type of wirelesses, but only a few had radiograms.

Gradually, the minds of the people in the community opened up to the outside world. Those who owned radios turned the volume very high for the benefit of those who did not have them, a gesture that was sincerely appreciated. Ours was a generous community indeed,

always ready to share. The sound of The African Broadcasting Service could be heard from *a*Mbewe's radiogram four houses away even though we also had a radiogram at home. Ours was a stereo that stood like a brown wooden coffin on four spindly legs that was placed along the wall, from one corner of the living room to where the window began.

The unevenness of the floor made it look as if one of the legs of the radiogram was slightly shorter than the other three, which affected the playing of records. A piece of paper was therefore folded several times and inserted in the gap between the leg and the floor, and the problem was solved. I bought records that I loved; LPs and SPs. The dinner plate size long playing vinyl records had several songs on either side while the short playing ones had a single song on each side.

The young people swapped records and invited each other to come and listen to music, to dance and to show off the latest dance moves. We had to be careful with the thinly grooved vinyls because they tended to soften in the sun and get scratched easily, which distorted the sound of the music and gave it a repetitive hiccup effect. Unplayable though the records became, we still kept them as a reminder of that which we had once owned but was now lost to us.

The usual Sunday tribal dances were gradually replaced by *marekodzi*. Some people bought vinyl records even though they had no radiogram to play them on. It just came to be accepted that on Sunday afternoons, men and children would gather at *a*Mbewe's place and dance to the music brought in by various people. We called it 'teen time', the equivalent of what today's youth call disco.

We shook our bodies in rhythm to the sound of music. We jived, shook the bottoms, swayed the hips and gyrated the waists. Sometimes we danced with frenzied vigour, at other times with a slowness that accommodated the pace

of the beat of the music. We clicked our fingers in rythm with the beat of the drums, the guitar or whichever instrument one's mind chose to focus on. Feet detached themselves from the floor and, directed by the music, planted themselves back again, on the same spot or a few paces away. We had fire in our hips and agility in our feet.

The music determined whether people danced in partners, individually or in a circle as a group. I enjoyed the bump-jive where we danced in twos, side by side and rubbed hips one against the other, first at hip level, then lower down at knee level and up again. We jumped and let the hips connect up there. Occasionally, instead of offering one's hip, one dancer would cup their hands and make contact with the partner's hip and bottom as if catching a ball. The bum-jive was very popular especially among those who were in love. Those were happy times indeed and we thrilled in the euphoria they enveloped us in.

We took delight in doing the modern jive to the tunes of Safirio Madzikatire, The Mahotela Queens and The Hurricanes. Most of us did not understand the words but that did not diminish the delight we got from the beat of the instruments.We made our own words as we sang along. It was during that period that I fell in love with Rojasi, a security guard from a neighbouring mining community. We were by no means Romeo and Juliet as I had been with Tatenda, but we were definitely *Solo nuMutsai*. We were deeply in love then and the song captured the intensity of our feelings for each other. The lives of my people were also mirrored in music.

'Achechure Anavhara Bhotomu' had us bursting with laughter as we conjured up images of the absurd idea of a frog hopping around the water well, dressed in bell-bottomed trousers. The pleading voice of Oliver Mtukudzi belted out 'Chido Chenyu Here?', sobering us up instantly and leaving us searching our souls from deep within. We

were sure he was singing about the plight of migrants. It was a known fact that our fore-fathers had roamed the wild forests and endured all sorts of difficulties on their way to Southern Rhodesia, so we agreed that the song was about us and we loved Mutukudzi and his music all the more.

It was not until years later that we got to know the song paid homage to freedom fighters during the war of liberation. There were also those songs whose tunes we enjoyed though we had very little or no idea what the lyrics were all about. We were never able to figure out the gist of 'Rusalina Soda' even though it was a rhumba song that blared out of the few stereos in the compound with much frequency, sending us shaking our bottoms with vigour. Our inability to understand the words of rhumba music from neighbouring countries, Katanga in the Belgian Congo in particular, did not prevent us from enjoying the beat.

The era of the platform shoes came and went, as did the era of the bellbottoms, of the afro-hair style and of the midi, which was later replaced by the mini skirt. The fashion trends for us females were more numerous and varied than those for men. We straightened our tightly coiled kinky hair with hot iron combs after rubbing lots of Vaseline onto the hair to make it easier for the comb to run through. Those of us who did not have the combs either borrowed from those who had, or we simply improvised and used heated stones instead. The more coarse the stone, the better it was for an easier grip on the hair. The stone was placed in the middle of glowing embers until it became hot. It was then carefully picked up with a damp cloth and placed directly onto the hair, rubbing gently from front to back, going through all the hair until it became straight and shiny. If it was not adequately oiled, the hair became singed and emitted a pungent smell.

Sometimes an accident happened and a hot stone slipped from the hand and slid down the back of one's head, past the neck and straight down into the space between the shoulder blades. In the majority of the cases the stone got lodged inside the dress, and the unfortunate person got badly burnt. Since the hairdressing activity took place while one was sitting on a chair, whenever the hot stone fell into one's dress, the victim would hop up and down to try and shake it off. It was a horrifying ordeal, but also a spectacle to watch. All that frenzied hopping and hollering like a mad woman, all in the name of beauty! Yet we persisted. The risks were great, but the results were even greater and worth the effort. The teachers' wives wore wigs and we envied them for achieving such elegance without the risks we put ourselves through.

With this new look, quite a number of girls discarded some of our time honoured traditions. We did not see why we should not. It was time for change all round after all. From the Bata Shoe Stores we bought *mariposa,* the cheap plastic sandals that we wore with pride. We painted our lips red and accentuated our waists wide figure belts. The more I embraced the modern culture, the more Father tried to drag me back in time. Everything modern, as far as he was concerned, stripped us of our culture, our morals and our identity. He claimed that by so doing we were slowly but surely losing our Chewaness. As if there was anything to regret in that, I thought, glaring at him, but not daring to utter the words in his presence. I soon got tired of his incessant preaching and I stopped caring about what he thought or said. I had tried earlier to change my name to Fadzai but my old-fashioned parents had declared that as long as I was still living under their roof they would continue to call me by the name they had given me at birth. I sulked and argued that everybody else was modernising and changing their names, including my

brother Chakumanda but they argued that I had no reason to discard mine which was a good name that I ought to be proud of. They had continued to call me Dhairesi, much to my chagrin whenever I brought home a friend that I had not told about my old name. The moment they got to know of it, none of them wanted to use my new name and I was back to being called Dhairesi.

Over the years my people had started speaking in a mixture of the languages of the migrant people and Shona. Our languages had gradually become diluted and no one spoke pure Chichewa, Chitonga or Chinyanja anymore. The letter 'l' in Chichewa was replaced by the 'r' of the Shona language such that the word *alibe* was pronounced *aribe*. This was especially so among people of the younger generation. However, my parents insisted on continuing with their dying language and demanding that my friends greet them with their heads bowed. They also had to speak in pure Chichewa. Father and Mother took delight in humiliating me and for that reason I rarely asked my friends to visit me at home. I resolved though to live my life the way I wanted. I defiantly painted my lips the brightest red I could find and I went off to dance at the shops.

"Iwe mwana uli nimwano iwe," Father would say, in the months following Mother's death. "You will surely come to a bad end if you continue the way you are going. Now you paint your lips a garish red, totter precariously on those silly shoes while wearing a skirt that stops almost where it starts! What message are you sending to the men out there? There is only one word to describe girls like you. *Pfambi!* Whores! How could I have fathered a child like you? I wonder who it is you resemble, honestly. Your own mother *ali kumanda*[96] was a woman of virtue, as was your *ambuya,* my own mother. Where did you pick up this

96 who lies in her grave

rot that contaminates your blood like anthrax? I just don't understand how it is possible for a mulberry tree to bear thorns. Had your mother not given birth to you in this very house I could have sworn you were switched at birth at these maternity clinics you have nowadays. One of these days the door to my house is going to be closed to you and if you think I am just making idle threats, just you try and dare me, then you will know for sure that behind these white teeth you see is a scathing tongue. O-hoo, you go on and try me. I will chase you away from here, then you can go and do as you please on the streets of Gatoma, far away from me. At least what my eye does not see, my heart cannot grieve over."

Father ranted on and on as the winds of change continued to blow into the compound, and as *isimanje-manje* breezed in too. I stopped paying attention to his ramblings since I had got tired of explaining that things had changed and that our age-old customs were changing as well. I was determined to broaden my mind and my choices at the pace the horizons were opening up. We were in the age of instant snaps, afro hairstyles, mini skirts, maxi dresses and jukebox music. Those were heady days indeed.

Every Sunday, most mine dwellers looked forward to the arrival of the photographer who came all the way from Gatooma to take pictures for a fee. It was an occasion so important for most of us that we dressed in our 'special' clothes for it, the clothes bought from *Mabhuruwayo* that most likely still had a few dollars owing on them. Many young people took advantage of this chance to freeze their youth in time and capture their happiness on paper. We merrily called out 'cheers' or 'cheese' and the photographer obligingly froze our smiles in time. I was never sure whether it was supposed to be cheese or cheers but it did not matter much, so long as the desired smile was achieved. Also captured for posterity_ I have to say

though, that at that time we were not thinking of future generations but boyfriends_ were a variety of poses ranging from standing behind a tree trunk and peering from its side in what was supposed to be a cool pose, crouching next to a bright shrub, holding a vase of plastic flowers, to extending one's hand to show a watch, borrowed or recently purchased, adorning the wrist.

The backgrounds to our pictures were chosen with care to portray us favourably. After all, these were the snapshots that we gave to our boyfriends who in turn gave us theirs which we treasured and kept in suitcases. Now and again we took the snapshots out last thing at night for a few longing glances and kisses. We also placed them under the pillow so that we would dream of our loved ones. This of course lasted until the man moved on to someone else and the snapshots were demanded back, to be forwarded to the new love at the earliest opportunity.

With this new way of life, the boundaries of our lives shifted and continued to do so, slowly but surely, letting in new ways and winnowing away others in the process. Father continued to see nothing good in this gradual shifting of values, and steadfastly persisted in condemning this new age. He did not understand this irrational need for change, he said. He still wanted to cling to an age that was slowly blowing out of our lives, which was why he had arranged for me to become the wife of *a*Mkandawire. I had just turned sixteen years old. I was shocked that Father dared suggest that I become the wife of a man aged over forty. I told him exactly what I thought of such an absurd idea.

"Dhairesi, when I married your mother I was already a man of mature years. She was at the exact age you are now. I do not need to tell you how happy we were together. You cannot continue living here and looking

after me when you could have a home of your own and a husband to look after you," he explained.

"You mean a husband for *me* to *look after,*" I mumbled, then loudly I said, "*Ababa,* I do not want to get married just yet and also, I do not wish to get married to a man chosen for me, a man I do not love. *Wanga mamuna nidhinga neka.* Yes, I will find a man for myself. "

"This is the stubbornness I talk about, Dhairesi my daughter. If your mother were still alive, I would not worry so much about you but on my own I feel totally helpless. I want to see you married and settled with a good, responsible man, not the layabouts invading our community nowadays. These young boys who flock into Patchway Valley from faraway places like Perseverance, Chakari and Brompton Mines at weekends are not good for you. They breeze in wearing bellbottoms wide enough to make two skirts for *Ambuya a*Cheusinje, big and fat as she is. With stereos perched on their shoulders belting *nyimbo zasimanje manje* at volumes high enough to make us all deaf in this compound, these young men behave as if they are gods. They buy you Canada Dry and Pep Soda just to lure you into a life of sin. In your naivete you go around selling your souls to the devil and entrenching yourselves deeper into a life of sin. You are knee deep in *mirandu* and the air you breathe is infested with the stench of *mirandu,* but do you ever lose sleep over your sinful ways? Do you, Dhairesi?" asked Father. I considered throwing a few retorts at him but I had already told Father everything I ever wanted to say about how I wished to live my life, so I kept quiet. One more word was not going to persuade him to see things my way just as one more utterance from him was not going to make any difference to the way I saw things, but that did not make Father give up. He went on lecturing.

"Do your sinful ways cause you sleepless nights? No. You sleep soundly as if you have the conscience of babies.

Your whole lives are nothing but *mirandu*. It is *mirandu* here, *mirandu* there and *mirandu* everywhere. The rotten ways of you children of today never cease to baffle me. You are willing to throw away just about everything, all for a mere bottle of some fizzy drink whose only benefit is in giving you wind. These goggle-wearing boys do not care one bit about you and they are the type who will ruin your lives before running back to their homes to marry the respectable girls known to their families. By coming here, they are just being careful not to foul the air they breathe back home.

"It is said that when a clever man relieves himself in the bush, he chooses his place with care, taking into consideration the direction in which the wind blows. By so doing, the inhabitants of his village need never know what he gets up to out there and what is not known about him cannot tarnish his reputation. We know nothing about these young men you seem to be obsessed with, nor do we know where they come from, and we have no way of knowing of their morals. They may be migrant labourers like us but they do not belong to this community. They are outsiders, unknown to us. Our own people are the best, Dhairesi, my daughter. At least we know their families."

I had listened long enough and could no longer contain my irritation.

"*Ababa,* what does it matter where they come from?" I asked. "It does not worry me. This custom of always wanting to stick with people from the same neighbourhood is history. It is dead and gone. Dead. Even your own fathers recognised the need to dispense with that life, yet you insist on dragging me back into it. The first labourers from various neighbouring countries, did they go back to their homelands for their brides? I am sure they married within each others' families with no qualms, creating a community as the years went by. Only you, *Ababa,* care about this past you are always harping on

about. For the rest of us there is so much to look forward to in the future," I argued. As descendants of migrants workers who were born and brought up in Rhodesia, we were familiar with the history of our people, thanks to the stories passed down from tongue to tongue and from one age group to another. For those of my generation, the distant past had no relevance to our lives.

We knew our history indeed, and we knew where we had come from but that did not mean we wanted to go back there. After I refused to become the wife of *a*Mkandawire, a widowed father of three, I continued to see the exciting young men who flocked into the compound at the weekends. A few other girls of my age also refused marriage to the older men to whom they were betrothed, choosing instead to go out with the new breed of suitors from elsewhere. A month after I refused *a*Mkandawire, I felt strange movements in my stomach. I consulted *Ambuya aFiripo,* who was horrified. She was the same woman whom Father had turned to when he heard about me and Giribhati. She was close to our family because Mother had regarded her as her own mother. The woman who had raised her was long dead. *Ambuya a*Firipo therefore filled in the role of the grandmother figure of our family. Father and Mother had often sought her advice on many issues, so it was only natural that I turn to her with my own problems. Mother's death had not reduced the high regard we had for her. One afternoon, I went to see her at her house. I chose a time when I knew she would be on her own, to ensure privacy.

"You say something moves within you, Dhairesi? Are you sure?" she asked after I had explained my problem to her.

"I am very sure, *Ambuya,*" I confirmed.

"Lie down and pull up your dress right up to your chest. I want to feel your stomach," she instructed, and I obeyed. I stretched out on my back on her reed mat, in

great discomfort. Her gnarled but firm fingers probed and prodded my stomach and kneaded here and there. When she was finally done, *Ambuya a*Firipo told me to pull down my dress. This must be a serious problem, I thought as I looked at her solemn face.

"For how long have you been feeling these movements, Dhairesi?" *Ambuya a*Firipo finally asked when I had pulled myself to a sitting position and sat facing her.

"I cannot say for sure, it could be a week or two. They were just slight movements at first but they have become stronger and more frequent since last Sunday."

"When did you last see the signs of womanhood, Dhairesi?" she asked.

"I am not sure, maybe last month, or perhaps two, no. I cannot remember, *Ambuya*."

"There is indeed a mass in your stomach...'

"Mama ine! Nimalodza. Amfiti have finally cast an evil spell on me. This is witchcraft," I cried, horrified.

"There is no witchcraft involved in the making of a baby, Dhairesi," said the old woman, her eyes glaring at me as if challenging me to call her a liar or incompetent. When I lowered my gaze and sat stunned into silence she continued, "If the baby has already started kicking you must be about four or five months gone. I must say this is a big shock, but then why should it be? I do not know how we all missed the signs. Your skin has the glow of a woman with child and you have gained weight although your stomach remains flat."

The shock of the pregnancy numbed me. I had been hoping that *Ambuya a*Firipo would tell me of an illness that made the stomach churn.

"Who is the father, Dhairesi?" she finally asked.

"I, I, I am not sure," I stammered, struggling to come out of my stupour.

"Surely you know the person you are seeing? It is he who is the father."

"Five months ago is a long time. I can no longer remember whether I was with Tomasi or Yona. Since then I have been with Rojasi. But I think it is Rojasi, the father of the baby. He is the one I am with now."

Ambuya aFiripo shook her head, wrung her hands together and waved me away saying how she pitied my poor father and what a blessing it was that Mother had not lived to endure the disgrace of my deeds. Still in a state of shock, I dragged my feet home. That night, the comfort of sleep eluded me. I kept tossing and turning for a very long time. My thoughts were in turmoil and for the first time in my life, I was forced to consider the gravity of my actions and their consequences.

Pregnancies outside marriages were very rare and considered scandalous if they happened. Most young girls were well ensconced in arranged marriages by the time their breasts started budding or soon after initiation, leaving hardly any room for pre-marital indulgencies and pregnancies before marriage. My main concern was that I had become pregnant outside marriage. I knew the chances of keeping the news secret were very slim, since the person who had diagnosed my condition was incapable of keeping a still tongue. However, I silently prayed she would keep my condition secret at least until lobola was paid for me. I resolved to tell Rojasi the news as soon as possible. He was due to visit me the next day. He did come but was gone within minutes of my telling him the news. He said he was sorry he could not stay longer because he was going to visit his uncle. Rojasi never came anywhere near me again and he behaved as if he had never been close to me before. I felt betrayed because all along I had believed he truly loved me and I had never doubted his promises. On numerous occasions Rojasi had repeated his intention to marry me as soon as we were both ready. I later heard that he was going around accusing me of attempting to trap him into marriage with

a pregnancy whose conception he had nothing to do with. He argued that he could not possibly be the father because he had been with me only once, which of course was a lie.

"I was with that girl only once. Everybody knows that it takes more than just once to make a baby. Dhairesi should look elsewhere for the father of her unborn baby. She could try Yona, or better still any one of the young men from Chakari Mine. Who knows, she might get lucky there," Rojasi was heard to say. I was shattered by his rejection of the baby and me. I was even more shattered when I realised that the whole of Patchway Valley Mine was talking about my pregnancy. Wild stories were circulating, with some people claiming that I was pregnant by no less than three different men.

"You wait and see what the whore is going to give birth to this year; a baby with a nose resembling Giribhati's, legs that resemble those of Rojasi, ears like Tomasi's, eyes like Yona's. It will be a whole mixture of fathers. Whoever is not represented is no doubt the most unfortunate man in the compound," some women said maliciously, in loud whispers that were meant to reach my ears, though. Women who had previously avoided me as immoral started approaching me to initiate conversation while at the same time openly scrutinising my appearance. The men who had previously sought my company changed direction whenever they saw me approaching. I had become a pariah, to be ridiculed or shunned. The number of men mentioned was wildly exaggerated of course, but I did not bother to correct the gossipmongers. I had long discovered that people always say what they wish to spread around, not the truth as it stands.

Whenever I was asked about my condition I denied that I was pregnant. I flattened my stomach by tying a big piece of cloth tightly around my waist. I ate as little as possible and hoped Father and his new wife would not notice the change in me. I had not yet decided what to do

about my situation. I toyed with the idea of secretly and quietly giving birth by myself, and then dumping the baby. It would not be the first time that such a thing was done.

The year before, a young unmarried girl at Eiffel Flats (Rio Tinto) Mine had dumped her newborn baby down a pit latrine. The poor thing was only saved after *achimbango* heard its cries from deep within the excrement. How the infant managed to survive in all that muck was a mystery. I tried to picture the infant floating on the surface of a pool of horrible faeces, and wriggling maggots crawling all over it, and the putrefying stench strong enough to suffocate and knock out an adult. That must have been the worst way for anyone to start one's life, but of course the woman who dumped that baby had not meant him to live. The news of the incident had spread from one mining community to another and at Patchway Valley we talked of nothing else for weeks. It was a callous thing to do, we all agreed, so the thought never really took root in my mind. I considered going to Gatooma to give birth and dumping the baby because no one knew me there. Though it occurred rarely, the few times it happened, the horror of dumped newborn babies made headlines on the news. After considering it briefly I knew it was something I could never do. My morals may have been slightly loose but my heart was not that hard.

Four months after visiting *Ambuya a*Firipo, I gave birth to a baby boy. Though Father was angry at first, he soon forgave me, to the chagrin of his new wife who thought he was being too lenient with me in the matter. He never tired though of reminding me of the many times he had warned me about my way of life. Although he was disappointed, Father disregarded advice from some that he chase me and my baby from home to face hardships on the farms, as that was the best way to deter me from having more of what they called the children-begotten-

from-the-bush. His response to them was always the same; "*Chaponya munzako chapita, mava chili kwaiwe,*" which means that the problem that befalls your neighbour today is as good as gone, tomorrow it befalls you. Father gave my son the name Mavhuto, which means problems, calamity, condolences or misery. Though it was far from what I would have wanted my son to be called, I consoled myself with the fact that at least Father had not decided to honour the memory of his late son Chakumanda by pasing his name on to my son, and he had not given him a name that depicted the unfortunate circumstances of his birth. I was grateful to him for being understanding and tolerant this time around. A month before it was discovered that I was pregnant, he had taken in *ma*Mpofu, a woman of the Zezuru tribe who came from the Zvimba Tribal Trust Lands near Sinoia. It was rumoured that her husband had gone to fight in the bush war when her little girls were still only a year old. When *ma*Mpofu came to live with us, her girls were about eight years old.

*Ma*Mpofu told us tales of the war of liberation that were as intriguing as they were alarming. Hardly anybody in Patchway Valley Mine had heard about this war and the few people who had a vague idea about it did not wish to discuss it publicly. I was not interested in it, nor was Father, but *ma*Mpofu switched on the wireless every evening. As time went by we got drawn into this nightly ritual. We listened to Radio Mozambique with little understanding at first. Gradually, we realised that black people were fighting to wrestle control of the country from the hands of the whites, one Ian Smith in particular. The voice over the radio talked about the black people in Northern Rhodesia and Nyasaland who had already been given their independence and whose countries were now known as Zambia and Malawi. Mocambique had done so too and had become Mozambique. Those of my generation learned about it from History lessons at school. What we

did not know much about was the war waged in Rhodesia by blacks against whites to get their land back. Listening to Radio Mozambique was therefore a revelation. There was a lot of music to go with the lectures. We were compelled to keep the volume down because listening to the broadcasts that incited us to rebel against the white regime could land us in prison. We would be charged with treason, so we were warned. Treason? Well, we were going to steer clear of it, whatever it was. We did not need to understand what it meant. It was enough to know the consequences of being charged with it.

The community that had been served by only four mine security guards for as long as I could remember was suddenly teeming with the British South African Police force of Ian Smith, commonly known as the B.S.A.P. We used to hurry indoors and shut the doors and windows whenever we saw a 'jeep'_ the notorious police vehicle_ cruise into Patchway Valley at neck-breaking speed that left a huge cloud of red dust trailing in its wake and whistling like a whirlwind.

Overnight, my people were no longer *vabvakure*. Under the black skin we became one people united by a common cause; to fight the white man and all of his kinsmen until they retreated to their homelands beyond the horizon. The news was received with caution and scepticism in some quarters of the migrant population.

"The natives here want to get rid of all whites because they are foreigners and because this land is not rightfully theirs, right?" *a*Musambakarume prompted his kinsmen, who nodded in agreement. "But who knows on whom they will focus their attention once they win their war? It could be us next being driven over to the border and all the way to Zambia, Malawi and Mozambique before you know it. *Abare vanga,* let us be cautious in this matter and keep ourselves to ourselves as we have done for years. Let us leave the locals to wage their war and let us not forget

that we are migrants here and we depend entirely on working for the white master. We are merely migrant workers who move from one place to another and wherever our jobs take us. We are not strictly for here or there."

"You are a coward, Musambakarume!" cried *a*Bhinari. "Why should we keep on slaving for *abwana*? This is our chance to be free. Have *abwana* not taken enough from us already?"

"Get away, *imwe a*Bhinari. What have you got that *abwana* could possibly want? What have you got that he could envy?" asked *a*Msambakarume with one hand contemptuously appraising *a*Bhinari from head to toe. "It is he, *bwana* who gives you shelter and wages. What more would you like from him, his wife?"

"He could at least give us decent houses," chipped in *a*Banda who had not said a word all along. "Our living conditions must surely be among the worst in the surrounding mining communities. Look at the living conditions of the workers at Chakari Mine. They have electricity in their houses and tap water right by the side of each house. We are told that over at Arcturus Mine they do not share toilets and bathrooms ten households to one. The classrooms there are not thatched with grass like ours here. They have proper asbestos roofs that keep out the rain during thunderstorms. Who can blame us for wishing for something better than these awful conditions we have here? We need better schools for our children, electricity in our homes and better toilets. Must men of our age be stared at by women and children whenever we walk into these communal compound toilets of ours to relieve ourselves? It may not embarrass you but I feel as if all eyes are on me, guessing at what exactly I am doing in there by the length of time I spend inside. Admittedly, *abwana* finally got rid of those disgusting pit latrines but what did he replace them with? Some kind of toilet with doorless

partitions that allow up to three people inside at the same time! It is still disgusting, though to a lesser extent but it is even more humiliating when a small boy comes in to squat in the cubicle next to mine, too polite to acknowledge my presence as I groan and struggle to ease my constipated bowels."

"It could be worse, *mubale wanga*," chuckled *a*Bhinari. "I would rather suffer from constipation than endure the discomfort and indignity of diarrhoea. Just last week *a*Kamanga was observed bolting at the speed of wind into the toilet. A moment later, a terrible rumble was heard by the women close by, followed by a stench so horrible it was as if a rotten egg had exploded into the air." The statement was greeted with loud guffaws and shrieks of laughter from the men.

"*Manje so?* It is a disgrace. *Abwana* should treat us with more respect. After all we are the reason they lead such comfortable lives. I say we should all unite under one skin and fight for better conditions!" declared *a*Bhinari.

"I think you are being ungrateful, my friend. How can you expect from *abwana* that which neither you nor your forefathers ever had back home? Moreover you are a free man, not a slave and therefore not compelled to stay on if you do not like it here. *Abwana* did not come to your village and march you all the way to this place. Your fathers came here of their own free will, probably even left their families in tears, and risked their lives to get here where they threw themselves at the feet of *abwana* and begged for jobs. Now you want to bite the hand that feeds you. No wonder *Masambadovi* say, '*ukarera garu namukaka mangwana bhasopu,*[97]' said *a*Musambakarume in his pidgin mix of Chishona and Chichewa which had become common to most migrant people.

---

97 *If you raise a dog on milk, it could turn on you in future*

"We may not be slaves, Musambakarume, but that is no reason for *abwana* to treat us worse than they do their dogs. I agree with Bhinari. We deserve to be treated better. We must all act with one purpose and support our kinsmen in the fight for a better life. After all one man's victory is a victory for all. Let us support the struggle," said *a*Kaunda.

"And if you should get *chigumura,* where would you go, to Zambia? Don't even put that idea into your head, *mubale wanga*. From what I hear, the people in Zambia carry bags full of Kaunda's money when they go to buy food," said *a*Msambakarume.

"Really? That would be wonderful," whistled Father, impressed. "You mean to say labourers like us can actually have so much money? I thought only *abwana* ever handled such large sums of money. Things are happening in our homelands." I too was impressed by what I could hear from the veranda where I was shelling groundnuts. The men were sitting on chairs by the edge of the veranda.

"The money is said not to buy much. I hear a carrier bag full of money buys only a single loaf of bread. That is how expensive things have become over there, especially food. "

"What! Is it paper money you are talking about, or one cent coins?" exclaimed *a*Kaunda.

"Paper money,"answered *a*Msambakarume, rubbing his forefinger against his thumb, with the smugness of one who has knowledge that no one else has.

"There he goes again! Surely you exaggerate?"

"Ask around if you think I am lying. I hear the headmaster read in the newspaper the other day that the food is so expensive over there that those who can afford it cross into this country to do their shopping in Victoria Falls town. Now if they send you packing back there with your whole pension stuffed in a small envelope you will surely starve to death within days. It is definitely not a

place to even consider retiring to, so you had better think of your future where this war is concerned. Here in Rhodesia you have no rural home to run away to and lick your wounds like the locals."

"Who needs a home in the rural areas, with a war raging over there as it is? The locals themselves are leaving their villages in ruins and coming to seek refuge with their relatives in towns. The rural areas have now become battlefields. The 'boys' come in from Mozambique to mobilise and recruit freedom fighters and also to launch their attacks from the mountains. Smith's soldiers go into the countryside where they brutally massacre villagers who give food and shelter to these *gorira,*[98] so I am told. At times the villagers are so brutally tortured for information that in the end, strong men break down and divulge the whereabouts of the fighters. Then the *gorira* are ambushed and if they survive the attack, they unleash their fury on the villagers whom they accuse of collaborating with the enemy and betraying their kinsmen. They string them up and kill them for being sell outs, so I heard. It is hell in those villages at present. It is one big vicious cycle in which I would not wish to be caught up."

"You just cannot win any way you look at it. You know, don't you, that Chivaura the compound security officer has a son who is on call-up, fighting in the Rhodesian Army alongside the white soldiers of Smith? Do you want to know what the fighters did to Chivaura's parents in Bhowera?" asked Father.

"*Ehe*?"

"Tell us."

"What?" chorused several curious voices.

"They beat them up and burnt down their homestead, making an example of them to those whose kinsmen fight on the wrong side of the battlefield. In this war, children

---

98

die for the sins of their parents and parents for their children's."

"But how do they get to know who's done what in towns and vice versa?" asked *a*Kaunda.

"O-o, we are our own worst enemies, *mubale wanga.* I am told they inform against each other, some out of fear, others out of pure malice and a big number do it to settle old scores. It is a sad situation when you can no longer trust your own brother or your neighbour with your life," observed Father.

"If the police get to know that your kinsmen crossed over to join the struggle in Mozambique or Zambia, they imprison you. Yet they force you to go for call-up themselves, National Service is what they call it. For this, your people get punished by the 'boys'. It is an impossible situation. These locals are caught in the middle, getting attacks from both sides."

"I hear that in some cases the *magananga*[99] themselves abduct the bigger boys and girls from boarding schools and march them across the border to join the war," said *a*Kaunda.

"*Ah ah ah, imwe a*Kaunda, don't you start now. That is just *'action'*. There is no truth in it. My kinsmen, do not believe this man's wild tales," cried *a*Musambakarume, shaking his finger at aKaunda.

"It is true, *a*Musambakarume. Ask *aTicha* Mabhachi and he will tell you. Just last month, I heard him tell the mine clerk that his own brother's son was taken to Mozambique from Mutambara Mission in Que Que just after Rhodes and Founders Day."

"Lies, all lies. Mutambara Mission is not even in Que Que. It is in Umtali."

"Whether it is in Fort Victoria, Umvukwes or Sipolilo, that is not the point_"

---

99 terrorists

"Let us just worry about what concerns us, which is how to survive in this situation as migrants. I think we are better off joining one side so that we can get protection from the other side should the need arise," suggested *a*Banda.

"Why don't we just stay right here where we are, in the middle? So far the attacks are confined to the rural areas and towns, not the mines. If the war comes to us then we fight. We should not even dream of taking sides with *abwana* against our fellow blacks. Meanwhile, if the war does not affect us, then we simply go about our lives as before," suggested Father. Everybody agreed that it was a sensible position to adopt.

Echoes of the war resounded all around us as it intensified; cars bombed and buildings reduced to rubble in cities and towns, buses torched and reduced to smouldering wrecks on a number of routes to the villages, people massacred here and there, and others blown to unrecognisable chunks of flesh by detonated landmines. Farmers were attacked on their remote farmlands and at times whole fields of crops were burnt down. Fear crept into people of all races and ages. The rich suffered alongside the poor as the country was swamped in a bloodbath. The two sides had reached the point of do or die. We heard about the terrorists and the effects of the war all around, courtesy of the Rhodesia Broadcasting Service. We heard too, courtesy of the bush telegraph, about the freedom fighters who were said to possess super-human powers that enabled them to disappear into thin air like mist. We marvelled at such a feat. However, this war was just like the famed *Nkhonto yaHitila* of many years ago in which my grandfather was said to have fought on behalf of Britain. Some people had only a vague idea of it. They had heard rumours about it and they knew it was being fought out there somewhere beyond the horizon but no one could say for certain that they had first

hand knowledge of it. So life went on as usual at Patchway Valley Mine. The hushed voice of Ticha Musazosiya urging blacks to join or support the struggle could be heard in the background as the song 'Tora Gidi Uzvitonge' crackled out of our small wireless as we listened to Radio Mozambique with great secrecy. We listened in awe as a long dead woman was eulogised in song. We had no idea women could inspire a whole nation like that. The more she and Sekuru Kaguvi were mentioned, the more we wanted to hear about them, so we took the risk, and happily sang along:

Mbuya Nehanda kufa vachitaura shuwa-
Kuti zvino ndofire nyika ino
Shoko rimwe ravakandiudza
Tora gidi uzvitonge

Mbuya Nehanda kufa vachishereketa
Kuti zvino ndonofire nyika ino
Shoko rimwe ravakandiudza
Tora gidi uzvitonge

On the other side of the compound, the defiant voice of Ian Smith vowing, 'Never in a thousand years!' boomed from the grand stereos of *abwana.* His son-in-law Clem Tholet's hit song 'Rhodesians Never Die' loudly and defiantly blared out of the big supersonic stereos of *abwana,* reminding the whites, and warning us, of their invincibility.

We'll preserve this little mission for our children's children too
Once you're Rhodesian no other land will do
We will stand tall in the sunshine with the truth on our side
And if we have to go alone, we go alone with pride

Because we're all Rhodesians and we'll fight through thick and thin
We'll keep our land a free land to stop the enemy coming in
We'll keep them north of the Zambezi till that river's running dry
This mighty land will prosper because Rhodesians never die.

Then in a matter of months, everything changed. The Zambezi River had not run dry nor did it look like it was on the verge of doing so anytime soon. It probably never would. A thousand years had not passed, not even a hundred or ten either when the leaders from both black and white sides met up to decide the future of the country, so the wirelesses informed us. The months that followed were supposed to be the beginning of a new era, but it turned out to be a period of uncertainty. We were not sure whether we were independent or not. Like Zambia before us, our country adopted a new name but unlike Zambia, the old one remained too, to be pronounced in the same breath as the new one.

The war limped on for several more months before it was finally all over. A ceasefire was declared and for the first time, the people at Patchway Valley Mine saw the evidence of the war, but I had seen it in its most brutal form at the farm. Only when it was over did we realise that the black people were divided in their fight for liberation. Two or three different groups came into the compound and each of them urged us to support their political party. This left most of us confused because we did not know what the difference between one party and the other was, or why we had to vote for one against the other. We learned to chant the various slogans and became adept at juggling the various parties to keep them all happy.

We bought cards for all the parties and we memorised and recognised their symbols and we sang praises to all

their leaders with equal passion. We listened with awe to the numerous promises of a better future, some of which left us dumbfounded as well as excited as never before. It was also for this reason that some of us bought membership cards for all the parties. We did not want to miss out on the grand promises by belonging to a losing party. Each of these parties expected us to belong to it and failure to do so meant that one was considered to be a sell-out. They all made promises of the same changes, and I could not understand why they did not band together against the whites since they seemed to have one aim but which they hoped to achieve through different leaders and different slogans. It was quite confusing but their promises were a good enough reason for most of us to take an interest in an issue that had hardly concerned us up until then.

The parties were promising a life we had never before dared dream of.

"If you vote for this party you shall take over all that the whites have. It is all yours after all, the result of your sweat of several generations and that of your fathers before you. The white man did not bring anything with him except a rifle in one hand and the Bible in the other. It is only those two items we shall allow him to take back with him when we dispossess him of everything that he stole from us. You need only point at something and it shall be yours. Vote for us and win your freedom, attain majority rule and what is rightfully yours," went the speakers of the various parties. We were overjoyed, needless to say. Women ululated as men stamped on the ground with their gumboots and their clenched fists punched the air. There were some who declared that they would stop work as soon as we attained independence. They had a few farms and houses earmarked for occupation. I too had a dream. I had lived on Chestnut farm for many years as a labourer therefore my dream was

not grand. All I wanted was a nice, clean house with electricity, preferably Mr Fred Taylor's, the Compound Manager at Patchway Valley Mine. If all the whites were going to be driven out of the country then he would not need it, I reasoned. I imagined myself living the life of *adona* and it felt good.

Victory with an overwhelming majority for one of the black parties meant the collapse of the white regime that had colonised and ruled the nation for almost a century. We celebrated our victory with the world behind us. The birth of our new nation had been a long awaited event among the black people not only in the country but all over the world. It was a birth that came after hard labour, many tears and much agony for all parties involved. Many lives were lost during the war just as many survivors were left scarred mentally and physically, but it was generally agreed that the birth pangs were worth the joy we felt at being a free nation at long last. The victory was like a mighty rapture that had the majority of the nation celebrating for weeks. Even the great Queen of England sent her son over to help bring down the colonial flag that had freely blown in the African skies, casting a shadow over the lives of the Africans ever since Cecil John Rhodes first raised it before naming the occupied land after himself. Many of the things we had not dared hope for suddenly appeared attainable. Light had come not only into our minds, but into our homes as well. The Mine Management had the public communal baths boarded up and the partitioned toilets replaced by outside bathrooms and toilets that were shared with only one other household. More water taps were installed and our lives improved, gaining us a measure of respectability. Proper windows with glass panes were installed to replace the wood and metal ones.

The great news was that we were all one nation, the blacks and the whites. We were one big happy family and

even the Prime Minister preached the gospel of reconciliation. Our town was Gatooma no more. Towns shed colonial names such as Umtali, Hartley, Shabanie, Gwelo, and Marandellas, the legacy of our oppression, and replaced them with the traditional ones the colonial regime had previously cast aside. We could, after all, cast off old skin and leave it behind. Upper Top secondary schools mushroomed in the country and enabled even the poorest among us to go to school and to be on the same level with the rest of society. On the surface everything was beautiful, especially as the Compound Manager and his kinsfolk no longer had Ian Smith as their leader. We replaced the heroes of the colonial regime with our own and we walked boldly and proudly down Josiah Tongogara Street where previously we had timidly walked down Moffat Street and David Livingstone Avenue to contemptuous sniggers of 'kaffir'. Apart from that everything else was very much the same as before.

Although independence brought electricity into the homes of the black people, the majority of the labourers did not have much use for it apart from lighting and using it for their small wirelesses. The women continued to do their cooking on open fires and they heated bath water in large tins outside and put hot embers in irons to press the clothes they washed in large enamel dishes. None of the labourers earned enough money to afford luxuries such as stoves, fridges, stereos and television sets. With time, they learned to go to town and get these gadgets and other bits of furniture on credit from Nyore Nyore Zimbabwe Furnishers, the first big store to extend credit to black people.

Girls continued to go to school until initiation time, after which, barely out of adolescence, they settled down to married life with mine labourers in much the same way their mothers before them had done. Boys as young as fourteen years of age continued to work for the *bwana* in

their houses and in the mines. Farmer Van der Byl continued to send his tractors to collect casual labourers at whom he snapped his dainty well-manicured fingers. He addressed them as 'boy' and they sprinted to obey their master's voice. Their pride at being the most liked servants showed in their over-eager, ages-old induced willingness to serve and obey. Mrs Van der Byl continued to frequent the Blue Jay Tea Room in Gatoo_ oh well, Kadoma now, where she met up with other white farmers' wives for tea and cake. The 'Whites Only' sign had come down, but the prices kept the barriers in place. So, as *adona* continued to daintily sip their tea, we hungrily tore into buns that we washed down thirstily with Coca-cola while standing outside by the window of the café and from which take-aways were served. The *picanini* Van der Byls continued to be chauffeured to the prestigious Sir John Kennedy Primary and Jameson High schools where upon entering the school gates, they headed straight to their like-skinned classmates, their glances wary of the dark-skinned new breed of classmates in their midst.

The daughter of the headmaster at the newly established secondary school at the Mine went to a former group A high school where she soon discovered that although the barriers had come down there, the whites were moving to some other places where they put the barriers up even higher, creating Lomagundi College here and Whitestone Primary School there. They really must shun us, I thought, but that was nothing new. We had always been shunned as foreigners, as blacks, as labourers, as uneducated and as, as... whatever one had against us. At Patchway Valley Mine, the Compound Manager, Fred Taylor still drove around with his beloved Rhodesian Ridgeback on the front seat while at the back of the truck his cook sat grinning like an idiot as heavy raindrops pelted his bald head. *Bwana* John Brown still lusted after the female labourers on his farm who in turn grinned back

because they considered it a special favour to be singled out for attention.

Even in death, the whites maintained their superiority by continuing to bury their dead in the prestigious cemetery next to the general hospital. They continued to erect expensive marble tombstones, the cost of which was enough to build a house for a family of Africans at Patchway Valley Mine. Meanwhile, we continued to bury our dead in a desolate corner of the compound, under red mounds of earth, with a perforated kitchen utensil as the only sign that the remains of a loved one were interred there. The people we had supposedly defeated kept their big spacious houses and frequented exclusive clubs in the privileged *mayadhi* area, and we still lived in our squalid dwellings under cracked asbestos roofs. The dogs of *abwana* bared their teeth and barked at black people with the ferocity of beasts that continue to sing their masters' song long after the masters themselves have learned to go mute, their true feelings only ever displayed in subtle ways. An old dog so set in its ways cannot be taught new tricks, and the rottweilers proved that to be true. By the look of things, we were destined to go on singing; '*Ndakarumwa nembwa kumayadhi, ndichitsvaga panoshanda sisi.*[100]'

Twoboy continued working as the overseer at Chestnut farm and at Patchway Valley Mine, and Father and his fellow labourers kept going down the mine shafts day after day to bring up the gold for *abwana*. The words of one observer, "*Chitima ndechimwe, chachinja ndidhiraivha,*[101]" summarised it all. With this realisation, we went back to our ordinary lives as the people who had

100 I was bitten by a dog in the prestigious white people's areas, while looking for my sister's work place.

101 The train is still the same, only the driver has changed

paid us so much attention that it was almost suffocating forgot all about our existence. Their goals achieved or defeated, whatever the case was, we did not see them again for a long time. Only one good thing appeared bright in my personal life; the fact that my son Mavhuto would go to school in a free country. I hoped with all my heart that his life would not be a struggle throughout as mine has been. Now that Father is dead my fears for Mavhuto have resurfaced. And they are greater this time.

MAVHUTO'S STORY

(1974- to-date)

Patchway Valley Mine. Kadoma

"Eh, Mavhuto *munyamata.*[102]" I turn my head slowly towards the voice that sharply displaces my thoughts. Two elderly men sit on a stack of logs, *a*Banda and *a*Kaunda. "Come and sit here, *munyamata,*" beckons *a*Kaunda, patting the space between them. I do as told. The three of us sit and stare into the distance like crows perched on the branch of a tree. The beauty of the orange hue emerging from the edge of the earth in the far distance contrasts starkly with the ugliness of death around us.

The earth gives birth to the sun with a gentle push, slowly and seemingly without effort. The sun, upon detaching itself from its mother, scales the horizon with ease. The word majestic comes to mind. I remember how, when I was a child, Grandfather used to tell me that the earth swallowed the sun in the evening and that once in the belly of mother earth, it would crawl backwards and be born again the next day. The sun lived a million lives. Born in the morning, dead by evening and born again after a brief period of darkness. So short a life but one lived millions of times, over and over again. I am lost in these thoughts when *a*Kaunda's voice, thick and stale from a

102 Boy

second night of keeping vigil over the dead, finally breaks through.

"Your grandfather has completed his journey, *munyamata.* This is the place where the footsteps of his own father led him many years ago. The soils of this land shall embrace the body of your grandfather. His soul shall finally be at rest. From now onwards there shall be no more swollen legs, no more panting and groaning in the shafts and no more congestion in his lungs. Those feet are rested forever," explains *a*Kaunda.

"*Uhu,*" grunts *a*Banda. I nod my head in agreement. Indeed, just like the sun, Grandfather had made his journey, but unlike the ever-rising sun, there would be no multiple resurrections for him.

"In a moment, before our shadows become visible on the ground, a few of the men shall go and check that the womb out there is ready to receive our kinsman. Creating a womb for a grown man at this time of the year is a difficult job. The task is even harder when the ground is thirsty. Fortunately for us, heaven saw it fit to soften the ground with its tears for the great man that our kinsman was. Later, when the sun peers no longer at the top of our heads, we shall be the feet of our kinsman as he takes his finally journey.

As humans, we do not live our lives the ways animals do. When our kinsmen depart from this world, we despatch their remains in various ways. Sometimes it is done according to the age of the deceased, but at other times one's position in the community determines how it is done. The little ones who proceed straight to the land of the spirits before they can be part of our world are laid to rest just before the dew is dry on the ground, but the bodies of grown ups are buried with the setting sun, for shadows ought not to fall upon a fresh mound on the ground. The spirit of the deceased is whisked away in the blanket of darkness.

Today, when we take the body of our kinsman to its resting place, *kumanda uko,* we shall observe our time-honoured burial rites. In the tongues of our mothers, and as one voice, we shall whisper softly to the winds from the north and implore them to blow gently and carry the spirit of our kinsman back to the land of his forefathers. Even though it is this foreign land that shall embrace his remains, we shall commit his spirit back to his homeland where it belongs. Then the wandering in the wilderness shall be considered to be finally over."

"*Ya,* *a*Kaunda, we *a*Chewa bury our dead *kumanda uko,*" says *a*Banda pointing in the direction of the graveyard. "*Ya!* We are not like *Masambadovi* who cannot bear to separate their dead from the living, *ya*. From what I hear, they bury their loved ones in their huts, right under their feet. Does my tongue not carry the truth, *a*Kaunda?"

"*Wayamba,* my kinsman. There you go again. That tongue of yours does go wild at times, as we all know!"

"It is true, *mubale wanga*. Why would I lie to you? They say the homesteads of the Mashona people are dotted with graves. One needs very good eyesight to be able to tell the boulders and the anthills from the mounds that hold the remains of the departed. If there is a hut to your left, you can be sure to see a grave to your right, three or four footsteps away. In what way then is that different from burying them right inside the hut? Those people feel they must live with their dead, side by side to bide them good morning before sunrise and to implore them to watch over them last thing at night. I hear they even invoke the spirits of their dead to come into their lives to watch over them."

"*Bodza!?*" gasps *a*Kaunda who, despite contriving to appear uninterested, cannot hide his curiosity.

"Why would I lie? Of what benefit are the lies to me? These things happen, you know. You just need to know which way to cock your ear if you wish to catch the voices carried within the echoes of the wind. The land is for the

living during daytime, but at night the spirits of the deceased reclaim their space. They say *Masambadovi* even brew beer and hold ceremonies in honour of the dead who are said to speak through the mouths of the living. The Mashona people beat drums all night and pound the ground with their feet, raising enough dust to make our Jakopo envious. It is a night when the dead commune with the living. Did you know that after burying the departed, and before sunrise the next morning, the relatives of the deceased set out back there to check the area around the grave for footprints?"

"But you just said the graves are just four footsteps away from the homestead_"

"Listen, *mubale wanga*. Listen!" *a*Banda cuts off his kinsman impatiently, and *a*Kaunda, preferring to keep quiet, sighs and rolls his eyes. "Ya, they say the elders of the tribe go to inspect the grave for footprints, and should there be any, then they know witches had visited during the night and_"

"Enough *a*Banda, enough!"says *a*Kaunda, getting up abruptly. I am glad of the interruption. With Grandfather yet to be buried, I find the talk insensitive. I get up to leave and *a*Banda's mumbling voice follows me as I walk away towards the house. The voice crawls up my back like maggots, sending shivers down my spine.

"These locals have strange customs and habits. Indeed they have. And they also say the dead..."

While the men busy themselves with preparations for the burial, the women are busy with the fires, water and the preparation of food. I have not been anywhere near Grandfather's body since he passed on. But now I decide to go indoors. Hesitant footsteps take me to the entrance of the house. Around the doorway lies an assortment of pairs of footwear placed in a haphazard manner. My eyes take in a pair of slippers, leather shoes and canvas shoes of

different colours and that are at various stages of wear and tear. Each pair looks forlorn and waits patiently for its owner to fill them again and find the familiar path back home. I lift my slipper-clad feet and step over them and into the kitchen. I immediately turn right and stand in the doorway to the sitting room. My hesitation is only momentary. A step or two finds me in the sitting room. In the far corner along the wall, Grandfather's body is stretched out on a reed mat on the floor, along the very spot where I lie down to sleep every night. It is covered from head to toe with the least worn-out of the only three blankets he owned. The room is lit dimly by a 40watt light bulb of the inferior quality we can afford. A metre or so from the body, women sit in a row, their ageing backs supported by the wall behind them. In front of them is another row of women. My gaze falls upon *ma*Mpofu's weathered face. The silent tears that collect in her eyes spill over into the grooves above her puffed out cheeks and slowly snake their way across the fine ridges and towards the ears in opposite directions where, upon finding no support, they tumble downwards towards the chin. *Ma*Mpofu wipes the tears with the back of her wrist.

I shift my eyes to the floor where they are immediately confronted by a row of pairs of feet of varying sizes and shapes; from smooth, cream coloured soles to soot-blackened or mottled ones. Deformed toes, ingrown nails and bunions glare at me as if defying my eyes to betray even the slightest sign of critism of the state they are in. Cracked heels yawn only slightly, but their mocking gesture is all too obvious. Opposite the women, and positioned facing their direction, are a few rickety wooden chairs that the elderly men of the clan are supposed to sit on. Only two of the eight or so are unoccupied. I ease myself onto one of them, which immediately groans and protests with a high-pitched squeak that squeezes out silence in an instant, filling the empty space. I try to jump

off but the chair holds my flesh in a firm grip and refuses to let go. A sharp pain sears through my bottom as I pull hard. More pain follows and tears gather in my eyes. The chair pinches harder with each attempt I make to free myself. My bottom shifts sideways slightly and the pain intensifies. The chair yawns and in so doing its grip on my flesh is loosened. Relief washes over me as I get up. I sidle down onto the cold floor and hug my knees and cross my feet at the ankles. The floor is cold but at least it does not pinch my bottom. Like *ma*Mpofu, I use the back of my wrist to wipe away the unshed tears welling in my eyes. A few tongues click and cluck. Sympathy is conveyed. The wordless gesture is understood even though the actual reason for the tears is misunderstood.

The women sit quietly. They are weary after keeping vigil for the third night in a row. *Amake* Chabwino tries to raise a song from her throat but her voice crawls out hesitantly. The other women do not add their voices to hers and as a result it falls flat on the ground, weak and unsupported. It curls inwards and slowly crumbles as silence reclaims the space. I am grateful for the silence which allows the thread of my thoughts to unwind and the space and freedom to roam. Suddenly, darkness fills up the space in the doorway.

The stooped figure of *Ambuya a*Firipo, now arguably the oldest woman in the community, inches forward into the room on silent, hesitant feet. Her bony fingers firmly support an enamel dish on opposite sides of the rim. From the dish, steam curls lazily upwards where it disappears but not before contorting itself into various shapes that edge sideways and upwards like a puppet manipulated by unseen hands. On one of the old woman's thin arms hangs a small towel. She moves towards the women sitting near the body until she reaches the outer row of feet. Her small bare feet search for gaps on the floor and when they find them, they immediately fill the spaces. Once her intention

is clear, the other women shift their bottoms this way and that way. Legs are placed one above the other and crossed at the ankles and space is created. Other knees are slightly raised, and the legs made shorter.

*Ambuya a*Firipo lifts one foot, moves it forward and the yawning gap closes like a flytrap snapping at an unsuspecting insect. When the old woman finally reaches *ma*Mpofu's side, she kneels in the space between her and the corpse. With great caution, she places the dish as close to *ma*Mpofu as she can and whispers to her words that do not travel further than her lips. *Ma*Mpofu nods and removes her headscarf, exposing what I know to be tightly coiled black hair with some grey around the temples. *Mhotsi.* Kinky hair. The old woman claps her hands slowly and with great reverence. She unties the knot at the corner of her wrapper cloth and takes out a bar of soap and a brand new razor blade. It is of the Lion brand, the type Grandfather liked to use. *Ambuya a*Firipo places the items on the floor with great care, then immerses the bar of soap in the hot water, rubs her hands around the soap and works a rich lather. She proceeds to rub the foam into the younger woman's hair. Before my eyes, *ma*Mpofu is instantly transformed into a white-haired widow. Bony fingers knead her scalp, each hand moving in a slow, rhythmic and circular motion from the temple towards the top of the head.

The procedure is repeated, this time from the forehead to the back of the head. *Ambuya a*Firipo stops for a while to examine her handiwork. Satisfied, she dries her hands on her wrapper cloth, rests her barely-there bottom on the heels of her cracked feet and unwraps the blade from its wrapping. Using her thumb and two fingers, she grips the sharp blade firmly and carefully. The fingers and the thumb meet in the hollow space that runs down the middle of the blade. The older woman walks on her knees,

closes the tiny space between her and the younger woman and positions herself by her side. With the right hand, she places the edge of the blade on *ma*Mpofu's temple just where the hair, now covered in white suds, starts. Her left hand supports the back of *ma*Mpofu's head. A deep sound threatens to rise from the pit of my stomach. I manage to stifle it and tuck it away unheard, but not without great effort. In one firm stroke, the old woman scraps the scalp with the razor from the temple to the back of the head. A path is formed and a bald patch is exposed. After each stroke, Ambuya *a*Firipo rinses the blade in the dish and carries on with the task until the widow's head is completely clean shaven. In the dish, the coiled hair clings to the suds floating in the water. This evokes the image of tiny black birds weaving their way in and out of a cluster of white clouds on a bright day. *Ma*Mpofu looks like I have never seen her before. Her new sculpted figure marks her as a woman touched by death, or to be more precise, tainted by grief. The black garments will mark her out even among strangers, as she who has been visited by death. From the day Grandfather took his last breath and for the next twelve months, the shadow that is death will walk closely by his widow's side.

After she is through with *ma*Mpofu, *Ambuya a*Firipo takes her razor blade to the mother-woman who lets out a panic-stricken shriek that rouses the ageing women around her from a state of semi-slumber.

"*Iyayi!* No, no, no! I will not have my head shaved."

"Why won't you, Dhairesi?" demands *Amake* Chabwino with indignation. "You know that tradition demands that the ritual be performed to show your state of bereavement. Your father's death has to be mourned in the proper way."

"*Ma*Mpofu is already doing that for him."

"She is doing it in her role as Masauso Nyirenda's widow, but you have to do it as his flesh and blood."

"No, I won't! I can mourn Father's passing in other ways except by shaving my head. I could even cut my hair short if that is of any help."

"Just tell us why you won't do it," insists *Amake* Chabwino.

The heated argument now has everybody fully alert. Heads turn, necks are craned, eyes are raised and ears cocked. Only the corpse does not stir. Silence waits too, equally alert. The mother-woman's voice, firm and clear bursts out, "because I have a perm."

Pairs of eyes seek each other out. Finding only bewilderment, they move on to those beyond, searching with raised eyebrows and unblinking stares for an explanation or an interpretation, in the mother tongue, of the small unfamiliar word still hanging in the air. Silence continues to wait, bewildered.

"You have a *what?' Amake* Chabwino's voice finally shakes off the silence. All heads turn towards the mother-woman, expecting the meaning only her lips can give.

"I said; I have a *perm*." With a swift movement, she rips off the headscarf covering her head to reveal sleek curls of shiny black hair. She stares defiantly at the numerous eyes fixed with fascination on her head. The texture of the hair feels, to the eye, slippery and rigid. Lips part slightly on some faces while on others open mouths expose toothless gums, stained teeth or perfectly chiselled front teeth. Eyes almost pop out on some of the faces and on others they squint till they are reduced to mere slits.

"What is that, a wig?" one woman finally finds her voice.

"It is a perm. I have already told you."

A few bony fingers reach out and plough into the dark mass on the mother-woman's head where they meet no resistance. The hint of rigidity is just an illusion. The fingers make their way along imagined paths in the hair,

parting it this way and that way, moving from ear to ear and from the forehead to the back of the head.

"How does it feel?"

"What is it like?"

"Can I feel it too, *a*Dhairesi?"

"Is it hard or soft?"

The questions are thrown together until they become sounds without meaning... a jabbering of old, faltering voices in the dim light. When the excitement finally dies down, *Amake* Firipo, who sits next to the mother-woman, extends her fingers towards the dark curls. Her thumb and forefinger grip the curls and feel them for texture. The fingers release the hair but do not move away. They hover above the curls as if pondering their next move. Then with a swift decisive motion, the gnarled fingers dig into the hair and tug at a few strands. The roots hold firm and the mother-woman yelps.

"Hey, it is not a wig. It is a perm. I told you that already," she explains. Ignoring the exasperation in the mother-woman's voice, the probing fingers raise the curls and stretch them to their full length. Breaths are held in what appears like a choreographed motion.

The women express awe at the length and the straightness of the hair. When the hair is slowly released, the strands twist and fold back on themselves, forming, not tight little coils the size of matchstick heads, but curls and ringlets. The mother-woman's curls differ greatly from the tight coils of the rest of the women.

"It is very soft, like cotton," in a loud voice, *Amake* Firipo finally gives her verdict. "But it stinks."

"What did you do to your hair to make it look like that, Dhairesi?"

"Is the hair in your armpits like that too?"

"What sort of magic brings about such results?"

"Do you lie down at night or do you spend the night in a sitting position?"

Questions rain down one after the other in a confused cacophony of voices. The mother-woman has a perm. I know what that is. A few of the female teachers at the secondary school have their hair permed. But until today, when I watched fingers explore the mother-woman's perm, I had no idea of its texture, or that the full length of the hair could be hidden in the sleek curls. Finally, one of the older women asks, "So it is for this smelly *pemu* of yours that you refuse to have your hair shaved?"

"Yes," the mother-woman replies matter of factly. She makes no embarassed apologies for her decision.

"*Eyi!*" a few voices shriek in unison while those still struggling with amazement manage a breathless gasp.

"Your father lies here, dead, and all you Dhairesi can think of is this silly *pemu* of yours. *Nxi*! Stubborn to the end, you are," chides *Ambuya a*Firipo.

"Why should that surprise you? That is Dhairesi for you… always going against our way of life," *Amake* Firipo adds, in support of her mother-in-law's disapproval.

"Not even the sacredness of death can make her sit up and reflect upon her stubbornness, just for once."

"Hey you people, it is you that need to sit and reflect here. This is Dhairesi whose waywardness we are all aware of. Nothing has changed about her. She is the same stubborn person she has always been; stubborn as a child, now possibly even more stubborn as a grown up. If her father, who lies dead over there, could not succeed in taming this wild spirit from his loins despite his many desperate efforts, what chance have any of us got? None. Let her be, I say," suggests *Ambuya a*Firipo. Many heads nod in agreement at the wisdom of the words but a few shake their heads vigorously.

"She shuns us, Dhairesi *uyu*. She thinks we are old, miserable and backward. We should leave her here alone with her father's corpse, just to teach her a lesson. It is the

only way she will realise how much she needs to be part of us," argues the wife of *a*Kaunda, our neighbour.

"*Mubale wanga*, the real tragedy of such situations is that whatever we do, Dhairesi here does not get affected," says *Ambuya a*Firipo. "The death of her father compels us to come together as his kinsmen and mourn him, then help bury him, for he was a wonderful man who was well-respected in the community. Had it been Dhairesi herself who had died, we would still be gathered here to comfort our respected kinsman as he grieved for his wayward daughter. Let Dhairesi keep her hair, I say. She has lost her father, and let it not be said that we made her lose her cherished hair as well," sneers the old woman. Several mouths droop at the edges. Eyes are rolled and shoulders shrugged. A decision has been reached. The old woman's age demands that her word be given considerable weight.

It is at this point that I decide to go back outside. For now, my eyes have witnessed enough drama in this tragic episode of my life. I step out of the door, seemingly unnoticed. Sharp rays of sunlight poke my eyes, making me blink. I take an involuntary step backwards before deciding to fight my way ahead. I walk into a natural light and seek out the men, *a*Kaunda in particular. By now he ought to know whether Grandfather's resting place is ready.

The remains of the deceased will be laid to rest today. Arrangements for the burial were made yesterday. I am told nothing about them though. By the look of things, the old man has ceased to be my grandfather. He now belongs to the elders of the tribe. He is their kinsman, their fellow migrant labourer. He is a victim of the mines like themselves and a fellow resident of the community. In that picture Mavhuto exists only as the product of his daughter's womb, a child-begotten-from-the-bush, a child of an anonymous man, whichever applies. I console myself with looking back to the fond memories of a life

shared with Grandfather and I am temporarily comforted. The old man had raised me to take pride in my name.

"Carry your name with pride at all times, *muzukuru,*" he used to say. I had oftened imagined myself heaving the name onto my head and balancing it there until it found stability. At times I imagined myself slinging it over my shoulder where it would perch like a badge of honour. There are a few occasions though, when I grip the name tight under sweaty armpits where it lies in danger of slipping. I am aware that I dare not lose this name that Grandfather claimed gives me an identity, yet I sometimes feel it slip off my shoulder and slide down my back and out of sight. I feel lighter then, as if a load has been taken off me. My connection with this burdensome name is broken and I ought to feel liberated and happy, yet I panic instead. I soon begin to feel like an impositor, a man sharing footsteps with the shadow of a stranger. Chabwino calls himself Chabs, but I am not Mav, or Marvin but Mavhuto. I revert to my given name and proceed to carry it with pride. The name feels heavy and steady on my shoulders. Balanced. In its heaviness lies stability and security.

The name keeps me anchored and it feels just right.

'Your name dates back to the olden days of the Federation.' Grandfather's words echo in my mind. He said he had insisted on calling me Mavhuto as a way of clinging to the world his father had left behind. On realising they could never go back to their countries of origin, most migrants made this land their permanent home. They had sought to fit into the land of their hosts by adopting the names of *abwana* which were adapted to our tongue. My classmate Yona's siblings are called Mereniya, Matiridha and Firipo. His own name is the shortened version for Yonatani, which itself is a corruption of the name Jonathan. Only a few of us have traditional Chewa names. In the last few years my people have moved on

even more. The nostalgia for the motherlands felt by our immediate forebearers began to recede slowly into the past and to fade with time.

In a bid to integrate even more with the black community of their adopted country, my people discarded the names of *abwana* and replaced them with their Shona equivalent. Muzarema is now more likely to be called Muchaneta. Ganizani answers to Rangarirai, while Kondwelani and Tsogolani answer to Farai and Tungamirai respectively. Because Grandfather had married a Shona woman, I benefitted from a fusion of cultures; that of migrants and that of the locals although Grandfather refused to acknowledge the fact. He stubbornly claimed that his was the dominant one, if not the only culture in the home. Admittedly, he spoke to his wife and me in the language he claimed to roll with pride round his tongue but his wife spoke to everybody, him included, in Chishona. I spoke to both of them in their respective mother tongues as I was fluent in both. This was because I learned the Shona language at school and spoke mainly Chichewa at home. My friends were speakers of either Shona or Chewa languages and I felt at home in either world.

I knew as much as any naturalised Zimbabwean about the history and geography of my adopted country and I knew their customs and their habits as much as I knew mine, if not more. *Ma*Mpofu boiled cassava tubers for Grandfather once in a while but our food was mainly the local staple diet of *sadza* and various types of stews. Sometimes *ma*Mpofu fried fresh beef in cooking oil and added onions, tomatoes and green vegetables. On other days she cooked beef that had been cut into long thin strips and dried in the sun. This was cooked in the same way as the fresh meat, but sometimes *ma*Mpofu substituted the cooking oil with peanut butter. On some days we had *sadza* with cultured milk that was bought

from one of the neighbouring farms. On rare occasions I would come home to find *ma*Mpofu sitting on the veranda and plucking feathers off a grisly-looking, recently beheaded chicken immersed in a dish filled with boiling water. She would fry the chicken and serve it with rice for herself and for me but she cooked sadza for Grandfather who always said a meal was not a proper meal if it was not strong enough to fill the stomach and sit there for hours. He said rice was that kind of food. He also hated it when his wife cooked okra which he claimed made people's heads soft and their thinking slow. He said pumpkin leaves ought to be grown for the sole purpose of providing shade for snakes in the fields, but certainly not for humans to eat.

The revulsion Grandfather had for certain foods did not extend to the silver-line, dried anchovies commonly known and packaged as *matemba*. *Ma*Mpofu liked them, as did Grandfather who ate them with gusto. I could never understand how anyone could find them to be delicious. Their stone-hard tiny eyes got stuck in the gaps between my teeth. It was difficult to avoid these eyes and whenever I bit hard on them it was as if I had clenched my teeth on fine grit. I hated them. Revulsion started as soon as I saw the silver line running along the length of the little fish. The food we ate and the diet of the locals only differed in that they ate dried vegetables with peanut butter while we preferred to eat the wild vegetable called *bonongwe.*

The opportunities previously closed to my people were open to those of my generation. There were no barriers in place. People of the older generation describe Patchway Valley Mine as a place that used to be fun to live in, with tribal dances taking place every weekend. The elders speak with nostalgia about those days, a period that I know nothing about. I grew up in a very different Patchway Valley. As a young boy, I looked forward to Thursdays when a bioscope was screened in the evening.

A wide brick wall erected near the beer hall served as a screen for the purpose of showing films that came as free entertainment for the miners and their families. The Compound Manager was said to provide these films because he wanted the workers and their families to get some relief from the monotony of compound life. The films became an event much looked forward to by both the children and the adults of both sexes. Men brought out wooden stools and took up position facing the wall long before the beginning of the film. Young women came out with their wrapper cloths or reed mats which they spread on the ground in front of the men. The sitting arrangement was carefully organised. The children sat or stood on the periphery because we tended to become rather excited and jump up and down if the action got a bit frenzied on screen.

Before the main film we were shown short comic clips featuring Fuzi and Tiki, the names by which we called the characters of Laurel and Hardy. We loved these short films because they made us laugh even if we did not understand most of what was going on. It was not so much what was said as what was done. The movies were silent anyway but it would not have made any difference had there been audible dialogue because very few people understood English and nobody paid any attention to the subtitles on the few occasions we got them. In the films with dialogue we hardly understood what was said because the voices of the white people came out clipped.

Our elders told us that the noses of the whites were not wide enough for clear speech. They were pinched and this defect probably interfered with the fluid flow of words, making it difficult for them to speak clearly. Others argued that their words came out boiled already by the huge quantities of tea they sipped from time to time. Such was their thirst that it was unquenchable. The workers spoke to their bosses and were spoken back to in

chilapalapa, therefore our ability to understand English as spoken by those whose mother tongue it was became almost non-existent.

Whoever ordered the films took care to choose those that focused more on action than dialogue and these tended to have Roman themes. We loved it when Hercules, whom we called Hekuli, took on an entire army with his mighty sword. Spartacus and the gladiators were favourites too. Then there were the western films whose cowboys we egged on in fights by repeatedly yelling out, *"Kaibho, kaibho!"* We fought alongside our heroes and urged them on when they seemed like giving up. We shouted abuse at the enemy and screamed until our voices became hoarse. We jumped up and down and sought to tread on the enemy who lay sprawled on the ground. At times, in the heat of the action, over-excited spectators aiming to 'hit' the enemy on screen whacked someone standing in front of them instead. A few fights broke out that way and the crowd cheered and took sides as the action tumbled from the screen to the brawlers within the crowd. In the dark it was always difficult to see who was hitting who and anyone was a target of the vicious blows and kicks that appeared to fly indiscriminately. Whenever that happened the film was halted and the crowds were told through a loudspeaker to either behave themselves and continue to watch the film or disperse altogether.

Our fondness for this weekly event always won in the end and back to our places we would go, to continue watching our screen heroes. Every film had an *ekita,* the one around whom the whole action revolved. There were moments though when the main actor was in such an impossible situation we feared he would not be able to get out alive. These nail biting moments made us tense and we held our breaths then, not daring to speak lest we gave his position away whenever he was hiding from the

enemy. Then someone would shout, *"Ekita haafe*[103]*!"* upon which we would sigh with relief and applaud resoundingly, remembering that the main actor always somehow found a way out of his predicament, however dire.

After watching these action-packed thrillers for some time, we soon realised that the more provocation the hero endured, the more incensed he became, and so too the more determined his quest for vengeance became. This heightened our suspense and anticipation for the confrontation we knew was sure to follow sooner or later, one that would inevitably end in victory for the main actor. We adored our heroes whose pain became our pain just as their victories became ours too. When our hero was raining blows on the enemy, we rejoiced and cheered, *"Chaya! Bhurara iwe chimamuna chamutima woyipa icho!*[104]*"* When he did not shoot the enemy as we 'advised' him to do, we felt terribly let down and in a kind of mass hysteria, warned him of the consequences of not finishing off his enemy when he had the chance. Whenever the enemy appeared to regain his strength and fought bravely, we held our breaths, then sighed with exasperation.

'We warned you, but you are stubborn,' we would chide our hero. If he was looking for an enemy he could not see but whom we were able to see, we lost patience with his apparent stupidity. We would point out where the enemy was and we could never understand then why he did not see thc villain whom we could clearly see. After all, they were in the same film! The screaming always got louder and more desperate before we turned our anger on the man who was our hero, *'Yangana kumambuyo kwako iwe!*

103the main actor does not die

104Hit him! Kill the cruel rogue

Look behind you! Oh, he is so, *so* stubborn. Let him get beaten up. We do not care!'

In the end when the main actor finally defeated the enemy, he was immediately embraced back into favour, his folly forgiven. We knew the words 'The End' would soon appear on the big screen, at which we all chorused *'the endi,'* as we rose as one big mushroom sprouting from the ground, our hearts filled with joy. Our feet carried our joyful hearts back home, the weary bones of the labourers temporarily numbed by the euphoria of watching a make-believe situation based on lives lived thousands of miles away and a million times detached from theirs. We would talk about the film all week, until the following Thursday. In some cases we were shown films in stages, one episode per week. The cut-off points always left us in suspense. We spent the whole week anxious to know what would happen next. We always knew a film was to be shown in stages when we saw the words 'To Be Continued' where normally the words 'The End' appeared. We chorused *'tu bhi kontinyo!'* as the crowd rose en masse with the swirling dust to wish friends goodnight before setting off for home. We referred to this kind of film as a 'to be'. We would tell our friends that there was a 'to be' showing the following Thursday and urge them to be there. The names of the people in the films also became nicknames for those amongst us who exhibited similar characteristics to our screen idols. Anybody who was funny in any way became Fuzi or Tiki. Once in a while we watched horror films of vampires. There was a lot of screaming and covering of faces with hands whenever a vampire bared long fangs dripping blood. I once woke up screaming one night. Grandfather was bending over me where I lay paralysed with fear. Concern was written all over the old man's face.

"There is a white man with blood on his long teeth, he is going to eat me, *Asekuru,*" I whimpered, holding on tightly to Grandfather. "He keeps grinning as he advances

towards me." Grandfather was puzzled and stared uncomprehendingly at me.

"He is dreaming of *dhirakura,*" explained one of *ma*Mpofu's twin daughters who had visited from the village. When Grandfather appeared even more confused, it was further explained to him that Dracula was the villain in the film we had watched the previous night. He then comforted me and explained that there was no white man in the house, and that I had had a nightmare. If this was meant to comfort me then it did not, for I had often heard adults interpreting their dreams before. Dreaming of white people was a sign of the presence of witches in the house. The presence of gory-looking white men, vampires or witches was the same as far as I was concerned. It was a bad omen. Grandfather gently wiped away my tears and held my hand until I drifted back to sleep.

Although Grandfather allowed us to go and watch the films, he did so grudgingly.

"I do not wish to appear too strict but I do not see what good can ever come out of *mabhaisikopo* that show a way of life which is alien to ours. The white women you all flock to ogle roam about in a disgraceful manner, dressed only in their under clothes. I do not know how any of you can bear to watch such acts of immorality. The white man's ways are different from ours. Our womenfolk never used to bare their flesh so unashamedly in public in the past, but they now seem to have no sense of decency. This alien behaviour stems from watching these abominable films. In them, if people are not fighting, they are licking each other unashamedly in public, like animals. What kind of life can that be, you tell me, Mavhuto *muzukuru*? If I appear rather strict and reluctant to let go of our way of life, it is because I do not believe progress means discarding those customs that are the basis of our culture. We should always take pride in our history, in our

language and above all, in our traditions. Your mother, poor soul, sought to shed off all traces of the person she was and in the process she ended up a caricature of the so-called modern woman; foul smelling oily hair and all kinds of brightly coloured powder on her bleached cheeks and around her eyes. There were times when I could hardly tell the difference between my own daughter and Jakopo. The resemblance was remarkable. All that was missing was the drumbeat to transform my daughter into a proper *chinyao*. From all the things that Dhairesi ever did to herself in the name of fashion, I think it was her head that suffered the most.

"My daughter became a stranger right before my eyes. At one point I wished she would embrace once again the frenzied religion of the white man that she had thrown herself into in the weeks following her mother's death. It probably would have curbed her excesses, though I had not thought so at the time she was deep in it. When some foot-stamping missionaries came into this community to preach, your mother was one of the first to follow them. I could not understand what solace she got from that happy-clapping type of worship where people screamed and became hysterical as if possessed by the devil. I was used to our own traditional kind of worship that was solemn and straight forward. A song or two to begin with, a reading from the Bible and a few more songs as the collection plate went round and the service was over. We then trooped out shaking hands and singing, 'God Be With You Till We Meet Again,' and that was it until the following Sunday. But in that new church there was singing, preaching, screaming, bible study meetings and public confessions and all kinds of things every single night.

The community became a crazed place. Those of us who worked full time could not keep up with activities that made so many demands on one's time. Mavhuto

muzukuru, I have nothing against church activities. God knows we need something to give us a reason for enduring the hardships of this world, but to throw oneself zealously into it to the exclusion of everything else left me bewildered. Despite her stubbornness, your mother was easily influenced by events around her. The easten winds blew her towards religious zeal, while the western winds blew her towards foolish romantic notions.

"When the excitement of the visit by the Dorothea Missionaries eventually died down, Dhairesi swapped her Bible for comic books. She resumed going to the bioscope and tried to emulate the ways of the women in the wretched films. I honestly do not know what you young people find to admire in them. The bioscopes seem to pull you and you just go along as if towards a force you have no power to resist. You only have to look at your mother to see the consequences of following blindly a way of life that is alien to ours. I blame those films for making my daughter shun our men. At one point she was seeing a Shona boy who came on school holidays to visit his uncle and his aunt here. That unsuitable association was very distressing for her mother and me. We knew the young man would never marry her, even though she claimed he intended to. We strongly believed that her rebellion against the time-honoured ritual of *chinamwali* had something to do with that boy. My own daughter refused to undergo initiation, a thing that had never been known to happen before, or since, among our people," Grandfather said, shaking his head as if after all those years he was still to come to terms with his daughter's scandalous rebellion.

"Such was the extent of the boy'sinfluence over your love-struck mother. As a parent I could not just watch while her life was hurtling towards ruin, so I did what any caring and responsible parent would do. I was aware of the extent of my daughter's stubbornness and I knew that

no amount of reasoning with her would make her change her mind once it was set. During the school term, the boy and my Dhairesi wrote letters to each other. I had always collected Dhairesi's letters from the Mine office whenever I was on a morning shift so I knew that she received letters quite regularly and with time I came to recognise the handwriting of the boy.

"At first the boy wrote to your mother twice a month. I kept hoping the relationship would fizzle out sooner or later but it seemed to get stronger and stronger instead. When the letters started arriving every week, I knew I had to do something. There was no point in waiting for divine intervention as there was nothing divine about that unsuitable relationship. I intercepted and went on to tear every single letter addressed to Dhairesi that I suspected was coming from that boy. By then I knew the way he shaped his letters. I must have torn up to a dozen of them before they finally trailed off. What a relief! It felt like a huge weight had fallen off my shoulders. In the weeks that followed I watched my daughter became morose as she pined for her lost love. Her heart was breaking at the apparent betrayal by the boy who had come to mean a lot in her life. It was sad watching her torment, knowing that I was responsible for it.

Although it made me feel bad, not once did I consider relenting. I had to think of the consequences of letting your mother place any hope in a relationship that I knew to be doomed right from the onset. The price of continuing with the ill-fated relationship was bound to be painful for all concerned at a later stage, if not earlier. The guilt I felt was not as a result of the broken relationship. It stemmed instead from the heartache I knew Dhairesi was suffering, but I had to think of her future. My naïve daughter was prepared to throw away chances of a good marriage for the sake of what was obviously a passing phase. Thus I resolved to be cruel in order to be kind. I figured that if I

acted early enough when her heart was still young and tender, Dhairesi would be hurt at first but she would eventually pick up the broken pieces of her heart and get on with her life. Young hearts tend to mend easily, sooner rather than later. My decision gave me an overwhelming sense of relief. I was happy that the nonsense with the boy was finally over. Little did I realise that worse was to come.

"When Dhairesi's heart finally mended, she embarked on affairs that did not seem to last long. I thought that with time she would eventually settle down and when that did not happen, I decided to take matters into my own hands once again. In the year that her mother passed on, it became crucial that I find Dhairesi a husband as soon as possible. Within months I had found her a man I deemed responsible and mature but to my embarassement, your mother laughed with contempt in his face before telling both of us that she would not marry *a*Mkandawire even if he were the last man on earth. She wanted to find her own man, she declared. I despaired over my daughter's behaviour. Her unwavering determination to distance herself from our way of life caused me many sleepless nights and immeasurable pain.

There was a period when I truly feared that my daughter had finally gone mad. Straight from the calabash-carrying phase, she started behaving as if all the combs in the house were at war with her. She would dance to a kind of music that had no discernible rythm to my ear. All I heard were the pounding of drumbeats and some kind of garbled chanting. Dhairesi would throw her head back and thrust her fists up and down as she jogged in one spot like a mad person. Such unkempt hair I had only ever seen on a witchdoctor or a madman. The only plausible explanation for my daughter's weird behaviour was that she was possessed by the spirit of my father, *a*Bhaureni Nyirenda who, by the time he died, was truly mad. I

thought the spirit of my father whom I had neglected in his old age had come back to haunt me. I was relieved when I realised that my daughter was not the only young person in the grip of this hop-skipping insanity. I was told by those who were in a position to know that the music the young were dancing to was banned by the government because it incited black people to rebel against their masters. Despite the threat of a prison sentence if caught, the youths still found ways of bringing that music into Patchway Valley. It must have been those young men invading the *komboni* who smuggled it in. So my daughter carried on dancing in the frenzied way dictated by the beat of the music.

Most of your mother's peers revelled in this alien kind of madness that was pacified not by the beat of the ancient drums of the times of our fathers, but by another intoxicating beat that was altogether different. 'Bob Mare, Bob Mari,' they shouted as they hopped about, their hair unkempt and brightly coloured strings tied to their wrists. I had never seen such kind of collective madness before, *muzukuru*.

"When your mother became pregnant by no one in particular, she plunged my sombre world into worse gloom. It surprises me today that from such despair could emerge something as wonderful as you, *muzukuru wanga*. Your birth was the single significant event that brought me back to life and made me begin to smile again. I regarded it as a new phase of happiness for me and the reincarnation of not only the son I had lost but also that of my wife, my mother, my father and all the rest of my family. In fact, it was like the sprouting of a new life out of an otherwise dying tree. In you, *Mulungu* gave me a reason to smile again, and to get up and go to work after my daughter had left home.

I should have named you Madalitso, for your presence in my life is indeed a blessing but I chose to call you

Mavhuto instead, so that you would always remember the plight of our kinsmen in their quest for what has turned out to be the shadow of a mighty dream in the wilderness. Our plight is the thread that has kept the fabric of our existence together in ages past. We are a hardworking people with a sense of honour and we take pride in our culture. That is why I am so adamantly against the rot that strips us of our traditions, the rot that stems chiefly from that despicable *bhaisikopo* that you are so fond of."

I let Grandfather rumble on without paying much heed to what he was saying. It was enough that he did not stop me from going to the film shows. I felt that there was no point in arguing about their influence, or lack of it, in our lives. I loved the entertainment and derived much joy from it. Grandfather had his own way of seeing things that was different from the way my generation saw things. He was a loving man who was too set in his own ways to ever accept that change was inevitable even though it was there right under his nose in all aspects of our lives. One only had to look at our diet, at the fusion of slang and foreign words with our languages, at the marriages between locals and migrants, at the songs we sang and at the way we embraced the various fashion trends that made our lives more colourful and less dreary. Many people were detaching themselves from the ways of the past and embracing a new way of life. Grandfather himself had done so by marrying outside of his tribe, although he chose to dismiss this as a minor and insignificant deviation.

"The choices of a *blati* ageing migrant labourer are limited," he mumbled.

Indeed the ways of the white man were different from ours, at times shocking and unbelievable. I had watched films where a man danced with another man's wife, his arms wrapped intimately around her delicate waist, and his cheek nestling against hers! It probably did not happen

in real life, I thought. It just could not. The white pastor who came to our church with his wife during Easter time exhibited nothing but respectable behaviour. I therefore concluded that in real life white people were not as immoral as the films made us believe. It amused us that there were habits we blacks deplored amongst ourselves.

The locals disapproved of us and called us by names that insulted us. They would often castigate their kinsmen by saying, 'Your behaviour is typical of that of *Mabhurandaya* who are ill-bred and shameless.' Our people, on the other hand, could not understand what the fuss was all about. We did not adhere to any specific protocol in greeting or addressing people. Bare arms and shoulders in our womenfolk did not offend us. The locals fussed over minor things, we thought.

I grew up going to church, C.C.A.P, one of the three popular churches attended by the descendants of migrants. The Church of Central African Presbyterian had eighteen members. Most of the people who attended church, such as Grandfather, did so to get a sense of belonging. The old man claimed that for him this world was not home but some place he had briefly stopped by on his way to his real home in heaven. He used to say that there were two things everybody needed in life; membership of his church and that of his burial society. He always made sure that his subscriptions were up to date at the burial society. The old man joked that it was money well invested in return for a guaranteed decent funeral. Indeed the burial societies played a major role in the lives and deaths of many migrant families, most of whom had only a few relatives.

"Bheriya izanipitisa kudziko lakumwamba[105]*,"* Grandfather used to say each time he set out to attend the quarterly burial society meetings. It was this society that

105 The burial society will give me a send off to heaven

took care of the costs of a member's funeral. The Mine Management provided a plain box which the Mine carpenter hastily put together using planks of wood. The body was placed in the coffin and a tractor ferried it to the graveyard. That was how most members of the community made their finally journey out of Patchway Valley Mine.

The role of the church, according to Grandfather, was to facilitate the passage of one's soul from this world to the next. However, for me the church services were some kind of entertainment that I indulged in once in a while, especially when I had a new item of clothing to show off. Church also offered a diversion from the monotony of compound life. At offertory time the collection plate was passed round for the church members to put their money in. It was not a real plate but a hat that belonged to the man who led the congregation. A sixpence here, a tickey there and one bob there was just about all most people could afford. It was not surprising then that we watched with amazement as the American Pastor gave as much as twenty dollars! Paper money. We could not understand how he could afford to part with that much money. Sixty dollars was more or less a miner's wage for the entire month. Anyway, Pastor Dickson belonged to a race that was privileged but despite that, he and his wife sat side by side on the same bench with black people. The pastor was fondly referred to as a white man with the heart of a black man, and one whose favourite hymn went like this;

The Servant Song

Brother let me be your servant
Let me be like Christ to you;
Pray that I may have the grace
To let you be my servant too.

We are pilgrims on a journey
We are brothers on the road.
We are here to help each other
Walk the mile and bear the load.

I will hold the Christ light for you
In the night time of your fears
I will hold my hand out to you
Speak the peace you long to hear.

I will weep when you are weeping
When you laugh I'll laugh with you.
I will share your joy and sorrow
Till we have seen this journey through.

I used to sing the words with no real understanding at first but over the years I have come to appreciate the meaning, especially in our lives as immigrants. We have had many sorrows as well as joys to share and our lives are like a long journey to some unknown destination beyond the horizon. We are on an everlasting pilgrimage to the land beyond this life.

When Grandfather's health started failing, he went through periods of talking about his father and when he did, he appeared melancholy and thoughtful. The dew had not been long dry on the grass when he asked me one morning to walk with him to the outskirts of the compound. *Ma*Mpofu had protested that the walk would wear him out but Grandfather dismissed her concerns with an irritable wave of his hand.

"The morning fresh air will do us good. Get a hoe, Mavhuto. We could perhaps try and ferret a rabbit or two out of their burrows," he said. I selected a hoe from among the several we had in the disused and derelict chicken coop. Grandfather took it from me and balanced it over his shoulder and we ventured into the woodlands adjoining the compound. We had done this many times in the past.

During previous forays the old man had walked with a spring in his step but lately, his slow feet hesitated between one footstep and the other. The hoe perched over his shoulder appeared to stabilise his gaunt frame and stop it from tipping forwards. Now and again Grandfather stopped to catch his breath but he was careful to make it look like he had stopped to examine the ground for the spoor of rabbits or mice. He bent down, steadied himself on the hoe, poked at roots, straightened himself up and continued ambling down the narrow path in the bush. Out there he spoke to me about the family in the homeland that his father used to reminisce about.

"Somewhere in Malawi, in Nkhotakota district, Nuhono village to be precise, are people in whose veins flow the same blood as yours and mine. My father left his first family there; a son, a daughter and an unborn baby. That was at the beginning of the century. He never went back and he never heard about them again. The children he left behind are obviously grown up now, that is if they are still alive. They are my siblings and I would like you to find them."

I did not respond to what was obviously more of a statement than a request. I had no desire to try and reason with an ailing man about an absurd desire to reconnect with people whose lives he had no idea or knowledge of, so I let him go on talking uninterrupted.

"It is not right that a man of my age should have no claim to family ties. I am an old man now. My bones are weak, my skin is wrinkled and my hair is slowly turning the colour of ash. I would not be surprised that my veins are almost dry of blood, yet there is no one to carry my name after me. My mother disappeared to the farms and we lost contact soon after. A few years later word of her demise filtered back to Patchway Valley. It was reported that my younger brother Wezi, my sister Nchesa, Mother and her new husband were burnt to death when the hut in

which they were sleeping caught fire after it was struck by a bolt of lightning. My only son Chakumanda died in what was reported on the wireless as the worst mining disaster in this country. For a long time after that, I rarely woke up smiling with the rising sun. Most of my days were gloomy from sunrise to sunset… until you came along.

"Mavhuto *muzukuru,* I have a few things that I regret in life, one of which is that I did not insist that Chakumanda remain in the same community where he grew up. I gave my son wings to fly, even though I did it reluctantly, and he flew very far. But what good would keeping him home have been? He would have been miserable, that much I know. All Chakumanda ever wanted was to play football, and Teasdale, one of the big bosses here offered him that opportunity. Maybe I should have made him realise the importance of education. It is not as if he was dull at school. He did not get good grades but that was because he did not care about education. As you know, we are a family blessed with sharp brains, *muzukuru*. Had my mother allowed me to work for my school fees, I would not have ended up a labourer. I always wanted a better life for myself and for my descendants.

One of my biggest regrets is that when your mother was in school, I did not regard education for female children as important. Yet your mother was the most intelligent person there was in the family, until you came along, of course. Your grandmother and I considered that intelligence to be an impediment to the virtues that a girl needed to have if she hoped to get a husband whom she would have to obey and respect. Now I wish I had given my daughter the opportunities the locals give to their female children. Who knows, maybe today she would have been working in a big hospital in town. An ailing old man can afford to admit to having made mistakes. There I was, willing to give everything for the advancement of a

son who was not interested in school, yet neglecting the same needs of his highly intelligent sibling simply because she was born female. I do not sleep well at night, thinking about my daughter's life. She never pleaded with me to send her to boarding school, and that was because she assumed I could never afford the fees. But I know that I would have somehow managed to get the money even if it meant I had to borrow from everybody in the compound. I hope that one day she can forgive me. Now I do everything I can to ensure that you Mavhuto get an education. It is my way of atoning for my sins, if you can call them that. Your birth was the best thing that ever happened since the death of your grandmother. You gave me a reason to carry on, and I became a new person. But since the crippling disease started eating my insides, my life has gone back to the days of gloom that I experienced after the loss of my son and my wife. Your grandmother was a very lovely woman. I could never have wished for a better companion in life." I smiled, because Grandfather did. Then almost as swiftly as it had appeared, the smile vanished.

"Mavhuto *muzukuru*, your *ambuya* was killed by the mines, even though she never went underground," he continued. I was confused, but chose not to ask for elaboration. He gave it anyway.

"You know about Chakumanda, my son who played soccer for the Mine team in the Chamber of Mines League, don't you?"

"Yes *Asekuru*, you mentioned him to me once, but only vaguely.

"I knew the boy was bound to leave this community at some point because of soccer, but I had hoped his feet would take him no further than RISCO in Que Que."

"RISCO? Don't you mean ZISCO, *Asekuru*? Zimbabwe Iron and Steel Company?"

"Eyi, Mavhuto, I do not know what they call it in those books you read these days but it was always called RISCO from as far back as I can remember. It was Rhodesia Iron *chakuti chakuti*[106]. Anyway that is not important," said Grandfather with a flick of his hand. We had by then come to an area with several trees whose leaves provided shade from the scorching heat of the sun slowly creeping over our heads. We stepped off the path and into the shade of a Musasa tree a few steps away and sat down with our backs propped against the tree trunk. Grandfather sat with his knees bent, almost touching his chin. He laid the hoe down between us and continued with his story.

"ZISCO or RISCO, whatever it is called does not matter. What is important is that Chakumanda left to follow Teasdale the Compound Manager to Shabanie Mine. When *bwana* Teasdale left, his departure was mourned by all the workers as if it were the death of a beloved relative. He was well loved as the *bwana* with the heart of a black man in a white man's skin. After only a few months at Shabanie, my son moved yet again, this time even further away to Wankie Colliery Mine when Teasdale moved there. Apart from his kindness, Teasdale was also fond of soccer and always lured his best players whenever he quit one job for another elsewhere.

"You must know by now that passion for football is in our blood. I had played the game as a young man, but I was never good enough for the Mine team. But my son, ah, that one!" From the corner of my eye I observed a wide smile and heard undisguised pride in the old man's voice.

"Chakumanda had the speed of a cheetah, the stamina of a raging buffalo and the agility of a monkey. He could dribble past all the defenders and go on to score brilliant

---

106 Something something

goals. My son dreamed of becoming as popular as George Shaya, Barry Daka, Peter..."

"Peter Nyama, *Asekuru*"'

"*Aha*, Peter Nyama, yes, that was his name. My son wanted his name on the lips of every soccer fan in Rhodesia, but most of all, he wanted to be like Patriki Dzvene, the player whose name was sung about in faraway lands like Zambia."

"I know about him. He was the first black person to play for a team outside Rhodesia."

"How do you know all that? That was before your time."

"Our soccer coach, Mr Mabhachi tells us many football stories from before our time."

"*A*Mabhachi. Yes, *a*Mabhachi is a wonderful man. Did you know that he used to be in the Mine team where he played alongside Seleta Banda, Bhesamu and Teddy? He made us feel proud that a teacher, educated as he was, was mingling with us migrants, playing football with us and speaking the language of mere labourers like us! He was the only teacher to ever play for the Mine, and such humility is not normaly found in the locals. He was a fantastic player. *Ehe*, that he was indeed."

"*ATicha* Mabhachi still runs very fast. He out-dribbles most of us in practice, *Asekuru*. As for *a*Seleta Banda, his fame is legendary as the first and only soccer player at Patchway Valley to play for the national team. What an honour for our community, *Asekuru*! Mr Mabhachi told us about this player you mentioned, Patrick Dzvene. He was bought by Ndola Club in Zambia. Later on, Aston Villa and Arsenal from England wanted him but Ndola Club, through their selfishness, refused to part with him. After all they had bought him too," I explained to the old man.

"We heard about these players over the radio. Our cherished but unreliable wirelesses kept us up to date with who was playing and how. You could say that Charles

Mabika brought the game right into our houses, *muzukuru*. His animated voice helped us conjure up the most vivid images of the dribbles, the brilliant passes and the near-misses that made us gasp with anxiety or punch the air with excitement. Ah, that Charles Mabika, who can claim not to have heard about him? The best thing about all this was that his wife and Seleta's were sisters, so it was claimed." Grandfather puffed with pride.

"Real sisters?"

"Yes, real sisters they said, from the same womb, suckled from the same breast, ha ha. On Sundays, Mabika's voice, as well as the voices of Jonathan Mutsinze and Evans Mambara, intoxicated fans with an infectious euphoria that swept *komboni yonse* on Sundays. Those men did not struggle to remember the names of the players, you know. It was through their lips that people like George Shaya and Barry Daka became more than just shadows. The men whose voices filtered into the otherwise stale spaces in our homes brought us news about what was happening in the football world, like the selling of this Patriki. I do not understand a thing about this buying and selling of people, though Mavhuto, but I doubt that Patriki would have enjoyed living among white people. If they can treat us so badly here in our own homeland, you can imagine how awful their treatment of a black man would be in the land of their ancestors. I shudder to imagine it. The whites would make him a footballer by day and a cook in the evenings. Tell me Mavhuto, do they have *nsima* in England, or Chibuku at least?"

I did not know, so I shrugged.

"Maybe it was a good thing then that Ndola refused to sell Patriki. He surely would have starved to death in the land of the white man, eating nothing but rice and potatoes. Such foods do not have a strong enough grip on the stomach to remain there for several hours I tell you,

Mavhuto. Ah, no wonder *abwana* are so thin. How can one get nourishment, or gain weight when one eats only those foods that pass right through the intestines? Whenever I eat that rice they seem to eat day after day, I am often hungry within a short time. I hear *vazungu* feed on potaoes and meat only. *Eyi,* can you imagine that, eating *ndiwo kupera, eh?* Only relish, eyi. No *nsima* and no rice? *Iyayi,* no!" Grandfather laughed so hard he began to cough. When the coughing subsided he cleared his throat, ready to continue with his story. I was anxious about him, yet I wanted him to tell me the story of his son, the uncle I knew nothing about.

For a man with a body that was wasting away, Grandfather had a surprisingly strong voice. He mopped his brow, rested his hands on his knees and continued.

"*Vazungu* and their rice, *eyi!*" The old man shook his head slowly. "Our womenfolk know how to feed their men properly. They do not serve light food to a man going to work underground, unless they wish him to perish down there for lack of energy. In general, our people are well-fed. One only has to look at how well-built our women are; full bossoms that can feed babies till the age of two, well-rounded behinds upon which a baby can sit in comfort while strapped onto the mother's back, and feet that can eat up the distance from one village to another with little effort and unfaltering rythm. The women of *abwana* are so thin that one would think they are starved all the time. No wonder they do not strap their babies onto their backs, otherwise they would snap into two like brittle twigs. Their feet on bare ground would result in blisters in no time. Ah, those people! The problem lies with their diet which makes them wobbly like porridge. Ya, it was a good thing Patriki did not go to their country. Why take him to England to play with white men when he could not even play for Salisbury Callies here in his own country? Was it not because Salisbury Callies was a team for white players

only? The big teams for black people were Dynamos and Highlanders. Chakumanda hoped to eventually play for either of them, hence his decision to follow Teasdale to whichever mine he moved to. Teasdale was passionate about soccer and my son realised that he had a much better chance of making his dream come true by following wherever Teasdale's itchy feet led him.

"Unbeknown to Chakumanda, he travelled from one mine to another as the spirit of death lured him. The unrelenting dark spirit that had shadowed him since birth intended to trap him out there where no one could hear his pleas for help when it eventually pounced. Your *ambuya* and I last saw our son after he had been at Wankie for barely a year. He came home for Christmas in 1971 and that was the last time we saw him."

I felt Grandfather lower his eyes from where they had previously been scanning the skies as he talked. He looked my way and gasped. I looked at him, wondering if he was about to experience another fit of coughing. His eyes bulged and his mouth hung open, as if struggling to spit out words. I followed his gaze to my left. Slithering into the bushes was the multi-coloured thick tail of what was, without doubt, a huge snake. Its trail was behind us, on the other side of the tree. We got up, me very fast on my feet and Grandfather with great effort. He grabbed the hoe and leaned on it as he steadied himself. He slowly went round the tree twice.

"The python was obviously up that tree. Its trail starts from here," he said, pointing to the base of the tree. "It came down and slithered away quietly while we chatted. Can you imagine what would have happened had it decided to come down on the side we were sitting?"

The possibity of the horror made my knees knock against each other despite my efforts to steady them. Grandfather slung the hoe over his shoulder and balanced it there as before. With the other hand he nudged me and

urged me onto the path. We were going back home, with the old man in front and me following behind.

"Stick to the path, *muzukuru.* Be careful not to step onto the bushes." I did as advised. Where the grass was longer along the sides of the path, the blades curved towards the path from either side and formed an arc that did not quite meet in the middle. Each time a blade of grass touched the back of my leg, I jumped and stifled a scream. I imagined it to be a snake slithering up my leg. Grandfather, however, appeared to have completely forgotten about the python. He continued narrating his tale.

"The following year, on 6 June 1972... That cursed date *muzukuru,* is forever etched on my mind. It was on that day that the mine swallowed my son." The old man went quiet for so long I thought he had probably changed his mind about finally telling me about his son. Knowing him as I did, there was no point in urging him to go on because he would not oblige. In any case he had deferred telling me about his son for a long time, promising to do so at some point in the future. When Grandfather finally resumed his narration, it was not without a slight quaver in his voice.

"Mavhuto *muzukuru,* when news of the disaster was announced over the wireless, I hoped and prayed that my son would not be among those miners feared to be trapped in the tunnels. A few hours later, word came to *kamupaundi* through the telegraph wire, confirming my worst fears. My heart went cold. Anxiety is supposed to make the heart beat faster, but mine went still. It was dead and lay heavy like a stone crushing against my chest. It was a struggle to breathe. I did not need to be told or to see the body to know that part of my own flesh and blood had ceased to exist. I feared for your *ambuya,* poor woman. It was a sad and difficult time for both of us. We got the news in the afternoon and by sunset we were on our way

to Gatooma. From there we boarded the overnight Rhodesia Railways steam engine to Bulawayo where we spent the whole day at the railway station wandering around like lost sheep while we waited for the overnight train to Wankie. I do not know how your *ambuya* and I managed to make that journey, dazed as we were, and with no idea how to get there. None of us had ever ventured further than Gatooma. However, trials and tribulations are slightly easier to bear when you have your life companion by your side, which I did. The poor woman, how she suffered! If I could tell you that I was the rock that supported her, and that during that terrible journey your grandmother drew strength from my bravery, it would make me feel better, but my tongue shies from carrying such an untruth. The mother of my son and I held onto each other for support. We both felt in the other's bones and heart, our own weakness and fears.

At Wankie Colliery Mine, we joined thousands of sympathisers and the families and friends of those trapped underground. We kept vigil day and night some distance from the mine shaft, hoping for a miracle that would bring our loved ones back from the jaws of death. The smell of hundreds of bodies that had not been washed for days mingled with the fumes hanging around us as we waited, anxiously and restlessly, for a miracle. Needless to say, the miracle never happened. In all that time, your *ambuya* and I did not eat anything. The food refused to go down. The faces of the wives and children of the trapped miners, *muzukuru*... those faces still haunt me to this day. Some nights when I lie down to sleep I still see their sorrow, their despair and the desperation of hearts that refused to accept what was gradually becoming obvious with the passing of each hour. The voices of the wailing women pierced the funereal air like a high-pitched whirlwind. Men and women paced up and down helplessly, trying desperately to cling on to hope that was fast diminishing

by day. The longer the miners remained trapped below, the louder the wailing got. The children looked on with frightened eyes at the horror unfolding before them, no doubt seeing their demise well beyond the current tragedy. A catastrophe of that scale had not been seen before. In those few days your *ambuya* aged right before my eyes. She and I stayed as close as we were allowed to get to Kamandama No. 2 mine shaft where the explosion had taken place. I looked at my wife and saw the woman in whose womb Chakumanda had nestled snuggly for nine months, forging a bond that was as close as one human being could get to another. I understood only then why they say the grief of a mother is different from that of the father. None is greater or less than the other in intensity but that of the mother springs from deep within the gut. Clutching her stomach, your *ambuya* lay prostate on the ground moaning, her legs too numb to support her. My grief threatened to suffocate me as it weighed down upon my chest. None of us had the strength to support the other but we drew solace from being in each other's presence.

"After a few days of keeping vigil, the Wankie Colliery Mine Management informed us that there was no hope of anyone making it out of the tunnels, dead or alive. The announcement merely confirmed in words the fears carried in our hearts but which our lips had dared not utter. Unbeknown to us, the rescue efforts had all along been aimed at retrieving whatever was left of the remains of the victims. There was no way anyone could have survived the explosion, we were informed. The Mine Management explained that a highly flammable gas had ignited somewhere underground and set connecting tunnels ablaze. A massive explosion was said to have ripped through the earth, sending tremours that shook the whole of Wankie. The blast triggered off landslides of earth and rocks that either killed the miners or trapped

them underground, my son among them. The fallen rocks would have trapped those who might still have been alive, though they could not have survived for long because the highly poisonous gas, methane, filters very quickly into space. Up to now I still struggle to comprehend the nature of that tragedy. Are you listening to what I am saying, Mavhuto?"

"Yes *Asekuru,* I am."

"Good. It is important that you know this. It is the events of the past that help shape the future." At this point Grandfather cleared his throat, leaned towards the left and shot phlegm into the grass. He did all this without once missing a step.

"*Muzukuru,* the faith of a man does not always come from his belief in the existence of the creator of heaven and earth," he continued, wiping his lips with the back of his hand. "There are times when faith is born of the desperation of one's situation. At Kamandama No.2, after all that had been explained to us, I still held on to the hope that my Chakumanda would somehow emerge from the vast tomb. I imagined him alone and scared, hungry, badly injured and slowly bleeding to death in a dark tunnel, and hoping for rescue that was not coming. I knew the feeling, having survived a collapsed tunnel myself in the early days of my job. I dreaded to imagine my own son in such a desperate situation. Parents strive to protect their children from all sorts of danger, yet I stood there helpless, unable to rescue mine. The untimely death of my son was a huge blow to your *ambuya* and me and it created a wound that no length of time could ever heal. That wound remains painful to this day.

"The whole tragic incident was made worse by the failure to get back the remains of our loved ones. Only a few bodies were retrieved, and those belonged to the few miners who were working close to the opening of the shaft or just outside of it at the time the blast occurred. When

they were brought up, the bodies looked so black it was not possible to say whether they were of black men or white men. They were buried with no names. The manner of the tragedy robbed the rest of the victims of a proper resting place. Normally, the shafts that suck our blood slowly, year after year, eventually spit us out when our weary bodies have nothing more to offer. Accidents and deaths happen too here and there, but Kamandama No.2 had chewed, swallowed and refused to regurgitate. Chakumanda_ sorry, I mean Mavhuto. No pain, *muzukuru,* surpasses nor even compares to that of losing one's child. The pain is made worse by the absence of a proper resting place to which a grieving parent can go and shed a few tears in remembrance of the departed soul. Only God knows how terrible my son's last moments were. The boy must have suffered. The last thing he deserved was a possibly cramped grave for his remains where we could never say prayers over them. No survivors, no bodies. It was as if the miners had never existed.

"Couldn't they have tried harder to save them, *Asekuru*?"

"O-o they did. They tried, Mavhuto. I know they tried the best they could but they were dealing with one of those monstrous forces of nature that are beyond human understanding. From what we were told, expert mining rescue teams flew in from South Africa to try and figure out if there was any way they could help.

After assessing the extent of the calamity, these experts advised sealing off the shaft. They said a rescue operation was too dangerous to undertake because contact with the noxious gas would have resulted in instant death for the would-be rescuers. In any case, the tunnels were assumed to be impenetrable due to collapsed roofs and rocks that were thought to be as hot as blasting furnaces. This would have made the retrieval of the bodies totally

impossible. I doubt there were any to retrieve though. Ashes. The remains of the miners were probably reduced to ashes. But who is to know for sure? The Mine Management took the experts' advice and sealed off the shaft, forever entombing the miners underground. With this decision, all hope died and a large dark cloud descended over the whole of Wankie and the rest of the country. Even the most hopeful of us were convinced there were no survivors. There had never been a mining disaster in the whole of Southern Africa of the magnitude as that at Wankie Colliery Mine, so it was announced over the wireless. Kamandama No.2 shaft remains sealed to this day.

"A plaque bearing the names of all those who perished in the disaster marks the sealed entrance to the ill-fated shaft that leads to the tunnels where the remains of the victims are entombed. Those of us who lost relatives in that disaster mourned our dead and the whole world mourned with us. One can only imagine how the next group of miners must have felt upon being lowered down the remaining shafts to continue working in the tunnels after that. It must have been like dying a thousand times, but what choice did they have? When a man knows the livelihood of his children depends on that job, not to mention the house the family calls home, he casts his fears aside and gets on with the job.

The months that followed were a difficult period as we struggled to come to terms with the tragedy that had left the whole country numb with shock. For my wife and me personally, the disaster had cruelly robbed us of a son we loved dearly. His death created a deep void in our lives that could never be filled. The greatest tragedy of our lives as migrant labourers is that the hazards of our job are many, and disasters occur everyday of our lives, though on a smaller, individual scale. No one notices or cares. Why should they? When one labourer dies, another one

takes his place. It is a case of picking up the pick-axe and shovel and carrying on. We breed in large numbers too so there is never a shortage of labour.

"Only when a disaster happens on a large scale does the world notice. *Abwana* for once is bewildered by the loss of such a big number of labourers because it affects production and the smooth running of the mine. Our lives are an enduring disaster that no one writes about in the papers because the mines kill us off one at a time in one way or the other.

"From the day Chakumanda was born, his mother and I knew we would lose him one day. What we did not know was that his death would be so horrendous. Although death had failed to snatch him at birth, it had stalked him all his life, ready to pounce at the earliest opportunity. It finally succeeded in luring him away from our watchful eyes and dragged him out there where it shoved him into a grave from which his cries for help could not be heard. Sometimes I wonder if it might have been better had we never had Chakumanda. His mother and I would not have known the pleasure of bringing him up nor would we have experienced the joy he brought into our lives. Had we lost him at birth like we did those unfortunate siblings of his before him, I would never have known the pride of holding my own son in my arms but I would not have had to endure the agony of his death either. Each time the pregnancies of your grandmother resulted in stillborn babies, it was as if a sharp thorn had been plunged into the centre of my heart. The pain worsened as we buried more of our babies. However, the pain of spending the rest of my life wondering how terrified Chakumanda must have been in that dark tunnel as death stared him mercilessly in the face is far worse than the sense of hopelessness that engulfed me at the end of each pregnancy. Yet in spite of that pain, I do not wish he had died at birth. I only wish he had not suffered such a

fate. I was fortunate to have been the father of such a wonderful son and I hope I was a good father to him. "My soul would be less troubled today if we had been able to lay his body to rest in a place where we could occasionally go to commend his soul to the gods of his fathers. To help ease our pain and sorrow, the elders at our church held a service to remember Chakumanda. To this day I still recall, word for word, the song that finally helped me accept that he was no more. It goes like this;

There lies beneath the shadow,
But on the farther side,
The darkness of an awful grave
That gapes both deep and wide;
And there between us stands the cross,
Two arms outstretched to save;
Like a watchman set to guard the way
From the eternal grave.

Upon that cross of Jesus
Mine eye at times can see
The very dying form of One
Who suffered there for me;
And from my smitten heart with tears,
Two wonders I confess___
The wonders of His glorious love,
And my own worthlessness.

I take oh Cross, thy shadow,
For my abiding place;
I ask for no other sunshine than
The sunshine of his face
Content to let the world go by,
To know no gain or loss.

"There is an emptiness that can never be filled and a feeling of disbelief in the hearts of those who never get to

see the resting place of the remains of their loved ones. When Chakumanda became an adult, he changed his name and called himself Petros. It was a decision his mother and I supported. After all, his had been a name given petulantly. When he was born, in my heart I had said, 'Here he is, take him! He is yours and always was before he was mine, just like his siblings before him.' I committed his body and his soul to death because I had expected to lay him in his grave not long afterwards. As the years went by and he survived, his mother and I rejoiced at what we saw as the defeat of the spirit of death. Yet death still had a grip on him. It pulled him back into its dark shadows and snuffed out his life because I gave him the name Chakumanda, which means he-who-belongs-to-the-grave. In a cruel twist of fate, he-who-belonged-to-the-grave would never have a grave to lie in.

His death was much harder for your *ambuya* to accept. By the time she did, the sorrowful woman had already started dying slowly from within. I never heard her laugh ever again right up to the day she took her last breath. My wife did not die suddenly in just one day, or in a week. Hers was a slow death that lasted from the time our son was entombed underground until the day her eyes finally closed and her heart went still, about two years later. They say a real man does not cry. I do wonder about that. God knows I am very brave, otherwise I would not be doing the job I do, but I shed tears when my wife died. I have long since come to realise that the bravery of a man does not lie in the tears he suppresses but rather in those he sheds before coming out to face the world, braving the curious stares and the furtive glances of sympathisers and remaining composed through it all. It is a brave man who says to his nearest and dearest, 'This is hurting badly. Please hold my hand and see me through it.'

"Mavhuto, I shed endless tears when my son died and I shed many more when I lost my wife a couple of years later. For a while I considered ditching my belief in God, but when you lose faith and hope what else is left but despair? It is those who lose everything that need God the most. With the passing away of those two, my family disintegrated. That is what drives this strong desire in me to reconnect with my father's family back in Malawi. The closer I get to the end of my life, the more I feel it my duty to urge you *muzukuru* to find our relatives back there. To the locals, we will always be *vabvakure.* It is a term I have grown weary of. Do not misunderstand me here. I am very proud to be of Malawian origin but I think those of my people who have been here for close to four generations should no longer be regarded as foreigners as if they are expected to one day pack their belongings and go back to their countries of origin. Our people have been here for almost one hundred years, living in this wilderness, going round and round in circles. Eighty years and more! That is twice as long as the period of time spent by Moses and the Israelites in the wilderness. We seem to belong neither here nor there. We are like a people who have no hope of ever reaching the Promised Land. We do not seem to be going forwards, nor do we appear to be going backwards, yet we cannot remain stagnant forever. We are slowly losing the idea of who we are. Look at you and the people of your generation. You do not speak our languages anymore."

"But we do, *Asekuru,*" I protested.

"No, you do not. The sounds I hear coming from your lips are certainly not Chichewa. You speak some curious mixture of Chishona, Chisena, ChiEnglish, Chibemba and a few words of our language that you try to pass off as pure Chichewa. It is as if you cannot decide what language you want to speak or who you wish to be. We

have to move decisively, either backwards or forwards. Only we can carve a niche for ourselves.

"The locals smile at us then go and make jokes at our expense. Their songs mock us and our way of life. That song *'Ndapita kumadzi, ndaona Chechure anavhara bhotomu,'* was played frequently and with great amusement in many homes in the mining communities. Following in its wake was *'APhiri Anabwera'* which became a big hit in the beer halls and even amongst our own people. While I am glad that my people can look at their plight with humour, I am exasperated and saddened at the same time by their willingness to passively accept mockery."

I felt ashamed of myself then, for I too was one of those that loved the songs. These were old songs from the mother-woman's generation but that made no difference. We played them over and over again at my friend's house and we happily sang along. I had previously not thought of the music as anything other than some form of amusing banter. With Grandfather's speech I was forced to consider the insinuations of the lyrics. As I played the words over and over in my head, I had to admit that while 'Chechure' was just harmless humour, 'APhiri Anabwera' was a sad mockery of the plight of most of our people.

APhiri anabwera kuchoka kuHarare
Anabwera ndisutukesi inalibe kantu shuwa
APhiri anaganiza, koma ine nizaenda kuti,
Makolo anga onse anamwalila kudala.

This translated to:

Mr Phiri came back from Harare
And brought with him an empty suitcase.
Mr. Phiri started wondering, so where shall I go?
All my relatives died a long time ago.

"Difficult to accept though the fact may be, the song '*A*Phiri Anabwera' captures the predicament of most returning migrant workers who stay away too long and have no contact at all with those back home," continued Grandfather. "It is a sad but true reflection of the situation most migrant workers find themselves in; nothing to show for all the hard labour of the years past, despair in the present and hopelessness in the future. The relatives left behind those many years ago all died at various stages until there was no one among the living who knew the returning descendants of migrants labourers. It is like settling among strangers once again, this time with nothing to do and with no purpose. We are like dead wood adrift in a flooded river; it has no direction, no purpose and is probably utterly pointless as well. What kind of people can we be, with no link to the past and unable to look back and say, 'this is the village from where my ancestors came, and in those caves lie buried the remains of their chiefs?' If we insist on cutting ourselves loose from our roots, we should then seek to enjoy the same privileges as the locals. We can only acquire these if we unshackle ourselves from the chains which fetter us to the cages that take us down the mine shafts, generation after generation. I have this great longing to visit the land of my ancestors in order to retrace the footprints of my father so that the souls of his parents may finally rest in peace. The more depressing I find my life here, the more I feel the spirit of my forefathers pulling me towards home.

"The urge to go to Malawi is much stronger now than it was when I was younger. When I lost my mother to the farms I felt lonely, but I soon filled the emptiness with my marriage to your Grandmother, *ali kumanda,*[107]" continued Grandfather. "Father, poor soul, lost his wits to alcohol and loneliness. In the job that had kept him sane and

107 Who lies in her grave

going, he was eventually replaced by the siren. Woo-oo-oo! the extraordinary crying machine would wail at certain hours to rouse the miners who were due on the following shift. Father was replaced by a contraption whose voice was stronger and loud enough to be heard far and wide. It was a voice that would never go hoarse nor quiver from the cold or from the weakness of the body. The tinned voice did not oversleep, nor did it need a house or a wage at the end of each month. It overshadowed the good service of the workers who had previously done the job in all kinds of weather; hot nights, windy nights, rainy nights and bone-numbing cold nights. But then *abwana* had made their choice. No one in their right mind could dispute the advantages of the tinned voice over the voice of *a*Bhaureni Nyirenda. The tinned voice never took a day off, it was never ill and it needed no pension at a certain age. We were aware that times were changing but we never dreamed the day would dawn when *abwana* would prefer a machine to shout in man's place. With the installation of the siren, Father's usefulness came to an abrupt end after more than twenty years of loyal service to John Mack and Co.

"What was a man of his age supposed to do? At over fifty years or so_ no one ever really knew their ages then_ Father had no home, no job, hardly any family and definitely no future. He only had a past that he had long since lost touch with. From his plight I had a terrible dread of *chigumura* for a long time afterwards. I preferred to die and be buried than be made redundant and homeless. Father was moved to a single room while the Management decided whether to pension him off or to find him something else to do. He was infirm in both mind and body and there were not many jobs a man like him could do. I had no room for him at my place, living in single quarters with a wife and a son as I did then. If he had been pensioned off, Father would have either been put on a

steam engine back to Malawi, that was if he could still find his way back to his village, or he would have moved to the farms. It was probably a blessing in a way that he died before a decision could be made. His death was caused by loneliness, despair and hopelessness, with a lot of help from alcohol. I have never admitted this to anyone before but I feel guilty at the sad end he came to. My guilt does not stem from the fact that he died, but from my neglect of him." At this juncture, Grandfather shook his head and adopted that faraway look I knew well enough not to interrupt with questions or comments.

"Look, who am I trying to deceive here?" The old man shook his head again before continuing. "I did worse than that. I did not only neglect my father, Mavhuto. I rejected him. I turned my back on him at a time when I should have embraced the poor man with warmth. It would not have cost me anything to show some kindness and concern for the man who had sired me. God knows he had become difficult on his return from the war but life could not have been easy for him. The demons that wrestled with his mind must have made his life an everlasting nightmare. Father died alone in his miserable single dwelling, with no one to care whether he lived or not. He had no one to answer his feeble cries for help, or to give him water for his parched throat.

"It was a miserable and lonely end for a man who had once fought bravely in the big war against Hitler's forces. Towards the end of his life, his brain had become so muddled up he could no longer tell whether he was back in his homeland or out here in this country. It was not known for certain how long Father had lain dead before his decomposing body was discovered, but the stench was overpowering and we were advised not to view his body. For a man who had braved the long journey through the wilderness in search of a fortune that had remained forever elusive, it was a sad way to go. Father did not have

much to leave behind. His old army trench coat and the medal were all that he had. We placed these items in his coffin and he took them to his grave. That was all he ever called his own, that and the small piece of ground his remains were laid on to rest. I hope he found in death the peace that had eluded him in the later years of his life.

"His demise made me realise just how terrible our situation is. The neighbouring farms have become a place of refuge for many of our people. In times of trouble and strife, the migrants take themselves and their families off to the ever welcoming and all embracing farms to live out the rest of their days. It is ironic that our fathers left their homelands to come all the way to Southern Rhodesia to escape the restrictions and impositions of taxes by the white man, yet it is at his feet that we finally seek to live out the rest of our days. We have to find the Nyirenda people of Nuhono village in Nkhotakota and try to regain what we lost in the quest for shadows and a dream that evaporated long ago into the mists of time. It is time we stopped sending our children down the mine shafts, generation after generation, forever and ever. I was born a child of the mines, as was your uncle Chakumanda and so were you but that should be as far as it goes. Surely there must be more to life for our people too other than just mine shafts, alluvial deposits and ore wagons! It is for this reason, to prove that we too can follow our rainbows and catch them that I struggle to buy you the school books, pens and everything else you need. If you should eventually end up stepping into the cage to go and work underground, it should be because you are doing the jobs previously done by *abwana* or because you choose to be a labourer, not because you have no other option. By the same token, the decision to remain here or to go to Malawi should be one that you make yourself, but whether or not, there is need for us to make contact with those of our relatives that we can still trace.

"This is something I should have done a long time ago but I never got round to it. I leave it to you now to do it. I do not pass on to you the pick-axe and the shovel in this relay, but the quest for reconnection with our kinsmen and for a place to claim as rightfully yours in this land where the winds blew us to. The sooner you do it the better. Leave it for another generation and it shall certainly never be done. Mavhuto, *muzukuru,* you are of a new and enlightened generation. You go to school and you speak proper English with the white man, therefore you are in a better position to think carefully about your dreams than I ever was. Let no man dictate to you the direction towards which your feet should take you. Do not be like my father who went off to fight for the white man in Burma without a clue as to why."

"He was fighting with the African Regiment to defeat Hitler," I finally interrupted the long narration in my eagerness to show Grandfather that my time in school was not wasted. After all I am considered to be an extremely intelligent student, the best in the eight year history of the 'upper top' secondary school at Patchway Valley. The teachers tell me that I possess knowledge and intelligence that is way above my age and class.

"You are right, *muzukuru,* very right. But enlighten me here. Who was this man Hitler whom the other great nations of Europe had to band together to fight against? And why?"

"*Asekuru,* that man was one of the most evil leaders that ever lived," I said, proud to show the extent of my intelligence. "Adolf Hitler was a tyrant who hungered to rule all of Europe. He occupied other countries after defeating the natives there and deposing their leaders."

"All right, Mavhuto. I understand that very well, so far. So Britain didn't like the rise of Hitler, Belgium did not either, nor did Russia. Is that what you are saying?"

"True, *Asekuru*. So they got together, formed the Allied Forces and set out to defeat this evil man and restore sovereignty to the occupied countries."

"Yes, yes Mavhuto *muzukuru*. I think I understand it now. So in order to win the war against this risen monster, the great nations had to enlist the help of the nations they themselves had conquered, the natives of the lands they still forcibly occupied and ruled in Africa. Hitler was a monster who wanted to occupy the whole of Europe, right?"

"Yes *Asekuru*, that is correct."

"Could this Hitler have been a kinsman of those leaders of the European governments that set up colonial regimes that displaced natives from fertile lands in Africa before they went on to greedily scramble for the most productive parts of the continent? My guess is that the blood that flowed in the veins of the European leaders was the same as that which flowed in the tyrant's. I suppose the rulers in the countries occupied by the evil Hitler in Europe retreated in the same way that the chiefs and the kings of the displaced African tribes did. From the little I still remember of our History lessons, in Germany, Hitler threw the evidence of his cruelty into concentration camps. Here in Africa those kinsmen of his who opposed his cruelty massacred the natives or drove them onto the barren soils of the Tribal Trust Lands. Many Bantu people were killed in large numbers as they sought to defend their homelands, a futile exercise when you consider what they were up against. Try pitting soldiers on horseback armed with rifles against bare-footed tribesmen waving assegais. There was no fair contest. Had Hitler sought to enlarge his empire by occupying large areas of Africa and displacing the natives as the other European nations were doing, I am certain that not one of those nations that fought him in Europe would have bothered to challenge him. Hitler was a stupid man who looked in the wrong

direction. The way I see it, his crime was not the deed but the target. Anyway, Hitler went much further by not only displacing and dispossessing the Jews. He sought to wipe out the entire race, admittedly, but his fellow rulers wiped out entire villages too. Is it not strange Mavhuto, how one notices the splinter in another's eye while completely ignoring the log in one's own?" Grandfather asked through clenched teeth.

"*Asekuru*, you mumbled the last bit and I did not quite catch what you said about logs," I said.

"Never mind, *muzukuru*. My mind tends to wander at times. It is the age factor, I suppose. Talking of which, let me take your mind back to what I was trying to say to you earlier on. I implore you not to be like my father whose destiny was decided all his life by others. Back in Nyasaland, he married a woman given to him, and he was compelled to leave his home and family in order to go and earn money for the white man's taxes. Years later, he was told that he had to fight in the white man's war in faraway lands that his forefathers had never heard of. He risked shedding his blood so that his colonial masters could keep their feet planted firmly in two continents; theirs and ours. That way, they could continue to enjoy the best of both worlds. Even after Father had survived the war and was sent home, he had a job he despised forced upon him. It was made clear that he had to either accept it or leave the mine house as the Management could not keep him if he was no longer their employee.

"You could say that my father's life was like the supple branch of a tree; billowing helplessly in the wind, swaying in no particular direction and bent as if bowing under pressure from forces greater than itself. But you Mavhuto do not have to endure the same kind of impositions. Education gives you the means to free yourself from shackles that have bound our people to their miserable existence for generation after generation. There

is no fortune to be found in the mines. The labourers get the minerals out all right but they hand them straight to those who own them. I urge you to walk away from the pits and not to look back. Lay the ghosts of our people to rest, make their sacrifices worth the trouble they took to get here, and the insults they endured with heads bowed like slaves. If you fail to free yourself now *muzukuru,* you shall live forever in bondage. It is the worst kind of bondage as it is wholly self-imposed. The greatest freedom comes from knowing who you are and where you come from, and deciding who you wish to be. There is no point in complaining that the locals shun you and call you *Mabhurandaya* or *Manyasarande.* How can you not be referred to as *Mabhurandaya* when you speak only *Chibhurandaya,* eat only the staple foods of *Mabhurandaya* and associate with *Mabhurandaya basi,* developing a cocoon around yourselves and creating communities that are impenetrable? Either you retrace the journey of our people and settle down among them, or you blend in and make a home among your hosts, mark your place and settle down. You cannot continue to exist as belonging neither here nor ther, as if you are waiting to go back one day. Should you decide to go home, Mavhuto *muzukuru,* do not wait until you become too comfortable. It can be a satisfying feeling at first but it can easily lull you into a false sense of contentment. The homesickness gets worse the older you get. The loneliness bites like a cold winter morning, numbing all feeling and leaving you stuck and isolated in your own misery." Were my ears hearing right, I wondered. Surely this could not be my own Grandfather urging me to discard the ways of my people!

"You surprise me, *Asekuru.* All my life you have done nothing but warn me about allowing new ways to rob me of my identity, now you say_"

"Nothing Mavhuto, I say nothing of the sort. I am in no way insinuating that our ways are inferior and should

be shunned. It is not adopting the ways of your new community while shunning yours that helps you fit in."

"I do not quite understand..."

"Be proud of who you are. Walk as a proud *Mubhurandaya* among the locals but whatever you do, do not shut yourselves away from the people in whose country you came to squat. Desist from creating a mini-Blanytre out here. Mix freely, learn their language, mingle with them and open yourselves to the opportunities available to them. And taking your place among them does not mean erasing your history from your lives. Now is the time to look for that which our people lost a long time ago as they trekked all the way here to follow their dreams. You Mavhuto can retrace the footprints of your great-grandfather back to the warm heart of Africa. The lost time between then and now is not important. Once a tree is planted, it spreads its roots underground and it thrives forever in the soil regardless of how often its branches are pruned. It will sprout over and over again. Only animals fail to trace the trail of their births through the ages, human beings do not. It may be that back in Malawi there may no longer be any living relatives who remember the departure of my father, but the spirits of those left behind will be appeased if you go and pay homage to their descendants who ought anyway to be aware of the story of their forefather who went to seek his fortunes over the horizon and never returned. The tears of the dead and of the gods would not have fallen in vain should you finally walk down the paths your great-grandfather *a*Bhaureni Nyirenda walked those many years ago in Nuhono village, gazing at this river, at that valley, at the moon on a cloudless African night, at the sun casting its shadow against the horizon, at the hills shimmering in the distance and at the shadow of Mount Mulanje.

"Do not misunderstand me and imagine that I wish you to go and bury yourself in some remote rural village in Nkhotakota. Far from it. I just wish you to go and reconnect with the land of your fathers and lay to rest the souls of the dear departed who mourned everyday for their loved one until they too died in despair. After that, you may go and settle anywhere you wish should you decide never set foot there again, it won't matter because you would have put a lid firmly on the past before you move on with your life. You probably wonder why I never did it myself, don't you?" asked Grandfather. Of course I did wonder but I chose not to say so.

"Like many people in my situation, I had a brother, a sister and parents here who were my whole world. Then I got married and started a family of my own, further entrenching my feet in foreign soil. Thereafter, it became impossible to do what I am urging you to do now. It is not an easy decision to make when you have loved ones you would have to leave behind. I had a family I wished to find back in Malawi but I also had a family I did not wish to leave behind while I followed an urge that burned holes on the restless soles of my feet. I was torn apart. I realised that I could not fulfil one dream without sacrificing the other. It is hard being a child of two worlds, which is what I was, with families on both sides of the Zambezi River.

"The best time to make the journey is before you have a family of your own, Mavhuto. Leave it later than that and you may never do it, and failure to do so will eventually start eating away at your heart like a maggot until it festers and threatens to drive you mad. Unlike me, you have nothing to tie you down to this place. Once I am gone you will be on your own. Dhairesi cannot start being your family now if she was never your mother all your life. There is nobody for you to regret leaving behind except friends and neighbours who will laugh with you by day then leave you alone at night to bury your tear-stained

face in your pillow as you find loneliness a constant pain. When you finally close the chapter on the past, you can begin a new phase, a new era. For four generations we have tried to integrate here, with great difficulty. The more I think about it, the more I feel that we could easily end up like the children of Israel who, after wondering for forty years in the wilderness, could no longer lay claim to any place. They were in no man's land for so long their existence was erased from the memories of the people in the land where they had come from and where they hoped to go and settle. If we do not seek to improve our own lives now we could end up being nobody, and belonging nowhere. Back in Malawi, those who stayed behind got on with their lives and can only treat us as despised returnees, more so if we go back only as burdens, empty handed and infirm. That is why I find that *APhiri Anabwera* song so insulting! What kind of people are we that grin like idiots in the face of such derision? Where is our pride? Our coming here to do the jobs shunned by the locals does not mean we lack self-respect. We should therefore not be regarded as inferior.

"Offensive though I may find this song, maybe it does not state anything less than the truth. The few labourers who managed to go back took with them almost nothing, and they returned to villages where they knew nobody. Most of the relatives they knew were long dead. I doubt there is a place set aside for returnees for that day in the future when they might wish to return and settle in the villages of their forefathers. We hear rumours about how those who go back are resented because their relatives are then forced to share whatever little or exhausted land is allocated to clans and families. That on its own is not really a problem. The problem lies in going back with nothing to show for all the years of toiling in the wilderness. Even though that may be the case, you do not relish the idea of anyone poking fun at your plight. It is

about time we changed the course of our lives. We owe it to ourselves to improve our way of life and it is up to you our children to do so because you are an enlightened generation. You have the opportunity to aspire to greater things. Independence is the dawn of a new era which makes that dream possible.

"Contrary to what most people believed in the euphoria leading to self-rule, independence is not about walking straight into ownership of factories or businesses forcibly grabbed from their proprietors. I was quite amused when I heard some of my fellow workers describe how, upon attaining independence, they would march up to Chimuromo, slap him in the face and demand the keys to his shop, his house and his car before sending him back to Europe empty handed. Some of my kinsmen must have definitely missed the message somewhere along the campaign trail." Grandfather chuckled before continuing. "Needless to say, those workmates of mine still troop into the cage daily with me while Chimuromo continues to run his shop supplying foodstuffs to the community. What independence gives to the majority of people, *muzukuru,* migrant workers like us included, is not the key to the former oppressor's shop but the master key to the doors leading to great and equal opportunities. Even with these equal opportunities, a great fortune does not land in your lap just like that, Mavhuto. You need to study hard and work very hard. There is no gain with no pain. For almost a century *abwana* had a head start over us.

"Independence gives all of us the freedom to choose what we want out of life. So if we are now free to change our destinies, why should we not grab the opportunity to lead better lives? Quite a number of our people are now daring to dream beyond the horizon, and that makes me very happy. Whenever I see *a*Kaunda's son returning from the college where he is training to be a teacher, my heart swells with pride. That young man's achievement brings

pride not only to his father, but to the whole community. His success is the success of all migrants. At last we can now stand shoulder to shoulder with our former masters and with the locals. In the past we did not dream of treading in other footprints except those of our forefathers. More of our people need to realise the importance of sending their children to school if we are to stand tall among giants. It is for this reason that I continue to work hard so that I can pay your school fees and provide you with all that the teachers ask for. I do not want you to end up like me. My teachers said I was bright enough to get the grades that were required for teacher training after Standard Six. I had wanted a different life for myself but my mother had no understanding of the value of education so she could not appreciate why I needed to spend money on books when she could use it to feed the family. Besides, with Father away at war, we did not have much money for food. I had to leave school early and work in the mine. Boarding school back then was for the rich because one had to go to a Mission school and pay not only the school fees but the boarding fees as well. Then there was the cost of the school uniforms, the bedding, the books, the pens and the bus fares to and from the boarding school. Hey, it was definitely beyond the means of us migrants. Independence finally brought this education much closer. There is nothing to stop you getting it too. Just work hard, *muzukuru.* Work very hard. You are no longer tied to the mines. You owe them nothing; not your existence, not your precious blood and not your sweat. The mines and the farms robbed us enough for almost a whole century. I sincerely hope that in the pursuit of a better life my people do not seek to detach themselves from their shadows. We should continue to be proud of our culture and of everything that defines us and which we identify with.

"Unfortunately, those of your generation do not seem to regard that as important. It would come as a pleasant surprise if you can still remember our songs and our dances. I do not believe that our traditions and our way of life are inferior to anyone's, nor is anybody superior because of the colour of their skin or because of the language they speak, or the country they come from. We are merely different... different but equal!"

We were crossing the road that led to Chakari Mine when I saw something huge crawl across the tarred road a bit further up. I screamed and Grandfather put his hand to my mouth.

"Shush, don't you know *a*Nkhata? Stop screaming," whispered Grandfather, removing his hand from my mouth.

"Who is he? I have never seen him before!"

"*A*Nkhata is crippled. He has no limbs below his knees. He shuffles his body on the ground to get from one place to the next."

"What, like a reptile?" I asked, puzzled.

"He had his legs chopped off at the knees so he cannot walk."

"Who removed them, *Asekuru,* and why?"

"It is a long, long story, Mavhuto. It goes back a long way." Grandfather became a bit pensive as he decided whether or not to tell me about it, and where to start from. He finally sighed, stepped off the road and beckoned me to sit on a boulder next to him. I did so but only after circling the stone and making sure there was no nasty surprise anywhere near it.

"Mavhuto, the story of *a*Nkhata is one that goes back many years. It is never discussed, except in hushed whispers and even so, only rarely. It began with the arrival of Chikanga who was said to be a witchdoctor who sniffed out witches. I remember the day *a*Nkhata and his wife were accused of practising witchcraft. They were booed by

children all the way from the clinic. I was one of the few adults who followed them to their house out of curiosity."

"Were they witches for certain?" I wondered aloud. My own belief in supernatural things was somewhat fickle. I was sceptical about the credibility of Grandfather's tale.

"Who knows whether or not someone is really a witch? There was Chikanga amongst us who was said to possess supernatural powers that enabled him to see what the rest of us could not. We followed *a*Nkhata and his wife to see if they would indeed bring back with them the charms they were alleged to use. It was one of the things Chikanga required of those he condemned as witches. The stuff was to be burned, the people concerned cleansed and warned never to take up witchcraft again for the rest of their lives, or else be prepared to watch their flesh rot, little by little, while they walked. I watched with my own eyes outside *a*Nkhata's house as he and his wife emerged some time later, their arms full of bundles of cloths. The children booed louder and the adults gasped in amazement. We do not know what happened inside the building where Chikanga was, but with the witchdoctor's departure from the mine, life went back to normal.

"For some months after Chikanga had left Patchway Valley, life was quiet, to the point of being dull after all the excitement of much activity. Then *a*Nkhata and his wife fell ill at the same time. They both suffered from the same flesh-eating disease which attacked only their lower limbs. No one could understand it at first, until *a*Mfitizarimba remembered Chikanga's warning. *A*Nkhata and his wife were first treated at the Mine clinic, and then later transferred to Gatooma African General Hospital when their legs got worse. They were a sorry sight, I can tell you. You know the green hue that some miners' heels turn from long periods of being encased in the hot, sweaty gumboots?"

I nodded impatiently. Even though I did not work in the mines, did not wear the gumboots and did not know about the hue he was talking about, I knew what he meant… gangrene. By then the shuffling figure of *a*Nkhata had disappeared from sight.

"Their limbs turned to a deeper shade of that colour. In the beginning some mine labourers feared they too would get the disease if it turned out to be an outbreak of one of the contagious diseases of the mines. At Gatooma General Hospital, the doctors told the husband and wife that their legs would have to be cut off at the knees. *A*Nkhata agreed but his wife refused, declaring that she would rather die with her whole body intact than go to her grave in bits and pieces at various stages of her life."

"Was she left to die then?"

"Yes she was. It was her decision. The woman was discharged from hospital and a few weeks later she was dead. She died with her body intact as she wanted but it was a body that had begun to decay. It let off a smell that assaulted the nose and threatened to bring up the contents of one's stomach. No one in the whole of Patchway Valley had ever heard of or seen a disease of that nature. We did not wonder anymore what happens to a corpse in the ground. We had seen it happen on the body of *a*Nkhata's wife long before her heart had stopped beating. *A*Nkhata had his legs chopped off. What remained of him is what you just saw crawling on hands, stomach and thighs on the ground."

"It must be hard shuffling on one's torso on the hard, gritty ground," I mused.

"It is just as hard on muddy ground, but such is life. Some penalties are harsher than others. *A*Nkhata wears mine gloves on his hands to make the crawling easier but he suffers from prolonged bouts of coughing from the dust he inhales. I would not be surprised if he contracts T.B sooner or later. It is one of the most fatal diseases of the

mines. Tuberculosis is very painful; there is the incessant coughing up of phlegm, the gradually wasting away of the body and the pain in the chest and ribs. I have seen many miners succumb to T.B. and finally die. The end is miserable, painful and prolonged, as you can see from my state."

Grandfather talked on about the diseases of the mines but I was not interested. I was not going to work in the mines anyway. I was still a long way from thinking about my future. It was the past and the present I found intriguing.

"Tell me, *Asekuru*," I interrupted him, "what Patchway Valley was like when you were my age."

"Um, it was an ordinary enough place during the day but it was a different place altogether at night. During the night, when I was much younger than you are, I often lay on my canvas tent shivering from fear of witches who were said to cast their spells on their enemies as they slept. There were many stories told of witches and witchcraft then. Our fathers, who went out on the early morning shift, used to talk of shadows that moved and made their hair stand on end as they passed certain places. Those were the days before electricity was installed. The Patchway Valley Mine compound was completely dark on moonless nights and shadowy trees breathed and sighed eerily in the night. The milk-producing hedges we grew to mark the boundaries of our yards became little toilets at night for children and adults alike.

"It was not uncommon to go out in the middle of the night and see the neighbour's wife, usually decently covered and commanding respect during the day, hitch up her dress and bare her bottom as she squatted in the hedge. These evergreen hedges harboured all kinds of evil deeds, human and supernatural alike. In the halo of a full moon the situation was not so bad. On the nights that I was too scared to go out, I used to wet my blankets. When

my mother realised that I was doing so while fully awake, she got me an old bucket into which I relieved myself. She herself had a chamber pot that she emptied into the hedge before sunrise. You are lucky *muzukuru* in that that you were born in a different age altogether, when tower lights brighten every corner of the compound. The fears I grew up with are obviously absent from your life."

* * *

My thoughts are jolted to the present by the sound of shovels scooping soil. Sombre eyes glance at the coffin with uneasiness. A myriad of colours is sprinkled on the ground a distance away from the yawning grave. The blues, greens, whites and blacks shift slightly as heads turn and bottoms shift to create space for one other mourner. The women let out a wail here and there in-between the reading of the final verse and the last song, and at any other time when silence threatens to trivialise the solemnity of the occasion. Some of the mourners squeeze their eyes hard, desperate to get a few final tears to fill the eyes before they roll down weathered cheeks. On the opposite sides of the grave are a mound of earth and the coffin. Two strong men lower themselves into the grave and two others above lift the coffin off the ground with their hands and pass it to those below. Wood creaks. Nails protrude. It is a poor man's coffin that contains the body of a poor man who once had big dreams. The hole swallows the coffin and the earth embraces Grandfather's body.

Mother earth welcomes back into her womb the son moulded out of her about half a century ago. She takes him back and cradles him, to rest in peaceful and everlasting slumber. The sweaty men are helped out of the grave. Men with strong arms shovel the soil back into the grave. The soil lands with a thud on the wood. A few scoops, and the men lower their shovels, lean on them and wipe sweaty brows with the back of their hands. They bend down again and continue to scoop the soil. Bend down. Scoop. Straighten up. Throw. Bend down. Scoop. Straighten up. Throw… Rest. Wipe brow. Bend down. Scoop. Straighten up. Throw. We get a glimpse of how the men work underground… of how much they sweat for hours on end. When the grave is finally covered, a friend of *ma*Mpofu hands over a plate, a cup and a dish to *a*Kaunda. The utensils are those *ma*Mpofu always served Grandfather's meals in. The dish is the one the men had used to wash his body for the last time after he died. *A*Kaunda crouches on the ground, a stone and a nail in one hand. He turns the plate upside down and balances the point of the nail on the base of the plate using his left hand. In the right hand, *a*Kaunda holds the heavy stone which he then raises till it is level with his temple. He brings the stone down hard, and with precision, on the head of the nail. The nail perforates the plate with a cracking sound and the paint chips off, leaving a black mark like an ugly wound against the light green colour. *A*Kaunda repeats the act and makes a few more holes. He does the same with the cup. Finally, he takes the dish, sets its rim on the ground with its base turned upwards. He throws the brick away and grabs the hammer by his side. He buries the claw of the hammer in the base of the dish and a hole gapes at him. With great care, *a*Kaunda places the perforated items at the head of the newly-created mound of earth. This marks the final resting place of

Grandfather's remains in the red soils of Patchway Valley Mine. A final hymn commits him to the ground.

His labours here completed
His soul to God committed
Voices of Angels whisper
Hush, no more pain or fear!

Refrain:
From the dust he was created
So His body is now entrusted
Ashes to ashes
Dust to dust.

His soul departs this world
His long journey at an end.
At the holy feet of his Lord
The servant rests his head

His journey now at an end
The crown of gold earned,
Angels cheer and applaud
For a reward well deserved.

As the last notes of the song die on their mournful tongues, the women uncurl stiff legs, heave themselves off the ground and rise like one giant mushroom. Their weary feet find the rarely trodden narrow path out of the graveyard and their sighs betray their relief that it is not their husbands they have just laid to rest. The men, their voices tuned to the right tone, their faces set to the appropriate level of solemnity and their heads turned to just the right angle, follow behind the women.

I take a lingering look at this place where I had never been before. It is cleared of shrubs and grass but the big trees with gnarled roots that sprout from beneath knobbly

trunks and thread their way along the ground stand firm and defiant. The clearing, a virtual village of what look like anthills in the early stages of formation, is home to inhabitants we cherish but with whom it is no longer possible to fraternise. The inanimate silent village and the surrounding living bush wage an ongoing battle. The bush which is forced to retreat from time to time creeps back furtively. The grass advances at a slow, steady pace. The creepers, mostly of the *chibayadhongi* variety, crawl with more determination and focus, feeling their way back along remembered paths, snaking around tree stumps, and up old and new mounds of earth in their quest to reclaim lost ground. Only the stones remain in their places of banishment, sulking while hoping for the miracle of a gust of wind strong enough to propel them back to yearned-for familiar spots.

Grandfather has joined the village of the permanently silent. With his death the great voice is forever silenced. The dream he had hoped to realise finally evaporated into the nothingness of time. His death takes him from a life of pain and for that, I am thankful. I hope his soul can at last find peace. With a heavy heart I prepare to walk the rest of the journey alone, not to lose myself in time, but to go all the way beyond the horizon. I shall not let Grandfather down by simply existing from one day to the next, drifting through time in no particular direction, nor will I follow the footprints of my people down the mine pits. The past should die with them, just as it did with Grandfather and his father before him. The mines shall not get the chance to claim my life and my soul, to suck them into the tunnels beneath the bowels of the earth as they did Chakumanda.

My determination to break away from the past transcends everything else and that means definitely not grasping for the future by travelling a century back in time. The mother-woman is an indistinct figure on the edge of my life and there she remains, a stranger and as

detached from my life as the past I want to leave unexplored. I shall move forward and make my life here, giving hope to future generations in a land that promises a new beginning to locals and settlers alike. Like the new nation that my country is, I shall grow and embrace each new day not with sadness, regret or nostalgia, but with the hope that the future is a better place to be in. Hope is the one invaluable legacy I can derive from the long journey that brought my people from across the great rivers on foot those many years ago.

If I am to retrace the footprints of my people and regain their dreams, I shall do it right here. Right now. The God who brought my people this far and saw them through their trials and tribulations will see me through. I do not have to grow old first in order to experience the loneliness Grandfather spoke about at length. I already feel it all around me. In spite of the presence of all these people walking besides me, I am very much alone. I have been mourning these last few days and feeling lonelier by the day. This is the isolation Grandfather warned me about, but I think I will fare better here than anywhere else. This is my home. It is the only place I know. Here I have fond memories that tie me to this place, contrary to what Grandfather thought. I am the reincarnation, not of the soul of his clan, but of his legacy.

Apart from what Grandfather told me as I grew up, school has taught me a bit about the history of my people. Our forefathers who found themselves here did not just come upon the mines by accident through following a railway line whose destination they knew nothing about. They were recruited through the Witswatersrand Native Labour Association (WNLA) which was commonly known as Wenela. This association was set up in 1910 and tasked with recruiting labour force from Mocambique and from the countries that made up the Federation of Rhodesia. The Native Commissioner in each of these countries was

responsible for recruiting young and strong men for work in the mines in South Africa and in the then Southern Rhodesia. To date, there exist places in these countries which are known as Wenela. In the then Nyasaland in particular, there were four labour camps set up, two of which were in Chitipa and Lilongwe. Whenever the Native Commissioner felt his recruits were not strong enough for the rigorous journey, he kept them at the camp for a while and fattened them up to his satisfaction. Documentation was then prepared for them and they came on six month contracts. There were however, those who did not come via the Wenela scheme and slipped into the country without any documentation. Whichever way one did it, most of the migrant labourers chose to stay on and make this country their home. It has been their home since then. This is where I belong. This is home. I am a son of this land whose soils have been nourished by the umbilical cords and the sweat of my people for generations now.

Grandfather may be gone but I shall see his smile in the rising sun and hear his voice in the chirping of birds in the sky and in the whispering wind. I shall feel his breath in the cool morning breeze. When I venture out into the surrounding woodlands, I shall remember each bush he gazed at. I shall savour the memory of his delight in nature and I shall remember always the names of the wild fruits he picked, and above all, the many dreams he shared with me. I shall remember too that home is where the heart is and for me, that place is here.

Home, sweet home.

THE END

ABOUT THE AUTHOR

Photo by Dave Harper

You can connect with the author on facebook under the name Spiwe N Harper, or through her author page; Spiwe N Mahachi-Harper.

Printed in Great Britain
by Amazon.co.uk, Ltd.,
Marston Gate.